MAN ON A TIGHTROPE

For years Cordell Hunt was a legend in the
world of international espionage. Until his cap-
ture and release by the Soviets bred suspicion
throughout the intelligence community...and
forced him into exile. But now certain people in
Washington want Hunt back. Safe, sound...or
otherwise.

To secure the freedom of the Russian woman
he loves from the arms of Innotech, his former
employer, Hunt must infiltrate the inner circle of
the world's deadliest terrorist network. Is he on a
legitimate mission or being set up for elimination?
Whatever the case, Cordell Hunt plans to give
Innotech the run of his life. Though it may very
well be his last...

ASSET IN BLACK

"Prescott ignites furious suspense in this com-
manding novel which catches the reader like a
well-oiled trap..."

West Coast Review of Books

ASSET
IN
BLACK

CASEY PRESCOTT

 AVON
PUBLISHERS OF BARD, CAMELOT, DISCUS AND FLARE BOOKS

*Grateful acknowledgment is made to the National
Strategy Information Center, Inc., for permission
to reprint from Frank R. Barnett's preface to* Intelligence
Requirements for the 1980s: Covert Action, *edited by Roy Godson.*

AVON BOOKS
A division of
The Hearst Corporation
1790 Broadway
New York, New York 10019

The Arbor House edition contains the following Library of
Congress Cataloging in Publication Data:

Prescott, Casey.
  Asset in black.

  I. Title.
PS3566.R368A9   1985   813'.54   84-21557

First Avon Printing, May 1986

Author's Note

The characters and events in this story are entirely fictional, as are Innotech/Triage, Nirvana, the NATO Intelligence Steering Committee, and the People's Crusaders for Peace.

Everthing else, however—all the technology, government and antigovernment organizations, and historical content—is real and portrayed as accurately as security considerations allow.

The author wishes to thank those of you from the various intelligence agencies, the Departments of Justice, State, and Defense, and the FBI, who gave their time, expertise, and encouragement during the preparation of this book but declined to be identified:

Thanks—you know who you are.

Prologue

ON the high steppes of Afghanistan's Kunar province, northeast of Kabul on the Pakistan border, even in summer the nights are always cold.

The American who slipped through the 0100 dark with the Afghan rebel *mujahedin*—the freedom fighters—had been colder, recently, farther north in Badakhshan where the Soviets were using chemical warfare on the mountain people of the Hindu Kush. His body was acclimated to the harsh climate; he shouldn't have been shivering as he scrambled with the rebel band down treacherous slopes toward the Russian garrison at Bari Kot.

The chill the American felt had more to do with his gut instincts than the weather. His name was Cordell Hunt; he was an American adviser without portfolio, in Afghanistan as an agent of a mercenary, multinational risk consultancy that did for the American government what it didn't dare do for itself. If Hunt was caught by the Soviets, he was on his own—the company that had hired him couldn't help him; the American government wouldn't help him.

And his gut was telling him there was something very wrong about this night action against a Soviet position. The Afghan Pushtuns called such a night action *shubkhun*—"blood in the night." Hunt's instincts were telling him there would be plenty of that.

He shouldn't have come along—he wasn't supposed to go raiding; he was supposed to unite the fractured militia groups and the Afghan Loi Jirga—the tribal council—so that he could put together an arms conduit for them; he was supposed to verify the use of chemical/biological weapons by the Soviets in the Kush; he was supposed to find out if the Afghans would consider responding in kind.

Yet here he was, sliding down a final arroyo, squinting at the lights in the Russian camp and trying to keep his balance with a full kit, including ninety rounds of ammo, strapped on him and a Kalashnikov assault rifle in one hand. In front of him, he could make out the gray-turbaned head of the unit's malik—the man who had challenged Hunt to prove himself by risking his life on this sortie. Behind were a dozen mujahedin with scavenged weapons, including a new Soviet shoulder-borne rocket launcher for which they had only three shells and which only Hunt, who read Cyrillic, had any chance of using effectively against its makers without the luxury of practice rounds.

But that wasn't why his hands were numb and his gut was ice cold.

On the trail, something had happened that felt so wrong to him that if this had been his mission, he'd have scrubbed it on the spot.

They'd met another traveling party on the narrow, mountainous trail and its leader had called out, "*Mandanaresh*," which meant "Do not be tired." When mountain travelers met, it was a commonplace greeting; when mujahedin met, it was the *only* greeting.

But there was something unusual about the other party, something that the leader of Hunt's band confirmed when he answered, "*Tashukor*"—a mere "Thank you"—rather than responding in kind.

Now, as they came down onto relatively flat ground where barbed wire was strung, Hunt told himself that his suspicions were unfounded—that the Kunar malik couldn't be a Soviet sympathizer; that what he'd heard was just happenstance, not a confirmation of a setup; that the operation against the Soviet camp wasn't being blown from inside.

But he couldn't convince himself of it.

Around him, pebbles rattled as the rest of the Afghan fighters came down the slope, whispering excitedly.

One mujahed tapped him on the shoulder, "Malik, the weapon," the freedom fighter murmured, his teeth flashing in the dark as he handed Hunt the long tube of the rocket launcher. The fighter had called him "malik"—"headman"—and this nickname, which the mujahedin had given to the American, was at the root of Hunt's difficulties with the group's leader. If it hadn't been for the rebel girl, Nasta, who kept smoothing things over, Hunt and the Kunar malik would have settled things between them long ago; but this was no time to think about Nasta.

Hunt hefted the rocket launcher, settling it on his shoulder, adjusting the infrared sight he'd adapted from the rifle he'd brought with him into Afghanistan.

When Hunt was ready, the mujahed, behind him, loaded it, then stepped smartly aside as he'd been trained, one of the two reserve rockets already in his hands.

Before Hunt in the dark, the rebels were spreading out, cutting wire and preparing to cut power lines; from Hunt's right and left, the sounds of men checking clips and of bolts sliding home were all that could be heard.

Hunt knew the position of the munitions depot by heart; he could draw a map of the compound in his sleep.

He waited for the leader's signal—a wolf's howl.

When it came, Hunt fired the rocket, knees braced against the shock and sound, head buried in the crook of his arm, then hit the dirt as it arced toward the munitions dump.

Nonetheless, the shock wave from the explosion buffeted him; the concussive roar of assorted munitions going up deafened him.

He never got back to his feet. Well before the ringing in his ears lessened, Hind helicopter gunships descended on them out of the black night, spewing cannon fire and antipersonnel explosives.

Hunt had time only to grab the man next to him, pull the mujahed down by the ankles, and bury his own head in his arms before the ground around him began to shudder with near-miss explosions and he was showered with clots of dirt and shattered rock and the occasional wet debris of a human body blown apart.

Just as he took his arms away from his head and neck to grab his rifle and shoot back at the gunships, now swooping with blinding searchlights while their gunners kept the mujahedin pinned, something exploded right beside him and the back of his head came off in a blinding shower of multicolored sparks.

Chapter
1

"HERE you go, sir. That's your Brit contact there, the one with the red T-shirt that says 'Cocaine' and the fatigues." The field agent/taxi driver bullied his clattering Peugeot into a taxi area across from the SATAS bus terminal on the Djemaa El Fna, Marrakech's main square, parked, scratched in his wiry black curls, and turned fully around to give John Shy a look of consummate Arab understanding belied by his Long Island glottal stop as he shouted above the *suq* noises: vendors hawking, bleating animals who somehow knew their hours were numbered, fortune-tellers beating drums to call their favorite spirits, brash young toughs

yelling over their comrades and their ghetto blasters. "Those are
all black-market currency dealers he's with, sir, so look a little
doubtful and suspicious and tell him 'Jerry' sent you in the worst
Spanish you can muster, then say 'dollars for dirhems'—just like
that, with the English preposition. Got it?"

Shy was already putting his foot out the door, nodding, sizing
up the motley clot of street people in which the dark-lipped Berber, an agent of Britain's Special Intelligence Services (SIS), lurked.

"And, sir?" Jerry, Shy's CIA liaison, added, "You gotta pay the
fare." Jerry tapped his cab's meter. "Otherwise *I'd* have to, outta
my own. This here's an up-and-up cab."

As Shy dug in his pocket and then held out some as yet mys-
terious coins, the shoulder holster under his jacket thumped against
his ribs. He readjusted it. In it was the blue Soviet-made Tokarev
automatic he'd found waiting for him at the Hotel de la Mamounia's
desk when he'd come in after paddling around in the hotel pool
for an hour, dodging the heat and his doubts.

Shy saw the driver's head shake, a look cross his face that was
half worried and half sneering. He let it pass, checked his Rolex,
and slammed the cab's door behind him. He'd like both this young
CIA man and his British contact (whom he was hesitant to call,
as he'd been instructed, "Ali Baba") to think as little of him as
possible. Then if he had to walk away from this whole messy
business leaving a corpse behind, he could claim incompetence—
or ignorance. It wasn't much, but it beat admitting to premeditated
murder.

The Berber with the comedic cover name airily proclaimed in
Oxford-accented English that he had been brought in "specially
to act as a go-between in this dicey little minuet" and proceeded,
during their ten-minute stroll through the cheap hotel district
that gave way to a featureless wall of poker-faced casbah houses,
to brief him.

Ali's information was quietly and concisely given, but the
American knew it by heart. John Shy, Western European regional
director of the multinational security consultancy known as Innotech, was in Marrakech hoping to retrieve a badly burnt asset
of theirs for debriefing in the States.

It wasn't going to be easy: Cordell Hunt, the asset in question,
was a second-generation spook, an ex–intelligence officer with an

aversion to acronymous organizations—in short, a rogue cowboy who knew altogether too much about the international intelligence community ever to be considered a civilian. But it was as a civilian that Innotech had contracted, through Triage (its paramilitary subsidiary), to send Hunt into Afghanistan.

Once among the Afghan rebel mujahedin, however, Hunt fit the definition of *mercenary* as stated in Article 47 of Protocol 1 Additional to the Geneva Convention. As such, the Russians who had captured him pointed out gleefully, he could not claim the rights of a combatant or a prisoner of war—they could have executed him. But they hadn't: Cordell Hunt was valuable, not only for propaganda and intelligence purposes but also as barter.

Innotech—a privately held corporation of exceedingly low profile—could do nothing to help him. The Soviets dealt with the United States government, forcing the Departments of State and Defense to publicly disavow him, and privately making his deportation contingent upon the release of two U.S.-held KGB agents.

By the time the Russian assets were cleared for Moscow, Hunt's passport had been canceled as a prelude to revoking his citizenship permanently, despite the face that Titles 8 and 18, U.S.C. (United States Code) section 1481(a)(c) could not, by Supreme Court ruling, be used to divest an American of his birthright. Hunt was in no position to argue.

When the question of where to deport him *to* was broached, friends he had made among the strong British intelligence contingent at listening posts in Pakistan suggested through back channels that King Hassan II of Morocco grant him asylum. The wily old *Sa'did* monarch was happy to oblige: Morocco had its hands full fighting a war in the occupied Sahara against the Polisario guerrillas, at risk in which was control of the phosphate-rich northern desert. Providing he recovered his health, the dispossessed American, an experienced counterterrorist, could be very useful.

But now that the spotlight had faded and heads had cleared in Washington, certain people very much wanted Hunt back home—safe, sound, or otherwise. *Otherwise* was the kicker, the uncertainty factor that had brought Shy out of his habitual shadows into the harsh North African sun where his cover was laughable and his European expertise useless—all because of a free-lance field agent code-named "Dropout."

Ali's advice, given without rancor in the dusty, lattice-covered alleys that got smaller, narrower, and darker as they proceeded into the casbah's maze, was free from censure, but realistic: "I should like to have a go at talking to him first, Mr. Shy. Just a moment, if it's agreeable to you. No one wants any plinking about." Ali's eyes indicated the almost imperceptible 7.62mm automatic under Shy's kid sports coat. "Besides, after six months sampling Soviet hospitality in Kabul and Moscow, he doesn't look too awfully much like his old photos—or didn't when last I saw him in Peshawar—so some positive identification *is* in order, isn't it? One would also like to be able to assure him of your good intentions, but I don't suppose..."

Shy looked at his Adidas, turning gray in the street before his eyes, and jammed his hands into his jeans pockets. Having bumbled of his own accord into every clandestine service professional's nightmare, Shy found himself harboring increasing sympathy for Dropout, who had been awarded two Intelligence Stars by the time he was thirty and now, seven years later, was holed up in Marrakech's casbah, expatriated and by all accounts unsalvageable.

"Cord and I are old friends," Shy replied, "but I'd like you to be able to assure me of his, or yours, or the Moroccans', for that matter. This is one hell of a 'favor' you people did him...."

Sidelong, Shy caught a glimpse of a thick dark eyebrow being raised and had the distinct impression that he was being reassessed. He wondered if a direct question as to the involvement, if any, of the local police in this affair would be worth the risk, and decided against it. Instead, he said, "I just want to talk with him. He has more alternatives than he knows."

"Really?" All interrogators practice, but few master, the stare that accompanied the Berber's response. In the face of it, Shy kept silent until his guide stopped under a Moorish arch where a peephole covered by an iron grate was set into a wooden door at about eye level.

The Berber knocked and stepped back. Even before the peephole opened, the *clack-snick* of something like a submachine gun being loaded and cocked could be heard.

"Smashing," smiled the Berber; "someone's home." He lifted both hands and, as an eye peered out at them, ostentatiously lit a Sobranie, cupping it against a nonexistent wind.

A brown eye scrutinized them, withdrew. The peephole shut without so much as a salaam having been uttered. Shy found his ears straining to catch sounds of movement, low exchanges behind the door, while his adrenaline-prodded instincts lamented the bright winter light at his back. The Berber must have been having similar thoughts, for he asked, blowing smoke through his nose, if Jerry had mentioned that the name of the square where they had met, translated into English, meant "Rendezvous of the Dead."

Before Shy could reply, the door opened inward and a tall figure swathed in traditional indigo robes motioned them in without speaking or coming fully into view. The lower half of the face whose brown eyes rested calmly on them was covered; the hand that motioned them in was fine and long and not sufficiently dark to be Berber.

In the moment of initial blindness, Shy experienced a vertigo of unreality, then fatalism as the door shut with a thud and rapid-fire Arabic buzzed in his ears. The woman was at the door's locks by the time his eyes adjusted enough to pick out the black Sudaev held familiarly, vented muzzle pointing upward, in the crook of a pale arm.

"She says he's resting, but we're welcome to wait. I had to vouch-safe your behavior with my honor, so do be good. We've been offered tea, coffee, or almond milk?..."

Unless his orientation had been in error, a woman of Marrakech wouldn't interpose herself between men. "Tell her he must be informed that we're here. Surely it's up to him to decide whether to see us or not. And tell her I have no intention of waiting." As he spoke, he watched her for signs of comprehension, and saw her brow knit.

The Berber calling himself Ali rephrased Shy's words in Arabic, frowning and adding a spread-armed shrug. She responded and he said to Shy, "We're to follow her; she doesn't want to leave us alone, it seems."

Beyond the shadowed foyer, filigrees of light from a second story spilled on the dirt floor; out of the unformed dark, he began to be able to see packing crates against the half-tiled walls. She opened a door and stepped into a brilliant oblong of white, a center court where a single orange tree grew and someone had been interrupted while kneading bread. Around the atrium the house sprawled; above his head a balcony curled; he didn't like it one bit. He craned his neck and wondered whom he could haunt if he died here, sinking glumly into apportionment of fault while his shirt grew clammy with sweat as they entered the rear of the house.

Crates here were larger and floors were tiled. Two low sofas were backed up against a whitewashed wall, expensive Rabat rugs slung over them and up three steps leading to them. A legged tray between the sofas revealed that they had been expected: three cups were laid out, and brass and copper pots. Shy sat there, not liking his Berber guide nearly so well as previously, while the woman, submachine gun cradled close, opened a door at her back and called softly through it. Shy heard his name among the alien words, and some not so alien: He was *haram*—bad; he was *ayub haram*—very bad. Even under the circumstances, his feelings were hurt.

The Berber called out a greeting, hurrying to the woman's side, palming the Sudaev's muzzle away from his chest, where she thrust it, with enviable aplomb, remonstrating that Shy was *hallah*—good; he was very good, a *malik*—a headman.

Then things began moving very fast, so that Shy had only time to note the use of the Afghan term *malik*, and that the woman knew it, and to wonder if any Moroccans spoke Pashto, before Ali was ushering him through the final portal on this interminable journey, into one more badly lit room like something out of an old movie, ceiling fan and all.

"John Shy, Cordell Hunt. I'll be drinking your coffee if you want me." Ali squeezed Shy's arm and closed the door behind him, leaving Shy facing a recumbent figure in a corner.

"Hi. Welcome to purgatory. Have a seat." Hunt gestured. Something in his hand reflected the one suspended bulb's illumination.

Shy approached carefully, slowly, zigzagging around wooden ammo crates and nondescript bales, trying to keep both hands in plain sight and a hold on his emotions. The man before him was lying under a striped blanket, propped up; he was gaunt, with sunken hazel eyes in a dark angular face, unshaven, unkempt, his spiky prison haircut just growing out. His nose seemed broader and flatter than his photos, and his arms, bare beneath an old black T-shirt gone gray with washing, showed fresh, livid scars. In his right hand, resting upon one updrawn knee, was a pistol.

Above his heart, on the T-shirt, his blood type was printed in red.

"Sit?" The papery voice was polite; the opaque, brittle eyes never left him. "Please. You're making me nervous, hovering like that."

Shy sat where Hunt indicated, catty-corner to him next to a table on which were bottles of Flagyl, chloroquine, and penicillin; a chipped clay chillum black with resin; two Seven Trees air-drop cans that had once contained, according to the labels, magnetic .45acp clips; a pack of unfiltered Camels; rolling papers and loose tobacco; and a two-inch cube of umber *kéf*.

"Why didn't you have your girl pat me down?"

"Would that be fair?"

"Meaning what?"

"Meaning that if you give me any grief, I'm going to put one of these hydroshocks right through that seven-hundred-dollar jacket, and I'd like to be able to look at it as self-defense." He didn't move anything but his head, rolling it just slightly.

This is *not* what I wanted, Shy thought; it's not going to work. What was he supposed to say to the poor bastard? "In that case, I'll be very careful not to. Now, with your permission, I'd like to take my coat *and* what's under it off. This really isn't my sort of thing, you know—guns and so forth."

"That's right. I remember. Funny how people change." Hunt's monotone suggested he saw nothing funny about it.

Shy wasn't imagining the wildness under wraps, the explosive potential Hunt was controlling with difficulty so that the result was an eerie stillness. "*May* I take off my coat?"

"Whatever trips your trigger."

Again, with the unfortunate euphemism, Shy recognized the end-game mentality of burnout; he'd seen it before, in a captured Turk withstanding sophisticated interrogation in Vatican City, in a Glavnoye Razvedyvatelnoye Upravleniye (GRU) assassin in Brussels: They clung to their training and their professionalism throughout everything calculated to neutralize it, desperate to redeem themselves from the agent's cardinal sin, error. To do so, they willingly crossed the borders of madness with no return visa. When he'd taken off his coat and shoulder harness and put the gun on the table, he had gooseflesh: This wasn't the same man he'd known. Sending him had been no better than sending a stranger; from Hunt's demeanor, it might be worse. The thing to do in situations like this was to get the other person talking, but he couldn't fathom how to manage it: Hunt knew the procedure as well as he—no, *better*. Any comment that even smacked of interrogation was going to be ill received. He sighed. "Can I trouble you for a Camel?"

Hunt's eyes indicated yes.

When he had lit it, he leaned back and said, "I came a long way to talk to you, and I can't do it with other people around. Are you well enough to have dinner with me at a restaurant of your choice?"

An appreciative smile touched Hunt's lips. "Don't look too good, huh? Well, don't let it bother you—nightmares are par for the course. Nobody's asked me"—he lay the handgun down, and Shy was able to identify it as a Colt Commander—"out to eat in English for months." He pushed himself upright, suddenly almost boyish, and reached across to get the *kéf*, papers, and matches. From under him he pulled a knife. He heated the blade and then the *kéf*, and pared thin slices into the paper, which he covered with tobacco, rolled, licked, and offered out.

Shy dared not decline it. When he passed it to Hunt, he realized how unsteady the man's hands were. The hash spoke for him: "You ought to consider letting me help you."

"To do what? Die before I hurt somebody else? It's too late. I must have blown everyone I ever knew." There was a catch in his voice.

Shy just waited.

After a time, Hunt cleared his throat. "How do you like the Red City?"

"I'd like to get you out of it."

"To some nice, quiet place where the best and brightest are lined up to fuck me? Thanks, no."

"I can't talk with you under these conditions. Can we get together later or not?"

"Where are you staying?"

"The Mamounia."

"My, my. No expense spared. I'll call you at six. Be in your room."

Shy stood up. "I'm glad." He reached over and picked up the Tokarev and his jacket, slowly, watching Hunt very carefully, and shrugged into them.

"No you're not. You're worried."

"I can't argue with that."

Shy did argue at length and, for him, passionately, with his Berber contact about the disposition of Hunt's case. Through lattice-covered alleyways and past red-clad water-sellers and over the chorus of minaret-high muezzins calling the faithful to prayer as the city turned ocher in sunset and his blood pressure rose, Shy made the customary disclaimers.

But his "plausible denials" were shrugged off by the SIS operative with an infuriating combination of British superiority and Islamic impropriety: "But, sir, if I may be so bold—we— that is, *you*—are underestimating him. He's a sodding chief of station—"

"*Was*, not *is*. He's had no official standing for years."

"Yes, sir. Well, we all know about Yankee ingenuity and black operations. Hypothetically"—Ali took Shy's arm, walking uncomfortably close so that the American had to remind himself that Muslims put much less store by "personal space" than Americans: He'd had a lecture on "high-context" Islamic cultures during his orientation—"let's assume that I *do*—that Special Intelligence does—know a bit about him. After all, it was to us, not you, he turned for help. Given that Cord is at least the equivalent of a deep-cover net chief, how can you expect him to walk blindly into so obvious a setup? A bloody *dinner date?*"

"You're assuming that he doesn't want to be debriefed by his own—absolved, if you like, by the act of confession. I've seen his sort before—they're all alike. He wants help, needs to trust somebody. He can't go on waiting for the day someone decides he's more dangerous alive than dead. There are too many likely candidates: If it's not a Soviet assassin from GRU or a KGB Directorate S *mokrie dela*—a 'bloody wet' boy, as the Russians say—then it might be someone he trusts from a friendly Western service...."

"Like you. Yes, I see. But I won't have any part of it, nor will my people, I'm sure. Do you occasionally wonder why the Soviets let go of him so easily?"

"Only once or twice an hour. There's Jerry, I believe."

By the time the cab pulled up at the Mamounia, Shy desperately wanted privacy, time to think. He left the Berber drinking coffee in the ground-floor lounge. Up in his room, he mixed a Jack Daniel's and Sidi Harazem water from his suite's service bar, then

took a long, indolent shower. Upon emerging, the charm of the
old renovated palace and the mash had done its work: He felt
human, if not good. Padding out into the sitting room in a towel,
he noticed that his message light was on. It wasn't the air condi-
tioning or the drops of water he'd been content to let evaporate
from his skin that made him shiver.

The red light glared balefully as he got his attaché case out from
under the bed. It was undisturbed, and he opened it. Before he
picked up the receiver to dial the desk, he fitted the modular
encoder to the phone and set the electronics that filled up the
case to record, stand by to scramble and transmit by virtue of one
of Innotech's own tap-free units that converted the analogue signal of the human voice to digital, silent pulses that would travel
undetected through any phone system's headers to emerge at a
compatible receiver, decoded and reconverted into analogue.

The message, when he got it, was simple: Call your aunt.

After he had been connected with the number appended and
the ringing stopped, he listened for a tone and dialed fifteen
additional numbers: his access code and the area and number
codes for the office he wanted. Then he engaged his encoder.
"What's up?"

A putatively female voice answered, "We've had EO incidents
at Fishkill, Tokyo, and Zürich. Given time zones, they're simul-
taneous. No proud parents coming forward. How are you doing
with my prodigal son?" ·

"Jesus." EO stood for explosive ordnance.

"What?"

"Ah—I'll be back tomorrow, with or without him."

"Make it 'with.' We've already sent out invitations to his home-
coming party. Everybody's anxious to talk to him."

A weight lifted from Shy's chest. "That's something, anyway.
See you." He put the phone down; disengaged his equipment;
spun the tumblers until a light-emitting diode blinked on, indicating that its locks were properly engaged; and slipped the armed
case back under the bed.

Then he called his pilot in a room down the hall and told him
to get the Falcon ready for an evening flight to Zürich. He could
hear the sleep snap out of the man's voice. Getting Jerry's boss,
the local CIA station chief, on the phone took a bit longer but

didn't require a secure line. Contingencies had been planned for
well in advance.

He felt a twinge of regret about implementing them, but in the
stomach-tightening distress his call home had produced, he paid
his conscience little mind. His previous concerns paled to insig-
nificance. EO's at Innotech installations? He made a mental note
to strangle with his bare hands the fool who had sent Cordell
Hunt into the field—then remembered someone had already
beaten him to it. With this kind of hell breaking loose, he should
have been minding his own shop, not out here playing who-do-
you-love with a bunch of borderline-psychotic black operators.

Clutching his towel, he made his way out to the balcony and
stared sightlessly into the famous gardens below, beyond which
the casino was just coming to life. Nobody gaming away their
jewels and Mercedes in there tonight would be playing such a long
shot as this junket had turned out to be. He hoped Hunt actually
knew something valuable enough to make up for the fact that his
fuck-up had maneuvered Shy into exactly the wrong place at a
crucial time. But then, that was what agents did, wasn't it?
Maneuver. He wondered if Jerry's boss, CIA's local chief of station, was right about Hunt's being doubled—coming out of Russia
turned, owned, KGB's man.

But it was too obvious, too stupid, and too archaic—not to
mention impractical: Cordell Hunt was blown more thoroughly
than anybody since Kim Philby; no reputable organization would
touch him. His picture had been on every Western and Warsaw
Pact newscast as an example of the mercenaries of American
imperialism. This, Jerry's boss had argued doggedly, could well
be the mechanism of Hunt's Soviet cover; like all old hands, the
Marrakech chief of station had lived in the labyrinth of deception
so long that his own logic was infected by it: Only things that
didn't make any sense could be trusted; only the illogical made
sense.

Shy turned his back on Marrakech's minaret-pierced dusk and
mixed a toast to his erstwhile brethren of all the governments of
the world, wishing them luck with their deceptions, every one.

* * *

In the Narodno Trudovoy Soyuz (NTS) safe house where he had sought sanctuary from the double-edged solicitousness of his Moroccan hosts, Cory Hunt turned his back on the submachine gun pointed at him and rummaged through his belongings for a clean pair of pants.

He was naked and tired and hungry and suddenly cold, and his wounds hurt where grenade fragments still remained. This plus the quality of the light thrown by the room's one naked bulb and Nasta's belligerent harangue combined to disorient him: For a moment he was back at 2-4 Dzerzhinsky Square in the Lubyanka's institutional-green interrogation cell, watching colors fill the air and alphabets spill out of his nose and knowing he wasn't going to be able to hold on to his sanity much longer. An instant later, bathed in sweat and shaking, blinking garish flashback residuals from his vision, he turned on her: "Put that lead-spitter down or use it. And speak English, can't you? We both need the practice."

Anastacia Martinova had discarded the indigo jellaba she wore like a Shi'ite whenever among strangers for her customary Afghan grays. Her haughty White Russian face, unveiled, showed no sign of softening, but she thumbed the Sudaev's safety and slung it back against her hip, her hand resting on it lightly as a Western woman would hold a shoulder purse. Undaunted, she continued, booted legs widespread, to assert in English that she couldn't let him walk into the murderous American's trap: "Malik, I'm looking out for your safekeeping, every time. Don't use with me that tone. Your worsted pants I have mended, but to you I shall not give these without your promisings you will not go. This is foolish thing. And the omens! These are—*haram*—bad! Just this day, early—"

"Nasta, your English grammar's worse when you're mad than it is in bed. I'm going. You can come, too, and protect me"—still naked, crouched facing her on his knees, he grinned slyly—"if you dress like a tourist and meet me in the Mamounia bar. We need a dry run at that anyway. I'll bet I can get Shy to buy you dinner, too—*if* you'll let me introduce you."

"No! This morning," Nasta enunciated carefully, brown eyes steady on him but narrowed, "I visited Aisha, who is finest of seeresses, as you yourself have agreed, and she threw the bones for you. So bad was the reading, we made the rhythm and summoned the spirit Isawa. The spirit spoke through Aisha's mouth to me, saying, 'Beware a pale one coming on the arms of a friend.' Dark wings for you, the omens hold."

"Shit." Shaking his head, he turned on his heel, winced, steadied himself with one hand, and with the other pulled a pair of khaki pants from under his bedside table. He wasn't going to argue with her, he told himself. But he did: "You sound like a regular Koran-carrying Muslim. Don't tell me you believe that crap."

"A leetle."

"Little. Say it."

"Little. Kori, do not do this. Since I came down from Kandahar, you have been my only concern. Narodno Trudovoy Soyuz needs you, the Afghan Islamic National Front needs you, my comrades of the Loi Jirga—the Grand Assembly—need you."

"Woman, *will* you face reality? Do you understand the word? NTS has been waiting since 1919 to reclaim Russia, and it'll have to wait at least until you Whites can say 'Popular Labor Union' in English. You dig? I can't help anybody anymore. I'm not even certain I can help myself. You and the Jirga—if it hasn't dissolved by now—are just going to have to get yourselves another boy, another go-between, because I was never, ever, much more than that. And then you'll have to wonder about who *he* is, and why *he's* doing it, and who's on the other end of that arms-conduit-in-the-sky you want so badly—*or* you can act like sensible adults and let me pass this thing along to Shy and see what he says. If what's left of my brain can still add two and two, it's his people you've been dealing with all along, or else he wouldn't be here."

He shifted his position, agony stabbed up his spine, and he sank to the floor. "Never mind, it doesn't matter. You'll never get the Soviets out of Afghanistan, much less free Mama Russia, going by the omens." He forced the words out over the pain to cover his enervation, but they sounded harsh and breathless. "As for me, even a dog who's been hit by a truck has enough sense to find a warm, quiet spot to lie down. I appreciate everything you people have done, but it's time for me to go. How long do you think *you're* going to be tolerated here, if this place is so notorious that an SIS contractee, a low-level agent handler, can waltz in here with a *very* high-up from the States?"

Morocco was technically still supported by the U.S., but they were better than two billion U.S. dollars in the hole to the Soviet Union and so far precious little usable uranium had come out of the Meskala phosphate deposits. Things were tense again with the French because of Mauritania, as well as with the Soviets themselves over their own Algerian "conflict of interest." He'd known that this could happen, half expected it. He'd been fooling himself, wishing it wouldn't, trying to recoup before it did. He felt very stupid, and Nasta bore the brunt of it.

"You think that if KGB asked for either or both of us, the Moroccans wouldn't hand us over with a smile, just think back a couple hours to what happened when America called. Now, are you going to help me find a clean pair of pants or am I going in there looking like a fugitive?"

He didn't look up to see the result of his words, but he heard her move away. Shaking his head, he let out a long breath, then started pulling on his socks. It was still difficult to bend over so far. Reminded of how much he owed her, he found himself on the verge of tears and pulled back from it determinedly, thinking that he'd told her the truth for the first time; in his business, a little truth paid a lot of debts.

A pair of jockey shorts flew in his face, then his tan tropical worsted slacks, then she knelt and put her arms around him. He didn't move or speak, distressed by the volatility of his own emotion, knowing he must somehow get control of himself.

But if he'd been able to do that, he wouldn't be giving up. For that was what agreeing to meet Shy was—a surrender. The better part of valor, he thought, and shrugged her wordless comfort away. Gracefully Nasta folded into a squat beside him and with downcast eyes handed him a miraculously starched green shirt. He'd taken away her revolutionary's militant armor when he'd talked her into his bed; even now she didn't complain. He wondered if he would spend the rest of his life looking for another woman whose grandparents had fled the Russian Revolution to settle in Afghanistan, prospered in Kabul, sent their granddaughter to France to study, imbued with their own indomitable will to struggle, despite personal hardship and impossible odds, toward an unattainable goal. He wanted to say something about personal honor, about respect and affection, but coming from him, what would it mean? They were both part of the same exploded cultural matrix—relics, souvenirs like the grenade fragments he was carrying around lodged near his spine. Homeless, disoriented refugees, they were equally uncomfortable with all the world's cultures and ideologies—they knew too much about too many. World orphans, their foster homes were dead drops and safe havens. Their friends all had war names, covers, and code designations, permanent seats in the floating poker game belonging to the shadow people, the counterrevolutionaries, terrorists, and spies. For better or worse, it was time for Hunt to fold.

Dressed, he was glad they had no mirror. The Hunt who wore jute sports jackets and loafers and good slacks was an old, half-remembered acquaintance, someone more efficient and ethical than he'd recently become.

Aware that he hadn't said goodbye to Nasta, he left quickly, still settling his Commander in its shoulder holster, wondering if he really believed he could conceivably shoot his way out of whatever he was walking into. When he closed the door, he saw her, back turned to him, taking a pair of high-heeled sandals out of her footlocker.

Ali's words to him in those few moments before Shy had eased through his door came back to Hunt as he headed out of the maze to where cabs could be found.

"Cord, old friend," Ali had murmured, striding forward with a business card in hand, "I've this American with me. Orders. Be a good fellow and see him. But do be careful; he's armed, I'm sure, and thoroughly dangerous, else my people would never have acceded to his people's *demands*"—he had paused for emphasis, card in hand but not yet offered—"that we produce you. It's not our business, is it?" He thrust the card forth. "Unless, even at this late date, you'd like it to be? Our offer is still valid ... No? Well, then, what do you think?"

The card said *John Shy, Risk Analyst* in the lower right-hand corner above the phone and Telex numbers; opposite, cities were listed: New York, Paris, Zürich, Tokyo; above these in modernistic lettering the legend read *Innotech*. Nothing more.

"I think," he had replied, "that you ought to stay out of it." He tossed the card and it sailed into one of the air-drop cans. Ali had flushed and spread his hands in a gesture of helplessness and finally said, while Hunt was fishing out his pistol, "I am filled with regret, my friend."

Hunt clicked off the safety and sighted open-eyed at Ali's midsection, balancing his cupped hands on an updrawn knee so that Ali would not see how badly he was shaking. "You ought to be. This is hardly going to be 'coffee with a friendly who may be able to help.' At least, not in terms of what I'm ready to call 'help.' Tell him to come in, then get out. Keep Nasta away from the door after you've locked it—it's old wood; anything can happen with these—"

"Please, for my sake and your own, don't let it come to violence."

"Go on. Get out of my sight picture."

So much for friends.

Recalling it had made him angry, and anger chased his melancholia. "The galloping angsts" he called the fearful depression that at times overswept him, and which, of all the aftereffects of his time in the Lubyanka, he detested most—more than the frags that grated against his spine or the migraines or the flashbacks.

If he could stay angry, he would be okay.

Upon reaching the Mamounia's end of Avenue Bab Djedid, the minicab slowed, then stopped: The street was blocked up ahead. He got out, gave the driver twenty dirhems, received a blessing in return, and walked across the street. Sauntering by the hotel entrance, he noticed nothing more unusual than a few patrons talking with the brightly clad doormen. A bit farther on, he saw a black Citroën being winched off the sidewalk; he got past a panel truck for an unobstructed view just as an ambulance started up, shrieking, and drove away, its lights bloodying the dusk.

He doubled back and crossed to the hotel, looking back frequently. On the well-lit Mamounia steps, he asked a ghoulishly happy woman with a red smile drawn high on her puckered lip what had happened in French. His guess was right as to her nationality, and she excitedly told him how she had seen with her own eyes the passenger shoot at the pedestrian, bystanders panic, the man in the T-shirt reel backward, the car chase him up on the sidewalk. "Yes, it was terrible. And then the Citroën hit the man, and the wall. But, yes, I saw it all: The man's face was no more, but still they ran him down, then they left the car and ran off—disappeared. It was horrible. My sleep will be disturbed for—"

"How difficult for you, madame. My sympathies."

"Tell him, honey," said a portly bald man sweating through a white tuxedo, "the good part." Hunt thought he detected a southern drawl.

"I speak English. Tell me the good part."

"The hoods—you know, the guys in the car—they blew this guy's face right *off*. Hit some bystanders, too—that's the live meat in the wagon. So they had some kind of pump shotgun, and from the spread and the damage I'd bet they reloaded their cartridges with six-millimeter ball bearings. Cop said could'uv been the KBG. Imagine that, a spy shoot-out, a goddamn *hit team*, and *I* saw it! Wait until the guys at NRA hear—"

"Excuse me, sir, but why do they think that?"

"You're not from a paper, a wire service by any chance? No such luck, eh? Well, son, the thing is—get this—the cops *knew* the guy from his cocaine T-shirt; they'd been tailing him earlier in the day. It was that American merc there was so much fuss over a few months back—the Ivans caught him in Turkestan, can't remember his handle. Good thing they knew who it was 'cause there wasn't enough of that poor sumbitch left to ID. Whaddaya suppose that guy done t'a—"

"Hunt," someone younger interrupted. Cory had started to back away, but there were unyielding bodies behind him. The younger voice continued, "Cordell Hunt was the guy's name. And you can tell the folks back home at the firing range that it was definitely KGB."

The newcomer turned a grinning Mediterranean face to Cory, saying, "Hi, I'm Jerry. John thought that I'd better come down in case you forgot to call first. Lucky I did. Right this way." A firm hand closed on his arm so that Jerry's knuckles were resting against Hunt's gun.

"Yeah?" The fat man, unwilling to be denied his audience, put a restraining paw on Jerry's sleeve: "*Yeah?* And who appointed you the expert, *butt-in?*"

"CIA," Jerry whispered, enunciating elaborately, and winked.

"*No* shit?" Cory heard the beefy tourist exclaim wonderingly as Jerry and his two backups crowded close, deftly extricating him from the fat American, the upper-middle-class crowd, and free society.

* * *

Hunt fought exhaustion in one of the Falcon's leather seats while
the Innotech jet winged toward Zürich. There had been no dinner, no long talk with Shy at the Mamounia. There'd been damn
little time for talk, let alone food. Instead, there'd been a waiting
limousine and Jerry's two large friends ready to hustle him into
it if he balked, Shy's brusque apology and a promise that they'd
"talk on the plane," an exchange of documents—his gun and
Moroccan papers for an American identity complete to (old) passport photo and pocket litter, congratulations all around in the
hotel lobby, and Jerry's instructions as to which customs official
they should approach. There'd been one particularly difficult moment, after he'd shaken hands with Shy's blue-jeaned pilots, when
Nasta came walking into the lobby.

She was as white as the dress she had on. He knew from her
face that she'd heard about the killing outside. Seeing him, she
darted forward with a little cry, then realized what the men in the
suits and the packed bags around him must mean, checked herself,
and sank into a lobby chair, where she lay her head back, fanning
herself in a good imitation of a tourist who hadn't been careful
about her exertions.

But he'd known it wasn't good enough; he saw it in Jerry's eyes,
sliding in her direction, in a nod from one of the quiet men in
sunglasses. Trembling from adrenaline he couldn't use, he verged
on freeze-frame panic: He didn't know whether his attempted
intervention would help her or hurt her. He had to let it go, walk
by her like a stranger.

In their car, he fought overwhelming nausea and rebuffed their
attempts at small talk, keeping his eyes closed. He had plenty of
regrets to keep him company. When it was handed to him, he
carried a two-suiter through customs, Shy speaking for both of
them, joking with the customs official about his companion's "weak
American stomach."

The blue and white Falcon took to the air with a leap that made
him grab his airsickness bag, but he knew it was his life he wanted
to disgorge. Ali's death was way too high a price for what was left
of him; Nasta's would be unendurable. He repeatedly reviewed
the consequences of mentioning his NTS contacts to Shy; in the
end he couldn't do it. He knew too well what salvage operations
like this entailed: What was waiting for him was a whole lot of

unpleasant SOP; he couldn't bear the thought of involving her in it. Even if Shy swore she'd remain unharmed, undisturbed, free of guilt by association, Hunt couldn't believe him. He'd wait and see if and how the subject of his NTS connections was broached—and by whom among what was going to be a nearly endless parade of interrogators.

It was beginning to seem as if he'd never left the Lubyanka's proletarian despair, as if there actually *were* no difference between one side and the other in this fucking covert war he'd spent his life fighting—a point he'd maintained to be false under corporal punishment the savagery of which, in his worst nightmares, he'd never dreamed he'd survive.

Then it occurred to him that maybe he hadn't survived it—that he was in a hell specially contrived for failed assets: Why should God show mercy to the men who maimed and murdered and betrayed in His image? But three or four times during his Soviet captivity, looking down death's brown tunnel, he'd thought he'd heard a compassionate voice reprieving him and sensed a serenity and an equanimity that had seemed, to him, eternal.... But then, it might just have been all the hallucinogens the Russians had pumped into him.

After a while, he wept silently, simply staring out the wing window and letting the tears his eyes couldn't contain flow down his cheeks.

Chapter
2

IT had been snowing all day in Zürich, and it was still snowing when two black cars pulled up under the Falcon's rapidly icing wing and five figures hurried down its ramp toward their open doors.

Snow gusted, and when its curtain parted, the Falcon's crew and two passengers had disappeared into the first car. It pulled away.

John Shy ducked into the second, mouton collar high against the storm, his naked fingers red on his briefcase's handle. The driver closed the rear door, came around and slid behind the wheel in the partitioned front seat awaiting orders. For some time he would get none. Sensing it, he picked up the paper on his seat and began to read.

"So you got him after all—Dropout," said Innotech's pale director to Shy. Sid Cannard preferred to be in bed by ten. It was one in the morning, and he'd had a difficult day, not the least of which had been tracking the progress of the Falcon and the storm, converging on Zürich together so that it couldn't be said for certain until the final moments whether the plane would be allowed to land: Not even Innotech could argue with the weather. "For a dead man, he's unusually troublesome."

John Shy had been blowing on his fingers. "Don't talk about him that way, Sid. He's a human being and he's used up. And you know damn well who did the using." He leaned his head back against the seat. "Jesus, that was hard. I haven't felt this bad since I left the service. I've got to know what's going on: Are we just handing him over to whoever would like a piece of him? And if so, why? I think Innotech has a responsibility to protect its people. He hired on to the Afghanistan team without the slightest notion of what the risks were—"

"John, forget him. He's old news. What he knows can't hurt us, and might save a life here or there, or so I'm told."

"Negative, Sid. I'm going to go to the wall on this one. I'm warning you. I don't like the precedent this will set: We don't need our people worrying that if things get tough, they're open to debriefing by agencies they've consciously chosen not to work for....*I* don't want to worry about it. No government is going to get close to thinking that they own us while I'm part of the 'us.' He was dispatched by my shop, and we'll take care of him. This once I'm going all the way with one of my people."

"John, you're overtired."

"Don't make excuses for me. Sid, I'm asking for your help. I've been up for thirty-six hours and I'm cranky, but I'm not any slower than I've ever been. I've put up with roaches in my couscous and I've smiled at submachine guns and looked the other way while ostensibly friendly services used us as an excuse to take out a troublemaker—"

"This is *not* a correct reading."

"Who cares about the reading? This isn't data, it's brains on sidewalks. In the final analysis, I'm the one who had to go clean up after someone else whose armchair analysis didn't convert to a real-time action very well. And I've been listening to Dropout; you haven't. Take a ride with him and come back and talk to me about analyses. *His* analysis is that the world is going to go to war over the Khyber Pass. I went down there thinking I owed it to him for old times' sake. And I wanted to feel better about what was really a pretty sad thing we did to somebody we'd heard wasn't in any position to be choosy and maybe wasn't as smart as he used to be. The last part is right enough—he's not smart enough even to realize what's happening to him, or he doesn't care. But whichever, he still thinks we're the good guys."

"We are. I've got three research labs with big holes in them to prove it. I'd like to think that matters to you."

"Sid, I told Hunt we'd take care of him. I had to tell him something—you should see those eyes. We had to trick him in, didn't have time to lay anything out for him—I got the recall message and we scooped him off the street."

"And very neatly, I might add."

"Tell that to the Berber's family. Or to Hunt. I asked him on the plane if he wanted to talk to me about what happened to him, and he just shook his head. The kid I had along for backup gets off the wall, comes over, and wants to 'tune him up' for me! What the hell is wrong with everybody? The guy's not a traitor, he just had a run of bad luck. The way he looked up at that kid, twice his size and eager as sin—it'll be a while until I can forget it."

"Your wife phoned when the news broke. Beyond assuring her that there were no casualties, we couldn't tell her anything. She didn't know you'd gone out of town?"

"You don't have to be that polite. No, I don't always come home, and, yes, we are trying to work it out. But I'll call her."

"Good."

"Are you going to give me an answer?"

"On Dropout? Not the one you'd like, John. Dear boy, you're a marvelous administrator and your sense of fair play is admirable, but this is *not* your problem any longer. I am beginning to think it was a mistake to send you down there." Cannard sighed and shifted, fetching out his pipe. "It's always a mistake to trade on personal loyalties, and yet, without them, where would we be?"

"Without them, there'd be no Dropout, that's for certain, just a dead retrieval party. You owe me something on this one."

"What would you like? A raise? I'll paint your office. You fancy a new car or a better terminal? Just speak right up. But the Europeans and your own nationals and various special-interest groups who feel that their people have been compromised need to know what has been leaked. A man who has been around and about as much as your Mr. Hunt could have endangered quite a number of innocents in place."

"That's the bottom line?"

"I'm afraid so."

"He thinks I'm the equivalent of his case officer. I told him the man who was handling him died in an auto accident, but I didn't tell him more than that. He doesn't need to know who fouled him up or how badly or for what kind of incentive. I want you to shift all his records over to me. As for what he divulged, he can't be certain. He assumes that everything he knew, they know. So just go down the list and see who's left of his old acquaintances and pull them off whatever they're doing, or alert their services to do so. Most of what could happen has already happened, we must assume—they had him nearly five months. It took them a month to decide to send him north, he thinks."

"What else did he tell you?"

"Too much. Ask me anything about Afghanistan—he's about convinced me that it's more important than the whole of Africa. Ask me about the quarrel between the Baluchi who want an 'independent Baluchistan' and the Pakistani Pushtuns—he doesn't say 'Pashtuns'—who want the border right where it is. Ask me about the leftists we *aren't* supporting and the right-wing fundamentalists of the various nomadic tribes and Muslim sects, all of whom have sent representatives to the 'Loi Jirga' to counsel different strategies, or the Raydoviki—that's what the Afghans call the *Spetanatz* shock troops that the Russians are putting in there. He thinks we're wrong in assuming Afghanistan is their Vietnam—it's their boot camp. Remember the old saw about the difference in the way we clear out minefields? The Americans bombard the field with mortars, and damn the expense; the Soviets march a company through it, and damn the casualties. They're not going to give up live ammo practice on those rebels, and the

Egyptian support the Afghans are getting isn't worth mentioning. Or let's talk chemical ordnance, CBW binaries—"

"Let's not. I get the point. He'll tell anyone anything they want to know, so it might be best to sort it out ourselves rather than letting the injured parties come to their various conclusions about interagency collusions. Is that it?"

"That'll do if it convinces you. Hunt's found out there's no holding back information after a point—*you* must realize it. Modern interrogation itself precludes heroics."

"You win, John." Cannard finally lit his pipe, the flame elongating his falconine nose and the graying bristles of his sixteen-hour beard. Watery eyes turned toward the younger man. "You always do when it comes to this sort of thing. I'm wondering, I must confess, why you haven't asked me for a site report on our damages, but I have the rest of the night free. If you wish to handle Dropout, you may do so with my blessings. Perhaps he could be useful, given that Saturday's EO's were what they seem— simple terrorist actions; and not what I fear—a concerted attempt by some one of our enemies, or even our competitors, to expose Innotech's somewhat privileged status to public scrutiny. You know we cannot tolerate that *at any cost.*"

Shy was already objecting that Hunt needed hospitalization, rest, moral and financial support when what Cannard was saying registered. He inclined his head and one eyebrow raised. Then he whistled a short, wavery note. "I was thinking about that and hoping no one else was. This is going to be expensive."

"Sabotage always is. Tragedy, too. Only violence is cheap in our particular market. Speaking of violence, did Dropout tell you what he was doing with a mujahedin demolition team trying to blow up a Soviet arsenal in Bari Kot?"

"He did, actually. It wasn't his operation; he was challenged by one of the Kandahar Province maliks as to his intentions, and went along to demonstrate solidarity—and to show them how to use a few pieces of advanced Soviet equipment they had captured but didn't understand."

The director grunted, touched a toggle, and told the driver to take them to the Hotel Baur Au Lac. The car pulled away. "I hope you don't mind, but we doubt that any of our executives' houses or our customary visitors' accommodations are secure right now. And we did think we only had to host your party until the weather broke."

"That's very generous. How long can I have him there?"

"Until I find a better place for him, or find out I cannot fail to produce him. After all, he *is* dead; it's on the wire. Let's not tell Mrs. Shy where you are just yet. One never knows how things will develop—but then, you don't need me to tell you what to do, only to assure you that I will do my best with the Dropout matter if you'll concern yourself with our mutual problem. Our computers were without power for a bit too long a time to assume that we don't have serious secondary problems. There's no telling what we may have lost, or what we'll have to assume we might have lost *previously....*"

"You think this bombing was someone covering his tracks?"

"We need to know what's missing and what's been destroyed before contemplating deception as a possible motive. One does tend to make suppositions of that type when confronted with this sort of circumstance. It's terribly inconvenient of them to have done such a thing, whether they're simple terrorists or not. Not one but three different groups have claimed the event in Zürich as their own—for such diverse reasons that it seems to some that professionals may have been responsible. And, too, the ordnances themselves were relatively sophisticated, not homemade bombs or simple plastique. Before we get into this, I've assumed you'd want to stop by your hotel and change. I've tried to anticipate your needs as best I could—food and that sort of thing. Additional room service isn't available at this late hour, but we do have a crisis team convened in my parlor nibbling my cupboards bare while they wait for you. I hope you don't mind that I took the liberty. I was on hand, as it were, and you were not."

"Did you happen to be in town by accident?"

"My daughter is having some personal difficulties, and I'd thought to help her straighten them out. Someday you, too, shall know true agony: the problems of one's child that neither money nor ingenuity can solve."

"Is she?" Shy had asked, and patted through his pockets for a cigarette. He didn't miss the sharp old man's deceptively gentle eyes weighing his reaction. If he had not been so tired and so disoriented by the abrupt weather change and the events of the past few days, he would have been more worried about it. But last Thursday seemed weeks away, and his old concerns flat and thin.

"Yes, she is. It seems a time for troubles." They rode in silence, until the old man chuckled. "Very unwise, very."

"*What?*" Shy said sharply, his head snapping about so that he dropped an ash on his storm coat.

"Dropout." The director shook his shaggy head. "Very unwise, but somehow charming—showing solidarity. Do you think, John, the Afghans would be willing to do the same for him?"

Always, she had known when to celebrate, and when triumph was premature. This evening, sitting in a suite at the Hotel Baur Au Lac with the Zürichsee's ice floes glittering like undulant marble beyond the park's silvered grounds, she knew the elation around her to be overhasty. Curled up in a chair before one window, she sipped champagne and wished the vicious children around her would get drunk enough to stumble off to bed: They had lashed out successfully at yet another capitalist target, sanctifying their muddled destructive ethics and proving once more the power of pampered mediocrity to obstruct what it feared. The People's Crusaders for Peace had wanted to bomb missile silos—they had settled for multinational Innotech's computers instead. They had done it with a little work and a great deal of luck and their parents' money—and some unobtrusive guidance by professionals.

She slipped on her shoes, having made her obligatory appearance, put down her glass, and said farewell to the young jackals, whose eyes were shining. Did she realize that this was the first time so great a blow had been struck against the *haut bourgeois* enemy? They had been successful in three countries, they were certain now! Soon the world would proclaim it!

She sidled past the dozen youthful radicals into the hall without having to answer, only smiling and letting the boys kiss her cheek and the girls assure her they would never forget her, ever. "Remember," one particularly fiery blond youth called after her, "what the Czechs say: A fistful of might is better than a sack of justice!"

Hoping there was no one around to overhear, she blew him a kiss.

When she had exited the automated lift at her own floor, pleased with herself for having endured their company for what seemed like far too many hours without once having pointed out that the only thing more boring in the universe than Communist rhetoric was terrorist dogma, she found her way barred by a group of men who filled the corridor with their bulk and their luggage.

They were speaking English, so in that language she asked them to make way for her. One among them was apologetic, well made with amorous eyes, and he gallantly saw her through the "little roadblock," promising that since it was *his* roadblock, he would not demand to see her visa for the other end of the hall. Among those who made way was an almost familiar face: a man, spiky-haired and painfully thin, who reminded her so much of Cory Hunt that she tripped on an overnighter's corner and was saved only by her self-appointed escort's quick reflexes.

He insisted on accompanying her to her door, penance, he said, for her "accident," clearly his "fault."

Then he introduced himself and her heart stopped still.

In the hallway, her body followed suit. Behind Innotech's John Shy, two large men in greatcoats yet remained in the corridor, watching them; the thin, rangy man in the green bomber jacket was gone.

"I have a confession to make," she said to Shy, smiling into his quizzical stare. "I have overindulged and lost every shred of decorum. The room I go to is not my own, and the man not my husband." She wore no coat, no hat, carried no bags; this one would not have failed to notice. "So you see," she continued in her most sultry voice, "your courtesy is awkward, here and now."

Thus she got away from him without giving her name, and when she reached her own door it opened before her and a man's head and shoulder peeked out. As she entered, she whispered to him, "Are they still standing there?"

"Who? Oh, them, yes."

"Close the door." She went to the curtains, drew them back to stare up into the steadily falling snow. He came up behind her, but when he put his arms around her waist, nuzzling her hair, she pushed him away.

"What is wrong?"

"I just saw a spook in the hall."

* * *

Every time Hunt fell asleep, one of them would wake him up. Dreams can be had in moments. He would be dreaming that he lay once more among his mujahedin, Plamya fire and Hind helicopter gunships lighting up the night, frag-riddled and doomed outside the Soviet garrison at Bari Kot, and they would wake him and he would blink until the Raydoviki disappeared and he realized he didn't have blood in his eyes and the Slavic face before him was not a gloating Russian ranger's or the Kandahar Province resident's, but a Western interrogator's face. If it was that dream, he was always angry and frightened that the men and their questions were so much alike.

But if he'd been dreaming of the labyrinthine KGB headquarters called the Lubyanka, walking the endless green corridors from one of the rear prison buildings to the old insurance-company building on the square for a session with Chebrikov in his office, he was always relieved to wake at all. Sitting there with Chebrikov while the quiet-spoken interrogator who'd brought him in from Kabul was explaining what would happen next—and why cooperation or lack of it was beside the point—he'd try to focus on the sealing wax diligently applied nightly to the old Mosler safe behind Chebrikov's desk and wait for the drugs to hit, or the equipment to arrive, or guards to come take him to an "observation room" where strangers would watch him sweat. Even in that dream, he'd pray that he'd have only Chebrikov to contend with—that his poor performance wouldn't result, as Chebrikov constantly warned him, in Hunt's case being taken from him and given to a less sympathetic interviewer, leaving Hunt to bear the brunt of Directorate S's anger and Chebrikov with a black mark on his record that nothing—not his Odessa connections or his diligence or his father's influence—could ever erase. Hunt had only to die or be traded and he was free; Chebrikov, who'd extracted him from the executioner's coffle and his rat-infested holding cell, who'd seen to it that he had medical attention and clothes and was not buried up to his neck for the Afghan Communists to spit upon any longer than was absolutely necessary, could find his whole career ruined by the selfish obstinacy of the man he'd tried unfailingly to befriend... When he dreamed of Chebrikov, he would wake in tears. He hadn't known enough then about Innotech or the NTS to save either one of them. But he had known he couldn't go back into the field run by the Soviets. He could agree to it *in extremis*, but when they put him under, his truth-drugged soul betrayed them both.

On the plane, it had been Shy who woke him with coffee or kindness, and there Hunt had been embarrassed if he found his face wet with tears or his arms up to protect his head. On the plane from Kabul to Moscow, there had been a big Slavic kid like Shy's bodyguard who had "tuned him up" real well. Of all his fears in those days, the worst was of losing his sight or his reason from continual blows to the head. The stitches holding the back of his scalp to the nape of his neck had just come out then, and when he would wake in the Falcon he'd feel, fugitively, all the phantom effects of his earlier, lingering concussion: His vision would be blurred, his stomach queasy, ears ringing, and his determination renewed—to make them kill him before he got to Moscow.

But now, in the hotel, it was not so difficult: He was beginning to believe the evidence of his senses, which told him he was safe in the civilized world, despite the disclaimers of his reason, which knew damn well that somebody was going to turn the big kid loose on him one of these times when he came up too fast out of his chair or just refused to sit. Sometimes his side would stab him with pain, and then he had to lie flat until the sweat on his upper lip subsided and the hot knifing sensation dispersed, but they thought he wanted to sleep and they weren't about to let him. A part of him was hoping they would sic the kid on him. A tangle would suit him, he'd feel a lot better if he could kick some ass, and bruisers like him went down easy, and satisfyingly hard. There was too much the youngster hadn't learned yet. He stood wrong, like a barroom bouncer, confident that his size and weight were sufficient advantage, flat on his feet, advertising his lack of finesse as if it were art, his blond head low and forward of his center of gravity, soft tummy hanging over his belt.

The younger man knelt over Hunt where he lay stretched out flat on the carpet beside his chair.

"Up now, please." A huge hand reached for his shoulder, hesitated. A toilet flushed in one of the bedrooms down the suite's hall. At the same time a phone rang.

"Get the phone, Bowser. I promise I won't take a nap."

Again it rang, and Hunt heard water running.

The baby-sitter looked over his shoulder, down the corridor into which the interrogator had disappeared just before Hunt had taken to the carpeted floor, then back at him. "You think I won't get a chance at you, man? You're dreamin'."

"Whatever blows air up your skirt." Hunt rolled slowly to one side, not wanting to start anything after all, the stitch in his side diminishing so that, as he got his knees under him, it no longer took his breath away. What was wrong with him? This wasn't the Lubyanka; there was no need to court suicide.

The baby-sitter looked relieved and backed toward the phone, snatching it from its cradle, saying, "Roger. Yes, sir. Will do," and such.

Hunt eased into the chair on which lamplight shone and slouched forward on crossed arms. They ought to let him sleep; he wasn't thinking clearly. Somebody was going to get hurt, most likely him. He tried to think about Shy, and that made him nervous; his head cleared a little. He ran down his stay-awake litany: This was big trouble, worse than it had seemed going in. The job description had been faulty: Shy had made him no promises, but in their first meeting he had sensed a gentleman's agreement that help was on the way. Then something had changed, and he didn't know what. Shy had seemed distant, preoccupied, as if he were just going through the motions.

It had occurred to Hunt that he was asking too much from his own side, but John Shy was a diplomat's son, prone to phrases like "frank and useful discussion" and the mind-set that went with them. Or so he had assumed. Seeing Shy's baby-sitters crawl out of the shadows on the Mamounia steps, he'd felt simply naïve. Now, after concerted interrogation that was too thorough to abate any time soon—and after what he'd seen when they were checking him in—he was beginning to put things together. And he knew he shouldn't. That was the last thing anybody wanted him to do.

In the hallway last evening, Shy had met a woman whose eyes, when they caught Hunt's, blew away the years like snow: Dania Morales, Angel's wife. He had said to Shy when he returned from escorting her to her room, "Got a good fix, does she?"

"What's that?" Shy had been rubbing a stubbled jaw. "I've got to go out, Cord. I'll get back to you as soon as I can. And I'll send somebody over qualified to continue what we've started. There's supposed to be food and coffee in here already; let's take a look." He had gently maneuvered him into the suite's "hospitality room."

Hunt hadn't pursued it. If he were wrong, he would be accusing Shy of quite a bit more than dishonorable intentions. If he was right and the woman was Dania, then it wasn't the fat kid with the big fists he had to worry about. But it made no sense for Innotech to hire somebody outside to kill him. They were perfectly capable of performing any indicated executive actions without resorting to contract agents. And the Moraleses' prior acquaintance with him, plus their well-deserved reputation for consummate unsubtlety, made them an unlikely choice. But Shy had made no attempt to explain her....

The Foreign Service type came out of the bathroom, tugging on his tie. Hunt's interrogator had introduced himself only as "assistant to the regional director," and it was not until the Zürich night, pale with clouds underlit by the city, had brightened into a gray day filled with the threat of storm and whiteout that Hunt realized the man's RD was Shy.

This impression was confirmed now as the ARD received from the big blond the message that the "follow plane" was at last on its way from Paris (to where Hunt assumed it must have been diverted during last night's storm) with the "additional material on board." The caller wanted to know where he was to deliver it. Glancing over his flanneled shoulder at Hunt, the wiry little sandy-haired man smiled. "Hungry by now? I know I am." He frowned at Hunt's headshake. "Well, be a good fellow and run along into the other room. The pilots ordered up enough breakfast for an army. Eat some of it, it's your party. Take him in there, son."

The big youth lumbered forward and Hunt, hands up, refused any forthcoming aid.

In the suite's living room, the bearded pilots stopped talking when he entered. On the table were newspapers with stripped side arms on them, leathers, gun oil, a box of Winchester .45 magnum slugs, a couple of swabs. "Hey, man, this yours?" One picked up the handgun that had been taken from Hunt in Morocco. "Nice setup. You get it done in the States? Looks like Clark's work, or Stark's." He was nervous, trying to be friendly, looking for something to say.

"Hard to say if it's mine, right now. But you're part right: Clark accurized it. They didn't have those night sights in the States then. I had the trigger reworked and that combat safety added in Berne." A warm feeling came over him, seeing it. The two things he had regretted leaving behind were that particular handgun and his Lebanese army T-shirt. He stood over the table cataloging what lay there: two S&W .38 snubbies with waistband concealment rigs— those would be the pilots' own, small and handy; a Wildey .45 magnum gas-powered auto, certainly the big kid's toy; an Ingram M-10 submachine gun with a LARAND suppressor on its muzzle. "You think we're in for a shooting war here, or is this all standard travel gear?"

By then the kid was growling at the two sport-shirted pilots to clean up the mess before their food came, and Hunt was easing into a chair thinking about being four stories high in the middle of town and how, if things kept up this way, that Ingram SMG could buy him out quietly, efficiently, and much more safely than trying to hand-and-toe it down the granite face of the Baur Au Lac with half of Zürich looking on. It was not until that moment that he realized he was considering escape.

Having faced his impulse, he pronounced it impossible, tactically, and ominous, emotionally. One of the pilots offered him a Marlboro from his floral shirt's pocket. Taking it, and a light, he turned to see which drawer the weapons went into.

Face screwed up, the blond stuck his head close to Hunt's. "Don't even *think* about it, buddy. As for that piece, it's mine, the boss says." He reached into the drawer and got Hunt's pistol, shaking it to dislodge its Null SMZ holster.

"It don't come out that way, dummy. Jeez, don't you know nothin'?" The pilot with the long black curls reached out and snapped the gun free of its sheath. "This here's *pro*fessional *e*quipment! You gotta unsnap this thing, or jerk the gun sideways. And you ain't—Ah, never mind. Shoot your *cagliones* off, son of a pig."

He sat back down, tucking the green/red/gold tropical shirt into his jeans, then stuck out his hand. "Glad to meet you, sir. I can't say what I'd like, but if there's ever anything I can do, once this gets straightened out—and I'm sure it will, sir—you know, like air drops or stuff, you just ask for Mino. Me and Flak admire the fuck out of the job you guys are doin' out—"

"That tears it. *You*"—the blond paused, trying to find room to stuff the Colt in his pants' waistband—"are going on report. No fucking fraternizing with this Ivan-sucker. Copy? Now, we're going to be real noncommittal while I get this food paid for."

He opened the door and a waiter rolled in a trolley full of food. "Take the old coffee urn, okay? *Okay?*" The waiter, holding out the bill for signing, was shaking his head, indicating that he didn't understand. "Take...the...coffee...urn!"

Neither Hunt nor the two pilots intervened, and as the waiter became more frustrated and the blond repeated more loudly and more slowly his English instructions, Hunt risked asking in groping Italian what was aboard the follow plane.

"Mino, don't," Flak warned. "Sir, I can't believe you're dumb enough to have this conversation, even if Mino is." He ruffled the other's hair. Both pilots were well set up, close-bearded and loose-limbed. There the resemblance ceased: Flak was wheatfield American—a brilliant smile, sunstreaked hair, and bright blue eyes, a lone-gun lady-killer; Mino was saturnine, Sicilian, and solid, with black hair curling in the hollow of his throat. "How many languages can you cuss in, sir?" Flak continued. "Me, I can handle anything from *stinkeballen*—that's stinky balls in Dutch—to *bisbis ager*—that's stinky toes in Ethiopian. But I missed Nam, so I can't say nothin' in Slope. Know any Slope swears, sir?"

Hunt told them he didn't know more Vietnamese than was necessary to order dinner in a restaurant, but offered to teach them how to say "Your father has tiny Cuban balls" in Russian, or "Move and I'll blow your homosexual ass to paradise," in Arabic. "In Pushtu, you've got to be subtle. In Pushtu, you might want to say that a man's balls were hairless, but he wouldn't mind it as much as if you told him you saw his daughter's face unveiled and noticed no resemblance."

When the blond broke in with food and red-faced hostility, Flak had just repeated both the Russian and Arabic phrases successfully, and offered his open hand—"Give me five—sir!"—and Mino was muttering that "speaking of undersized balls and such, look who's here."

Hunt looked up, and remembered where he was, and why. The Baur Au Lac's food was as good as its reputation, and as they ate, a silence descended that was more oppressive for the interval of normalcy that had gone before. Hunt nibbled a brioche and drank a lot of coffee, and wondered what the follow plane had aboard that could matter. The answer kept coming to him, but he pushed it out of his mind.

To survive, he must collect no information, collate no data, put none of the questions he had to bed. At the end of everything else, they were going to ask him what he knew about Innotech, and he didn't want to know any more than what the scuttlebutt and the Russians had told him. When the guns were on the newspapers, he had seen the word *Innotech* in conjunction with a photo of a bombed-out wall. He hadn't been in any position to move the Ingram that obscured the article, but its gist was clear enough: Three Innotech facilities had been hit by terrorists, multiple groups had claimed responsibility, and investigations were under way.

Now he knew what had distracted Shy. He hoped no one had decided it was his fault: It would be hard to argue that the information extracted from him might not have been at least incrementally responsible for Innotech's sudden popularity as a target. He began to know what he should try not to say, and as he thought about it his throat closed up: They always get what you hide hardest of all. The Soviets had gotten everything he knew about the members of the Afghan Jirga, about his little group of army infiltrators, about the NTS's effort to rally the Muslims against the godless Communists. Even now, he sympathized with the Afghan Pushtuns' problem: To fight the Soviets, they would go to any lengths, but they were appalled by the excesses of the capitalist societies that offered to help them, uncertain if democracy could coexist with their religious beliefs, unwilling to be corrupted even in their most difficult moments. Only a few years previously, their country had been neutral and free. It was easy to forget, as was the fact that most of the army holding Afghanistan was made up of conscripted Afghans, Muslims and brothers, when they were firing fragmentation grenades at equally Muslim mujahedin from Russian-made Plamyas with a cyclic fire rate of three hundred rounds per minute.

After the phone rang again, the interrogator came to get him. "All done, then? We've having some visitors, I've been told, so let's get started before they show up." Behind him was someone with a pipe and a fat black bag in his hand. "Would you like to go with the doctor into the bedroom? Take him in there, son."

Still seated, he experienced a moment of vertigo and his mouth went sour. When he looked up, he saw the two pilots watching him as if the light were too bright. He slid from the chair before Bowser could help him up and went with them. If they stuck needles in him, he didn't know what he would do. He thought of a number of things to say—warnings, pleas, threats—and said nothing, just proceeded, feeling his bare feet hit the floor and the big blond breathing down his neck and fight-or-flight mode come on him so hard that his teeth ached.

In "his" bedroom he managed to ask, "Where's Shy? Does he know you're doing this? Please don't give me anything until—"

The baby-sitter grabbed him and tried to hold him, he thought. Later he was told they were only trying to get him to sit on the bed. At that moment, he saw the bag and a syringe and he chopped the kid straight across the larynx and grabbed him by the belt long enough to get a hold on the Colt Bowser had stuffed there earlier. The kid, gagging and eyes defocused, clutched at him.

The safety had not been on, Hunt found as they grappled, and he shot the baby-sitter in the gut.

By then the doctor was backed against a wall and the two pilots were in the room, one with his little snubby and the other—Hunt heard the clip slap in and a round being chambered—with the M-10. The distressed interrogator type stood between the beds wringing his hands and telling everyone to "be calm, it was only one report, and deny any problem if the hotel security people come by."

The blond was holding his belly together; his sobs and the smell of excrement filled the room. Hunt crouched down over the baby-sitter doubled up in his own fluids. "You want to deny any problem, better get some towels under him." There was no exit wound: Hunt's bullet must have bounced around inside him like a pinball. Both index fingers meeting at the trigger, he gestured with his Commander's barrel. "Go on, go." The interrogator had laced his hands over the crown of his head. Slowly, he took them down and sidled toward the bathroom.

In front of him the two pilots were whispering to each other, Flak with the Ingram on his hip but pointing left of Hunt; Mino with his elbow locked out straight, the S&W's barrel trained on

Hunt but wavering in a nervous figure eight. "Your ARD's worried about the noise. You want to put those down before one of them goes off?"

Flak widened his stance. Mino muttered, "Fuckin'-A," and put one hand on his hip, sliding one foot back to improve his sight picture.

"You two want to stand there, faced off with me, while this guy bleeds to death, I don't mind. But I don't think you want to hurt anybody—or get hurt." The blond baby-sitter groaned. "So why don't you just put those on the floor and go stand against the wall and I'll let the doctor see to his patient."

From the bathroom doorway, the interrogator suggested that they do that. Flak puffed out his cheeks and knelt down very slowly. "You want me to break it down, sir? I'd be glad to do it ...sir? *Mino!*"

"Mino, Mino," Hunt murmured, "just relax. Let's not make this worse than it is." Mino's gun came down and Hunt leaned back against the wall behind him. "Okay, Doc, come look at him. You, too, Flannel. Then you get Shy on the phone and tell him to get his ass up here."

HEADING down the Bahnhofstrasse in the back of a NATO armor-class-five Mercedes 600 with consular corps plates, Shy couldn't see five feet through the limousine's privacy glass. It was Sunday noon, but it might have been dusk, so hard was the snow falling, unremitting white from a leaden sky, concealing the railway station and the fine shops and cosmopolitan restaurants as it masked the park in which the Baur Au Lac nestled at the bottom of the hill.

Under its portico an ambulance was being loaded, and Shy was reminded of the Mamounia. At least there he hadn't been the one

on whom the onus of explanation, bribery, and deception had
fallen. He wasn't worried about covering it—the Swiss had a simple philosophy: Come, spend your money, spy as you will upon
one another; so long as one was not after Swiss intelligence or
short of funds, Swiss authorities could afford to be very tolerant—
but he was apprehensive about Hunt, who had already forced him
out farther on a limb than he liked, into fallbacks he had hoped
not to need.

In the pale cherry-paneled lobby, he spoke to no one, leaving
his friend from 141 Zollikerstrasse to smooth things over with the
management. Though the Swiss francs being lavishly dispensed
were Innotech's, the consulate staffer was discharging a personal
obligation to Shy. Had the doctor not also been Innotech's, the
ambulance private, and the pressure inordinate, no amount of
indebtedness would have sufficed to enlist aid from that quarter.
As it was, Shy had had to lie to him.

When he had gotten the news in Crisis Committee at Cannard's,
he had excused himself, saying that the backup he had taken to
Marrakech had shot himself in the stomach, and little more. There
were some titters at the idea of a gunshot in the Baur Au Lac,
where international arms deals were made by men who had never
so much as handled a weapon.

He had been lying ever since. The subscription list—those with
need to know—he had drawn up with Cannard for Dropout was
exceedingly short: those invited to the hotel suite, necessarily;
himself; Shy's own opposite number in the States; two assistants.
Since he had taken that phone call, he had emended it further.

He was the only one outside the suite who knew what was actually happening there. Despite the cautions of tradecraft, he
wanted to keep it that way. He could have waited until the management agreed to clear the floor, sent in a Triage antiterrorist
unit with rubber bullets and stun grenades; he could have thrown
up his hands and called in the locals to handle a psychotic killer
who was holding five of his people at bay; he could have ignored
Hunt's request and sat by until Hunt either killed his hostages or
escaped with them. Any of those would have been safer, but all
of them had overt consequences.

As the elevator opened, he took off his overcoat and his jacket
and stepped out, obviously unarmed, in his shirtsleeves. He thought
he should have shaved, or at least called his wife. There was no

one in the hall. He loosened his tie and knocked on the suite's door. While he was here, he could give Michele a ring—that is, if Hunt didn't shoot him.

Mino Volante, his pilot, answered in an open Hawaiian shirt under which was a T-shirt bearing the legend "Injection Is Nice But I'd Rather Be Blown" in white letters on a black ground. "Sir, we're sure glad to see you. We didn't dare start anything, what with the penetration problem of these flimsy walls." Walking backward, he whispered, "Watch out sir, he's cocked and locked."

"Is everyone all right?"

"This way, sir, okay? Yeah, no harm except to Tubby's tummy. The doc thought he might live, but Hunt doesn't think so. We all went into one of the bedrooms when the ambulance guys came, so that was cool, but the head of housekeeping keeps calling— wants to know when they can make up the beds."

"Son?"

Mino stopped, turned around, jammed his hands into his jeans pockets, eyes on his boots.

"Mino, is there something you want to say?"

"Yes, sir, that is—no, sir, I don't want to...but, I mean—I would'a done the same thing, sir, if I was him. That fat schvantz said you told him he could have Hunt's gun.... That reads like he ain't gonna need it where he's goin', don't it? I can't suss it out any different. You copy this? He could only figure we were gonna take him out...I mean the guy's been real upright with us, no hassle. Man with a piece like that is committed to controlling his environment, sir. But nobody's tied up, or hurt, or even been threatened. Those medicos come in and he's cool as a line louie, takin' us in the other room and talkin' muzzle climb with Flak—"

"I see. Thank you, Mino." By then he had spied Hunt in the next room sprawled across two chairs at the dining table, head back, seemingly half asleep. Hunt raised the automatic he was holding to eye level in a casual salute, then lowered it.

Before him on the table was a hellish quantity of small arms; opposite him sat Shy's sandy-haired ARD. The Swiss doctor's salt-and-pepper head turned and red-rimmed eyes indicated Shy eloquently from his seat on the ARD's right. "I vas just giving him vitamins! I demand an—"

The ARD silenced him with a touch. Flak, at the table's foot, raised his tousled head from his arms. "Hi, boss." Flak grinned uncertainly, then shrugged and spread his hands, palms up. "Guess we fucked up, huh?"

Shy ignored them all. "Cord, you've got yourself into one hell of a mess. Let's clear the room and start working on how we're going to get you out of it."

"Not just yet, Shy." Hunt's enamel eyes slowly widened. "I asked the 'doctor' if he wouldn't mind taking those vitamins, if that's what's in that hypo, and he refused." He picked up a cup and sipped coffee. "Would *you* like to prove to me that's all it is?"

"Cord, we're wasting time."

Hunt sighed like crumpled cellophane. "Everybody out, but don't leave the rooms—except for you, hypo-jockey. I don't want to ever see you again." He said something very uncomplimentary in German.

The ARD cast Shy a commiserating glance and left him his pen, tapping it pointedly on the table.

"Sit down, Shy," Hunt said as the others began to file out. "Before you start, let *me* tell *you* something."

"You've got the gun, as usual."

"What choice did you give me? I know what's happening, don't make any mistake about that. I've been trying to keep things as low-profile as possible under the circumstances." Shy saw his thin lips twitch. "Let me lay it out for you before you insult my intelligence: You're here because you've got some leverage coming that's going to neutralize any amount of firepower, you think. So you'll talk me down until they get here and then I'll hand everything to you, right?"

"I'm here because you asked me to come. I would have been here sooner, but I was all the way across town. I'm sorry this happened, you don't know how sorry. I'm sure it *was* vitamins, perhaps with a little amphetamine to keep you awake. We had hoped you might be up to a few visitors."

"It's hard to believe you think I'm this stupid." Hunt leaned forward, resting his head on one hand. "That baby-sitter of yours dies, what happens?"

"Nothing whatsoever."

"Where am I, the USSR? You're treating me just like they did: no sleep, no privacy, no reality.... I really believed you, you know—

that it would be different. I can't handle any more chemicals—
you don't understand what you're asking. I asked them if you
knew what they were doing.... *Did* you?"

Shy cleared his throat. "No, Cord, I didn't. Just crossed wires.
We don't want to take chances with your health any more than
you do. But you just shot someone, and I have a feeling you didn't
mean to do it. So give me all this hardware and let's get down to
business."

"Can you guarantee that nobody's going to dope me?"

He meant to, but he said, "I wish I could. While I'm handling
things, I'll watch out for you, but you're making it very difficult."

Hunt laughed his papery laugh. "A goddamn honest answer,
at last. It *was* an accident, Shy, the kind that can happen to any
asshole who sticks a gun in his pants without checking the safety."
He was running his finger along his own handgun's barrel. "I
can't say I'm sorry about it, but I ran the details down myself: It's
all coverable, except maybe the part about the guy having a burst
appendix; I told that shaman he'd have to keep it simple, but I
couldn't be there when the ambulance people took Bowser out,
so I can't testify to the legend being plausible, casualty-wise."

Shy fingered the pen before him. Hunt would know as well as
he why the ARD left it. He pushed its button with his finger and
nudged it until it rolled off the table onto the carpet. "I'm impressed, but you must realize you've complicated things."

Hunt shrugged and picked at a piece of lint on the Commander's black slide. "You complicate things, your type. You honchos,
sending guys out on drops fifty miles from where we're supposed
to be, into hostile territory that's supposed to be friendly, to contact
people who don't want to talk to us, without having anything
concrete to offer in the way of help. And you're scared of turn-
arounds. You should be—the other side takes good care of their
assets. You write me off so easy the first time, and I buy your line
a second time. Then I see that Morales girl in the hall and you
pretend you don't know who she is, so I say, Okay, this guy's living
in the zone anyway, maybe he doesn't truck with low types." He
licked his lips. "But I'm scared, I don't mind telling you. If I just
wanted to get myself killed, I could have managed it in Marrakech.
What fucking right do you have to tell some security type with
an IQ of *maybe* a hundred twenty that he can have my pistol—

unless I'm walking dead and you just haven't told me? I know
money means nothing to you, but that's eight bills-plus there, and
it took me six months to get the work done on it. So when Bowser
decides to give me a bearhug, I'm not exactly in a positive frame
of mind. You've got me here with phony documents and I'm dead
as far as my Moroccan citizenship goes anyway. What assurances
can you give me that this is just another sloppy semiprofessional
operation and not serious ill will?"

"None, except that I want you to work on something with me.
I think you're well enough, and I know you're mean enough, and
I'm going to give you a chance to prove that you're good for more
than just reminiscing to joint committees from the Joint Chiefs,
Central and Defense Intelligence, the National and International
Security Agencies—"

"Shit. You suicidal?" As Hunt spoke, his pistol's muzzle came
up and Shy stared calmly into it.

"Shoot me. My wife will get my pension and I won't have to
feel guilty about you. But *you'll* learn something you haven't figured out yet: The Soviets are primitives when it comes to psych-
war. Otherwise, put it away. I can't do anything constructive while
I'm wondering if my will is up-to-date." Shy's solar plexus felt as
if it were fibrillating. He had no right to ask for Hunt's trust, and
Hunt knew it.

Cordell Hunt took his feet off the chair and with pistol in hand
rubbed his stomach. "I don't know. I'm all pumped up. Why didn't
you just play me straight to begin with? *Who's* coming here? What's
the 'material' the follow plane brought in? You think I couldn't
have walked out of here with those pilots and held off an army
from the Falcon? I'm still here, so I guess I'm listening, but I'm
going to need some damned cohesive answers."

"To begin with, I didn't have the authority. I'm trying, now, to
remedy that. You'll see only Innotech people. If we can give out
certain kinds of information, we may be able to avoid producing
you in person. As for the follow plane, I think you know: We
couldn't leave a loose end like that girl in Morocco after the trouble
we went to, clearing your deck, so to speak. And speaking of
speaking, her command of Russian is remarkable for a Berber,
I've been told. A house full of assault weapons, some of them
Soviet AK-74s, rented in the name of one Martinova and protected

by a woman passing for Muslim who might just be KGB is an odd place to find someone like you, unless you've actually made some sort of deal with the Soviets?..."

"I won't bother to answer that," Hunt said pityingly. "You poor, naïve sons of bitches would be pathetic if you weren't so damn dangerous."

"Then take the safe route: Cooperate with me—so far neither you nor I have broken faith—and I'll see you through, I promise."

"Shit."

"Indeed. Now, can we get ready to move you? You certainly can't stay here any longer. You've involved those pilots, I'm sure you realize, to the extent that at least for a while their fates hang on yours...."

"I didn't tell them anything."

"They know you."

"They think they may have guessed."

"They know you. Now give me the gun and let's clean off this table and pretend to be civilized."

"Sorry, Shy, it's not good enough. I'm *un*civilized enough not to put myself at the mercy of somebody whose lip curls when he looks at an honest weapon but will sign off on some 'cost-effective and politically sound' recommendation to desert whole networks in the field or bend over while entire populations take it up the ass from our friends and foes alike."

"Just like old times. All right, Hunt, let's start at the top and talk it out once again. Whatever you think of my politics, right now I'm the only friend you've got. And this time, tell me about Martinova—*and* the Morales woman: who, what, why, how and when."

"Speaking of old times, did you marry that girl we both liked and have lots of little third-generation diplomats?"

"As a matter of fact, yes. We'll have you to dinner when things calm down."

"Then maybe you ought to think about your family—widows and orphans don't get much comfort out of pensions. Or maybe, being married, moneyed, and overeducated, you've forgotten that nothing—no person, no pressure, no principle—gets in the way of somebody like me taking care of his own butt. I'll give you cooperation, but I'm keeping my gun."

"We'll see."

"Why don't you tell me I won't need it?"

"Because you should take it as an article of faith that I'll keep my word. We're going to sit here until we work this out—"

The phone rang; they eyed each other. Hunt slowly and deliberately slipped the flimsy-looking little holster over his shoulder and clipped its strap to his belt. "Let me tell you about—"

Mino came to the doorway. "Sirs? That was Mr. Shy's office...."

"Go ahead, Mino," Shy prodded.

"Well, sir,"—he looked at Hunt—"you were right, that guy just died." Mino's pupils had consumed his eyes; wide and staring, they seemed coal black in his paled face.

"That's what serious social ammo is for, Mino—you carry that snubby to balance your wallet, or what?"

"Yes, sir. I mean, no, sir. It's not that. Shy's office was adamant— that's what they said to say, sir—*adamant* that we 'vacate immediately.' There's a car downstairs and a guy at the door who says he can't wait much longer."

Hunt snapped the Commander, muzzle up, into its scabbard and reached behind him for the bomber jacket Flak had loaned him. "I'm ready. Get Flak to help you pack up this stuff." He pointed to the guns on the table. "Don't leave anything behind. Shy, if you're nervous, take your pick."

"Somehow I have to make you understand that it *cannot* be this way," Shy said slowly.

Hunt, standing, zipped his jacket, shaking his head. "Maybe some other time, some other place. This is your show; you want to close it down, it's okay with me. *You're* going to have to explain how and why you smuggled me in here. I'll just scream to every newsie I can find that I was kidnapped. Two can play, you know."

Shy started. "Two Can Play" was the name of the project that ended with Hunt in the Lubyanka. "Bastard. Mino, get Flak in here and be very thorough. We'll wait for you in the car." He ignored Hunt's offer of a side arm. That was what the Hunts always tried to do: drag you down to their level. "When we get out of here, try to speak a little higher class of English, I know you remember how. These affectations of yours must all be kept under wraps—the man out there waiting is a friend of mine; I'd prefer not to involve him more deeply than is necessary."

"*Who, what, where,* and *why?*" Hunt had not moved.

"In a consular corps car, driven by my friend's chauffeur, to a house out of town, where every one of you"—Flak had just come in—"is going to act like the well-bred, well-mannered representative of your nation we all know you're not."

Hunt made a derisive noise but went with him, pausing only long enough to pick up the ARD's pen from under the table: "Wouldn't want to leave this." He clicked it back onto "transmit" and handed it to Shy as they left the room. The worried consulate staffer's expression became even more grim when he saw Cordell Hunt.

In the hall, the elevator, and the lobby, Cory Hunt had been ready for anything—muscle types or medicos or full auto fire stitching him up the middle. Undesirables bought it publicly in the European theater all the time, and he was certainly that. But no one came out of the woodwork the way he'd once seen a scratch specialist do in Vienna on a walk-up (afterward simply sauntering off, pieces of cranium and pink brains and blood speckling him, two cartridges short of his standard load). In fact, nothing more untoward occurred than Shy's friend's comment when Hunt offered his hand: "Pardon me, but I don't shake hands with ghosts."

After that, the little balding man with the worried look ignored him, hissing at Shy that he considered this "a breach of protocol" and that Shy should *not* feel free to call on him again. Moreover, under the circumstances, he would not accompany them; Shy should simply bring back the keys when he was finished; hopefully, that would be very soon; meanwhile he didn't wish to know anything about anything—even diplomatic immunity could be stretched only so far.

The ARD (whom the angry, balding man called Hubble) pointed out the cameras in the elevator's ceiling, and the little man pulled on his cuff links and fumed until they parted in the lobby.

At the curb a group of limousines was parked, dusted with the snow still falling, uniformed drivers scraping their windows desultorily. Among them, only one had gunports, small rectangular seams showing their placement by the doors.

In it, heat-shocked after the cold, Hunt sat as instructed in the

middle of the back seat. Shy and the ARD got in the front; the
driver locked the rear doors from behind the wheel. Cory could
see their mouths move beyond the partition, but he wasn't a good
lip-reader. By the time Flak and Mino appeared with a porter and
their bags, he was dozing intermittently, snapping to when his
head fell back against the seat. Fighting the cozy warmth was
difficult; he hadn't slept since Friday evening, and then he had
not slept well. When the pilots slid in on both sides of him, he
welcomed the frigid air. He had been dreaming that he was back
in the States at China Lake, taking a short course in mycotoxins,
trying to tell by its symptoms if the dog behind the glass was dying
from the T_2 toxin trichothecene or something else: The sound
the door locks made being popped up by the driver's remote
sounded like the noise the dog's paws had made jerking against
the glass.

"Hey, man, it's okay." Flak squeezed his arm, then patted the
flat black Zero Halliburton camera case he balanced on his lap.
"We got everything, even to the rags."

The pilot's voice echoed in his head, reverberating like a dream
voice. Hunt knew he was losing it: Sleep meant vulnerability, but
he couldn't make his body understand. The heat lulled him and
the quiet car pulled out into traffic and the tires whispered rhyth-
mically like the easy breathing of the men on either side of him.
He sat up straight as long as he could, but his head was heavy on
his neck and when at last he leaned it back to devote all his attention to the assessment of his position he was still trying to make,
he dropped off somewhere between estimating how thoroughly
he had jeopardized his chances of reaching an accommodation
with Shy, and what, if anything, he could do about it.

The Mercedes' fishtailing woke him before Flak's gritted "Hope
that *na he* up front listened good at defensive-driving school," or
the snapping of the Halliburton's lid as the M-10 and the Wildey
came out.

Then a round hit the passenger side from somewhere out in
the snow; Mino's frame shook, but he continued trying to slide
the impacted gunport back to get the Wildey's seven-inch barrel
through it. "Armor-piercing, yet," Hunt heard, and saw the blood
begin to soak through Mino's coat.

He snapped his Commander out and pounded with it on the

partition's glass. Shy, face expressionless, turned around, as if in slow motion. Hunt gesticulated that he slide the partition back. While Shy unlocked it, Hunt was conscious of the two pilots crouched at the side ports, of the whining ricochets and smacks as the car took hits, then of Shy's hand coming back through the opened slider for one of the snubbies. Through the windshield he could see two Audis nose-to-nose across the road.

He slammed the slider in the other direction and lay his Commander's muzzle against the base of the driver's skull. "Let's just hit 'em straight on, right in the middle there, like you're supposed to know how to do, big fella. Move it! Come on, floor this sucker!"

The car, which had slowed almost to a stop, accelerated. Hunt clutched the window frame and hoped Shy would understand that a .38 wasn't pertinent to this sort of action unless the car was disabled or the chauffeur tried to do a handover by rolling out of the door with the keys. When the speedometer read straight up, he let go of the partition and felt around in the Halliburton for the handguns, but the pilots were wearing them. By then Shy had extracted his wrist and was rubbing it, and the ARD was yelling that everyone had better get their heads down and brace for collision, and Flak was ready for another clip and wondering where the fuckers with the big stuff *were* in all that terrain, and Mino was muttering over and over that he was god-fucked *shot* and pleading with the snipers to show themselves and "*Die*, motherfuckers!"

They hit the Audis at better than 130 kmph and the lighter cars blew apart and spun back against the rear of the limo with their bumpers, giving Hunt just a glimpse of balaclava-covered faces and assault rifles and maybe a recoilless rifle in a depression by the roadside before they were gone and Flak yelled, "Down, fool!" and grabbed Hunt by the belt as the car began taking machine-gun fire from the rear.

When he had scrabbled back up, the rear and supposedly bullet-proof window of the limousine looked like cracked ice and the ARD's head was nowhere to be seen. "Don't slow down, sweetheart," Hunt suggested, not caring if the driver spoke English: The Commander spoke everyone's language. He knew the right rear of the car was giving the man some trouble, but it wasn't until they had rounded two curves and no more shots were fired that he looked away from his driver's-eye view long enough to see in the side mirror the crumpled fender and chewed-up tire. The ARD had taken some splinters in his forearm from the fractured partition and Shy had his own head down, brushing glass from his hair.

"I'm putting in," came Mino's pain-gritty bravado, "for fucking *hazard pay*, boss. *Haz*ard pay, and that won't cover the half. Low-*pro*file or not, sir, I got to do it. Goddamn degrading, shot by a pissant terrorist through a car door."

"Mino," Flak demanded, "you okay?" And to Hunt: "Sir, would you sit back and put your gun away?" Then: "I'd thank you if you'd let me get over there."

"How about some kind of medal or citation, sir? Can guys like us get 'em?" Mino rambled.

Hunt sat back, letting Flak climb over him and the discarded Ingram with its spare magazine and the Halliburton.

Shy turned and put his head on his hand, staring back at Hunt silently.

"Christ, I think you're really hurt," Flak whispered, while Mino grunted, "Naw, I don't feel a thing. They wouldn't give contract agents Intelligence Stars, would they?—Ouch!"

"Sit up," Flak urged him. "There you go. Lean over, man, I want to see if that bullet's in you or what—Damn!"

Still, Shy was eyelocked with Hunt. "There's just no telling," Hunt murmured, "whether they were your fans or mine." He broke eye contact and slid across the glass-strewn seat to where Mino sat on the floor, his left jacket and shirtsleeves cut away, blood everywhere.

"Let's see, Flak. Let me look. Okay there, Mino. Can you lean forward?" He bent down and cleared the blood away, then said, "Lean back, if you want." He sighed. "Whatever it was, it was solid metal—went clear through. What's left in there is car and bone chips. I think they just got lucky and it came in through the port. But you got lucky, too. A little lower and you'd have a hole in your lung—a little meaner, like an incendiary round, and there'd be nothing to talk about."

"Here's the slug, sir." Flak was clambering around over Hunt on the seat. "It's not lookin' too identifiable, maybe 7.62-millimeter NATO." He put away the pocketknife he had used to dig it out of the upholstery.

"Lemme see, it's mine, ain't it?"

Hunt smiled and wound down to the floor of the car, where he began automatically collecting the spent spare magazines. "See if you can't pack it with something. Shy, have you anything clean and white up there? Shirts are fine."

A medical kit came into his field of vision. "Flak, will you see to it?" Shy's voice accompanied it.

"I'll do it," Hunt said, conscious of the car's speed and the freezing air coming in the shattered window, which hung in strings that tinkled as they blew, and Shy's odd tone of voice. He put the magazines carefully in their foam beds and slowly hiked himself up onto the seat, empty-handed, then added, "I don't mind."

"Well, mister," Shy said quietly, "I *do* mind. You've done more than enough already. More than enough, Cowboy Spook. That's the problem with *your* type: Everywhere they go becomes a war zone. *And I will not have it here.* This is my territory, I call the shots. All of them. Understand?" He rubbed his wrist, which was perceptibly swelling. His lips were blue, his face was white, and his voice was trembling. *"Well?"*

Hunt said, "Mino will very probably make a full recovery," as calmly as he might.

"I doubt it. I doubt any of us will fully recover from you. You're a carrier of a virulent disease. Certainly this vehicle is not going to recover. I don't want to see you *touch* another gun, not if you're all that stands between me and my Maker, not if World War Three is about to start and you could avoid it with one 'well-placed' round of 'serious social ammo'—not for any reason. *Am I making myself understood?*" He snapped about, slammed at the spider-fractured partition, and picked up the mobile phone.

"Christ, these guys are too intense," Hunt heard Flak whisper, and Mino grunt in reply.

After a time, Shy hung up and, twisting, said to Hunt, "I insist that you apologize to Mr. Helms, whose credentials are too impeccable to ever have been impugned at gunpoint in such a cavalier fashion—and to Mr. Hubble, who is in no way impelled by honor or duty to continue risking his life for yours."

Hunt closed his eyes and counted slowly backward from ten, feeling Flak's fist strike his calf and withdraw. When he opened them, the limousine was turning onto a mountainous side road, and he had missed any indicator of what its name might be. He took a deep breath and then expelled it. "My apologies, Mr. Helms. And you, too, Hubble."

He wanted to say again that it could well have been Shy who was drawing the fire, but he didn't. Shy wasn't in any state to listen to reason, and Hunt was simply too tired to acquit himself well in verbal battle, let alone a battle of wits. In his own adrenaline aftermath, he felt helpless and hopeless. He watched the empty shell casings and the loose Ingram jitter on the Mercedes' carpet, and he watched to see that Flak did a competent job on Mino's shoulder. Thus again he missed a crossroad in the lowering dusk, and began studying landmarks only as they came down a long drive in which three other vehicles with their lights on were already parked: a Land Cruiser, a Rover, and a Seville with MD plates.

People began getting out of the cars as they pulled up before a snow-frosted chalet set into a mountainside.

Later he would recall his arrival there and wonder how he could have been so unobservant as to have missed the helicopter pad like a bull's-eye in the center of the circular drive, or the gates that silently shut once the battered Mercedes had passed the natural choke point of convening ridges behind which the house was set. But at the time, his teeth were chattering and his fingers felt numb and his eyes kept refusing to focus; the only thing that had kept him conscious this long was the cold wind stirring the shattered glass curtain at the back of his neck.

And because he was approaching the limit of his endurance, he tried to make light of what his instincts were telling him about the chalet and the cars and the dozen people pouring out of them, teasing Flak: "I'm disappointed you lied to me."

"Never, sir. What do you mean?" They were getting ready to help Mino out into the arms of the two men in overcoats dispatched there by a waiting woman who had dashed up to the car, peered within, run to the Seville, and reappeared with a doctor's bag.

"*Na he:* You said you'd never been in Nam."

"That's not Vietnamese, it's Thai, sir. It means—"

"Watch it." The door opened. "I know what it means, and we wouldn't want to say that with a lady present."

She was furred and elegant, tawny and sweet-smelling, and she gave Cordell Hunt a look loaded with commiseration and despair at the ways of the world as Mino was objecting that he was *walking* wounded, anybody could see. She bent over, leaning into the car, saying, "There, there, you'll feel better soon," and gave Mino a shot, stabbing a loaded syringe into him so expertly it seemed like sleight of hand.

"Aw, no," Mino protested, but the woman had stepped back and the waiting man lifted him effortlessly and took him up the path toward the big carved doors where Shy already stood with his ARD talking to five or six people, pointing and pounding his fist into his palm for emphasis.

"Okay, sir, let's slide out nice and easy," Flak whispered.

"My friends call me Cory; let's cut the shit—you know me."

"I couldn't do that, sir. I—" He slid out first, and as Hunt was following, the woman in sable came forward from inspecting the rear of the ravaged limousine.

"What *happened* here?" Her voice had an accent that could have been Barnard or Beverly Hills or Bonn, the sort of diplomatic nonaccent that embassy people cultivated. It was to Hunt she had spoken.

"We took time out for a quick game of hardball on the way."

"Well, you and your friend there"—Flak was crouched by the rear tire—"seem to be none the worse for wear," she pronounced brightly. "Poor Dropout." She indicated with her head the path down which Mino had been taken. "But we'll take good care of him, you and I. I believe I'm supposed to call you Flak. I'm—"

"Christ, lady, *be cool*," Flak broke in, craning his neck to frown at her. "Go find some candidates for your first-aid station, if that's what you're doing here."

Her manicured eyebrows wriggled, then she nodded. "So *you're* Flak." She held her hand out and he scrambled up to take it, wiping his palms on his jeans before presenting one. "I've heard marvelous things about you."

Hunt leaned back against the car's misshapen fender, his vision filled with red and white lights, all sounds far away. He estimated, from the direction of the oncoming darkness and the fact that they had gone south from Zürich, that they must be in the Albis, but that would mean he'd slept longer than he'd thought. It seemed almost like being back in the Hindu Kush in winter—except that everything was smaller, fuzzier, and the air wasn't so thin, and there were trees and limousines and people who spoke deception as well as any other language.

Flak was dressing down the woman without regard to profanity, but in an undertone.

Hunt caught the end of it: "*Mino* was the guy you gave the goddamn shot to, lady!"

"So—oh, my! Then...*this* is Dropout? I'm so sorry." She stepped toward Hunt and behind her he could see Shy and three men coming down the steps. "Dropout, we've been so looking forward to meeting you—"

He shook his head at her, still needing the car to prop him up, but angry enough to cross his arms and glower down at her outstretched hand. "I don't want you to call me that. If you don't want to call me by my name, then pick a war name—God knows I've had enough of them. The Pushtuns call me 'malik,' and the Arabs call me 'Abu Ifrit,' and in Delta they used to call me 'Scratch.' Or call me whatever the fuck is on these papers.... Ask Shy, I forgot. Shy, you'd better muzzle this bitch before you don't have a card left to play.."

"Beth, fix up something for our friend to keep him awake. He's so sleepy he's cranky. I want you to see something, cowboy, before we go in the house—*if* you're up to it. Flak, you'd better come along."

Flak walked beside him, their shoulders brushing, the corners of his mouth pulled in, kicking gravel and watching where it flew. "*Fluff-head, na he, schvantz*—"

"That will do, Flak," cautioned Shy.

"He's perfectly right in complaining, Shy. Who vetted these operatives, your worst enemy? If I were you, I'd sit down and do a radical reappraisal of who is doing what for whom, and why."

"You and I are going to bounce that ball around as soon as this is over."

Hunt didn't like the way Shy had said it. He zipped his borrowed jacket against the chill and stuffed his hands in its pockets, trying to control the shivers that had begun to wrack him. Flak offered him his overcoat, and when he refused, Shy said softly that he had taken care of that, too—that Hunt would soon be warm and dry and rested and well.

"Even some of your things from Marrakech came in on the follow plane. Flak, get the duffel bag out of this trunk." It was the Rover they had halted beside, and inside it something lunged against the glass. Shy took Hunt's arm and said, "I expect you to control yourself. If you act in any way aggressively, you shall be quite dead. Look behind you."

"I saw them, I don't need confirmation."

"But I want you to know that they're Triage—stone professionals; if not of your caliber, then certainly of your cold-blooded ilk."

He had stopped listening; he just waited for Shy's voice to cease. Through the blackout glass, he couldn't see the car's occupant, but he knew who was going to come out that door.

As it opened he said, "Give us a moment; we can't possibly coordinate our stories in a couple of minutes."

"Sorry. I wish I could."

Nasta needed help to get out of the car; she was pale and wild-eyed and dressed in Western clothing someone else had bought for her: The coat was too big and the pants dragged in the gravel and snow. Two baby-sitters and Shy and Flak formed a half-circle around them. She stood unencumbered for an instant, then made a move toward him. Cory Hunt had never seen anything as damning as the accusation in her luminous brown eyes.

In Pushtu he said, "I did not mean this evil. How is it with you?"

"They abuse me." Her chin was up, her eyes sparkling. "Very bad, these friends of yours."

He walked toward her, his hands negating what she had said, and his arms went around her. In his grasp she struggled briefly, then subsided, her head pressed to his chest. "You are foolish," she said into his coat. "They will use us against each other. They are devious. They think—they think I am a spy for the Schurawi, a—"

"Schurawi" was what the Pushtuns called the Russians. "You mustn't make them hurt you. Tell them whatever they want to know. You don't realize how they can hurt you. Please, promise—"

She struggled backward, glaring at him but with tears in her eyes. "You said they would help us, that this one"—she inclined her head toward Shy—"was the one who sent you. . . . It must be

that you, too, are as they. Abu Ifrit,"—she shifted to Arabic—
"you are as they call you, a demon, an evil spirit. I promise you
nothing; you are full of lies." Tears ran down her cheeks as she
spoke.

Abu Ifrit, his Lebanese war name, meant roughly "father of
demons." He wanted to know what they'd done to her, but he
didn't ask. He put his hand under her chin and said, "If you hate
me, I can bear it. But if you resist them to punish me, I cannot
endure the thought of what will happen to you. It is you they use
against me"—even in Arabic, he was stumbling, at a loss for
words—"and I'm helpless before them, because of you. If you
don't tell them who and what you are, I must, to save you. You
can*not* resist them, Nasta—"

She was shaking her head so that her black hair flew, writhing
to free herself from his embrace.

He let her go and she staggered backward abruptly, wiping her
nose with her hand. He wanted to say how sorry he was, somehow
to protect her. He spread his hands and let them slap down to
his sides, then turned away so that if the baby-sitters had to wrestle
her back into the car, he wouldn't be forced to watch.

"Let's go, Shy. You've made your point."

Though he heard her cursing, then a gasp, then the car doors
shut, he did not look back, but walked meekly between Flak and
Shy up the driveway, the path, the stairs, and into the chalet,
through a door whose thick glass side panels each bore a decal
proclaiming: "These premises protected by Triage Security Systems."

Chapter
4

"DRINK?" Shy wanted Jack Daniel's, but settled for Glenlivet, straight up.

"No thanks, never touch it. When I was working with Delta, we used to call the Department of Defense the 'Ditsy old Drunks.' That's part of the problem: Half the world's policymakers are on their asses by lunch. Maybe one of the 'pilots' could spare me a line or a joint?"

"Screw Delta," Shy said as he tossed off his shot. He'd been up for thirty-six hours, but he couldn't possibly look as bad as Cordell Hunt, slumped down in a wing chair before the hearth's crackling fire, chin resting on his laced fingers as if his elbows on the chair's arms were all that kept him upright, moss-agate eyes red and puffy above a two-day beard.

"Screw Delta," Shy repeated. "The 'Working Group on Terrorism of the Special Coordinating Committee of the National Security Council' did—that's why you quit them, or so your letter of resignation said."

"With twenty-nine agencies having to okay it before Delta scratched its nuts, and seventeen subordinate committees each lobbying for their own interests, and the chair of the Executive Committee having changed five times in the two years I was there, Delta never had a chance to do its stuff. You can't do counter-terrorism by committee."

"At least we agree on something." Shy crossed the paneled library to its sliding doors and asked the man posted outside to find Flak. Beth was perched on the little Chippendale settee left of the door, her sable coat and medical kit beside her. She got up, and Shy met her. As soon as the man was gone, he kissed her. "I'm glad you're here," he said, "but I shouldn't be. Did Sid send you to keep an eye on me?"

Beth Cannard gave him her half-lidded wicked-lady look, giggled, sobered, then said, "I'm sorry about the mix-up at the car. I was so worried about you, I wasn't thinking. How's Dropout? You should let me examine him...." She heard footsteps and stepped back.

"Later. If I have to stay here, you can stay with me. I'll take you home when I leave." He leaned close—"God, you smell good,"—and whispered, "You don't have any illicit substances, do you—for Dropout?"

"What do you mean? Marijuana? No, nothing like that, just sedatives and interrogation aids."

Flak and the sentry returned, and he patted her arm. "Just an hour or so, doctor, and he's all yours. In the meantime, could you supervise the kitchen staff? Dinner at seven, if you can hustle them. Espresso, ASAP?" He turned to Flak. "Coming?"

In the library, Hunt's head snapped around as the doors opened. From the window, he returned to his chair and eased slowly into it. "Quite a safe house. Yours or the local station's?"

"It's a bastardization, actually. Swiss on the outside, but built to

Triage specs for some friends of mine who decided they wanted a French country house"—he gestured to the tall arched fireplace—"with all the security money could buy. We gave them a rate and they let us use it now and again."

"So that little incident on the road could have been a case of mistaken identity—a move against the local station or the diplomatic mission?"

"I doubt it. Did you want to ask Flak something?"

"Got any crank?"

Flak had been pacing off the mahogany book walls; he stopped and flashed a disingenuous look first at Shy, then Hunt. "Sir?"

"Crank. Blow. Snow. Toot. Speakee English?"

Shy nodded. "It's fine if you do, Flak. In fact, it would be helpful. And some pot, too, I believe our friend wants."

Both assets grinned, and Shy had the uncomfortable feeling that his terminology was out-of-date.

"Thai stick, sir, is what I've got. It'll lay you flat out, after being up so long." Flak, looking doubtful, scratched his bearded jaw and approached the desk, which dominated the south corner of the room. Reaching it, he threw one leg up, took a pack of Marlboros from his shirt pocket, and extracted a folded American bill. He then took a pocketknife from his hip pocket, a Swiss five-hundred franc note from his wallet. "There's the coke. I'll have to go back upstairs to get my smoke—that is, if Mino hasn't toked it all. You want me to go now?" As he spoke he was emptying crystalline powder from the folded bill onto his wallet and separating it into powdery lines.

Hunt joined him and rolled the Swiss note into a tube through which he sniffed two of the white stripes while Shy watched, curiously uncomfortable.

Four little piles remained when Hunt straightened up.

"You, sir?" Flak asked of Shy. "Keep you sharp. No? You mind if I do? Thanks." Having vacuumed three of the lines into his nose, he handed his wallet back to Hunt and sat up blinking. "Guess I'll go upstairs, then. You keep the rest of this for later, sir," he said to Hunt.

"I think I'd like you to stay, Flak," Shy decreed as Hunt thanked the pilot and made a self-sealing envelope out of the American ten with practiced skill.

"Just to get that Thai, sir, like you asked me."

"Go on then." He turned away from them and went behind the desk to pour himself a second drink. When he came back with it, Hunt was fiddling with the fire, poking logs, which cracked and sent sparks bursting upward.

"He's good," Shy heard Hunt say of Flak as the doors slid shut, and wondered how perceptive someone in Hunt's condition could possibly be. It was a nagging question that perplexed him more and more as he watched this peculiar man, who had been out of circulation for six months in the most arduous of circumstances and before that had spent eight months in the most demanding physical venue the world had to offer, the Hindu Kush, and despite it all was running the rest of them ragged.

"Why do you do it, Cord?" They were alone, Flak gone and the doors closed. "Why the risk, the violence, the fearful stress, when you know very well it's not going to change anything? Surely not to save the world?"

Hunt stared at him from his chair, chin once more propped on hands. "No, not to save the world," he agreed. "To save myself, maybe. What else would I do? I've always done it. I grew up with OSS tradecraft, and my dad...well, you know how he got his ticket punched. I was the youngest agent handler Angleton's shop ever had. When he demanded and got the Israeli account, my father was the CIA station chief in Tel Aviv.

"But it's not like it used to be—the Agency's not what *it* used to be. For a while, it *was* the ability to make a difference—to save lives that mattered or support the America I believed in; then it was the precision, when nobody believed in that America anymore. Where were you when a thousand agents got the ax overnight and nobody knew shit about what was going on in Israel? Our deputy director of operations wasn't about to let anybody run his black ops: No paper work; everything was in his head. And nobody gave a flying fuck about him, or agents in the field, or anything but their nice stateside desks.... That was it for me with CIA."

"But you keep busy."

"I do what I'm hired to do, the best I can. Better than most. I've got so many enemies that someday somebody I don't even know is going to pop up behind me to collect his blood debt: some father, mother, sister, or brother I blew, or got killed. It's practical now. If I've got any protection from the scratch artists and the fanatics, it's that I'm working—makes me a little scary."

"But Afghanistan? Why there? Why Triage?"

"Afghanistan's a different story. *You* watch those Ivans laying T_2 toxins like we used to lay napalm: yellow clouds of it. Badakhshan mountain people bleeding from the eyes, nose, mouth—even their skin, before they fall down and die in convulsions. It's genocide, like it was in Laos. Blue-X just puts the rebels out—I could walk away from that, maybe. But the T_2 program—even the Russians are afraid of it; that's why they burn off the evidence afterward.... Ah, fuck it—I'm high on Flak's blow and, by the look of you, you could walk away from Armageddon as long as WASPs were exempt. Anyway, it's all old news."

"I asked you," Shy reminded him as Flak came in and closed the doors. "And you're wrong—we all feel that way: everyone who's chosen to go independent, and certainly *any*one who has on-site knowledge of Soviet order of battle in that particular theater—

"Sit down, Flak, if you will. I was just agreeing with Cord that it's discomfiting to ponder Soviet chemical-warfare tactics. Once they've worked out their binary delivery systems and decontamination drills where no one can stop them—or even verify for certain, beyond classified satellite imaging and overflight pictures, what they're doing—what they do with that technology's up to them.... Central Europe, China—"

"Pakistan, sir," Flak corrected quietly. "Take a look at the secret protocol State's got to the 1940 Soviet/German/Japanese/Italian pact. They still want now what they wanted then, fucking admitted to wanting... I can quote it: They said their 'territorial aspirations center south of the national territory of the Soviet Union in the direction of the Indian Ocean.' That's in *Nazi-Soviet Relations 1939–41*. Just 'cause it was never signed don't mean it ain't pertinent. They'll destabilize Pakistan through the Baluchistan border dispute and go all the way to Karachi—then they've got their warm-water port and a choke on the Gulf of Oman. They're dug into Iran now, those mullahs are happy enough dialin' for rubles. They'll 'help' them like they started helping the Afghans...so it's kiss the Persian Gulf goodbye."

Shy saw Hunt's analytical stare and knew Flak had been too

forthcoming, well-placed "ain't" or not. So did the asset, who raised one hand, palm up. "Sorry, sirs, I know it's none of my job to give opinions."

"Go right ahead," Hunt said. "Talk all you want." He shot Shy a wicked smirk. "Tell us how *you'd* save the world."

Flak chuckled. "Wouldn't I like to, sir. But you almost brought a whole planeload of T$_2$s out of Afghanistan, so the rumor runs ...that would have helped some."

"Almost doesn't count, unfortunately," Hunt replied, his flippancy suddenly replaced by the more familiar brooding watchfulness. "I need some rack time, Shy. If you want to 'bounce' your 'ball' around, trot it out."

Beth chose that moment to appear, smiling and silken with a silver tray on which were two Meliors of espresso, steamed milk, and porcelain cups—four. "Coffee, gentlemen?"

"Just leave it, doctor," Shy snapped; then was sorry, but dared do no different.

She cast him a reproving glance: Shy felt it through his jacket. Not looking up, he took it off and rolled up his sleeves, concentrating on making his cuffs even, until he heard the doors close behind her.

"Before we get to Innotech's troubles, I'd like to hear what you have to say about the Martinova woman. We've been getting a surprisingly good intelligence take, I've been told—KGB take." Shy dropped a lemon peel into his espresso and pulled a chair close to Hunt's by the fire.

Flak said, "Black or white, sir?" to Hunt and brought two cups with him, sitting on the floor by the hearth. When Hunt took his cup, it rattled in the saucer so that he had to hold it with both hands, and Shy felt suddenly sick to his stomach: What he was doing to this man was inexcusable, whatever the reason—and the reason was personal: It was Shy who needed Hunt; Cordell Hunt needed only to be left alone. All the horror of the last thirty-six hours crowded in on him, his doubts, his suspicions, his italicizing brush with death on a quiet mountain road. He repeated, because Hunt had made no reply, the subject he wished to broach: "What *is* the story with you two? You've just given me your anti-Soviet line, but you're obviously romantically and politically involved with an enemy agent—I have a list of the armaments found in that hovel, and the balance of them were Soviet-made."

"I can't tell you anything about her."

"She admits to being KGB. Did you know it, or not?" Out of the corner of his eye, Shy saw Flak settle back as if he might become invisible.

Hunt said, "That's the bitch, isn't it? You'll never know for certain if your 'take' is any good, whether she's telling you what you want to hear, whether you're getting anything of value. Try to trade her, and if the Soviets say yes, you still won't know—they might want to ask her the same questions you're asking."

"Cord, don't fight me on this. It won't be worth it to you."

"Maybe she's a provocation, you think—entry to you through me to give you bad information, or give me bona fides. I know *I* got those assault rifles transshipped from Libya, so she's not guilty of that. The Libyans aren't hesitant to deal with me, after the way my own country treated me."

"And what were you going to do with them?" Shy knew his tone was too abrupt, he was out of his depth, but there was no one to trust with this....

"Air-drop them into Kandahar, maybe. None of your damn business. You think she's *mokrie dela*, I'll never change your mind. You think I'm a doubled Soviet penetration, you've got to ask yourself what the fuck you've got worth penetrating. I sure don't know. But I know that when an interrogator thinks he's got all the answers, the easiest thing to do is agree with him. Maybe Nasta knows that, too."

Flak murmured, "Sir, take it easy. He's got to ask you, and you know it."

"Don't you good-cop/bad-cop me, kid. You're good, but you're not *that* good."

Flak got up to refill his cup, looking over his shoulder at Hunt reproachfully. When he came back, he lit a joint. Hunt accepted it from him, toked, then passed it to Shy, who handed it on.

"Don't make things more difficult than they have to be, Hunt—for you *or* her."

"*Phew*, at last! I don't care if you put her in your Cuisinart feetfirst, Shy—" He paused, raised cup to lips, the saucer held under. "Yeah, I do. I'm so tired of this....She's NTS. At one time your organization had some interest in them. I got a lot of them iced, so when I got my back pay, I bought them some hardware to take up to Afghanistan. They'd sent her down to look after me, which is more than any of my old buddies in a dozen high-rolling services had seen fit to do. So let her go, leave her out of this. She can't hurt you and she doesn't know anything. She's a child, a card-carrying innocent. She speaks Russian because she's of Russian extraction. And she'll die to protect her pathetic little column, which is more than I've got the guts to do—for anything or anybody."

Shy was suddenly conscious that the man with the emotion-thickened voice was carrying a gun, but Flak had his wallet out once more, offering Hunt a cigarette and taking the cocaine to apportion for them both.

Hunt said, "Can I get some Camels? Straights or filters, I don't care." He spoke from between hands covering his face, bent forward. Flak promised to get him a carton in the morning. And: "Easy, sir. That's why they call it 'crank.'"

The two repeated their cocaine ritual.

"Okay, what's next?" Hunt asked Shy after a quiet interval: The second dose seemed to have calmed him.

"Dinner, soon, then sleep, you have my word. Just tell me about the Morales woman and give me your estimate of what was happening out there on the road today."

"Here comes *your* problem? Angel and Dania Morales are independents, scratch artists, used to be terrorists, trained in Aden for Habash and Haddad, onetime heavies at Camp Khayat. From what I've heard, they're open market: any job for a price, ComBloc hit folk turned nonsectarian. So when I saw you talking to her, I made the assumption that you wanted them to put me down 'accidentally'—total deniability if anyone should find out I made it out of Marrakech."

"Why would I go to all the trouble of getting you out of there if I were going to do that?"

"I don't know, you tell me."

"They're capable of staging an action like the one we encountered on the road on such short notice?"

"It's their style. They're very overt, publicity-conscious types. But it could have been meant for whoever normally travels here in that car. You're saying the Moraleses aren't yours, but you're not saying anything about Innotech's troubles, and if you didn't sic them on me, it's not me they want: I'm not worth their kind of money to anybody else. Can we assume that you might be? And that the demolitions I saw pictures of in the local paper are part of what you want me to 'work with you on'?"

"You were worth something to whoever 'scratched,' as you say, the man responsible for your part of Two Can Play. How, by the way, did you learn the name of the project?"

"The Soviets told me, or rather, they asked me more about it then I knew. If you're telling me I was blown from inside, you're going to make me very concerned about your aid and comfort, such as it has shown itself to be."

"Then I won't tell you that. But I will tell you we've had a lot of casualties—some accidental deaths, cars, a plane downed; some not so accidental: A man of ours—a Triage control, actually— was found in a multiple-murder sex-scandal sort of configuration. It did our public image little good."

"Sirs, keep in mind that it was a thuggee-style killing," Flak put in. "No blood, strangled with red scarves, right out of deepest India, only it happened in the States and the newsies didn't pick up on it—scandal is more their angle."

"I don't think that's germane."

"The hell it's not. Someone was sending you a message through back channels, Shy," Hunt disagreed. "I can't sort this out without some sleep. Find out who was in the Baur Au Lac with us—in that Morales woman, you just might have a thread worth unraveling. But if the Soviets are coming at you via terrorists, I don't know what you can do about it. They only have to suggest that you're target of the year, then lay back.... Are you hot enough to be worth it? Troublesome enough? Are you doing classified technical services development the way they think you are?"

"I can't talk about it with you yet, but your guess would be sufficiently educated. We do very much need to know exactly what the Soviets were asking you."

"I'll help you as best I can, if you'll skip any protracted debriefing and turn Anastacia Martinova loose."

"Just say you'll put yourself at my disposal. No conditions. I have to meet my own superiors' requirements as far as you're concerned. I'm going to try to use this as a lever to pry you away from them, but I may not be able to do it. I've got to make you realize that this isn't a field operation and I'm not a miracle-worker."

"I can't tell you any such thing. You've got leaks in your

organization the size of the Suez Canal. I might be signing my own death warrant. You do whatever you've got to do and I'll comport myself accordingly," Hunt said in a slow, tired voice. "I'm still experiencing flashbacks, but I've had the tumors the rough stuff gave me removed. Now, if you'd keep in mind that I've been mortared and starved and beaten so that my ears ring if I turn my head fast—just in case you might want to be *able* to send me into the field on this, you understand—I'd appreciate it. I don't want your dinner, I don't want your company, and I don't want your veiled threats. If you don't let me go wherever it is I can sleep, I'm going to pass out right here." He leaned back in the chair, closed his eyes, and waited.

"All right, all right, Cord. Flak, help him—"

"I don't *need* help."

"Make up your mind."

Cordell Hunt blinked fiercely, stood up, and had to steady himself on the chair's back. Flak was up immediately, and Shy was surprised to see that Hunt allowed the pilot to slip an arm around him. "That's it, man," Flak murmured, "no shame in it. Everybody needs a little hand once in a while."

Shy sat silently until they were gone. Then he palmed his eyes and waited for the ache in his throat to subside. When Beth peeked in, saw him alone, and entered, he didn't know it until she stood beside his chair. "Is it going to be all right?" he heard.

"How should *I* know?" He shot bolt upright so that she stumbled backward. He didn't move to help her. Sitting abruptly in the chair that hit the back of her knees, her hand to her mouth, she stared up at him wide-eyed.

"I'm sorry, Beth, I really am. I've had a difficult day—days. And I'm frustrated: The bastard is making me feel like an amateur. It's been a long time since my professional performance has been called into question, and I don't like it. I really wonder," he continued, lifting her upright, "if I haven't already fouled this up beyond repair."

"You need to rest." She nuzzled him. "We're too old for all-nighters. You were almost killed today, and adrenaline can be a tricky drug. We'll be having dinner soon—"

"I don't want dinner. I want to save that poor bastard, and I don't think he's going to let me. And if he doesn't, we might lose

Innotech. If that doesn't take away your appetite, you don't belong here."

When the chopper dropped into his dream, Cory Hunt was hearing from Chebrikov how the unrequited loyalty Hunt felt toward his country was ruining both their lives. When he spoke to Cory, he would blink rapidly, the little pink mole on his right upper eyelid fluttering. They were walking in the Lubyanka's exercise yard, alone, and the sky was the color of old cell-water. He said Hunt's behavior was going to force him to allow the use of neurokinin by those who felt the prisoner needed an object lesson. Did Hunt realize what kind of pain was in question? Capitulation was a certainty: Under neurokinin, a stone statue would talk and talk and talk. And for what? Hunt's nation had disowned him— here was a stat from the *New York Times*.

Hunt took it, looked at the wriggling lines of print, handed it back unspeaking. Chebrikov suggested that gentler methods were still a possibility: Hunt could salvage something yet; seductive psychochemicals could be administered, and thus he would never have spoken except under duress. What was the hold Innotech had on him? A proprietary of the American intelligence community run by an ex-CIA "supergrade," Innotech had used him as a giveaway, paid him no better than a mercenary, and lifted not one of its multitude of covertly gloved fingers to aid its asset in distress. Hunt said, for at least the twentieth time, "I was a Triage contract agent. That's all I know."

Up above, guards with AK-47s stood indolent watch. Chebrikov didn't believe him, couldn't believe, but Hunt must believe that Chebrikov was not exaggerating. The little pale man looked grave and began quietly to suggest that Hunt put himself in Chebrikov's position. His father had not sent him through Odessa High Artillery Military School and the General Staff Academy for nothing. KGB Chairman Chebrikov, among others, was personally concerned that this younger Chebrikov make a success of his interrogation. One had to comprehend the Soviet military elite, and the desire of the KGB's gerontocracy to rejuvenate its ranks, to understand how great an affront to both groups Hunt's destruction of young Chebrikov's reputation would be. It should have been obvious to

Hunt that a KGB colonel who had gone to Afghanistan as part of the military mission chaired by Pavlovskiy and come back declaring that a limited contingent would be successful there *could not* fail in such a paltry matter. It was bad enough that the Hunts and the mujahedin existed at all; for him to defy the mighty KGB was simply not a possibility acceptable to Chebrikov's superiors. Nor would death be permitted: Hunt would end up a drooling idiot, unable to guide a spoon of gruel to his mouth, and Chebrikov would not get his division command before the cutoff age of forty—in which case he could never become the *vozhd* of tomorrow he was expected to be.

"What's a *vozhd*?" Hunt asked.

"A great leader, American, like Lenin," Chebrikov replied as the chopper buzzed the compound and from above a dozen rifles tracked Hunt as he hit the deck.

Cordell Hunt awoke crouched below a curtained window, lining up the three tritium-gas dots of his pistol's night sights. He didn't remember getting out of bed or grabbing the gun stuffed between the mattress and headboard above his pillow. He didn't know where he was. The window didn't open; he rested the pistol's muzzle on its sill and watched the chopper come down on both skids, trying to determine its manufacture. It was four, five in the morning, and the landscape was snowbright, brighter than the sky's clouds—somewhere, there must be a moon.

He thought this was the best skew yet that Chebrikov had dreamed up for him—but he had his Commander, his carry-gun, not some sterile ops gun or expropriated Soviet hardware. He leaned his head against the cold glass. Snow, okay, he thought. The helicopter out there was a Bell AH-1T Improved—it set down slowly in the pad's center, showing off its spectacular capacity for hover and maneuverability. The marines had them, so did some of the contract airlines—so did Triage.

Maybe it was a Triage chopper, come to get him—but that was crazy. *Where* was he? He crouched there, places and situations spinning around and around in his head, dripping sweat and shivering, watching the chopper disgorge three people and the lights go out and his breath make mist on the glass, until the door opened and a silhouetted figure said, halting, "Aw, Christ," and very slowly brought one hand up to turn on the lights. "It's okay, man," he heard as the light flooded his eyes and he refused to blink, taking the tears instead—he could still sight through watering eyes.

The man at the open door wore no shirt and his jeans' fly wasn't snapped. "Sir? It's me, Flak." He had his hands clear of his body and was squatting down in the doorway. Behind him, somewhere beyond Hunt's view, people were moving: He heard lowered voices, shuffling feet. "Cory?" With one hand the man was waving behind him.

Hunt thumbed his safety off. He didn't know whether that hand was going to come back with a pistol pulled from the jeans' waistband at the small of the guy's back. The man had sunstreaked hair and a scruffy beard and he thought back over what he had said: *Flak.*

He knew that sounded familiar; Flak had called him Cory. Where the fuck was he and what was happening to him?

"You don't want to shoot me, sir. I'm the best friend you've got. That's just our taxi being delivered out there, honest, sir. No funny stuff. Let me come over there and talk to you? Then I can close the door. Sir, please? Okay?"

Hunt nodded, and while the man cautiously did what he had said he would do, Hunt found his fix on reality and began to think about covering the lapse. Flak was Shy's pilot and they were outside Zürich. He sank down, his back to the wall, knees up, and rested his pistol hand on one knee, safety engaged.

The pilot came cautiously, steady eyes friendly but pupils pinned, and slid down the wall beside him. "Okay? I'd have told you if I'd known, sir. Surprised the piss out of me—I was out of bed lookin' for some kind of cover by the time I knew what I was hearing. Shit, choppers just always sound like trouble, once you've been where they habitually go. They don't mean to freak you, sir, they just don't know what they're doing, I guess. . . . I mean, with guys like us, you don't spring eggbeaters at 0500 in a civilian neighborhood. You want some joint?"

"Thanks."

"I hate to smoke alone." He lit it for Hunt.

"I don't mean that, I mean the plausible rap. Even if it's not true, you're making me feel better." He passed Flak the joint.

"Here's a cigarette, sir?" Flak had lit two, and exchanged the joint for one, toking deeply. "I'd like to do that, sir. This is a damn fine outfit, on the whole. What happened to you—you know Murphy's law, sir...." He flicked ashes into his open hand.

"Better than most. How's Mino?"

"Good as gold, sir. He's been asking about you. Wants me to tell you that he'll take your shots for you anytime. He's been spacin' his brains out, on the house."

"I figured. Is that woman here—my friend?"

"Ah—no, sir, she's not. I believe the ARD's with her—at least, he got in that car and I didn't see him get out. If you want a lady, sir, I'm sure they'll oblige you. They want you to be comfortable. That dinner you wouldn't eat was the best I've had in weeks. If you'd like something now, I bet I could get you—"

"I keep getting the feeling that you and I are fraternity brothers. Is that so?"

"Might be, sir. Would that make any difference?"

"Maybe."

"Pro or con?"

"That would depend on how this turns out, wouldn't it? Unless you could keep tabs on my lady friend?..."

"Negative, I'm afraid, sir. But if you figure that those Triage surveillance stickers mean they've got audiovisual aids, sir, you're right."

Hunt chuckled. "Well, if they do, they're about to see a man take an inordinate amount of time in the shower." He levered himself up, using the wall for support.

"How about that snack, sir? I'm due to be checked out on the chopper in an hour, anyway—it's no trouble."

"What I'd like is some plain rice on a hot plate with a raw egg on the side and some black coffee. Think you could manage that?"

"My pleasure, sir. And, sir—"

"Flak?"

"Why don't you give me the Commander and I'll clean it for you and give it back full up. You're down a round, and we wouldn't want a misfire—nobody would."

The loose-limbed pilot looked up at him, hand outstretched, ingenuous yet pointedly suggesting that Hunt wasn't in any condition to determine such things for himself. If they were going to disarm him while he slept, he couldn't stop them. At least here and now, maybe, he'd have a chance of getting it back. "Lose it and I'll bust your butt for you." He snapped it down on Flak's steady palm and without a backward look took joint and cigarette into the bathroom, which was filled with toiletries and grooming aids and harmless analgesics, but had no razor blades or sleeping pills or even a comb or the ubiquitous American traveling hair dryer; he thought it must be because of the cord.

He knew what was happening to him: They were treating him like a prisoner and he was reacting with the too-familiar syndrome—picking his favorite jailer, responding to all the cues. There wasn't much he could do about it. The situation had been altered by their acquisition of Nasta, but that was not why he had let Flak have his gun: He needed to see if they would give it back.

Chapter
5

"JACK, I can't tell you how much I appreciate your coming out here," Shy said to the man he'd rousted out of bed and flown in from Mons. "An opinion from you is going to mean the world to me. I really don't know whom else I can trust."

Jack Fowler—director of the Intelligence Steering Committee, NATO Supreme Headquarters, Brussels—judiciously quartered the Kansas rib-eye nestled between two over-easy eggs on his plate. Wind-scored and devoid of fat, he seemed hardly to age—one more line around the green, farsighted eyes; a bit more silver in his gray crew cut. "It's always good to see you, son, especially when you've got something on. What is it?"

"I've got a hypothetical question for you."

Fowler nodded with mock gravity, laying aside his knife to tap freckled knuckles against his perpetually chapped lips. "Steak and eggs, helicopter ride, hypothetical question. Right, John, I'm with you so far." A ruddy sun, coming up beyond the lavender-sprigged curtains, flooded the chalet's genteel, floral-papered breakfast room with amber light.

"Say that I had a pulse on the Innotech bombings and I wanted to isolate it myself, but I wasn't sure where it might lead me...."

"You mean, it might lead you right back home to Innotech?"

"I don't know, Jack, that's what I'm saying."

"If you're really dealing with a terrorist infestation, they'll have gone to ground by now, you know that."

"What if I had the right tool for the job—an experienced penetration agent, an ex-Agency deep-cover net chief?"

"Then I'd go with it, put him out there in a triad configuration and give him whatever he wants." Fowler, food forgotten, looked fondly at Shy. "What's the problem?"

"First, Innotech's not cooperating: We don't have a charter for this sort of thing. Triage is our strong arm, and they're not subtle by nature—the closest thing they do to what I'm proposing is the clandestine courier service; otherwise, it's overt and covert paramilitary support and electronic surveillance, ordnance and transport."

"Yes, John, down-links and up-links and no government oversight—I know the litany. If you want a good hypothetical solution, you must at least give me an honest assessment of the problem."

"I'm telling you what the shop has been saying, Jack. I told you I need a second opinion." Shy drank off half a glass of milk. "They're stonewalling me, stalling. Someone else wants this asset—in fact, it seems like a lot of people want him not to exist, or, failing that, to be quickly stashed somewhere soundproof and sealed."

"Let me see if I'm still on course: You've got an operation on the boards your people don't want you to run, centering around a potential security risk. Is that so?"

"That's what they're saying."

"You don't think that's an in-depth analysis?"

Shy toasted him with a goblet of fresh orange juice. "It's really good to see you, Jack. If we ever got together, I bet we could get the UN out of New York."

Jack Fowler went back to his congealing eggs. "Is Michele still insistent on letting that article of hers for *International Security* on totalitarian-bloc tactics in the UN go to press without the deletions I suggested?"

"My wife still thinks she's Crusader Rabbit."

"She's going to be a rabbit-skin coat if this keeps up. Tell her I strongly suggest she leave the sniping to boys with Kevlar vests and high-powered scopes. Or take a position with us, so I can give her some security coverage."

"I'll tell her." He addressed his steak and poured them both coffee. When they had finished eating, small-talking, and testing each other for conflict of interest in the way of their kind, Shy began taking chances.

"Jack, in the first twenty-four hours after recovery, the asset in question has cost two lives and an armored limousine, plus lots of jet fuel, miscellaneous property damage, lost sleep, and frayed nerves. In other words, the whole damn thing might be a diversion. . . . Guess who oversaw the retrieval?"

"*You?* Isn't that rather like sending an SR-71 Blackbird to pick up a routine diplomatic pouch?"

"Which brings me to point two on my list of problems. The treadmill they've got me on goes like this: The asset might be a Soviet penetration, the terrorists might be Soviet-directed, the big bad Bear is after my poor little defenseless company."

"So you're afraid they'll tape your wrists to your ankles with it, like Angleton over Golitsyn. But why?"

"I don't know. I can't see Innotech skipping off through the meadows, net in hand, chasing the elusive butterfly of World Communism. It isn't what we do, I wouldn't know even where to start. But the hitch on this asset, they tell me, is that he's got Soviet connections. If so, so what? I'm saying, and everyone is looking at me like horns just sprouted from my forehead. I've got to vet this asset or forget him—and if I do vouch for him and I'm wrong, it's the end of me, Innotech, everything."

"I'll give you a job, maybe not at your current astronomical salary, but you won't starve, so it's not the end of everything. Are we still speaking hypothetically?"

Shy held his hand out parallel to the table and rotated it sixty degrees in one direction, then the other. "Do *you* think technology transfer from Innotech to ComBloc agents is what I'm being diverted from? You would have heard something if anything like that is happening."

"Ah, I see where you're taking this—the bombings are just cleanup, so whatever is missing can't be pinpointed. What are you doing worth such a convoluted and expensive scenario?"

"Lots of things, and nothing. Supercomputers—superconductors, very high speed integrated circuits ... Our R&D program *was* a year ahead of IBM/Navy's; our cryptography section has a new publishable dual code, the encoding portion of which has already been disseminated to a number of sensitive receivers; then there's technical services and satellite links—it could be any damn thing at all. But what we don't have is a government umbrella to stand under if it starts raining. If we begin looking like our security's questionable, we'll be a shop without customers. We've done lots of work for you, Jack. Is this kind of talk making you nervous?"

"A little, I must admit. But we need you, too—organizations like Innotech serve our general welfare: no charterbound restrictions, no public to whom you are responsible, no fears that if we have a developmental problem you're solving, the high-end results will be skimmed off by your own government sponsor. And Innotech tip sheets have come out at every board-of-estimates meeting I've been to in five years as corroborative evidence in cases where there are no other concurring sources. Nobody in NATO would like to see an end to Innotech, even if Sid Cannard is a hard case."

Shy sighed. "That's nice to hear. I wouldn't have called you in on this if I wasn't afraid I'm being overly paranoid." By his chair he had a briefcase; from it he pulled a black folder with an Innotech decal on it. He handed it to Fowler, who opened it long enough to see the red inner cover and the NO DISTRIBUTION—EYES ONLY stamp, then let it fall closed. "I don't know, John. You're putting me in an accessory position. You hope, if I read this, I'll pull strings for you."

"I think you'll want to, Jack, I really do."

"What if I don't agree with you? I would still have to refrain from acting in my own best interest in order to respect your confidence. What do you envision wanting me to do?"

"I need help. I want to put this asset out and I don't want anyone to touch him."

"My dear John, this is getting very delicate."

"That's why I asked you out here. I can't trust Sid, even if you do. I had to call on the cousins in Morocco; when I got back here, I borrowed one of their consular limousines, on the spur of the moment at one P.M., yet I was attacked by terrorists around four P.M. That's some operational mobility for swacked-out kids. Maybe my own people were responsible, maybe our customers, who feel they've a vested interest—"

"Who is it you've got, John?"

"Somebody you'd want to help if you could, Jack. I don't want to compromise you or pressure you—and as you pointed out, too much information is going to do just that."

"You are keeping this asset from debriefing by agencies whose help you employed to acquire him?" Fowler's eyes sparkled angrily. "Are any of them ours? No, never mind, don't answer that— of course they are." He poured himself a second cup and, stirring brandy into it, stared out at the snow-covered tennis court gleaming in the sunlight. "I'm beginning to have an awful suspicion as to whom you've got here. May I assume he *is* here?"

Shy, breathing shallowly with an appreciation of danger far greater than he had ever experienced from Dropout, nodded carefully. "Jack, get them off my neck."

"Impossible."

"For *you?*"

"For a lot of reasons—yes. But, damn you, I want to *know*—" Jack Fowler snorted irritably and cursed the doctor who had taken his cigars away.

"Jack, somebody almost killed me yesterday, on purpose, either to shut me up or just because I happened to be in the car with this asset. Either way, I don't want it to happen again. The cars used for the blockade were Audis, not cheap little terrorist-type cars, and I've got the plate numbers. Do you want me to run them through Interpol?"

"Maybe you ought to, son, just to make yourself feel better. I'll ignore the implication—you're right, you're paranoid. If *we* came after you, you wouldn't have time to wonder about who was doing it." Fowler's tongue flicked in and out like a lizard's.

Shy knew he'd made a mistake—he had only half of one license number, and he'd played it too early. "I'm sorry, Jack. I'm not in any position to try to get heavy. It's just that I can't think of anyone else whose help I'd dare to have, and it doesn't seem like I'm convincing you. So..." He started to get up.

"No, not yet—" Fowler's hand vise-gripped his arm. "Sit back down and let's make a deal. ... I have to be able to show worthwhile incentive. What can you give me?"

"A woman who just might be Afghan NTS, a high-up with negotiating power, if she's not KGB." He forced a grin. "A year's membership to Innotech's freebee club—whatever you ask for, as long as I'm still alive and well and employed by them."

"Get Michele to make those deletions I suggested and I'll do what I can."

Shy closed his eyes. "I can't get her to give me a kiss, Jack."

"I'm sorry, I didn't know."

"Me too. If there's anything else you want..."

"Maybe after I look at the catalogue. Okay, tell me."

"Tell you what?"

"Is it really old Percy Hunt's kid you've got here?"

"Read what I gave you, then we'll talk."

Chapter
6

BY the following Friday, Cordell Hunt was feeling acclimated—not good, but better. His situation in the Zürich safe house was not unique—he'd often been without any appreciable future. He apprehended it with a cold, vacant knottiness where his stomach should have been: He had no alternative. Once in west Beirut, doing reconnaissance for the Israeli invasion of Lebanon under Pierre Gemayel at Sharon's request, he was taken prisoner by a PFLP (Popular Front for the Liberation of Palestine) column he'd penetrated and his situation had been much the same: no fall-backs, no options. In that case, the cell leader had eventually been overruled by his superiors and Hunt had received voluminous Arabic apologies along with his gun and his freedom.

Somehow he didn't think that was going to happen here, although Flak had been true to his word and returned Hunt's pistol with the breakfast tray, muttering excuses for having taken so long and explaining that there wasn't any way he was going to match Hunt's handloaded, fully jacketed, high-velocity hydro-shocks, but that he'd asked around among the Triage sentries and borrowed a 145-grain Glaser Safety Slug from one and an armor-piercing 183-grain KTW from another. Hunt politely sat through Flak's conveyed warning from the two shooters that, because the points of impact varied so greatly between the Glaser and the other, loading them consecutively would be a mistake. Then, on the pretext of adding the Glaser to his magazine, he checked his own expanding loads to make sure Flak hadn't emptied the powder from the cartridges.

Beside the bullets on his black lacquer breakfast tray had been three capsules. At Flak's urging, Hunt consented to swallow the "Vitamins."

Soon after that, he was visited by the lady doctor, who insisted that he call her Beth and wanted to examine him. Since they left him alone with her, he had to assume that Flak was right and they were under surveillance. She did a thorough hands-on, which he found so ludicrously suggestive that at one point he told her he hoped she was kidding; he wasn't interested in making training films. She didn't even blush, but took her gloved hand away only when she was done probing.

By then he was feeling a little woozy, but he had expected it. In came the voice-stress analyzers, a gurney on which he was told to lie, and a portable ultrasound rack through which she proposed to determine if he had sustained internal damage without subjecting him to X-rays. She rubbed oil on his belly and ran the microphonelike metal sounding device over him, while behind on the monitor a picture of his insides built on the screen.

"So?" he said when she switched it off. He could have sworn she was turned on to him: Her lips were puffy and her chest rose and fell in a pronounced fashion.

"So," she concluded in her ambassadorial accent, "you are healthier than you have any right to be, if what you've been telling

John is true. What makes you think they used two-four pyrolo or neurokinin on you?"

"Just a guess. There's a lot I don't remember." She was squeezing what seemed like soapy water onto him, cleaning away the oil on which the sensor had slid, and she kept stroking downward. "Come *on* lady, this isn't funny. Jumping a man's bones for information went out with Mata Hari." To cool himself, he thought back to the neurokinin interrogations, when it had seemed every muscle was going to rip itself from his skeleton. It worked, and she saw the result, but made no comment about it, telling him to get dressed, her back turned, fiddling with her machinery, keeping up a steady stream of questions: Where did it hurt, when did it hurt, how did he feel today?

He knew damn well she was just waiting for the drugs they had given him to kick in, but he had been glad to slide off the table. In the duffel bag that Nasta must have packed for him in Marrakech were jeans and combat fatigues, three T-shirts and a sweatshirt, underwear and socks. None of it was clean, but he was grateful to have it. He had pulled out an ancient white Airborne sweatshirt, with its gray and yellow eagle's head, when his workbelt with its SSS speed scabbard and magnetic double clip holder, full up, fell to the bed. He blessed Nasta, and felt guilty, then dizzy, then sat heavily, trying to see only two feet on the floor. Later they told him he had imagined the workbelt, but he knew better.

It became his routine to see the woman in the morning and Shy in the afternoon, the ARD Hubble at night. He began to suspect that Beth was a psychiatrist rather than a medical doctor, and that Shy didn't care whether his take was any good or not.

At one point, as lucid as he ever was those first days in Zürich, he suggested to Shy that since they were just going through the motions, there was no need to continually juice him. "It's quicker," Shy replied, "and unassailable. I feel as badly about it as you do, Cord. We've got to convince these people that I know all there is to know about you."

"Why?" he'd asked, trying to guide his fork to the general area of the plate on which his food rested.

"We've been over this before."

"Not to my satisfaction," Hunt said slowly and distinctly, "maybe to yours. I just about begged you not to do this to me. If you want

my help—and God knows you need it with this crew you've got—
you're going about convincing me the wrong way."

"Don't you think *I* know that?" Shy's fork had clattered to his
plate. He had stood abruptly and left the room.

Hunt thought that might have been Wednesday. Thursday they
stopped giving him "vitamins." Thursday night he woke from a
more coherent nightmare than those he'd been having recently
to find that he was not alone.

He didn't move, just lay listening. The Commander might be
in its niche above his head, it might not. He thought about the
car's driver, the man Shy called Helms. The one thing that seemed
hopeful to him about the Innotech/Triage team's performance
was that the driver had disappeared from view after the first day
and Hunt hadn't seen him since.

The breathing he was hearing was heavy. He waited. Even considering the shape he was in, his odds were good in any unarmed
combat: When he'd chopped Bowser in the larynx at the Baur
Au Lac, he hadn't meant to do more than back the bruiser off a
little.

He let his attention focus on the motion in the dark, relaxing
until he could almost see the energy patterns of the person coming
toward him: Hunt was no ninja, but he'd spent the best part of
six weeks in a ChiCom internment camp learning Dim Mak tech-
niques from his cagemate. The art, variously called Poison Hand
or Death Touch in English, was something he hadn't had much
opportunity to practice: If you impacted the target properly at
the right time of day on the requisite Chinese meridian, he died,
sometimes instantly, sometimes up to four months later. You
couldn't dry-run it; you just saved it for a rainy day.

He estimated the hour and he estimated what impact point
would give him a quick takeout, and he waited for the person to
make a move: If weapons had been on the agenda, he would have
bought it in his sleep, so it was certainly a contact sport the adversary had in mind.

He "made the weapon" by bringing the thumb and fingertips
of his right hand together so that they resembled a bird's beak,
then shifted as though in sleep to free his hand from restricting
covers and position it. He was hoping for a solar-plexus strike—
Hee Hu Hsin Hsueh—or a Ho Fee Hsueh, which touch must be

made an inch or two lower, depending on the size of the adversary. Either one was an instant kill, but in the dark he might be a little off, so he needed a touch with a built-in margin for error. His backups, a hit down into the clavicle or a good head touch, depended somewhat on the time at which they were inflicted.

Just as his wide-open eyes were beginning to make out the approaching outline—a phantom form, pale and tinged with passionate red—a voice whispered, "Scratch?"

"Crazy bitch."

"Ssh," Beth Cannard pleaded, and he felt the mattress dip as she sat down. "Scratch, please..." Her voice was trembling and he felt her fingers stroke his arm.

"I can't believe you're this hard up. You can't get it anywhere else? Or do helpless victims turn you on?" Her finger stopped where that sort of woman's would, on his biceps. She didn't say anything, just sat there. He thought about infrared cameras and the pale reddish tinge he could almost see on the white sheets and expelled a deep breath he had been holding: He didn't really want to chase her away. He had scoped what was happening between her and Shy; they stayed away from each other too carefully, were too formal for people working together; there were too many penetrating looks. But he mustn't buy himself more trouble, he thought as her hand started to move again and he found himself curious to know if she might have something soft and silky and expensive over that thoroughbred body she had been throwing at him since he was brought in here. She caught his hand and, bringing it up to her lips, kissed his fingers. *Shit,* he thought as her hair brushed his neck; the least he could do was ruin Shy's good thing. He did his best to make sure that Beth Cannard was never going to be the same.

On Friday she didn't come in the morning; it was the ARD who was at him about where Chebrikov had gone to school and did he know that KGB's chairman had the same name?

In the afternoon she appeared with a bright-eyed smile and an armful of packages, dumping them on the floor before the huge stucco mantel, stolen from some sixteenth-century French château, which dominated the library where Hunt was on his lunch break, watching the fire and wishing he could escape. He had given the window in his room a good clout with his gun's barrel and succeeded only in making alarm bells ring. The ground-floor windows were decoratively barred with wrought iron. If they didn't let him out of this cage soon, he was going to start climbing the walls. He had asked the ARD about it and the man had spread his hands helplessly: Ask Shy. There was a Triage soldier over in the corner, silent and motionless: He had gotten used to them. It wasn't their fault; as long as they didn't muscle him, he was content to let them do their jobs.

"Well," she said, "come take a look." There was something hesitant and puppylike about her. For a moment he didn't understand, then he did. This morning the sports coat and slacks the Brits had bought him for the trip to Morocco hadn't been in his closet when he got back from breakfast; in fact, everything but his black Kataebe T-shirt and the jeans he was wearing had been taken.

He sat on the hearth and opened the first box, from some exclusive store he'd never heard of that took great pains with its packaging. Inside was a sweatshirt, mottled gray and unremarkable except that it was cashmere. The price tag was still on it and he shuddered. "Don't buy me presents, lady. So far we've been trading even."

"Be gracious. Try it on."

"I don't have any use for something like this. That kind of money—"

"Since John couldn't be here today, he sent me out to get some things for you—special-purpose items. It's on Innotech, and it's part of your cov—your *project* budget."

"I keep telling you people, there isn't going to be any 'project.'"

"Flak has been pestering John all week to let him take you to town this evening. If you don't agree to go, he'll be very disappointed. Mino, too."

Hunt looked over his shoulder at her. Her face told him no more than her voice; he shouldn't have gotten loose with her.

"That so?" He hadn't seen Flak or Mino since his first morning here, and he'd missed them.

"If you don't take the qualifier, you can't pass the test," she intoned gravely, then smiled again, too carefully. "At least look at the rest of what I brought you before you turn it down. The tickets are still on them in case of size error. If price really makes you uncomfortable, I'll take all the tags off—just close your eyes."

He almost told her that it made him damned uncomfortable—compromised, in fact. He said, "It's just that I don't have two Swiss francs to rub together. I don't want to find that this came out of whatever Innotech thinks it still owes me."

It didn't. There were expensive twill slacks and designer fatigues that nevertheless might be useful, a good expedition parka rated to 80° below, a lighter leather field jacket filled with down, merino socks with silk liners, some shirts in neutral colors, and a catalogue from the safari/ski outfitter who was responsible for blending "fashion and serviceability."

"Let me get this straight. You're giving me clothes so I can look like one of the Refugee Rich that clutter up this town when I go out with *Flak*? Why don't you just shoot me here?"

But it was with Flak that he found himself, at eight that evening, driving into town in Shy's silver Ferrari Mondial, Mino sprawled in the back of the 2+2, hanging over Hunt's seat, trying to get someone to take his bet that this wasn't the "end of the bullshit and the start of the high-rollin', blowout good times" all three of them were going to have.

"What are you supposed to do if I try to split?" Hunt asked Flak, whose close-trimmed beard let Hunt see the stress lines running down his jaw from cheekbone to chin.

"Drill your ass, sir. Don't make me find out if I could do it."

Mino snorted. "Flak's the coldest sucker I ever met, sir. He's bein' polite, but he'd shoot God if John Shy told him to—ain't that so, Flak?"

"Mino, shut up, if you don't have more sense than to say something like that."

There was a tic under Flak's eye momentarily as he swung the Ferrari around a turn. "For a ground vehicle, this surely is one fine piece of transportation. Watch the route, sir, and you can drive back if you want."

"*I'll* drive it—right now, in fact," Mino said. "Pull over, Flak, and let me have a go."

"*You*? You scare me enough in the air. It's a good thing that chopper's 'Improved,' the way you were kissing those snow peaks, or I'd be hiking home from Mount Whatever-the-fuck."

"It's the improvements that ain't Bell's that threw me. But I've got it down now, even you said so. What it's got, sir, is this Collins automatic IFR approach-and-hover from Rockwell. You know choppers, sir?"

Hunt said he had a passing acquaintance with them but that was all.

"Well, this new autopilot's more like playing a Lunar Lander— you know, the electronic game, sir—than like flying a real—"

"*Okay*, Mino! He doesn't care about it like you do. Sir, I thought we'd hit the Bazillus—the jazz is great and the food's good, for Zürich."

"And Flak brought his sax. Gonna sit in with the band, I bet."

"Why are we doing this?" Hunt asked Flak quietly, and saw the pilot's hands tighten on the leather-wrapped wheel. "Or, more specifically, why are *you* doing this? I'm not real happy here— they're giving me some grief. You know it, yet you'll willingly risk your life for them? Because that's what you're doing: I'm about at the end of my leash with Innotech."

"I know, sir. That's why I volunteered to get you out of there awhile, where you can think a little straighter. They didn't—*Shy* didn't ask me to do this. I just want to help, sir. What they're asking of you—it's a lot. I thought maybe it'd be good if you knew that somebody understood how much—"

"What are they asking, Flak?"

Mino said, "We're gonna get to go with you, sir. All the way."

Flak, without looking away from the road, felt for his cigarettes, mouthed one out of the pack, dropped the pack in his lap, then lit the one between his lips. "Mino, one of these days I'm going to get smart and shed your ass. Sir, if you operate for Shy, we're both in—they asked us if we wanted the job. It's quite a step up." He looked away from the road, hard into Hunt's eyes. "We could— *I* could learn a lot from you."

"You could get killed."

"Yes, sir. That, too. I'd be dead but I'd be an up-scale asset and not just a pilot who's handy around the edges."

"I'll let that pass," Hunt remarked, and looked out the window. "If they want to regain my confidence, tell them I want to see Martinova again. I want to verify for myself that she's all right."

"I bet they'd let you if you'd take this op. It sounds like it's doable to me, sir, but it's not my area of expertise."

"*What* sounds doable?"

"Picking up on the Morales angle. I'm going to sound some people I know about her—tonight, sir, at the club. I thought if you were there, I'd be sure that I did it right." He reached backward, grabbing Mino by the hair. "And you, brother, you be *cool* in there." He let him go, and no one spoke for a time as the car sped through the slushy night, almost alone on the road, just the steady taillights before and corona behind, which had been there since they pulled out of the chalet's private road.

After a while Hunt said, "You still carrying that snubby?"

Both of them said yes, they were.

"Ought to get something done about that, if you can. They're not real controllable in urban situations where you might want to get four or five rounds off fast." As he had hoped, his critique changed the subject.

When they had gotten into Zürich traffic and through the Friday night chaos and narrow cobbled streets to the Bazillus, he found it in no way resembled the Lubyanka's basement cafeteria, which was the most public place, save airports, he had been in more than a year.

The bad light and the number of strangers daunted him. He demanded and got the single table, stage left and near the fire exit, from which he could, sitting with his back against the wall, keep an eye on the bar, the balcony, and the stairs down to the front door. But the unstructured situation was almost more than he could bear: He had gone out infrequently in Morocco—and if at all, he had gone out only in daylight and kept to the casbah sections where other foreigners were instantly recognizable. The one time he had varied that rule was taking a taxi to meet Shy, and that had been a disaster, in retrospect.

He wondered if it was just because of Nasta that he didn't shoot Mino through the ear while Flak was behind the bar in the band's dressing room, jumpstart that fast little car, and run for it: He could give them quite a chase. The documentation he had wouldn't get him through the first checkpoint, but he knew where, with money, he could get counterfeits; he'd run more borders than John Shy had teeth, and money was where you found it. . . . There would be no more painful itemization of his failure, no more roll-calling the agents whose lives he had destroyed—and he would be stone-dead within forty-eight hours, free at last. There was nothing he could do for Anastacia Martinova, now that someone thought it was worth peeling back her brain, layer by layer, to see if anything interesting might be found.

He closed his eyes against the disorienting surrealism of the club, against the earnest young peace freaks and the smoky light and the purple air, leaning his forehead on an icy hand.

"You okay, sir?" Mino whispered. "Sir, I can't keep calling you 'sir' in here."

He raised his head. "No, and it'll be a relief to me: Cory will do fine. How's your shoulder? Stiff and sore, I'd bet."

"I've got Percodan for that, sir—*Cory*—so it's like a distant twinging. I'm kind of relieved that it happened—I always wondered how it was going to feel, whether I could handle it. Sort of like flying, I guess—guys don't mind any little accident you can walk away from; cuts down the odds of having all that bad luck you haven't been getting come down on you in one big one that's gonna write you out of the game, if you know what I mean."

Hunt did. Someone came toward them and he sat back, the leather jacket brushed out of his way, ready. But it was only the waitress. He let Mino order for him. He didn't like this place; he shouldn't be here unless and until he was operational. These two were pushing him into something before he was ready. He almost told Mino to cut the crap, that he knew what was going on.

But then he wondered if he truly did. "Mino, Innotech isn't like a government service. If anything goes wrong, you can't even tell yourself that it was in a good cause. And they haven't got squat for bailouts. Don't get in over your head. Fly for a living—that's what you know how to do."

"Or I'll end up like you? That doesn't scare me, sir. And Innotech's the best, sir. Didn't they get your government to bail you out—under the table, maybe, but they traded for you, two for one ... well, Cory, didn't they?"

"I don't know, Mino. There's no way of telling how those guys think or what they do as opposed to what they let you think they did, might have done, are doing, or even intend to do." He had been trying not to let his bitterness surface, but he saw the troubled look in Mino's eyes. How many times had he tried to talk a potential agent out of getting himself killed? It never worked; they just thought you'd lost your nerve. "I sure as fuck know I'm no longer a citizen of the Land of the Free."

"I heard that! . . . Can you tell me how come you weren't carrying a nine-millimeter side arm, considering the foreign venues and the availability of ammo that's NATO standard?"

"There's ten years' worth of forty-five acp anywhere the American military's been stationed. But if I were operational, I'd have whatever I was told to have, or what suited the legend, or what was ultimate for a particular purpose. Off-hours, I want to know that if I have to put somebody down, he's going to stay down. I start loving my enemy right after I've put a round in him, so I don't like to have to shoot him twice."

Mino puffed out his cheeks. "Are you trying to spook me, man? I know this isn't African handball we're playing."

"You asked me," Hunt reminded him, certain now that Mino meant well but thought with his mouth. He saw Flak threading his way between the tables toward them, the case he had been carrying nowhere in sight. Onstage, someone, crouched low, was doing things with microphones.

Flak, sitting, leaned forward. "We're rolling, if we want to be. Somebody's going to set it up for us to meet a couple of the right people. . . . Cory, what should I tell them? I don't want to make a meet and then have you decide not to show."

Hunt stood up. "I'll be outside trying to figure out how I can leave you both here looking exceptionally stupid. You want to deal with consequences, deal with that. I'm not ready for anything else, and neither are you."

He had to cross the crowded room, dim and full of tables; he had to descend five steps and get through the front door, all with his back unprotected and unknowable conditions before and behind. The muscles along his spine twitched; he knew what it felt like to have a bullet slam into him. When he had pushed through the open door into the street reflecting light from its cobbles, he sidled left down two steps and leaned against a wall, breathing hard and feeling perspiration dry on his face.

Across the Stampfenbachstrasse, before the night-lit boutique, the Mondial waited. When they had driven slowly toward the Bazillus Musik restaurant, Flak had flicked the high beams, exclaiming that at last he had found them, and a car had obligingly pulled out of its convenient parking space. Behind it, a pair of longhairs studied the boutique's wares; two cars down to his right, a motor went on and lights flared. For the first time in days, his back betrayed him, sending a debilitating shock of pain from his right knee up along his spine so that his vision blurred.

Someone got out of a BMW Bavaria, which had been parked there when he had arrived, and walked toward him, hands in his coat pockets, just as Mino came skidding down the steps, cursing and entreating him breathlessly. When the overcoated figure saw Mino, he stopped where he was and leaned against a parked car, frankly watching them.

"Go tell Helms it's a false alarm, if he's part of your team," Hunt said softly to Mino, not looking one way or the other, waiting for the red stars to clear from his vision and not caring too much if push came to shove. One shot through the boutique's window and the local shields would be on their way; the alarms would bring witnesses; Mino was blocking him from Helms if he was the only designated shooter; the car in front of Hunt was a 4 × 4 with high ground clearance—he could dive under it and wait for the soldiers to disappear or the police to show or a good sight picture to come his way . . . *if* he made it to the car, and *if* the shooter didn't put one in its gas tank, and *if* there weren't a dozen more soldiers out there, duly cleared through Innotech or some agency to raise hell here without anyone blinking an eye, and *if* the police, should they consent to come by, didn't just hand him back to Innotech or the consulate general the way his papers said they ought to, instead of letting him try to talk somebody in the Moroccan Embassy into believing he was alive and well and had nothing to do with the blow-away on the Mamounia's steps while at the same time admitting that he was in the country illegally. The Swiss would deport him to Morocco; and the Moroccans would shut him up in one of their infamous prisons, where people were "lost" all the time; and the prison warden would, as probably as not, have an auction to determine who got him. No one with whom Hunt dealt need know that some crazy claiming to be Cordell Hunt had ever come into Moroccan hands, and Hunt would end up back here in Zürich—or somewhere inestimably worse. "Shit." And there remained Nasta. "Well, Mino?"

"Not that I know of, sir, he's not," said Mino, abruptly composed. "I've got the keys here. What say we just walk over to our wheels and ease on in? Flak'll be right out, sir. I think I'll just stay between you and him, and we'll—"

Flak came shouldering through the door, case in hand.

"Look who's here," Mino began. "Did you know Helms was—"

Flak, shaking his head, wondered once again why these "fuckers" were "so radically intense," then told them both to get over to the car.

Hunt declined to move. Mino touched his arm tentatively: "Don't let that *malaka* Helms get to you, sir. He's still pissed from when you backseat-drove his ass through the roadblock."

Hunt looked down at Mino's fingers on his arm, then at his deep-shadowed face. "I wouldn't call *any*body a jerkoff right now if I were you." He saw Flak's signal, and saw the man known as Helms saunter slowly back to the Bavaria.

When they crossed the street, his two companions flanked him, and when the car's doors were opened, Hunt demanded the keys: "I'm driving; Flak's navigator; Mino, you're tailgunning."

When he had started the engine and pulled out of the space, the Bavaria and the car farther back, which had been idling throughout the sidewalk exchange, both pulled out behind them. "Let's have some directions, Flak."

"The chalet's—"

"To John Shy."

"Sir, I don't know.... Yeah, I do, but we can't go there, sir. Honcho parties like that aren't for the likes of us."

"You think not? You're either going to see Shy with me or going into deep shit with me, because I'm going to run my butt off"— he reached under his jacket and snapped the Commander free of its sheath, laying it, cocked but not locked, between his thighs— "unless I get some straight talk, now, from somebody who can put me in the picture. If you mentioned my name in conjunction with Morales in there, you can get out now, because if I have to think about it, I'll lose my temper.... No? Okay." He accelerated. "If anybody even suspects they might have recognized me and knows who you are, I'm in worse shape than I was an hour ago."

"Sir, that's not so. I—"

No directions were forthcoming. He pulled the car over. "You want to call Shy for authorization, there's the mobile unit. Call."

"Christ." Flak began to recite the complexity of the routing procedure he would have to employ to get Shy on a secure line, looked at Cory's intently watchful expression, and picked up the phone. Five minutes later he put it down with a rueful grimace. "Yes, sir, you're right, sir—we're all in worse shape than we were an hour ago." Then he gave Hunt directions to Cannard's on the south shore of the Zürichsee.

Chapter 7

"WHAT *is* it?" Beth whispered.

"Dropout," Shy responded, still with his eyes closed. He'd had an enervating week; tonight had been the worst, not the best, of it. He was drunk and he was exhausted and he'd been negotiating all evening so that his throat was sore and he wasn't yet sure whose support he could count on—he was totally unprepared for a confrontation with Cordell Hunt. This was going to be some "party."

To make a difficult situation unbearable, his wife was here. He had taken the day off to see if there was any chance that he could convince Michele to help him do Jack Fowler a simple favor—

deleting a sentence here or there didn't seem to be too much to ask. But Michele was Michele: uncompromising, lover of abstracts and principles, not so much ungiving of affection as forgetful of the need to express it. It was not that she'd fallen out of love with him, she had said, just that she couldn't spare any attention from her project. She *had* found time to clip the London *Times* article on Hunt's death ("Ex–CIA Adventurer Slain in Marrakech," in which an "unidentified intelligence source" was claimed to have told an American bystander that the "soldier of fortune" had been killed by KGB) and tape it to his mirror with a crabbed note in the margin—*"John!"*—and Triage's name underlined in the text.

Seeing it, he'd experienced a palpable chill, then realized that it wasn't a security leak, just Michele being Michele. But he had to say something, so he'd gone into her bedroom, awash in print, and said, "Do I console you about this? Is that the point?"

She had looked up from under her tortoise glasses, sprawled on her bed in jeans amid a dozen open books and paper-clipped magazines and three-by-five cards. "There but for you went I? Hardly. But he *was* a friend, and it *was* a raw deal he got. Don't you oversee Triage's adventuristic antics? They pay you for something up there on Innotech's top floor, I assume."

"How good a friend was he?" He had never asked her; they didn't discuss what they'd agreed to term "peripherals" to their relationship.

"At one time, before I met you, it was...childish infatuation on my part, expediency on his—not that I minded knowing that. Nobody gets the Hunts of this world; they're—" She broke off, blinking rapidly. "Sorry. It's not your fault. God, I hate dead puppies." She sniffed, and crawled off the bed, carefully maneuvering among her placed papers.

"But somebody gets the Shys? I was a safe bet?"

"The safest. Look around you."

"Make Jack's changes?" he asked once again, tempted to tell her about Dropout, although they never, ever talked about his projects in specifics.

"Absolutely not. If I come to your party, I'll be forced to tell Jack he should be ashamed of trying to influence me through you, and that when I can, I'll return the favor."

She had told Jack Fowler exactly that.

It hadn't gone down well.

Nothing had since Thursday, when he'd argued with Beth and the discussion turned personal. He'd reiterated his position, that he'd never divorce, and she'd said she thought that would be best for them both, and they'd ice-packed the whole matter as best they could. Tonight, in her gold-spangled gown, she was looking as if she were just what he needed, which meant he was about as drunk as he could afford to be, because his next move was to make her realize that her behavior with Dropout was counter-vailing his strategy, and that under the circumstances he was going to ask her to leave the project; and when he'd said that, she wouldn't be amenable to any amorous suggestion he was moved to make.

So he said it, flat out, in Sid Cannard's magnificent white kitchen, and watched her flinch as if from a physical blow, look away, touch the marble-topped table, nod her head: "All right, I deserved that. But don't try to pull me off the project. I won't go."

He thought that over. "Then let's consolidate our efforts, starting immediately. You book the hotel."

She looked up slowly, not smiling. "It's not wise, but if you say so, I will."

"Do. Now. I'll go put Dropout in the bag and we'll have all night to figure out what we're going to do with him."

"I don't agree with you, John, that he's capable. It's not fair to him. He's not ready."

"I won't accept that evaluation. We've been over this."

Then a Germanic servant came to get him, as he had requested, when the Ferrari pulled up the long drive.

Outside, under the portico, Hunt sat on the car's fender. "I hope your evening has been more pleasant than mine, Mr. Shy," Hunt said in his best bureaucratese. "Since the experiment I just underwent was too ill-conceived for Flak to have thought of by himself, I'd like to talk with you about it. Invite us in."

"Certainly not." Shy shrugged into his coat. "Let's take a walk." Behind him, as he stepped off the curb, he heard his bodyguards' tread; since Monday he had been able to go nowhere without them. It was unpleasant to be continually under guard, to take precautions against the likelihood of bodily harm. He said honestly, "I'm not at my best tonight, Cord. What in particular is the problem?"

"I'm not drugged and I'm not stupid."

"Yes, well...could you be more specific?"

"Were you trying to flush Morales with me as bait? I'll ring her on the telephone, as long as it's your line and your nickel. Or were you just curious to see what I'd do—and what, if anything, someone might try to do to me? Or do you simply not give a shit in general—so little, in fact, that you'd try to operate me through Flak without having to tell me anything, as if I were a civilian cutout, ignorant of even the rudiments of intelligence tradecraft? Agent-handling is something I've forgotten more about than you'll ever know. *Is* that what you think you were doing? Because Flak's not up to it. I thought for a while he might be—"

"You're paranoid."

"You said it. But I know you knew about this; Beth told me it's been in the works all week—that I had to pass muster. I don't want to work for you under these conditions. I can't. You're too maladroit. Don't you know who the Moraleses are? It's not some spoiled rich brat you saw in a fancy hotel you're talking about prodding into action, it's Angel Morales' wife. I almost scratched him once five years ago, during the culmination of an eight-week attempt to flush him that turned overt when he kidnapped a communications exec in Bogotá with the pro-Soviet FARC guerrillas—call themselves 'Colombia Revolutionary Armed Forces.' We chased them into Brazil, hooked up with a Brazilian CODI—that's 'Internal Defense Operational Commands'—counterterrorist team, and put lots of holes in his Cessna. If you think he's going to be real thrilled to see me again, you don't understand what it's like to trade that many bullets. I sent him away with a souvenir or two: He's not likely to forget hydrostatic-type wound trauma. So if you want me to go after him, give me either an armed and trained team or a legend that can stand up to some very exhaustive scrutiny."

"You *will* do it under those circumstances?"

They walked between two Mercedes onto the snowy lawn.

"For certain considerations."

"Which are?"

"I want my American citizenship back—my own name. I want to see Martinova now and leave with her under no compunction when I've neutralized Morales. I want the arms and ammo confiscated from the NTS safe house to go to the people waiting for them—air drop into Kandahar or to an address I'll give you in Peshawar. And speaking of *my* money, I want a half-million Swiss francs, half now and half later—if I don't live through it, you can give my second payment to NTS. And I want an end to interrogation, threats of interrogation, or even contemplation of interrogation. I have had enough."

"I wish I could do those things, Cord, I really do. The money's no obstacle. I'll get you your team, whatever support technology you want—you can call your own shots. I'll even negotiate with Morales, buy them off, if that will end these attacks on Innotech."

"Fuck Morales. What about the rest of it?"

"I'm working on the interrogation matter—please bear with me. You're still here, and I was only slated to have you overnight, so I've already demonstrated both good faith and substantial progress. Arming the Afghan rebels without the secure conduit Two Can Play was supposed to ensure is an impossibility, even if we had your munitions, which we don't; the Moroccans claimed them. As for American citizenship, I think that's an impossibility—there's been too much publicity; you would stand to lose it under the Agee decision even if you got it back—you've blown plenty of American agents. But some friendly nation...I think I might be able to do that. Again, it will take time."

"And Martinova?"

"Utterly out of my province, I'm afraid. I traded her to keep you. Seeing her is out of the question, but she's in good hands, I assure you—*Cord!*"

Shy stood, amazed, watching the man walk rapidly toward the parked Ferrari, Shy's bodyguards parting hurriedly to make way for him. Beyond them, he turned and, walking backward, called to Shy: "What bothers me the most is that in the final analysis it's going to be one of you moralistic, liberal bastards with your clean hands and your closed minds that gets me killed." He headed for the car.

"You'll never find her without me," Shy called back softly. "You'll never get to her on your own. You need me for that." Hunt stopped but did not turn. Shy continued, conscious that he was risking everything: "Anyway, you told me that nothing—not Martinova, not anything—was worth your own ass to you. Don't make me scrub this offensive—if I do have to, you'll go with it."

"I know," he heard Hunt say quietly, his back still turned.

Shy had a ludicrous vision of himself chasing the burnt-out, alienated asset to and fro in Cannard's gardens until hell froze over, trying to reach some accommodation with this creature from another world before Hunt, true to type, pulled out his over-powered handgun and shot him. Drunk or not, he decided, he had done the right thing by telling Dropout about Martinova's disposition. He walked slowly and determinedly to where the man in the leather jacket stood hunched against the cold. "Let's nail this down, Cord. It's now or never. What kind of legend do you perceive as viable?" The thing to do, Shy was sure, was to keep Hunt talking, keep him from doing anything irremediable. But the field agent, with a shake of his head, moved off toward the waiting car.

Shy was damned if he was going to *run* after him. Coming abreast of his bodyguards, he avoided their questioning looks, increased his pace, calling, "I'll let you talk to someone about her if you like." It was a desperate gambit. Shy had never done any-thing remotely like it in his career. But then, he'd never handled an agent like Cordell Hunt. Some analysts contended field men like Hunt were a dying breed, made obsolete by satellite over-flights and the microprocessor revolution. But they, like Shy him-self, best and brightest of their law-school graduating classes, had been taught at an early age that anything could be settled through negotiation.

Shy had no compunction about using Dropout. Hunt knew the risks better than anyone Shy had knowledge of; he'd worked at one time or another for the most exclusive of the American in-telligence clubs—from the Joint Chiefs' own spook shop to State's Bureau of Intelligence and Research (INR) and for nearly a dozen intelligence-sharing services abroad.

Agents like Hunt all had certain things in common: They kept asking why they weren't allowed to do their jobs; they had recur-rent nightmares of betrayal, according to Beth, of being stranded in the field, deserted by even their memories, somewhere an em-bassy or a mission had suddenly been closed. They were paranoid and they were violent, part of the shadow world they penetrated. When they went renegade, they were inestimably dangerous: They knew both sides of the game, every angle, every weakness, every potential scandal and pressure point. That was why Hunt would never get his citizenship back: The senators and congressmen who exercised intelligence oversight would never permit it.

The asset had reached Shy's Ferrari; Flak and Mino were getting out of it at his order. Shy hurried.

"You know better than this, damn you," he whispered, reaching the open passenger door, holding on and leaning in toward Hunt, who was fastening his safety belt. The buzzing of the car's warning system ceased.

Shy got in the car and slammed the passenger door shut, thinking, *Agents maneuver,* but saying, "I can't let you do this, and you know it. Help me keep you alive. Don't fight me."

"You don't know what you're doing—that's not my fault. I don't want to pay your bill. I sure as hell don't want Martinova paying *my* bill. Get out and let me calm down before I do something you won't live to regret."

"Some people think you can't do the job, can't do *any* job—you know, that you're incompetent after Moscow."

Hunt draped an arm over the wheel. "Analysts will be analysts."

"So far, you're the only one who thinks *I* can't do my part. Your attitude entitles me to air my own analysis: You're in no position to bargain. If you're finished with your Lawrence of Afghanistan act, we can go in and see about Martinova—assuming you *do* care about anything but yourself, which I am beginning to doubt. I've met two of your five conditions fully, and agreed to work on the rest. I'm not accustomed to *paying* for this kind of treatment. From now on I want cooperation from you."

"As long as it doesn't interfere with my survival, I'll cooperate with you. I have been all along."

"Is that so? How is it that I've gotten more relevant information from you in the last few minutes than in the entire time we've had you?"

"I told you not to dope me. Now I'm telling you that I'm unconvinced you can back up what you say, what you promise, or even what you'd like to be able to promise. Convince me."

"Tomorrow I'll bring you the Triage roster and you can put together the team of your choice. I took the chance of those pilots fouling up because you seemed so sympatico. I'm doing everything I know how, believe me."

"I don't want a team from the Triage roster. You don't listen well. I said I needed an armed and trained team. I don't consider Mino and Flak properly armed or trained, but I can fine-tune them. They'll be all right."

"Good. We've got to get moving on this."

Hunt leaned back and fished out a Camel, offering one to Shy. "Who's in there from the community besides Sid Cannard?"

"A few people. But at this juncture, it might serve us just as well to let the right people know you're alive and on staff here, the implication of presenting you publicly being that we intend to keep you that way. There'll be some looks askance, I imagine— you're rather underdressed. But once in a while representatives of the paramilitary are invited here."

"Pretty last-ditch, isn't it?"

"You insisted on forcing the issue, now I'm accommodating you."

"So it's arms dealers and political whores?"

"On the whole. My wife is in there—would you classify her as either? Never mind, don't answer that. Now, I'm going to be as impolite as I can manage and not introduce you to anyone. We'll find the man I want you to talk to, you'll satisfy yourself as best you can that nothing else could be done, and then you'll get back in this car with those two youngsters and go directly to the chalet. Acceptable?"

"I'll have to see what the 'man' says."

"You do that," said Shy, a surge of anger driving the last of the drink out of him. When this was over, he might just be glad to see the end of it—however it turned out.

He took them up the bluestone stairs into the palatial paneled hall and endured many stares and Flak's whispered attempts to explain that he'd done the best he could to allay Hunt's suspicions, but it had worked all too well. Shy silenced him irritably; he knew that.

Beth seemed to materialize, all sparkling beadwork and thick-waved hair, in their path, kissing Flak and Mino as if they were school friends of her social stratum, and Hunt with something more like passion.

"Find Fowler and have him meet us in the kitchen," Shy said to her when his turn came.

"This is mad; Dropout's contagious," she replied, but disap-

peared into the crowd of gowned women and men in black tie,
which was thickening almost imperceptibly around them. Shy kept
them moving, wishing Mino wouldn't crane his neck so obviously
and Flak wasn't the sort whom every woman's eyes followed. But
Hunt was professionally unremarkable, taking advantage of the
two pilots' attention-drawing configuration, moving off to the side,
neither purposefully seeking shadows nor ill at ease, but floating
in their wake.

At the door to the kitchen, down a long hall along the length
of which the real heavyweights from NATO at Brussels and Bonn
and Paris talked percentage points of arms-market losses to the
Soviets, Shy saw Sid Cannard and took a deep breath.

Here, as had not occurred in the reception room, men occasionally broke off conversations when Hunt went by. Shy hoped
he was doing the right thing. Once Hunt stopped to receive a
bear-hug greeting from a representative of Israeli Military
Industries (IMI) who'd been a Mossad control agent as late as
the '67 war and, for all Shy knew, might still be. Standing at a
polite distance, Shy caught occasional phrases—"data pull"...
"Moraleses"..."deep hush"—but when at last Shy moved in to
extricate him, their talk was of the new Galil SAR's (short auto
rifles). The Israeli greeted Shy coolly, though he evinced no surprise at seeing Hunt alive and the two of them together, but
referred to Dropout as "Abu Ifrit" and warned Shy to take "good
care of this boy, who is like a son to me, from when he was *this*
high."

Strike one, Shy thought.

Strike two was a pair of unlikely bedfellows: a cabinet-level
German involved with Grenzschutzgruppe-9 (GSG-9 was
Germany's elite antiterrorist squad, Israeli-trained and, if one
judged them by their widely circulated training films, surpassing
their teachers) and a CIA man, deputy director of foreign intelligence. By the time Shy had extricated himself from the wickedly
smirking Israeli purposely detaining him with arms-market small
talk, the German was scowling, and when Shy interposed himself,
the American was saying, "...talk to you about Two Can Play,
Scratch, at your earliest convenience."

"Hi, Shy. You know these two. This Agency type thinks he wants
to talk about 'Two CP.' Doesn't understand that I gave at the

Lubyanka. Give him your number, okay?" And Hunt slipped away, leaving Shy returning two very disquieting stares.

Then the American asked him what he thought he was doing, *told* him they'd have to have a breakfast meeting tomorrow, and wondered if he'd share Innotech's technique for raising the dead. The German glowered, muttering something about blackmail and Mauser 66S sniper rifles.

Cannard was definitely strike three, frowning in his most forbidding fashion and calling Hunt "Dropout" to his face and questioning whether anything Hunt could do would be worth what he'd already cost Innotech.

In the kitchen the brighter light confirmed Shy's gut analysis: His hands were shaking almost as perceptibly as the asset's tended to do; he was blowing it. Hunt didn't miss the signs: "Easy, big fella. Chebrikov and I know enough about Sid Cannard to make his mother disown him." Hunt's eyes had that NO EXIT look and his lips were tightly drawn. He sat at the breakfast bar, perched on a leather stool, and asked one of the women in white organdy aprons to give him some coffee before they left.

Flak had just run the gauntlet, and was backing into the room still assuring some "sir" or other that he would take care of everything, yes indeed. Mino was lost in the shuffle, and Shy hesitated to wonder where the irrepressible pilot might have gotten to—he had enough trouble on his hands. He thought of calling the chalet and having the helicopter sent to pick up Hunt, but dismissed the notion: They had to start trusting each other. He prayed that his wife wouldn't drift in here and see them.

"I hope to hell Sid didn't hear you say that," Shy said to Hunt, sliding into the adjacent stool.

"Better hope he did. That bastard would as soon blow me out of the water as look at me. My dad taught me to hate his guts in the old days, and he knew the types of whom he spoke."

Flak, squinting, asked Hunt for a light and agreed to go find Mino.

As he was leaving, Beth and Jack Fowler came in.

Cordell Hunt snapped to, purposefully sat back down, and gave Shy a long and scathing look. Thereafter, Hunt ignored him. "Good evening, sir," he said to Jack Fowler. "I wasn't told it would be you."

The two shook hands, the bar between them. Beth caught Shy's eye and smiled encouragingly.

Fowler relishingly lit a cigar. "I'm not supposed to do this, you know, Cory—my doctor's forbidden me the noxious weed. You shouldn't either; Percy would whip your insolent arse if he were alive."

"Yes, sir, I know he would. But my odds are a lot worse on a dozen other fronts. I'm sure you know the score, since you're here."

"So you can be sure the fire's not coming from my soldiers. I hear you've become quite the *cause célèbre.*"

"No, sir, I don't think so. Can we talk about Martinova?"

"You don't think *what?*"

Hunt closed his eyes, opened them, and told Jack Fowler that in his best estimation, after months of close observation, Anastacia Martinova was a Narodno Trudovoy Soyuz operative with substantial connections in Southwest Asia and Eastern as well as Western Europe, but nothing more.

Fowler replied that he would keep Hunt's analysis in mind but that no final determination was going to be made for quite some time in the Martinova case.

Hunt said, "So she's a case? That's what I'm telling you: She's not, or shouldn't be; not unless the mujahedin don't matter anymore."

"Having nothing to do with what I personally hold to be true, or what does or doesn't matter *anymore,* she is presently under observation. More than that, Cory, I'm not at liberty to divulge or discuss right now. When you can, come up to Mons and we'll have some long talks—privately, off the record. Any light you can shed on the voluminous mysteries surrounding that woman will be very welcome. We've been trying to convince John to let us borrow you for a few weeks. You do have a unique perspective and we're looking forward to sharing it."

What Fowler was saying could be construed as either aid and comfort or threat and warning, but it wasn't the sort of temporization Shy had expected from NATO's top intelligence gun. And Hunt, lighting another cigarette before he stubbed out his butt in a saucer, was cautious and respectful as he ventured: "I can't do that. What would you do, sir, if you were in my place?" with just a trace of a Brahmin accent as if he'd been thrown back into an earlier time, reminding Shy of Hunt as he'd been the summer Michele, and then he, had first met Percy Hunt's son during what Cord referred to, in supercilious undergraduate fashion, as his "short-lived American exile" at Harvard, when Shy had been doing his postgrad at MIT.

Fowler pulled a stool around the bar's end and sat opposite Hunt, face propped up by one palm, examining his broadleaf cigar. "I think if I were you, I might have done pretty much what you're doing. But I'm not you, and I wish you had come to me first."

"I didn't come to anybody, sir. I wouldn't. I still can't. I'm having a crisis of confidence."

"So I surmised. Be terribly cautious—you're the last of a fine old line. I still think about your father. I don't want to think about you the same way, Cory. Don't make me regret my noninterventionist nature the way he did." Fowler got up, carefully put out his cigar, and slid his hand inside his tuxedo. Shy saw Hunt tense and wondered if the asset could possibly be expecting violence from Fowler.

When he had replaced his cold cigar in a silver case holding five others, Fowler said, "You did this to me, John. I *had* quit. It's on your head." And he shook Hunt's hand again, then Shy's, then kissed Beth on the forehead, telling her that he was leaving straightaway and she must give his thanks to Sid.

When he had stepped out, Mino and Flak, kept waiting outside by Beth's strategic position in the doorway, slid within, wondering if that "guy" who had just left was who they thought he was.

Hunt said he doubted it, and asked Shy elaborately for permission to return to base.

Shy gave it, and when they had gone, he lay his head on the counter atop folded arms, slumped over, not caring who saw him. His stomach was full of road-racing midgets and his mouth was sandpaper-dry; he was going to have to stop drinking until this operation was over.

He noticed tha⸱ Hunt had left his cigarettes behind just as the asset returned alone to retrieve them. "I forgot these," Hunt said quietly, "and I forgot to give you my shopping list. So if you're serious and I'm operational, get out your onetime pad or whatever you jot on and let's shape this up—Hello, Cannard."

Innotech's director did not respond to Dropout directly. "John, what *do* you think you're doing?"

Shy recited from rote his blanket justification: Incontrovertible proof that the terrorist international was, in any single case, responsive to Soviet direction would be of inestimable value not only to the Western intelligence community and the governments it served, but to the weapons-technology industry of which Innotech was only the most overtly beset. He couldn't very well tell Cannard he was turning Hunt loose on all of the above.

Hunt didn't even wait until Shy was finished before decreeing, "We might as well start right here. Cannard, have Angel and Dania Morales put through the Octopus. I want everything they've done or even might have done in the past five years."

Cannard, looking only at Shy, demurred, saying that the Octopus was a CIA computer and Innotech could hardly access it at whim.

Hunt sighed, observed that nothing ever changed in this business, and announced that since he hadn't really expected substantive aid from Innotech, he was prepared to "access" his own information. "But I won't tolerate interference. The next time I see Helms, I'm going to shoot him." He brushed past Cannard and out without a farewell.

Fishing out his pipe, Cannard said around its stem, "John, I can't *have* this sort of thing. You've upset certain customers tonight, flashing that man overtly. What can you be thinking of? A procedural error during a crisis of this magnitude could cost us everything. You can't put Dropout in so sensitive a picture—he's a rogue, that much is obvious. And you know it: You've had the Octopus data for days."

"You suggested using him on this terrorist matter—it's what he does, after all. I can't show him anything that will add to his information on Two Can Play, but I *will* show him the Agency data-pull—I needed to check his story against it. Sid, I want you not to ask me about this—not about what I'm doing, or how much it's costing, or what the potential repercussions might be. As you pointed out previously, you don't want to tell me how to do my job." He wondered if Sid would fire him; then he told himself he didn't care; then he heard his voice speaking, as if of its own volition: "None of those *banditti* out there care about how we do what they ask. They care only that they can pick up a phone and get things done, or write a purchase order and sleep at night without submitting to government clearances. They're more concerned over what the policy shift from restraint of arms sales to third-world nations by America to open competition with the Western Europeans for developing nations' business is going to mean to their own countries' bottom lines."

"I never meant you to take this so far, John. My Lord—deals with Jack Fowler!" He raised a palm. "No! I don't want to know the specifics. You're right, I suggested that you extract whatever pertinent information Dropout might have. Now I'm suggesting that in view of these developments the prudent move would be to cede him to those prepared to cope with his sort. We can't have this turn out badly. We can't afford to lose any friends . . . *I* can't afford to lose *you.*"

"What developments?"

"Beth says Dropout's urinalysis reveals extraordinarily high levels of beta-phenethylamine, a prime indicator of paranoid schizophrenia. If he *is* schizophrenic, stressing him could trigger a psychotic incident."

"I read Beth's report, too. But I read it with an open mind. I'm willing to accept the milder diagnosis—that Hunt's a stress-seeker, certainly, and that he's been *so* stressed lately that the abnormally high concentrations of PEA in his urine are simply a reaction to what we've been doing to him. He's healthy enough for someone who's been through what he has. His kidneys are functioning, his knee jerks when you hit it, he can put a three-inch group in your choice of targets—prone, upright, or standing on his head. And unless there's something I don't know about, there's no reason for you to oppose this operation at so late a stage. . . . Is there?"

"I only wish there were."

Chapter
8

MAYBE because they'd stopped drugging him, his nightmares got worse. He dreamed of Nasta repeatedly, of being helpless and standing by while Chebrikov or Jack Fowler put her through her paces. Then he'd dream she was lying in the dirt beside him at Bari Kot, or that he'd been talked into sending her out with one of his Afghan deep-cover teams and she came back, like some of his boys had, one limb at a time. He told himself it was the training sessions out behind the chalet on the snowy slopes that were stirring up his dreams: The terrain was similar; about this time last year he'd been doing pretty much the same thing in the Kush. His equipment here was better, but his physical condition was worse: He found himself having a more difficult time in this generous air than he'd had there at higher altitudes.

Save for the Israeli intelligence take on Morales, which had come in with the Galil SAR's undetected, as the old Mossad man he'd approached at Sid's party had promised, Shy's project was beginning to seem like a textbook go: Hunt was being dispatched into the field with agents about whom he knew virtually nothing under the vaguest of orders. He wasn't taking Shy's offer to negotiate with Morales seriously; "executive actions" were always mounted this way—total deniability demanded that no assassination order ever be given in so many words.

He still wasn't sure if Shy truly wanted a successful operation, but Hunt was going to give him the run of his career. Claiming that he wanted all his hardware to come from outside the Innotech corporate structure—that he preferred not to have to worry about sabotage—had given Hunt the chance to tap the Israeli IMI man and the German for "favors": It hadn't been the Galils, Mini Uzis, and Mausers he wanted as much as a look at both country's files on the Moraleses, but when the Israeli arms came, he curtailed the climbing and rolling and signaling and crawling drills he'd instigated and got serious with his two trainees.

He'd set up a combat course covering the ridge in back of the chalet, but first he took the two pilots to the top of the hill where the wind was tricky and let them get the feel of the different windage settings on the sniper rifles he'd borrowed from the Triage sentries, close enough to Mausers for training, and watched them find out what a Star-tron night sight could and could not be expected to do. They spent the night up on the hill: What he really wanted to gauge was their performance under hardship conditions and the disparity in their training.

When dawn broke, unsatisfied and stiff with cold, he took them over the combat course using the Galil 7.62s and the little Mini Uzis, retraining them not to pop up from cover like jackrabbits to make their hits; to roll, fire, and roll; to think always of concealment; never to be directly left of the last muzzle flash from their own weapons. When the German Mauser 66S's came, they were going to be in for a pleasant surprise. Until then he was content to push them physically, probe them mentally, and compare his performance to theirs.

They were younger, but it was Mino who complained first, lowering his soaked, aching body slowly to the floor before the library fire, that Hunt was going to kill them all before they ever engaged the enemy. "I'm gonna die of exhaustion or overexposure before I get to put any of what you're preaching into practice. If I'm too burnt out to lift my arm, too shaky to hold it still, what good's a stun grenade or a fancy side arm? I can't shoot nothin' but my foot in this condition, let alone some arcane shit like a three-inch oblong between a guy's 'upper lip and *occipital lobe.*' What's wrong with the old two-shot burst to the chest? I fly good, I'm not supposed to have to be James fucking Bond. Ain't shit about bein' no commando in my orders."

By then Hunt was shivering before the blazing hearth in his sweater, sweatshirt, and parka, glumly realizing that he couldn't take another day of the regimen he'd prescribed for them, handguns arriving tomorrow or not. He hadn't the strength or the inclination to pounce on the opening Mino had given him by asking what orders the pilot *did* have. He told himself that he didn't care whether they demonstrated personal survivability or not; as long as they didn't take him down with them, they could go get themselves killed.

Flak responded to Mino quickly—perhaps covering a breach, perhaps only as irritable as the other two: "You can't figure three rounds per enemy takedown, asshole, in an urban situation where all you're likely to have is a handgun with possibly one extra clip. Two-shot bursts to the chest aren't going to stop somebody on angel dust; he'll just keep coming. I had a guy get up off the ground once with a hole you could *see through* in his chest and take another shot at me. Head shots are what you call a 'no-mystery takedown': save time, ammo, and nerves. That right, sir?"

"Sometime," Hunt replied, "you've got to tell me how you got so smart flying contract, Flak. Mino, after what I saw in the Baur Au Lac, you ought to be grateful somebody's taking the time to help you. Panic is the absence of training."

"I *heard* Hubble." Mino rolled over on one elbow, scowling. "I just wasn't sure I agreed with him. You've put us through all this because of that?"

"That was then, this is now. *Now* I want you at least Camp Peary—competent. My life may depend on it." He pulled his Commander

out and extracted the magazine, ejected a cartridge into his lap
with the slide, locked the slide open, peered into the chamber to
check that the gun was indeed empty, and handed gun and magazine to Flak, who had displayed not so much as a flicker of
recognition when Hunt mentioned the Farm. "That's the way I
want you to clear the accurized handguns you've got coming.
Remember, there's no firing-pin block on a Commander. Still got
that stopwatch, Flak?"

Flak nodded.

"Good. As of today, neither of you can change clips fast enough.
I want you both down below three seconds per exchange, *with* a
round still chambered when you pull that magazine out. If you
can't make the time, or you let your gun empty, you're liabilities
and I'll leave you here."

"I can make it," Flak murmured. "You're not stretching *me* too
thin. I've had autos before. Just aren't the safest thing in an airplane—they'll go off if they hit the deck right, or sometimes if a
cabin depressurizes, or the—"

"How many safeties are there on that gun?"

"Two," Mino said. "Grip safety and thumb safety."

"Three," Flak disagreed. "You forgot the half-cock notch."

"Four." Hunt shook his head despairingly. "You both forgot
the disconnector: It stops the hammer from falling when the slide's
retracted." He held out his hand to Flak, reclaiming his side arm.
"I'd leave you this to practice on, but you'll have your own tomorrow. If you can't qualify, it won't be because of the equipment.
You'll be getting my setup, from three-pound trigger pull to be-
veled magazine well. The gunsmith will be here to handle any
ammunition-feed problems. I'm real tired of arguing about this.
If either or both of you want out, I'll be pleased to dismiss you,
but you'll disappoint a few higher-ups, I'd bet."

He excused himself, full of doubts, and headed off to bed,
wondering where the Mausers and the accompanying German
intelligence were. The rifles were twenty-four hours late. If the
two pilots passed muster and he himself did not, what then? If
he had been controller rather than operative, he would have dis-
qualified himself. On his way up the stairs—beneath which, in a
computer-locked room, the surveillance command post was located—dizziness overcame him. He grasped the banister and

leaned against it while his perceptions dissolved into gray, into
black, into red-brown mist. *Standing, you're standing,* he reminded
himself, doing what he knew he must to keep his legs under him
although he couldn't feel the knees he was locking or the mahogany banister at the small of his back. When the waterfall-
tingling had faded and grainy light began to coalesce into shapes,
leaving him with a light-headed sense of fatalism, he went back
into the library and told Flak to set up a meeting with Shy for
tomorrow—he had some things he wanted to say.

On Tuesday morning he woke stiff and weak and reeled out
of bed, his sinuses aching, his internal gyros askew. Tne Mausers
were in the front hall. He couldn't have cared less.

Using Shy's imminent arrival as an excuse, he sent Flak and
Mino out to the tennis court to put a few hundred rounds through
their new guns while the gunsmith was standing by. "If the tang
on the grip safety bites the web of your hand, Mino, say something;
now's the time to fix anything that needs to be fixed." He was, in
his way, compensating for his harshness the day before.

Mino grinned, understanding. "Yes, sir, I'll do that. Don't worry
about me, I won't shut down on you."

"Flak," Hunt continued, "yesterday you were flinching." The
pilot, who had been zipping his jacket, looked at Hunt with controlled incredulity, but said nothing. "It happens to everybody—
it happens to me every now and again. A person can be fine for
years and suddenly reinvent report-related flinch. Wear those ear
protectors and shoot until you've shot fifty rounds without a flinch.
Mino, you'll have to watch and tell him when he's doing it—that's
what's dangerous about it, you can't tell yourself when its happening. Go on, go. I'll watch from inside."

But he didn't. He collapsed onto the library sofa and thought
dark thoughts. He had to find some better way to get a look at
the German intelligence-pull on the Moraleses than staying out
in the cold all night the way he'd done when the Israeli take came
in; he couldn't read it here, where everything he did was taped.
An arm crooked over his aching eyes, he thought about Martinova,
up at Mons in Jack Fowler's care, and wondered what would be
left of the woman he'd known when he got to her—because he
was *going* to get to her, if he had to put down half of NATO.

He must have slept; the next thing he remembered was Beth's

cool hand on his neck. She took his temperature and told him he should be in bed. He knew that. "But my back doesn't hurt."

Though he didn't trust her, for far more serious reasons than he didn't trust the rest of them, her cool hand and solicitousness had a certain charm. When she let him lie back, she said, "As far as your back goes, I'm forced to concur with the Russians: When and if it becomes imperative that the shrapnel you're carrying be removed, you'll know it. Whether or not you'll pay attention to what your body tries to tell you is the question. If you want to cripple yourself for life, keep this up. By the time you have those two apprentices trained, you won't be *able* to go out and make John happy."

"I'm scared to death. Where do I throw in the towel?"

"Scratch! I'm serious."

"So serious you'll go on record with this?"

"The ethics of my profession require it."

"Which one? It's hard to believe you're daddy's little girl. I've never seen a more obvious spoiler. 'Confusing' me with Mino that first day at the car; then hitting on me; then when Shy didn't go for my throat because I'd had you, all these medical qualms... Shit, lady, you're more pathetic than danger—"

"*You* think—" She broke off, eyes very bright, and stormed out. He was glad to be alone.

But soon after, Hubble appeared, precise and punctilious, carrying a sheaf of papers in black-and-red Innotech covers for him to "go over" and a summary sheet of the Octopus data on the Moraleses, which the ARD was prepared to let him keep.

With burning eyes, taking aspirin and drinking juice, he stayed there all afternoon committing to memory the relevant portions of Innotech's Crisis Management Committee's report on the three EO's: site damages; options suggested, discarded, and pursued to "affix blame and prevent recurrence"; updates on all ongoing police and Triage investigations. It occurred to him that he might find himself interdicting either group once he got into the field, but the data were so laundered and the police involvement so minimal, he knew he couldn't make any assessments from it. So did Innotech.

He was more concerned with the Morales take. In general, it matched the Israeli data, but it was up-to-the-minute in a way that unaugmented American take just couldn't have been. Therefore, they were giving him data from Innotech's own covert sources while seeming to withhold it. He studied the sheet: who had checked in within six hours of her arrival at the Baur Au Lac; points of embarkation and debarkation of those listed above; Morales' traveling companion of record, one Rainer Diehl, to whom, according to the Baur Au Lac's records, she was wived; their departure by rental car for Cannes only an hour before Hunt left the hotel in the consular limousine.

There was no way to determine that she had, or had not, been involved in the incident in the Albis Mountains; only that she might have had the opportunity to be. Those who had checked in during the targeted hours included nearly a dozen junior members of the international diplomatic set: a son of a second secretary, a daughter of a chargé d'affaires, two scions of cabinet-level northern Europeans. Hunt realized why no one had said anything about going after the terrorists who comprised the international called People's Crusaders for Peace: Politically, it was impossible.

He hadn't seen John Shy since Cannard's party, just Beth and the ARD and those involved in procurement for the operation. Having scanned the data, he was beginning to understand why. More and more, the situation was seeming familiar: He couldn't trust his staging team, his controller, or even the policymakers acting behind the scenes—but then, neither could anyone else.

He'd sent word three days ago via Beth that he wanted verification that Martinova was alive and well before he took his little show on the road, but had received no response as yet.

Before he proposed his scenario and his legend to Shy, he was going to extract a commitment. If they expected him to mount this operation in the most dangerous of possible venues under extremely hazardous conditions (and from the data they had submitted to him, they expected exactly that and knew as well as he what necessarily would be involved), they could damn well humor him as far as Martinova went.

When Shy arrived at the chalet, it was nearly eight in the evening and the atmosphere was akin to that he had left at the Arianespace test site five hours before. Waiting for Aérospatiale's rocket-

launched spy satellite *Sortilege* to "turn the corner" on its journey
to a stable niche in middle space, Shy had found himself hoping
the French mission would abort: The key algorithms on which
Innotech's new dual codes were based would take a century of
computer time to discover, but part of what had been lost in the
Zürich EO was the *Sortilege* software decoding program.

He felt almost that way about Dropout, who was finessing his
mistress and distressing his wife, and whose unpredictability
threatened everyone about him, including Shy. Handing his coat
to the Triage sentry, he slid his hands into the back pockets of
his chinos and stepped into the gently lit foyer, quiet and lined
with closed doors. He didn't need to ask where everyone was.
Reflected in a Spanish mirror, he could see Flak slouched against
the wall opposite the under-the-stairs surveillance center, one leg
up like a stork, arms crossed, headset on, intent on whatever Beth,
beside him, and the men within the electrooptical command post
were watching.

Flak took off his headset when he saw Shy, and came to greet
him. "Hi, boss. You haven't missed much." Flak's eyes were
smudged with weariness, his insouciance worn away.

"Of what? Do we need to talk?"

"Too much talk." Flak shook his head. "*He's* got Mino in the
library alone—for a talk. Yes, I guess I'd like a minute if you can
spare it."

They went into the breakfast nook, where Flak punched up a
security block on the little encoder set into the wall beneath a
Hiroshige eagle diving over Edo, leaned back against a bleached
breakfront, and said, "I've been thinking maybe you should cut
me some new orders, or let me call it a miss. The fucker's a genius.
I'm not."

"Really? I've seen no sign of it. Don't let him psych you."

"Did you hear me out there, sir? He's got Mino alone, asking
about when we met each other and how long Mino's known me
and he never *did* believe my dumber-than-thou act. I can't get
anything out of him—he'll only talk hardware with me. I asked
him when we were going to get to tradecraft, and he said he
thought *I'd* be giving that part of the course."

"You're tired. You've been getting good take. I've been reading
your reports."

"I've got an accurized handgun with every pertinent modification known to man, but I've got no idea what he's doing. I don't even know what he wants to talk to you about."

"He probably doesn't know himself."

"Don't kid yourself." Flak's mouth pulled in at one corner. He fished out a Marlboro and lit it. "Can I ask you if Jack Fowler's sharing the take on this?"

"Yes."

Flak nodded, blowing smoke through his nose, squinted against the plume rising before his face. "How far do you guys want me to take this?"

"As far as it goes."

Flak tapped ashes into his palm. "It's already gone beyond Camp Peary. It's going to go to fire fights, if his preparations are relevant. You going to keep me out of jail if I have to pillage and murder in order to stay with him?"

"Just stay with him. That's what you're being paid for, that's what you came aboard for. Even if I wanted to, I couldn't let you out now. And I don't. He likes you."

"Yeah, I like him, too. We're both real likable guys. If he asks me straight-out questions, I'm going to have to give him decent answers. I don't want him deciding I'm a liability—he's used that word to me once already."

"Give him *plausible* answers."

"Take Mino off it and I'll feel better. I don't want him going down if I fuck up."

Shy wished he had a drink. "Don't act like some skittish trainee." He hitched one leg up on the table. "This is going to get worse before it gets better. You two stay with him and do your jobs as best you can. The only clarification I can give you on your initial assignment is that we do want this operation to succeed—specific methods, from here on, are the operatives' choice. Now, let's get out there before we become too obvious. You shouldn't need to be asking questions this late in the game. I thought you people were inured to second thoughts."

"I wish." Flak started to revert the surveillance to its standard mode.

"Wait one second. Call routing and get together with them on an itinerary I've called in as 'Log B-one.' They'll want a flight plan. You might ready up the chopper, too."

"Tonight?"

"If possible. Feel better?"

"Christ, yeah. Why didn't you say so in the first place?"

"I thought you might run screaming out the door home to mama. Now let's go rescue Mino from the big bad Hunt."

Shy wished, preceding Flak down the hall toward the library, that the asset had had the intestinal fortitude to keep his own counsel. But what was one more doubt?

When he saw Hunt and Mino sharing a joint before the fire like old friends, he didn't wait until Hunt had finished speaking before interrupting—the asset had a good view of the door, and Shy could get the substance of Hunt's interrogatory from the tapes. "Mino, if you're flying us anywhere tonight, I'd prefer not to have to worry about your reflexes."

"Sir?" Mino got hastily to his feet, blinking.

"I'm not going anywhere until—" Hunt began.

For once, Shy knew he had all the cards. He hadn't been able to say that about his dealings with Cordell Hunt since the Mamounia. He cautioned himself that he mustn't enjoy it too much as he said, "In the first place, you certainly can't stay here any longer; you've drawn complaints from numerous quarters with your weaponry drills. This is hardly the place for a firing range—noise travels quite far up here, and the neighbors have a right to demand peace and quiet—they're paying enough for it. By tomorrow *no one* will be here." Shy saw Mino shuffling his feet, an exchange of glances between the two pilots, Mino sidle away, and Hunt put out a restraining hand, his eyes never leaving Shy's face.

"And in the second place?" Hunt shifted position.

"In the second place, I've arranged the meeting you requested. We'll leave directly after dinner, if that's agreeable to you. The chef has gone to great pains to prepare the Moroccan meal you asked for. I wouldn't want to disappoint him."

"Is there a 'third place'?"

"There is, and it is substantively the same infrastructure of security-related concerns you yourself have been displaying. I'd prefer not to discuss any pertinent details until we're under way. I'll be flying the short leg of the journey with you. We can talk then. I believe I've anticipated your needs adequately."

"I hope so, Shy. The last time you told me we'd 'talk later,' I had occasion to regret trusting you even that far."

"*Mino,*" Flak hissed, "come *on.*"

"I'm sorry you feel that way. I'm also sorry you found it necessary to go to your friends at Bonn for corroborative data. If
you had not done so, we might be able to proceed at a more
leisurely pace." Shy spoke to Hunt, ignoring the pilots.

"Somebody on your tail, big fella?" Hunt said as Mino slipped
by Shy and from behind him he heard the beginnings of Flak's
angry dressing down.

"No more than usual—or no more than what has come to seem
usual. Just don't solicit the help of any more unwilling government
officials—no matter what you think they owe you. They don't
like it and I don't like hearing how much they don't like it."

Hunt's offhand wave seemed to say, "You can't blame me for
trying."

Shy found himself over by the bar, asking Hunt about the dinner menu. He remembered that *tagine* was a mixture of lamb,
olives, and artichokes in, perhaps, yogurt sauce, and that *kefta* was
shish kebab, but beyond recognizing *harrira* as some sort of soup,
the rest of Hunt's Arabic buzzed meaninglessly in his ears. There
would be no wine, of course, with a Muslim dinner. Just as well.

Outside, Beth called him aside. "John, he's been running a fever
all day. Can't this wait?"

"Anything serious, do you think?" Her perfume was one he had
bought her; her silk and suede rustled; he never tired of watching
her eyes. "I want to get rid of my competition."

"Influenza, but he hasn't got a great deal of resistance."

"He's not your patient anymore, Beth. He's about to be dis-
charged." He let her come along as he told the Triage supervisor
to shut down the project: Everyone but the perimeter guards was
free to leave after dinner; the supervisor himself was to deliver
all the video cassettes to Shy, surrender his single log copy at that
time, and supervise the cleanup before he left.

He could feel the end-op ennui come down over his personnel
like a shroud.

Beth said she wanted to go with them. He said no. She asked
him if they could speak privately. He said yes. In the ensuing
argument in her bedroom, he mentioned, despite himself, that
he was thinking about closing down his house for a few months.

It was not Beth who had caused his troubles with his wife—if Michele's own words could be believed, it was all his own fault and had nothing to do with either Beth Cannard or Cordell Hunt. It was Shy who must bear the brunt of her outrage at having been lied to about Hunt's death, then ignored (or gone unrecognized) by the agent at Sid's party. Shy had let her believe the newspaper reports; Shy had turned an old and valued friend *(Hunt?)* against her. It was Shy who had become a prime example of the enemy Michele had been fighting for years, a "profiteering death merchant" without even the common sense to pretend to a moral imperative.

When he had come to Innotech, he had promised there would be no more clandestine meets, no more "friends in trouble" half a world away in the middle of the night, no more guns in the house or security personnel masquerading as domestics, no scruffy desperadoes in the sitting room or armored cars that must be started remotely from a safe distance and whose windows would not roll down. He had promised they could bring the children back from their boarding schools and get rid of the attack dogs this year, and she had believed him—until she had seen Cord Hunt, obviously operational if he could not chance a soft hello, a short reunion. Through it all, Shy had kept silent—the safest thing she could do was leave; he couldn't respond to her demands for an innocent explanation, if there was one, in the matter of Cordell Hunt.

But though it was not Beth's fault, he felt her in some wise contributory to his difficulties, both with Michele and with Sid Cannard. He brought up her congress with Dropout and the complications her impropriety had caused in his dealings with her father: "Sid didn't like this gambit from the outset. Now he's breathing down my neck every minute, just waiting for one of us to make a mistake. I can't take the chance that that person might be you. And it's too bad; I'm going to have a number of free evenings in the next couple of months—I'd thought we might share them. But you've made that impossible."

He stormed out, thinking that he was a nicer person when he was drunk—more patient, more easygoing, more communicative. By the time he had reached the staircase, she was already on the phone.

Chapter
9

THEY had hashed it out in the chopper—to Shy's satisfaction, anyway. Hunt was aware that he was going to have to take what he could get; annoyed that, such being the case, he'd put so much time into thinking about the way he would have preferred to run it.

When they changed to the Falcon at the Zürich airport, Hunt stayed on the tarmac until he was sure that all the equipment they had brought in the chopper was off-loaded and that what went into the Falcon was exactly that—no additions, deletions, or substitutions.

Sitting alone with Shy in the Falcon's leather lounge seats, he remembered the flight here from Morocco. He was always glad to leave Zürich, a surly tightwad of a town more German than Swiss, but never more glad than this time.

Their flight was carefully orchestrated so that he had no chance to identify the landing zone: Most forward bases within an hour's jet of Zürich look pretty much alike.

In the headlights of the jeep and staff car that came to meet them, he looked for unit patches or division insignia, but saw none, not on the MP's or the vehicles, whose plates were obscured with dirt.

He stopped trying, listening, as he knew he must, to Shy, who was doing his part by continuing to dole out last-minute instructions: Triage importation invoices for their class-three weapons; carry permits; keys to vehicles and safe havens; emergency phone numbers that could not be written down; bailout procedures involving Innotech branches; a piece of Shy's letterhead on which were written three numerical groups that, according to Shy, entitled the bearer to whatever was desired from Triage's electronic arsenal when presented to the proper individuals.

Hunt watched Flak out of the corner of his eye as Shy, in high gear, disseminated, finally, the tradecraft provisions crucial to their survival. He saw no sign that Flak was having trouble absorbing the codes, dead drops, and fallbacks, even at the rate Shy was throwing them out.

Mino had been left with the Falcon; things were shaking out as he had known they would. This would be the chain of command from now on; like it or not, Flak was going to be running him on-site; Shy was returning to Zürich. Hunt didn't argue about it; he had accepted it, de facto. Whenever he wanted to communicate with Shy, he had gone through Flak. Their inclusion of him in this part of their preparation was mere courtesy.

Looking back through the rear window, he saw a fuel truck pull up to the blue and white Dassault Falcon 50 to top off her tanks; in the ramp lights, her Innotech insignia, crossed lightning bolts, glowed electric blue. He'd had to leave his side arm on board with Mino or forfeit this meeting, even after all Shy must have gone through to clear it. He didn't like it, but he told himself it was an understandable precaution.

He wasn't thinking about much but Martinova; his concerns had dwindled, telescoping in on the moment to come. He said, as they drew up to a long, low concrete building's rear and the motorcade stopped, that he'd like to be able to give her some hope.

Shy, ducking his head, blew a frosty breath and told Hunt to convince her to tell them the truth.

It was a dozen fluorescent-lit Lubyanka-green corridors later that he asked how long he could have with her.

Shy took his arm and pulled him aside; the half-dozen white-coats around them moved discreetly away. "You have twenty minutes; if you can take it for fifteen, I'll be surprised. Just remember, when you're in there, that you insisted on this. And don't blame me for what you see, either. Try to remember that it could be you in there, that I'm not God, and that not even God can control Fowler's ISA boys when they've got a KGB agent to debrief." The International Security Agency was one of Jack Fowler's babies—some said he'd gotten his fifth star for delivering it. It was exceedingly interested in Southwest Asia, one reason why Fowler and ISA/NATO had been Shy's logical choice, but Hunt started visibly to hear Shy admit in an open corridor that Martinova's disposition lay in ISA's hands. He had hoped against hope, all this time, that it wasn't so.

She wore a hospital johnny and they talked through a perforated Lexan barrier. The light was dim, but he could see some fading bruises, green and yellow, on her cheek. She was standing, leaning against the partition, her forehead resting on the clear plastic, when he was let in.

The door behind him closed and she raised her head, her eyes wide, palms spreading before her on the window. It was a small room, for this purpose only. He wasn't more than a dozen feet away from her, but she wasn't sure of his identity. "Kori? Kori, is that you?" in Pushtu. "*Inshallah,*" in Arabic—"If Allah please."

He found himself up against the barrier, his mouth to the little circle of holes, with nothing to say but "Yes." She was weaving on her feet a bit, though he knew they would have eased up on her in the last day or two in anticipation of his coming. Her brown eyes were inflamed, and he hated his society, which took a people who bowed only before God on pain of losing their place in heaven and showed them man as their master. Then he watched her lips, and not the injection marks on her neck. "I should tell you to cooperate with them," he whispered. *"Allaho A'alam."* Allah *will* forgive the hidden things: What he was saying might not be true.

"No, malik, not from you, too." Her eyes, crowded with tears, betrayed her. Fiercely with her wrist she brushed them away, leaning into the perforations so that he felt her breath on his lips. "Kori, I don't know what we have done . . . what they have done to me . . . what I said. Kori, help me to do what is right. I am shamed. . . ."

The back of her hand was swollen and discolored from a careless Pentothal hit. He remembered the feel of it and his stomach rolled. She was asking for death; he shook his head: no.

She leaned heavily against the partition. "I cannot—Everyone who dies as a *shahid* on my account shall curse me. I am lost."

A *shahid*—a slain innocent—went to a special part of heaven; their blood, some maintained, ran fresh for days. She had already told them what she knew. It was then, when there was nothing more to give, that things became unbearable. He put his pinkie to one of the holes, pushed it in until he could brush her cheek. "You . . ."

She raised teary eyes to him, crying freely now, and he whispered, *"Dashe, dashe"*—"Stop, stop"—a Pushtu command the Russians had adopted. Heard often in the streets of Kandahar and north of Kabul, frequently it was followed by a sharp report: a Russian soldier's rifle. It brought a trace of anger to her eyes. He had needed to know it was there, that she still could be rallied. He said, "So you crave a *shahid's* easy place in heaven, with so much left to do? Where is my freedom fighter? I warned you this was a terrible fate."

She licked her lips and squinted at him, her head cocked, her cheek puffed with bruises. Then she nodded calmly, suddenly speaking English: "Truth you did speak. My English has had much practicing. Is it ill with you, too?"

"No," he said, "it's not." He wished she had stayed in Pushtu, but what difference did it make? "I—" He almost said it: I love you. He couldn't say it, not there, not then. He couldn't afford it and neither could she. But she rubbed her lips against his finger and told him she was pleased, that he must make a great revenge upon them for her and pray that she would be granted a "soon-coming death."

He thought, *I've got to get out of here.* He said, "Hold on, Nasta. Just hold on, do you hear me?" He repeated it in Arabic to be sure. "On New Year's Day—" it was *her* New Year he meant, the first day of spring— "on New Year's, I'll be back and I'll get you out of here, I promise. Please believe me, Nasta. Look at me."

She looked up and he forced himself to hold her gaze. Then, despite all reason, he said, "I love you, I'll take care of you, I swear. No matter how it looks—wait for me. Promise?"

"Kori, it is impossible."

"It's *not* impossible. Tell them what they want to know. If you don't have answers, make some up."

"As I cannot eat their food, I cannot eat their hatred and I cannot eat their lies."

"They'll just feed you intravenously. Don't you understand what can happen to you?" But she did not understand, and he couldn't make her understand that just because she didn't remember what she had told them didn't mean that what they later *said* she had told them had come from her mouth: The subtleties of it escaped her.

"No, it is so. I have done it. I have betrayed everyone. And I do understand what is happening to me—it is God's will. I have sinned."

With him, she meant, he knew. For all her Western education and her spurning of veil and sexist Muslim attitudes, she was still half a Shi'ite, having grown up among them.

He managed to say, "*I* betrayed you; *I* betrayed whoever is hurt through you. Yet I will not sit down in my tracks and say, 'God, take me, life is too foul and I am too weak.' I am not a coward."

She threw her hair back, the old Nasta for one moment, and made an ululation. "But you are a liar."

"Yes, that. Do you think I lie about coming back for you?"

"I think you would like to come, Kori. As I would like to go. God is good"—she sniffed, then straightened up—"but he has made of me a woman: I am weak—they have shown me that I am weak. Once, I did not think it so. Before them my courage is nothing and my spirit defiled. You cannot... love... such a one."

Shit, we're two of a kind, too proud and too obstinate and too opinionated even to survive. "I'll be back," he murmured, retreating from her before he lost his last shred of composure. Shy had been right to insist he leave his handgun in the Falcon. He would have tried to give her what she wanted, otherwise. He knew she thought he could.

"I will not be here, malik. They say they will move me—tomorrow."

"I'll find you. I'll make a deal with them. Please believe me, Nasta."

"Kori—"

"Yes?" He was at the door and he didn't want to go out there looking too distraught. He leaned his head against the doorjamb, then looked back at her.

"I tried not to believe them when they told me about the bargain you made, yet I was angry. But now that I have seen you, I am not. And I will not be afraid....I wish you to go without..."— she searched for an English word—"...burdens."

He would carry that moment—the image of her softened behind the Lucite, her shoulders hunched up and her chin high— with him for the rest of his life. He couldn't say anything else. He lifted his hand, let it fall, and slipped out the door.

It was Flak who saw him slide through, Flak who joined him against the wall and lit them both cigarettes despite the multilingual "No Smoking" sign. "You okay, sir?"

Hunt nodded, though he was not, watching the whitecoats converge, wondering where Shy was.

As if reading his mind, Flak said, "He's gone off with somebody—said not to wait. We've got to hustle—okay, sir?"

"Okay, Flak. Okay." He forsook the wall's support and Flak paced him, the whitecoats keeping their distance—two before, two beside, two behind. Raising the cigarette to his lips, he noticed how badly his hand was shaking and thought to himself that this time he deserved whatever aftershock his body was going to give him: Not for any reason, no matter how humanitarian, should he have said those things to Martinova when his own chances of surviving *this* operation were marginal. The first day of spring, not three weeks away...if he could make good his word on that one, it would be a bona fide miracle. He wondered if Shy and Fowler and whoever else was in this would get a kick out of watch-

ing him make a fool of himself on tape. They had taken away his
final option, that of failure. He told himself that if he hadn't
pressed for a meeting with Nasta, they would have engineered
one, hoping for this very result. Now they didn't even have to
worry about him; they knew from his own mouth that he couldn't
walk away from the go.

At least things were getting simpler: Given the foregoing epi-
sode, he had to succeed, or die in the attempt. He couldn't leave
her like that—not Nasta; not when it was his fault that they had
her; and not, most of all, when he knew what lay ahead for her.
He tried to estimate what kind of leverage he might be able to
apply to Jack Fowler, but put the inquiry aside. Nasta's distress
was still too real. He saw her everywhere he looked, an overlay
of his inadequacy. *He* had crumbled despite years of lesser hardship and privation, despite two decades of experience and intel-
lectual preparation for just such an event—what could he
realistically expect her to endure? For he wanted her to endure.
He would take whatever was left when they were done with her.
No one understood the final humiliation of betrayal and treachery
better than he; he could help her without condemnation, without
reservation, no matter what they made of her—no matter what...

Absently, pacing Flak through the corridors, he realized he was
doing the proper things, the habitual conduct of tradecraft that
made him a survivor: He was comparing this hallway with others
he had walked in Belgium, and in Wiesbaden, Ramstein, and
Frankfurt. Maybe they *would* move her, maybe they merely told
her so, knowing she would tell him, diverting him so that they
felt comfortable leaving her right where she was.

The pilot, meanwhile, kept one eye on him, walking close. Once,
as they came in sight of the doors beyond which the night and
the Falcon waited, Flak reached out to touch his shoulder. "If you
ask me, sir, this was a rotten idea. But nobody ever does." Frowning, he took his hand away and looked askance at Hunt. "I was
getting cigarettes and one of the intelligence types came up and
told me she fell, sir, that they didn't get physical with her at all.
... I don't suppose it helps.... Sir, did you know all along we were
going to the States?"

"No. Does it bother you?" It bothered *him;* he hadn't been to
the U.S. in five years—except once, briefly, nonstop to China

Lake and then back into Southwest Asia. He didn't consider the technical-services research installation "America." Like this corridor, it belonged to the community, subscribing to its laws, posting them multilingually whenever it chose—and when it did *not* so choose, cloaking all in shadows. He didn't blame Flak for being nervous. Going with him to the States was like moving into a free-fire zone. He had hoped they might catch Angel and Dania Morales in Cannes or Nicosia, relaxing, or at work in Beirut or Panama City—anywhere, in fact, but America; there was just too much light there, too much to go wrong. Flak hadn't answered. He asked again, gently: "Does it bother you?"

"A little."

"We'll be all right."

"Yes, sir, we will—if you say so, sir. Do you think we could—" —the doors drew open before them; a jeep with MP's in it came to life, pulled up to the curb; the whitecoats melted away—"—go over things a little more, come to some sort of personal understanding? I'm just doing my job, and I want to do it the best I know how—or maybe what I'm trying to say is I'd like to do it the best *you* know how."

Jacking themselves up on the tires, they climbed into the jeep's rear seat. The air was cold; brilliant stars littered a cloudless sky. Flak said he'd seen a satellite report and it was clear all the way— no "red" weather between here and their destination.

Hunt looked at the earnest young asset, willing to walk into incalculable danger with little or no information and untrustworthy allies simply because he'd been tapped for the assignment, and saw his younger self. *It's not that you don't know how foolhardy it is, it's that you've been trained not to care.* Hunt said: "Since you'll be busy on the flight deck, I'm going to try to sleep until we get there—I've got to put some mental distance between me and what's happened here this evening. Once we're somewhere I consider secure, you can ask me all the questions you want and I'll do my best to answer them. Don't worry, Flak, I'm not going to take this out on either you or Mino."

Flak raised one eyebrow and puffed out his cheeks. "Yeah, I guess I know that, sir. But Mino's going to need a little bit of extra help—beyond being comfortable point-shooting a Mini Uzi—you copy?"

"Loud and clear." The jeep lurched around a hangar toward the Falcon, hunched like an apocalyptic eagle on its runway, engines beginning to whine. "Its just the three of us from here on in."

Chapter 10

"THEY'RE in," Shy sighed to Fowler, crumpling the digitized message in his hand. The runner who had brought it was already disappearing behind the cars parked on the stableyard's thawing sod. Beyond Jack Fowler's back, one of his Hanoverian stallions took a six-foot, two-inch jump and sailed over the ditch on its far side to land perfectly, nary a tic nor a stumble, arrogantly adding a buck calculated to unseat its rider. The rider cursed the horse and Jack Fowler peered over his glasses at the talented, ill-tempered show jumper. "*Formidable!*" he called to the rider, relegating his reading glasses to the breast pocket of his Donegal tweed jacket,

pale and speckled as the snow melting into the grounds of his
Mons estate. He turned to Shy: "I wish we could stop him from
doing that—reminds me a bit of our Dropout—so good he thinks
he can afford a bad attitude. That horse lost himself Madison
Square Garden last year, screwing around because he was the class
of the field and he knew it. Let's hope we don't have similar
problems with your asset. That was quite an extraordinary performance he put on last night." The big bay thundered by, spray-
ing foam and sod, precluding an immediate reply.

Shy had spent the night at Fowler's, doting on each piece of
news as it came into Jack's homey "situation room." In all that
time, this was the first subjective reference Fowler had made to
the Hunt/Martinova interview.

Both men were strung tight as piano wires, paired by their
mutual involvement, grateful not to have to pretend to calm, or
to sleep, or to optimism. So much was at risk; anything could go
wrong. They had listed possible disasters on yellow legal pads:
The plane could crash (though Fowler had his "eyes" out—follow
planes to spot the wreckage); Hunt could hijack the multimillion-
dollar long-range aircraft to wherever he chose and demand
Martinova's release on pain of unbearable publicity (though they
were prepared for that eventuality with a Triage demolition/
antiterrorist squad standing by); bad weather could blow up suddenly, forcing the Falcon to divert to some purely commercial
airport where Innotech did not commonly do business (though
their documentation was up to entry standards). Even if all the
radar handovers were flawless and they landed without incident
on Hanscom Field's seven-thousand-foot runway in Bedford, Mas-
sachusetts, at 1:00 A.M. EST and taxied into Innotech's hangar,
difficulties could crop up: The FAA official Innotech owned at
Hanscom could fall ill or die or have car trouble—or he could
balk. Hunt could blow it somehow, if he turned sour and decided
Martinova was right, revenge was all there was left for him.

Now that none of these had happened, both men were free to
speculate on the next group of contingencies with which they
might find themselves concerned. Glancing at his watch, Fowler
suggested that they walk back to the house for breakfast; the driver
would bring the car. Shy could just make out the château's four
chimneys among the evergreens across the groomed meadow's

upward slope. "Do this every morning and not only will you work up an appetite, you'll keep your heart in top shape." Fowler fumbled for his cigar case. The morning was unseasonably warm and hence moist; Shy could see the snow evaporating. Spring made his nose empty promises—as with Dropout, it was too soon to know for certain, too soon to trust his instincts.

"What did you mean back there, Jack?" He strolled away from the paddock beside Fowler, who seemed to be in gentleman's camouflage, white and gray from his crew cut to his rubberized terrain boots. "I don't think that was any kind of performance— I think he finally found out that he's as human as the rest of us."

"You'd better hope not. I knew Percy Hunt a long while, as intimately as I fancy anyone ever knows an agent of that caliber. They're a lot alike, father and son. The only one Percy ever cared about was that kid, and he hated himself for it—couldn't afford to be vulnerable, couldn't afford to be afraid...but up until he was executed by the PLO, Percy ran interference for that young rascal like I've never seen—obsessive, you might say. What do you think is going to happen when Cory Hunt finds out his true love is a Soviet plant?"

Shy tripped over an arching root, recovered. "Come on, Jack, not that old saw. After what we've seen, you can't think—"

"I don't 'think,' John, I evaluate data. I'll let you talk to a functionary from the NTS émigré clearinghouse in Frankfurt—they've never heard of her. NTS Afghanistan swears every intimate of hers is...'disappeared,' as they say—arrested or executed. Now, before you interrupt me"—Fowler held up a hand—"let me finish. I'm perfectly well aware that the apprehension of those Afghans could be Hunt's doing—we can't be sure how much the Soviets got out of him. I'm also aware that *I* don't want to believe that he knowingly took up with a Russian NTS penetration, so I'm discounting the possibility that such is the case—perhaps wrongly, I don't know. I do know that no matter how strong our evidence is, this isn't the time to tell him. If he's known all along and they're playing us for fools, I'm going to skin him with my own two hands."

"Jack, I asked you in on this because I thought you were too sophisticated to buy this bullshit....*I* can't believe, after dealing with Cordell Hunt, that anyone could sucker him for long. And for what reason? He didn't have much left to give when the Russians got around to trading him. Surely they, better than anyone, would have known that."

"Given the shape he was in by the time he got to Morocco, she must have seemed like an angel from heaven. Maybe they didn't get anything substantive out of him—*you* certainly couldn't, unless the take you've been forwarding me is laundered—and were quite simply trying another tack. Maybe it's purely revenge—did you know Nikolai Chebrikov, Hunt's interrogator, was judged to have performed so poorly that he was given a choice of Gorki or Kabul? A relative of the KGB's top gun, disgraced and demoted—how do you think the old man felt when the kid (he wasn't more than thirty-five, that's a kid to me, these days) shot himself in the mouth in the Kabul station after what old Chairman Chebrikov must have gone through to get him even a resident's post? You don't put a kid through two staff colleges amid that kind of internecine warfare and then take it lightly when he blows his own head off."

"How did you find this out?"

"From Martinova. Don't look at me like that—we confirmed most of it. Chairman Chebrikov is in retreat, or in disgrace, or dead—we can't find out which. But if Innotech is now the object of a personal vendetta from some Black Sea villa, then items of information that have been keeping me up nights lie down in nice, precise slots. Say something."

"No comment.... Jesus, all right. Jack: your ghouls are leaning on her so hard, she'd implicate the Easter Bunny if it were suggested to her adroitly."

"This way." Fowler ducked under a branch into a shadowed path. "Fair enough, that's so. But didn't your troubles with Two Can Play start while the Soviets had Hunt?"

"Don't *say* that out loud."

"It's safe enough, John. I have the grounds swept for bugs every other week. A man's got to be able to speak freely somewhere, or else screws start to loosen in the old head." He tapped his grizzled temple. "And I like to talk to myself, another perquisite of reaching my age in this business. Are you going to answer me?"

"About Two Can Play? I'm not free to discuss it...." Fowler threw him an amused look. Shy took a deep breath and wondered whether he was going to have an ulcer by the time this operation was over. "Cards down, then: Innotech feels that the 'accidental losses' we sustained during Two Can Play's inception and early stages are unrelated to the recent EO's. I don't."

"Yes, I had lunch with Sid, and that is his position. Why did you people get involved with so perishable an operation in the first place? Certainly you must have realized that at the first whiff of trouble, your U.S. backers were going to pull out. They're experts at it. It's one thing to run arms to the rebels—even the American public has a vague idea that we ought to do something— but quite another to use that Southwest Asian conflict as a smoke screen for mounting a destabilization effort against the Soviet Union."

"Jack, you know more about this than I do. I was only put into the picture at the shutdown. I didn't hear about it soon enough, or follow it closely enough. And that, I am willing to admit, is my fault. I didn't know they were going to play Hunt as a giveaway to save somebody else's ass, and I didn't know—I still don't know— who vetted the case officer's decision. But I do know that every- body who did know—the other net chief, the handlers, Hunt's case officer—is dead of the usual "natural causes": auto accidents, plane crashes, heart attacks, and just plain bad luck. And I know what kind of money was involved. And I know one more thing— I'm scared half to death. My life has become a shambles since this thing started; on the bad days, I think that having Hunt in the field might be the only thing keeping *me* alive."

Fowler's head, before him on the path, nodded. The old warrior stopped, turned, said, "Have you thought about what you'll do if you find out Innotech sabotaged its own go?"

"Holy Mother of God, Jack, is that what you *really* think? Then why did you give me that Soviet revenge story?"

"Both things could be true." Fowler shrugged. "Neither could be true. You know how it goes, John. Nobody ever really knows how these things will develop. And by midgame, often enough, all the parameters for action have changed so much that focuses tend to shift. I need to ask you some blunt questions. I don't care so much if you answer them now as I care that you start thinking about them."

Shy had the feeling that Fowler was about to open up; a shiver coursed him. "Shoot."

"Not funny. *Have* you thought about your recourse?"

"Are you still offering me a job? Jack, I've gotten used to living beyond any reasonable means. I couldn't ask a government agency for that kind of money. I have three children in very expensive private schools and a dangerous wife—politically, I mean. I guess if I found something nasty enough to make me think about leaving, I'd just extort a retirement fund from Sid, button it down with a couple of lawyers, and play a lot of chess."

"That won't be good enough."

"*What* do you know that you aren't telling me?"

"That you've got very good instincts, that what you guessed at the outset is on the whole accurate, and that they've fallbacks in place on this that would make sure you never got the time to give your version of the official story to any lawyers. Level with me and I'll do what I can."

"But *why* would Innotech sabotage its own operation?" he asked innocently.

"Politics. Money. Deception. Discretion. You ought to start asking yourself some hard questions."

"Like? You're beginning to sound like a pop conspiracy theorist."

Fowler, snorting, began again to walk, preceding Shy, his words floating backward. "You know as well as I that conspiracies exist only in hindsight; that at the moment, one makes the best decision, scrambling from one nominally secure position to the next. In the process of doing just that, I had a chat with the Two Can Play backers—your customers, or *ex*-customers. I'm now representing them. Their interest, you *must* understand, is to bury this whole escapade with little or no fanfare."

Shy cursed under his breath.

Fowler neither slowed nor looked around. "You realize, I had to find a way to make my involvement acceptable to Sid Cannard— official, if you will. My 'official' apologies, then, about—"

The flash was instantaneous; the shock wave threw Shy to the thicket floor, flare-blind, then showered him with debris; he didn't hear the snap his ankle made—it was drowned out in the percussive roar from the explosion. He knew he was cut, seared, and groaning; he wanted desperately to be able to see more than just the white explosion's imprint on his retina, centered by a silhouette of Fowler's flung form. He thought: *Land mine? Grenade? Dear*

Jesus, let me not be blind. Then he opened his eyes and saw leaves around the edges of his vision, his bleeding hand.

From somewhere, he heard a soughing sob. Good, then his eardrums weren't punctured. "Jack? Jack?" he called, spitting out snow and turf, and a rasping voice answered: "Don't...move ...boy...Aaah—"

Oblivious, he started crawling, trying to blink away the residual overlay before his eyes. Tiny sounds from far away grew louder: men yelling; a horse's thundering hooves; cars starting; a chopper's thick-throated whine. He crawled until he reached Fowler, crumpled in the snow and mulch, everything around red and the stench of fried flesh and chemical-explosive aftermath in his nostrils along with pulverized dust and rock and his own terror, subsiding now as he realized he could put weight on his swelling ankle, that he could see, and sit up, and think again.

He whipped off his belt and cinched it around the stump of Fowler's left leg, gone nearly to the knee, and took the old man's hand. Jack's grip was crushingly tight. Maybe he wouldn't die. Maybe....Then he realized what Fowler was doing: pressing something into his palm. Jack's hand fell away and, despite himself, the old man sobbed. Shy looked down and saw a key in his palm, pocketed it, dragged Fowler's head into his lap.

By the time the converging security started shouting orders from beyond the copse, Shy was weeping freely, more than willing to "stay still until the chopper drops a line to you," as the agitated men intermittently advised, barking through their bullhorns while they swept cautiously closer with their bomb sniffers and mine detectors.

He was trying to make Fowler understand how sorry he was when the old man, pink spittle in his mouth and a trickle of blood oozing from his right ear, reached up and pulled Shy's head close. "Go look at what...my desk drawer. John, promise...."

"Sure, Jack. Anything you say. I'm sorry—you don't know how much. My fault, all of it....Forgive me?"

Fowler made a gagging sound and the grip on the back of Shy's neck relaxed. "Not...if you don't...win this one for me....Promise, now...." Jack Fowler heard Shy answer "Yes," then went limp in his arms, eyes closed. "Good," he may have whispered. Later Shy told himself he had imagined it, that it was only a final anguished groan as a man who could not bear to lose was defeated by his body and passed out.

It took six minutes to get the unconscious, maimed man off the forest floor. The helicopter couldn't see them, and Shy's sprained ankle, engorged, made it difficult for him to hail them. By the time he got Fowler into the sling and the helicopter began to lift him through the trees, the minesweepers were in sight. Shy ignored them, wrapping himself around the injured man in his harness at the last minute. He couldn't bear it if Jack died fouled in his beloved trees.

He didn't go to the hospital; he pulled rank and made them drop him at the house, where he hopped and hobbled, oblivious to the solicitations of the nervous staff, into Jack's study and locked the door behind him.

In the drawer that Fowler's key unlocked, he found a cheap manila folder with "Cosmic," a NATO security clearance, scribbled on its cover in Jack's sharp script.

He had to hold it with both hands, so terribly was he trembling. All his senses seemed hyperacute; the gauze someone had wound around his hand in the chopper was soaked through with blood; his face stung from multiple abrasions and the kiss of thermal flash. He sat for a few moments quietly, recouping, the folder unopened before him on Jack's desk, trying to reconstruct the event and the conversation preceding it in his mind, chasing away his confusion, his shock.

Eventually he nodded to himself and picked up the phone. When he'd verified his impression that no assassin need have been on-site, that the ordnance was not radio-detonated but a small air-dropped mine containing chemical explosive such as a Soviet antipersonnel nondetectable plastic mine (APNDPM), he rang Triage and had them dispatch two teams: one here to Mons, and the other to go pick up one of the Zürich terrorists they had identified but not brought in because of politics.

The Triage VP questioned him laconically but specifically about what he wanted done, until Shy, exasperated, told him to "haul him in, kick him in the balls, and when he's told you everything you want to know, let him crawl away. I want to know who did this and why and where I can find them by morning or what passes for Triage's intelligence section is going to be out on the street. You read me, mister?"

After he slammed down the phone, he reflected that nothing he could do was going to help Jack Fowler, under some surgeon's knife by now.

"Win this one for me," Jack had made him promise.

Sure thing.

Chapter 11

"WHAT'S so funny, sir?" Flak asked Hunt as Cory swung the Wagoneer into the right-hand lane. Coming off the ramp from Route 95 onto the West Side Highway, he always drove as close as he could to the Hudson; New York unfailingly came into focus for him right here, as filthy and mean as the river.

"Excuse me, Flak?" He was busy with the traffic; among the low-riders and fragile Japanese cars and government compacts with G-2 plates and limousines was one fast blue Plymouth that had been popping up in Hunt's vicinity now and again ever since Groton.

"You've been smiling since we hit the ramp. I could use a good chuckle myself right now." Flak spoke quietly, sprawled wide on Hunt's right; behind them Mino snored softly, stretched out in back, one leg crooked over the Halliburton gun cases.

"Have I? I've been estimating the odds."

"Better than you thought?"

"Worse. Get a plate number on that Plymouth."

Flak shifted, pulled out a pen, his wallet, turned back. "Done." He stared out at the river where men fished for eels from crumbling docks. "I thought we were going to talk, sir."

"You 'sir' me in front of Morales, you'll have 'sirred' me to death. We'll talk when Mino wakes up. I don't want to go over this more than once."

Flak hissed through his teeth and shrugged one shoulder irritably without looking away from the window. Hunt was considering getting off at 96th Street to see if the Plymouth would follow when Flak slid down in his seat, staring up at the roof. "*Diu lai,*" he whispered: It meant "fuck you" in Cantonese.

"*Diu lai lomo tchow hai,*" Hunt shot back, using the same verb to insult Flak's mother, hoping to bring things to a head there and then. Flak put his thumb and forefinger to his eyes, rubbed them, and made no reply.

Hunt took the 96th Street off ramp and the Plymouth didn't follow. "He's gone on by, Cory," Flak said in a strained voice.

Ever since Mino had come aft in the Falcon and shaken his knee, saying, "Here we are, sir, safe and sound in the U.S. of fuckin' A.," Hunt had been countermanding Shy's instructions to Flak with little or no explanation. Flak's resistance had been substantial. In some instances the pilot had won out: They wouldn't put down at an "uncontrolled" field (where no FAA official was on duty) just long enough for Hunt to slip away, avoiding customs; they wouldn't fail to declare him on the "crew" list or let him avoid having his cover passport stamped. Eyeing the cockpit recorder, Hunt hadn't risked explaining to Flak then that Shy's idea of "security" wasn't his. He didn't want Innotech to be able to keep track of him. He wanted to drop out of sight as of Zürich so that no one could ever trace him to the States.

By the time Portland ceded them to Boston Approach, "flight plan as filed," Hunt was back in the body of the plane, sunk in deep meditation, coaxing away the residuals of his fever. Up until then, while they were still on vector 205 from Greenland, he had seen a chance of convincing the pilot. Once they were cleared for Hanscom, it was too late. The only thing he had accomplished on the trip, beyond raising Flak's blood pressure, was familiarizing himself with the Falcon 50's cockpit in case something happened to one of them and he had to fly backup on the way home. He hadn't flown anything this big or complicated for years, but the new instrumentation was actually simpler than the generation on which he had trained, and it didn't take him long to realize that the "navigator's console" where Mino suggested he sit was actually an ECM (electronic counter measures) and aerial surveillance station: Passive defenses, side-looking radar, jamming, counterjamming—Innotech didn't miss a trick. Neither did Mino. It was clear to Hunt after the first ten minutes that Mino was the flying talent—Flak's, as Hunt had long suspected, lay more in operational realms.

"We're all tired," he offered, heading into Manhattan's crumbling midsection. He had come down the West Side Highway because he was headed to Central Park South; he was riding Flak because he wanted to open him up; he was pretending to be concerned about the Plymouth because after the first few minutes of playing hide-and-seek with it on the Groton bridge, he was not—he had expected to be followed. He needed to sleep, but he wanted to stay awake; twice he had refused Flak's offer to drive—he saw Martinova everytime he closed his eyes.

He was still trying to restructure the op around the tradecraft problems Shy had injected into it, attempting to make positives out of negatives. He was bringing his life into focus, as he always did when he was in danger of losing it. He had been smiling because he was on the defensive; it always made him feel like wreaking some gratuitous havoc along the way, his form of graffiti. He'd been ready to run the Plymouth off that metal bridge into the channel where a behemoth destroyer sat at anchor in the predawn light; the Wagoneer was an Innotech Class Six Armored, heavy as a tank. They had swept it for bugs and sniffed it for bombs with Triage ("Helping Those Most Likely to Survive") electronic detectors, only the first of many miniaturized surveillance/security devices Flak produced from his shoulder-slung "effects bag."

"Anything in that magic bag of yours to wake us up?"

As Flak leaned forward to rummage through the bag between his legs, Hunt heard "...tired of this bullshit," and saw, as Flak's sweater rode up, the butt of an S&W revolver protruding from a holster tucked inside the waistband of the pilot's jeans. Flak straightened up and Hunt said, "I see you've still got that snubby."

"I don't leave home without it. And don't you derail my ass with this hardware rap—you've got a backup gun on you.... Oh, yeah, by the way..." He reached into the effects bag and pulled forth Hunt's Marrakech workbelt with its speed scabbard and double magazine holders, displayed it, let it fall. "Nobody there knew how to give this back to you. I told them you'd be glad to have it, no questions asked. The house'll be soon enough—unless you're hot to change clips in the car?"

"Thank you. I can wait."

"You're entirely welcome." The pilot began to apportion cocaine on his wallet.

"I'm not in favor of going to that address today." Hunt did not pause when Flak, with a lopsided grin, said he'd thought as much. "I'd like to check us into a quiet hotel suite overlooking the park, where we can talk about amending our procedure until we're both satisfied with one another's logic and good intentions. If we can't come to some accommodation, we'll scrub it right there. Until then, there's no need to check in with anyone—understand me? No phone calls, no contacts of any sort."

Bent forward, Flak snorted two of the lines on the wallet balanced in his lap before answering: "I sure am learning my craft." Rubbing his nose, he lay his head back against the seat, eyes closed, pulse rapid in his arched, stubbled throat. "I can't believe I volunteered for this duty. If you don't kill me, or get me killed, following your advice is going to make the shop think I let you turn me out—that I've flip-flopped—"

"That would be nice," Hunt said wistfully as he stopped the car at a light and Flak, eyes slitted against the harsh morning glare, handed Hunt his wallet and put on his mirrored sunglasses. "That's better," the pilot sighed as Hunt ducked down and ran a rolled dollar bill over the smudged lines of powder. When he sat up, the first thing he saw was a ragged bag lady stooping to root in a wire garbage can, talking to herself, pausing occasionally in her scavenging to shake one sooty fist at the traffic. God bless America,

Hunt thought, letting the short rush of anger the drug always endowed him with pass harmlessly away over the fate of one of New York's walking wounded. He heard Flak waking Mino— "Come on, Ace, drug call; this is one reveille you won't want to miss"—and then the asset turned to him: "What about your old lady, Cory? If you scrub, I mean."

"Is that what you think she is? Don't jump to any conclusions." He gunned the Wagoneer's motor as the light changed to green and Mino came to life, yawning elaborately and complaining that two lousy lines (sniff) were hardly enough (snort) to make up for all that he'd been through; he wanted a bathroom, food, and a bed with a girl in it—now. But since Flak—whose fault all this was ("You call this *fun*? You call this *educational*? Seems like down-and-dirty fuckin' shit to me—and this is just the git-go! Armed and dangerous in NYC! If it wasn't so real, I could pray I'm still asleep!")—couldn't produce even one of those things, the least he could do was give Mino two more lines.

Complaining that he'd be lucky if he broke even at this rate, Flak acquiesced, while Hunt, taking a right, headed south on Broadway toward Columbus Circle and all of them fell silent before the city's morning pathos: shopkeepers in dirty aprons desultorily sweeping sidewalks piled with splintered fruit crates and rotten produce; junkies hustling their morning score in the doorways of boarded-up buildings; prostitutes in leopard leotards shuffling bowlegged home to bed; flocks of yellow cabs headed downtown, off-duty lights lit like defenses against the poor and the vile; trucks and trailers headed uptown, riding low with heavy loads, anxious to be away; and on the meridian "green," pigeons vying with derelicts for bench space, oblivious runners in head-phones stepping in place, waiting for lights to change with pimps on one side and dog-walkers on the other. "Home, sweet home," Mino remarked. "Cory, sir, how long's it been since you've been back?"

"So long that what I'm seeing doesn't bother me—everybody picks their own hell, I guess. It's not home to me; I'm not an American citizen, if you recall. Maybe I never was—I only had visiting rights in the old days anyhow, the occasional semester here or there. If you're feeling displaced, it's only natural. The American community overseas tends to reinforce the mythic

America we'd all *like* to be from—there's more wishful thinking now than ever, what with so much anti-Americanism abroad."

"I heard that!" Mino agreed grumpily, rubbing his face with his palms.

No one said anything else until Hunt pulled up in front of the Essex House on Central Park South, where he told Flak to slide into the driver's seat and went in alone. He could see them talking together, Flak leaning over, his head bowed.

At the desk he asked for a two-bedroom suite in front near a fire exit and gave both his Innotech Amex card and the car's plate number without qualm: The card's imprint wouldn't be entered into any data base until he signed the bill at check-out time; since he intended to pay in cash and reclaim the imprinted slip, his risk was minimal. As for the car's license number, the chances of Innotech or anyone else being able to locate them through a check of garages in the metropolitan area were, in his estimation, vanishingly slim, surely no greater risk than standing on a street corner with class-three weapons and rifle cases looking for a cab would have entailed, had he ditched the car at some parking meter or in a downtown garage where eventually it would have been towed away, the owner of record notified....

He smiled at the girl and told her he wouldn't be wanting house-keeping services, that he had expensive equipment with him he intended to protect with a doorknob alarm system, and that he was counting on her to ensure that no one was going to bother his party, all of whom intended to sleep round the clock. She made a note, patted her hair, and asked him how long he would be staying. He replied that he expected to be in town three days but would notify her immediately if he needed to extend his stay, and let her know that the nightly rate was acceptable to him. She called, "Front," and he went with the porter to get the black Halliburtons, the hard Mauser cases, and their luggage out of the Wagoneer.

On the way back in through the quiet, chandeliered lobby's natty elegance, she called to him discreetly. He left Mino and Flak to go up with the porter, telling Mino to give the man a five-dollar tip and make sure that Flak didn't use the phone. The cover ID he was carrying was the same one that Shy had given him in Marrakech, an old fallback ID from Two Can Play's beginnings;

he couldn't imagine there being any problem with the "Ashe" documentation that a hotel could have caught so quickly—he cursed Shy for insisting that he come into the country under an Innotech-generated cover.

But the woman, this time leaning close over the marble-topped desk, only wanted to explain to him that the suite she had given him was one of their finest, and that housekeeping would gladly come at a prearranged hour of his choosing, but come they must. He agreed, set a time, wished her a good day, and headed toward the elevators, cursing bureaucracies of every sort under his breath and regretting the necessities that had already made him conspicuous.

When the elevator's brass, graven door opened, he saw a camera in its corner, stepped in beside a pair of European businessmen wearing too much Italian gold, and out at his own floor, still not sure that he wouldn't have been better off walking through the lobby to the rear, turning right by the bakery, and disappearing into the streets.

In the suite, a quiet place of Chinese Chippendale and high ceilings with graceful moldings, the curtains were drawn back, exposing Central Park's expanse. The clop-clop of horses drawing carriages came in through the window before which Flak was standing; on the wheat-toned couch behind him, Mino sprawled, grinning widely. "Not bad, man. Not bad at all. Look at the bedrooms and pick one, si—Cory; we'll take the other."

Flak had taken off his jacket; he stood loosely, the sleeves of his V-neck black sweater pushed up, his thumbs hooked in his belt loops, his automatic holstered behind his hip in a weak FBI carry, his backup gun invisible under his sweater's blouse. "Let's shake it out, Cory. Now."

Mino made a face, then shook his hand as if he had scalded it. His own weapons were not in evidence. He picked up the room-service menu. "Can I order? What's 'shirred eggs'?"

"They're good, you'll like them. Order them for me, too, with croissants and juice and two double espressos—you may have to fight for the espresso, this early, but don't take no for an answer." Mino, relieved, nodded and beat a hasty retreat to the bedroom. "And come right back in here when you're done. This concerns you, too."

Hunt's workbelt lay on the couch. He picked it up and joined Flak at the window. When the asset had spoken to him, his voice had been thick. Hunt had expected some anger, frustration, perhaps, but not the degree of distress he now sensed in the pilot. Before he could say anything, Flak gritted: "I can't have you telling Mino to keep me from picking up the phone. I've got a job to do and you know it. You sat there while Shy briefed me—no one's holding out on you, or messing with your head, or fucking you any way at all. *Why* are you doing this to me? If you don't want a 'handler,' I can understand that, but if *I* weren't here, you'd have somebody who'd really make things hard for you. If you want, I'll leave; you can run the whole thing like the singleton you want to be, and take your chances with Innotech on your own recognizance— Aw, Christ, you make me so crazy I don't—" He turned from the window, faced Hunt, his eyes glittering.

"What do you want to know?"

"I want to know what you're planning to do with all that firepower. Is this a sniper team, or what? Is that what the go is?"

"We've got to look like business people, Flak. Let me start a little before that. Mino, come over here. Okay. Now, here's my feeling: Either you both realize that I don't want *any* help from Innotech/Triage—not a piece of information or a phone call or a fallback or an armored car—and reason from that base, or none of this is going to make any sense to you. You've both got a choice: You can hang in, *incommunicado*, or you can go over to one of the safe houses, get your 'pursuit Porsche' out of Shy's garage, put yourself under surveillance by any number of interests—I don't care what you do. But the minute one of you checks in with them, I've got to lose you—I can't take chances. From then on, we'll run it like a European net: I'll call you from phone booths, leave one-time signals at dead drops, but I'll shoot you on sight if you come near me except on my explicit request. Questions?"

"I'll stick around," Mino volunteered.

"What's the point?" Flak asked despairingly. "You won't answer them."

"Is that a yes or a no? Are you in or out?"

"I'm in, I'm in. Otherwise I'll never find out what the fuck is going on."

"I've been assuming that's important to you," Hunt said, and then: "Mino, there should be some hardcopy printout in one of those Mausers' barrels. Will you get it for me please?"

Flak said, "If anything happens to him, I'll never forgive myself."

"If you care that much about him, you ought to shoot him now. Otherwise, sooner or later, he'll get you killed. And if you can't see that, you're in the wrong business."

"I've been thinking that myself, lately," Flak said as Hunt took off his field jacket. "The way this thing's been going, the way they treated you—the way they *feel* about you ... I wish you didn't think of me as one of them. I want you to know that I don't condone what's happened—I'm just doing what I can, the best I can." He spread his hands, ran one through his hair, leaned back against the windowsill. "Despite everything, I'm downright honored to be working with you—I just wish the circumstances were different."

Hunt looked at him steadily. "So do I. Don't worry about the small arms; they're just bona fides, so Angel knows I'm serious. What I want you two to do— Hi, Mino."

Mino had the tightly rolled green-and-white sheets of computer printout. Hunt tapped them. "This should be a Bonn's-eye view of Angel and Dania Morales' career these last few years. If you've got moral qualms about taking executive action, what's here should allay them. But first off, see if you two buy this legend and think you can handle your part of it.

"I want to go in there with as much as possible up front. We saw Dania in the Baur Au Lac—she was on our floor, so we can assume she heard the single report, as well as recognized me and maybe Shy. Even though you don't remember her, she might remember you. So our story goes that I'm offering myself and both of you, whom I've charmed away from Innotech and convinced that mayhem might as well pay highly. We want work as a team, but we've got a real problem: We're on the run from Innotech/Triage. That way, there's no chance of getting our stories screwed up. I'm going to tell them the truth as far as it goes, from what Innotech did to me up to and including Martinova being handed to ISA, if I have to—I couldn't make up a better reason for finally deciding it doesn't matter who you grease, only how much you get paid for it. Can you handle it?"

"We're going to penetrate their organization?"

"We're going to try. Angel might kill me out of hand; he and

I had a little altercation once." He shrugged. "Business is business, so there's a chance I can talk my way past it. There aren't that many guys with my sort of credentials. But even if he won't talk to me, you two might still be able to get in this way—long enough to do the job."

"If, after he shoots you, we can convince him that we're just two happy-go-lucky contract killers," Flak added.

"Something like that. They're too professional to waste you just because they met you through me."

"That's real reassuring, sir," Mino said.

Hunt couldn't tell if he was serious. "But if they've got someone in Innotech and that insider's high up enough, they'll know the operation was originally aimed at them. Even so, we'll have confused them, but if you think or hear that they're on to you, get out and just keep going. Don't go back to Shy, because it'll mean his shop's either run or penetrated by a terrorist sympathizer. You could try a government agency, but they don't tend to believe walk-ins."

"You really think Innotech's chewing off its own leg?"

"I can't afford to discount the possibility, Flak. Neither can you or Mino. Mino, any questions? Objections? Doubts?"

"What if it works and they give us a job? What then?"

"Then we do it, or seem to be doing it, until we can get Angel Morales in our sights."

"Even if it's robbing a bank or something? Terrorists rob banks a lot. American banks have all those videotape cameras—"

"Even if it's robbing a bank and shooting everyone in it. You can't do it any other way, Mino. Are you up to it?"

"I—" Mino took a deep breath, looked from Hunt to his feet, then back to Cory. "Yes I am, sir—or I want to be. How can I tell? I've never done anything this open-ended before. Cowboying around like this . . . What happens if we get caught? This ain't no sanctioned operation where some nice Agency guy is going to come post my bail and give me a ticket for R&R in Hawaii because I've 'added most significantly to the bodycount.'"

Flak winced. Hunt indicated Flak. "He's right. Don't mention things like that. The most difficult part of doing this job full-time is that you can't talk about your past. Any little thing could trip them to you. You've *got* to watch what you say."

"I'll work up my John Wayne, boss. Honest." Mino unrolled

the printout, scanned it, started to shake his head and swear. Handing the intelligence report to Flak, Mino said, "My German's rudimentary. You telling me they think he did *all* that? There're an awful lot of terrorist organizations on that list. What are they, some kind of paramilitary comptrollers?"

"Think of them as a low-signature counter-Triage. They black-market arms, expertise, and personnel. If you kept reading, you'd begin to wonder whether they're not commissioned officers in Al Fatah, they've been in and out of Beirut, Nicosia, and Damascus so often in the last few years. They don't need to rob banks—they could start their own with what they've made helping Arafat arm twenty thousand full-time soldiers. They are professionals of the highest order—no proof of their direct participation in anything illegal exists. They've built a small, compartmentalized organization of high-caliber people who are committed to staying alive. They're contractors: They farm out work to their friends in third-world countries—they've got lots of 'em. Angel and his wife used to be patriots—I don't want to get into the terrorist-versus-freedom-fighter debate, but they look on themselves as 'activists for justice,' whatever that means. So do a lot of other people; I just don't happen to be one of them. Taking him out might fuck up the terrorist international's supply line, but remember—that's *not* why we're doing this: We're doing the work we've been hired for, just like he does."

"You know so much about him, you don't even want to look at this?" Flak asked, slapping the rolled printout against his palm. "And you're saying what this guy's been doing's no worse than what *we're* doing?"

"I'm saying politics doesn't enter into it—not for me, not for you, not for Angel, anymore: The Moraleses don't play favorites, they'll work for anybody, even the Soviets or the Americans. No government will tell you they use people like the Moraleses, but nobody'll tell you squat about Triage ops, either. I don't want you embellishing this legend with any political orientation, no story about being fed up with this or that ideology. I first met Angel in Kissinger's office upstairs in the Semitic Museum at Harvard—the old Center for International Affairs. He's got a double doctorate, poli-sci and philosophy. If you get fancy with him, he'll tie you up in knots."

"What's he look like?"

"Like a half-German, half-Argentine: black hair, blue eyes, my build plus twenty or thirty pounds as of five years ago. Had a Ché Guevara beard then, but I've seen him without it. Anything more? Something bothering you, Flak?"

"Yeah. It sounds like it could happen, we could go to work for them...*You* could— Never mind." Flak pulled at his lip. Mino mumbled something about calling to check on the food, and Hunt asked him to take his workbelt and put it with his luggage. When Mino had gone, Hunt said, "Never mind what?"

"I don't see how you can chance it, unless there's something you're not telling me. You're going to walk in there and hope this guy doesn't kill you before you get a chance to ask him not to? What if he's not inclined to listen?"

"That's my worry, isn't it. Like I said, Angel doesn't believe in guilt by association."

"What kind of 'altercation' did you have, exactly?"

"I shot at him some; he shot back. The usual thing."

"I don't like it."

"I'm not real fond of it myself, but there's nothing else I can do. Relax, friend. None of this is going to be blamed on you."

"We'll see about that when it's over. Shy's going to have a shit fit when he realizes he's lost us. Procedure says I have to clear something like this with the desk in charge, you know that."

"Let me tell you an operative's secret: If it goes well and they get what they want, nobody will ever know you didn't play by the rules, because Shy will take all the credit—tell them the whole penetration was his idea, everything else an internal deception to defuse saboteurs and leakage."

"If you say so, Cory, but I want to know exactly what the circumstances were the last time you and Morales were together—if I'm betting my life on this being doable, a whole fuck of a lot better explanation than 'he shot at me, I shot at him' better be on your agenda."

"All right."

Just then Mino came out of the bedroom, saying room service was on its way up and everybody "better secure arms—we wouldn't want to make them nervous."

As they did that, Hunt explained about Bogotá, then picked up his jacket and headed for his bedroom. Sitting on the foot of one queen-size bed beside his bag, he shrugged off his exhaustion and exchanged the two magazines of Glasers for the two of handloads that had come from Marrakech. He put his field holster with his luggage; it had no provision for the suppressor screwed onto his Commander's barrel and it wasn't time yet for an open carry. In his jacket pocket he had a compact ops gun, a Detonics Mark VI, and an elastic "Leech," a supplemental holster, hardly more than an elastic strap, to secure the little .45 wherever he needed to secret it. It was nice to have his workbelt back; though he'd nearly duplicated it, he appreciated Flak's gesture. He lay down flat and watched the dark dots in his vision crawl across the ceiling. He had everything he needed—every relevant piece of support gear, two good backups, enough working cash to have hired this six-hundred-dollar-a-night suite without batting an eye—but he wasn't optimistic. *Nasta, I'm doing the best I can.* Right then, he wasn't sure it was going to be good enough.

When he heard the door shut, he went out into the parlor and leaned against a wall, watching Mino discover the nature of shirred eggs and waiting for the dizziness that still came over him if he rose too quickly from a prone or sitting position to pass away.

As the buzzing, electrified feeling left him, he joined them at the table, no longer hungry, but mindful that if he did not eat, his physical condition would deteriorate further—he couldn't afford that.

Having drunk his first espresso, he entered the conversation. "We're going to need additional bailouts, and I want to do what I can on that today. If either of you feels you have to sleep right now, it's all right with me, but I won't be able to relax until I get things shaped up."

Mino mouthed, around half a croissant, that he was up for anything, too excited to sleep, and   glad Hunt had suggested they go out—he wanted to walk around.

"Fine. Flak?"

"Whatever makes you comfy, slave driver."

"That's my line."

"Not anymore. What have you got in mind?"

"Burn the Mauser printout. Find a travel agent and book three one-way flights apiece—I don't care where to, as long as one flight is for all of us and the other two are singles. Don't tell me where your single flights debark. Pay for them on the spot and get the executed tickets."

"You think the Falcon won't be there?"

"I don't know. I don't want to worry about whether it will or won't be there, or whether it's been tampered with, or anything else. Paris will do as well as anywhere for the group international. Okay?"

"Okay." Flak nodded knowingly. "How many days apart?"

"Three days apart. Then we're going shopping for clothes; there's no reason to match any description Innotech might see fit to broadcast. Wear your work gear; what you buy's got to conceal what you've got to conceal as well as make you look like local upper-class marauders."

"No shit? Clothes? On the budget?" Mino grinned widely.

"Innotech loves you. Just pretend it's Christmas. After we shop, we sleep. Get back here by four and rack until nine, then dinner, then we'll make the rounds. I haven't been here in a long time, so it may take a while to plug ourselves into the scene." He poured himself more espresso and lit a smoke.

"I thought you knew where the Moraleses were."

"I do, Flak. They're right above us in the Essex Towers, along with Gulf Oil and similar corporations and consultancies with that kind of money to write off."

"Phew," said Mino, looking up at the ceiling.

"Everything above the thirty-ninth floor is corporate condos. You can't get to them from here—they've got their own street entrance next door. We've got to get ourselves invited. There's a slim chance a man could rappel his way *out* of there, though, so we'll keep this suite even if Angel invites us to stay there."

"I wouldn't want to try it," Flak muttered, putting down his fork and going to the windows. He opened one and stuck his head out, came back, sat down. "I *won't*. You couldn't, without serious climbing gear, and we didn't bring it."

"Buy some if you want—this *is* New York. Or don't," he amended, judging the stony look on Flak's face. "It's just a last resort, emphasis on *last*. I'm trying to tell you everything I've been thinking about that you might need to know."

"I don't need to know your suicide alternates; I'd rather get blown away than spatter all over the fucking pavement."

"It'll be your choice, I'm sure."

"I guess." Flak took his Marlboro pack from his pocket and shook out a joint. "Anybody? It's 'Lamb's breath,' Jamaica's finest."

Hunt declined; he was too tired.

Forty minutes later, outside their hotel, Hunt ignored the waiting cabs, walking slightly ahead of his two assets. It was nice to have his back covered. Still, he had doubts about this phase, though he knew he had to do it: He hadn't handled his last sortie into an unstructured public situation very well, and the streets of New York made the Bazillus look like a safe haven. He turned a corner, headed downtown, keeping them close behind, hearing Flak explaining *sotto voice* to Mino how to "act covert."

On the corner of 57th, he chose a moving cab at random and told the driver to take them to Bloomingdale's. Its radio was on and Spanish-speakers discussed local issues emotionally. Under the radio's cover, Flak suggested other stores, insectlike in his mirror shades.

Hunt didn't respond, just stared out the window. He could lose them in Bloomingdale's in seconds; he'd chosen it for that reason. Keeping Flak in check for the duration of the op was an impossibility—he might as well start taking chances now.

When the cab disgorged them into the thronging sidewalk crowds, he was still thinking about a peroxide blonde he'd seen in a silver Subaru outside the hotel. Busy applying vermilion lipstick as his party went by, she'd pulled away from the curb and taken the same route he did. He'd be glad to be rid of the jackets Beth had bought him; the broad-band bug-sweeper Flak had brought was fine as far as it went, but Innotech could have secreted a side-band transmitter anywhere in the clothes they'd given him—in a lining, disguised as a button or snap. Even his own personal effects, taken away, "cleaned," and returned, could conceal some kind of tracer.

Upstairs in Bloomingdale's travel agency, they bought tickets to Paris for Messrs. Speer, Remington, and Hornady from a girl who gazed at Flak from behind candy-red glasses with such wistful longing that she could barely type. The two assets responded unconsciously, puffing out their chests while Hunt paid with traveler's checks, showing his "Ashe" ID. She hesitated momentarily, then asked him conspiratorially: "Are they in a band or something?"

He winked as if he knew what she meant while Flak hitched up his pants and said *he* wasn't through with her yet. Hunt, his Zürich parka draped over one arm, field jacket unzipped but too hot for the store's confines, drifted away while the other two detailed their bailout flights. They'd be all right, whatever he did, he decided.

Slipping through the crowded store alone, into and out of dizzying labryrinths of neon and mirrors, it was all he could do not to hurry. Strangers pressed close on the escalator; his pulse pounded; arm tensed over his shoulder harness, he waited for the jab of muzzle or knife against his spine.

On the street, he took deep, measured breaths and began looking for a likely indigent to give the parka to—someone who'd wear it despite the day's warmth. He found a wino in a thrift-shop overcoat and offered the suspicious drunk an even trade, coat for coat. He had to throw in two dollars U.S., and wait while the bum transferred a pocketful of personal treasures. It took too long.

Trotting across the street amid stagnant traffic, he disposed of the drunk's topcoat in a trash can, hailed another cab, which took him to 66th and Madison, where he tried on two vented, distressed-leather flight jackets at North Beach Leather; decided on the larger, which would conceal his workbelt's high-riding speed scabbard if he were reasonably careful; changed into it in a fitting room; and handed the salesman his field jacket, asking him to dispose of it, keenly aware of the large young man's close attention as Hunt laid out four hundred-dollar bills: The canted leather clip holder for his spare Detonics magazine would have been partly visible on his right hip as he got out his wallet.

But the clerk only thanked him and wished him a "nice day."

"Safe" on the street, he wanted desperately to sit down somewhere quiet. He got another cab instead, giving the cabby directions to a corner in the seventies off Fifth Avenue, following his ingrained procedural tradecraft: Never take a convenient cab sitting right where you'd like it to be; take a cruising vehicle—if possible, one that has just disgorged a passenger; if not, one headed away from where you want to go. Waiting on the sidewalk until the yellow cab disappeared, he lit a cigarette and wondered where Mino and Flak were by now. He hoped they'd had enough sense to finish their errands before returning to base. Catching the first brown and white cab he saw, he traveled another six blocks, endured the black man's ire that he needed a cab for such a short distance, got out on yet another corner, and walked up the steps of a limestone building that might have been an embassy, a corporate headquarters, or a sumptuous private house. He rang the single bell.

Within the double glass-and-mahogany doors, a liveried Semitic type looked at him doubtfully and reached under his desk. The speaker enclosed in brass by Hunt's head came to life: "Yes? State you beeznis, plise?"

He spoke a single word, hoping the man would remember so ancient a code—it was SOP to change them every six months or so.

The doors' buzzer indicated he might let himself in; the attendant never left his bulletproof cage. Cory crossed the travertine-marble foyer and trotted up the stairs, disregarding the elevator in which a squat old man sat reading a foreign-language newspaper.

On the third-floor landing, he stopped, turned right, and knocked on a door. The little man who answered it was unfamiliar to him, but agreed to tell the Russian he served that "Scratch" wanted to see him. The short Jew disappeared into the inner sanctum, returned almost immediately, still poker-faced but with dancing eyes, and ushered him in.

The room was dark, heavy silk drapes drawn; the swivel chair behind the desk was turned away, facing a samovar on a sideboard; the samovar's contents filled the room with the aroma of tea.

Cory slid into a Queen Anne chair before the desk. The one opposite him swung about slowly, revealing its tiny, wizened occupant, stirring sugar into a cup. "So? Back from the dead, *meshugener?*" frowned the old man, then broke into a smile that crinkled his face as if it were an unaccustomed, and painful, thing for its owner to ask it to do.

"Yes and no. I came to leave some money." He took a cashier's check drawn on a Swiss bank from his wallet and put it on the antique ash of the English partner's desk.

"In that case, help yourself to tea."

"I need documents."

The gnarled hands reached for Cory's check, glanced at the amount. "So? You think it will cost this much? I am a thief, but not that much of a thief."

Hunt got up and served himself from the samovar, took the delicate cobalt cup back to his seat. "You know what would happen if I tried to cash that. Get me some bailout papers, route the disbursements in the usual way, and keep what you think is fair."

"When do you need it and how complete must the documentation be?"

"I'm in an awfully tight spot."

"Instantly, and complete, eh?" The old man wheezed. "Being your lawyer has not always been pleasant, but it continues to be interesting. Where can I find you, in your crypt?"

"I'll come by when I can." He sipped from his cup, watching the gnomish septuagenarian over its rim. "Can we give a quarter of that to the NTS émigré organization in Frankfurt?"

"Which will leave you with a quarter for yourself? Have we become philanthropic in our old age?"

"If I make it through this, I've got that much more coming to me. If I don't, the balance to be deposited by John Shy of Innotech, Zürich, into my account will go instead to NTS—unless you can get to it first. How's your wife?"

"How should she be? She asked often of you; she mourned your 'death.' Since your resurrection, have you changed your mind? Do you wish me to make inquiries on your behalf toward restoring your citizenship? The jeopardy is great, but for you I would—"

"I know. No, just leave it the way it is. I've got to go now." He stood up. "Thanks for the tea."

"Are you sure you don't want the documentation delivered? I know how you hate to come here. I must confess I am wondering what lured you to the United States, let alone moved you to come to me in broad daylight."

"Don't remind me of my stupidity." He had reached the door. He turned back when the old lawyer called his name: "I *said* I'll pick it up. If I can't, proceed in the usual way with the rest. It'll mean only that things are a little tricky."

"I was just going to wish you Godspeed."

Hunt, lifting his hand in farewell, slipped out the door and took the stairs two at a time. He couldn't help reacting to the old Russian as he always had to his own father; by now, his lawyer should have been used to it.

He walked to Fifth, absorbed in his thoughts. During the first nineteen years of his life, he had witnessed five "bloodless" coups; three bloody ones; four "revolutions"; and, in the Middle East, three shooting wars, in one of which his mother had been killed by a piece of random terror: blown apart by a bomb in Tel Aviv along with other civilian noncombatants. He didn't doubt that he had done the right thing by coming here, although visiting the ancient who had handled the Hunts' affairs, father's and son's, for nearly forty years always evoked memories better left unstirred; he didn't doubt that he must discourage any misplaced compassion, any intervention on his behalf that could cause harm to a valued family friend.

When Cory had been eleven and Isser Harel and Jim Angleton had first hashed out with Allen Dulles the intelligence-sharing agreement between CIA and Mossad over a transcript of Khrushchev's anti-Stalin speech, he had first met his father's adviser—they had gone to breakfast at the King David, and later skeet shooting outside of Jerusalem. Even then, the man had been avuncular, aged and wrinkled and full of cares. By eleven, Cory had been a crack shot, charged with home defense, since his mother was categorically opposed to violence and refused even to touch a weapon. He was the man of the house, wherever they were, because his father was seldom home, and servants could not be trusted, and bodyguards came and went. He had shot well, and basked in the praise of the two adults. He remembered his father's hand on his shoulder, the evocative smell of pipe tobacco, and the tiny smile dancing in the corners of the elder Hunt's clear hazel eyes as he agreed gravely that young Cory would "be all right."

He took the first cab he saw, rebellious and full of the past, leaned his head back on the seat and closed his stinging eyes. At Madison and 56th, he got out, walking in what seemed like an aimless fashion, found Sulka, bought a half-dozen "dark shirts with dark buttons" from an old man whose memory was prodigious enough to be jogged by his request: "Ah, yes, sir. I thought I remembered you. It must be five...six years since we've seen you, but I'm sure your pattern is still on file."

He didn't have time to have anything made up, he explained; he was living abroad, in for the day. He paid with his Innotech card and an almost savage satisfaction at the total cost, choosing a tie and a bathrobe at the last minute, which brought his bill to nearly twelve hundred dollars U.S. The clerk had to call in his number to run a check on the card.

When he came out of there, the noon rush was on, the streets overflowing with folk. All the preparations he was making seemed suddenly risky; he was determined to take no more chances with credit cards. He fought his way through the press to a safari outfitter, completed his "blacks": field pants with roomy shell pockets, a camouflage stick, soft canvas shoes with thin, silent soles. He got Flak some climbing gear on the upper floor, added a box of Winchester .308 Accelerators, interchangeable with the NATO caliber the Mausers took but having the added advantage of a plastic sabot that separated from the bullet a few feet in front of the muzzle, allowing the shooter to pick up the plastic, with its incriminating rifling, and the unmarked bullet to travel on its untraceable way. There he paid in cash.

He wanted to go back to the hotel and sleep. It was easier to walk than fight for a cab in nearly motionless traffic. Turning onto Central Park South, he tried to shake the feeling that someone was watching him, but there were so many people and so many cars, he couldn't disprove his instinct.

The Essex House doorman smiled at him politely and the hotel's continental quiet swallowed him up. Heading for the elevators, he felt rather than saw a man rise from one of the wing chairs in the lobby and follow him, newspaper rustling as he folded it.

Hunt didn't turn around until he'd shifted all his parcels into the shopping bag in his left hand and thrust his right into his jacket pocket. The man was tall, with the tight upper-body posture and slightly protruding lips of a native French-speaker; he wore Carrera sports glasses and a good flannel suit. Hunt leaned against the wall, watching the opposite bank of elevators before which the two-meter man stood squarely on both feet. Others drifted up: women in new spring coats and men in tweed jackets; a porter with a cart helping an incoming couple with many leather bags.

The man who'd followed him caught Hunt's eyes and inclined his head slightly. When the first elevator came, neither took it. A second opened on Hunt's right and he stepped in, not punching a floor, and backed into a corner under the camera where, his left shoulder braced against the corner, his right hand still in his pocket, he could cover the other man from the camera's blind spot.

Smiling as he stepped in and pressed "Door Close," the man asked, "What floor?" and the elevator shut them off from the world.

Thinking *It's about time,* Hunt said: "That's up to you. I just come here to ride the elevators." He'd heard no trace of accent, but the gesture that answered his initial probe, a Gallic midlevel-irritation twitch of shoulder, confirmed his feeling that the man was middle-European. He pressed 10 and pulled down his flannel sleeve over a gold cuff link, newspaper still in his right hand.

Hunt disengaged the safety on the Detonics in his pocket and the man eyed him openly when he heard it click, shifted his gaze to the camera above, and stepped toward him. Finally, Hunt was certain. If they hadn't sent someone, if the cars were just cars and not a radio-dispatched follow team, it would have meant that Hunt was a giveaway, a sacrifice; now that they had surfaced, he could send an explicit message to Brussels and Zürich and even, possibly, keep them from killing him with solicitude—*if* the man represented Innotech....

"And whose little boy are *you?*" Hunt asked softly.

"We were worried—"

He'd heard enough, then, to know he wasn't going to shoot some civilian. "Drop the paper, don't move suddenly—you know the drill."

"In a lift you would chance such a thing? Under surveillance?" But he let the newspaper fall and stood motionless. "*Incroyable! Alors...* what *is* the problem? Where are the others? DARLING"— he spoke the last word as if in capitals: It was someone's code designation—"failed to report. I—"

The doors opened at the tenth floor. "Out," Hunt said, closing on him, letting him exit first. "There's the fire exit. Nice and easy, don't make me nervous. You want to talk—" The man, hands carefully away from his body, opened the fire door, and Hunt, letting his shopping bag go, braced it with his left hand as he followed him through.

"That's good enough. Over there, assume the position."

"*Pardon?*" The man took off his glasses and cased them fastidiously, slipped the case into his breast pocket.

Hunt looked at the man leaning on the balustrade and shook

his head. "Over there, against the cinder block, face the wall, hands flat beside your head, legs spread."

"Surely this is not necessary; we are your support infrastructure, not an enemy."

"We'll see." He had the Detonics out in plain sight. With his left hand, he began patting the Frenchman down, first extracting a wallet. He flipped it open and saw the man's ISA card, took the card, then let the wallet fall. Reaching under the agent's coat, he found a self-suppressed Ruger Security Six; on his hip was its nasty little sidekick, a silenced Standard Model, a scratch gun that took .22 longs and came from the factory sterile: no serial numbers, a favor from Ruger to the governments of its choice.

Stepping back, he emptied the .357 wheelgun of bullets over the stairwell, put it in his belt, and pocketed the tiny assassination weapon. Then he moved in close, carefully, his Detonics at the man's neck, and, unbuckling his adversary's belt, jerked his pants down.

"*Sacre bleu! What* are you doing? You mustn't! If those bullets are found ... *mon Dieu!*"

Revealed were boxer shorts. Working his way downward, his gun between the agent's cheeks, Hunt came to an ankle holster. "Shit, you're a regular little armory, aren't you, sweetie?" He got the final snubby, thumbing the cylinder open and ejecting its shells into his pocket. This time it was the gun he let fall ten floors. He'd hoped for this confrontation; he couldn't have Shy and Fowler thinking he'd doubled on them, gone out on his own or crossed to Angel Morales' or any other side. But he hadn't thought they'd put an ISA man out where he could get him; he had been prepared for the possibility that he was interdicting some special agent from the FBI or another service's agent in place.

The man started to straighten up; Hunt pulled him back out by the underpants. "You stay here, honey. I want you to listen very carefully. If I see any more of you, or another blue Plymouth or silver Subaru or what have you, I'm going to walk. Nobody's gonna have anything to do with someone as hot as you guys are making me look. You tell whomsoever that I don't report to anybody until this is over."

"Tell them yourself. To take a man's issue weapon and— How will I explain this to—"

Hunt chopped him in the left kidney and the man crumpled

down the wall. "I told you to *listen.* I'd put a couple of your own twenty-two longs in your ear if I didn't need you to deliver my message. Get up. *Now!* Or you won't be able to."

When the man, his nose running and tears in his eyes, had tried and failed, Cory, ignoring gasped French threats, leaned down-long enough to pull the belt around his ankles tight. "You're telling me you're going to do *what?* That friend of mine ISA's got *better* be healthy and happy when I get back there. Meanwhile, you just reminded me." He kicked the man. "Crawl over there by the stairs. ... That's good enough. Now put your head down on your arms." The man, cursing tremulously, did so, his striped boxer shorts shivering as if in a gentle breeze. Hunt thought about Nasta, and how she had needed to support herself against the Lexan. He put his foot on the ISA agent's upraised buttocks. "Don't forget to tell them that nobody got physical with you—you fell," he said quietly, and pushed the asset down the stairs. When he'd watched long enought to be sure the man was still alive and conscious, he backed out of the fire exit and picked up his packages, summoned the "Up" elevator, and got off at his own floor, relieved that his temper had not gotten the better of him.

At the suite's first door, he hesitated. He listened and heard voices, then put down his things and got out his key. The doorknob alarm was gone or disarmed. He let the door swing open.

Mino was on the telephone in the parlor; from one of the bed-rooms, a quick-talker announced that it was one thirty-five on a beautiful day in Manhattan, fifty-two degrees and "holding steady here at WBLS."

Flak was nowhere in sight. Hunt closed the door, and Mino, signing off, put down the phone and the pencil with which he had been jotting, turned: "*Sir!* Cory, man, am I glad to see you!" The pilot, in briefs and a "Take No Prisoners" T-shirt, tore the note off its pad and folded it, coming toward Hunt. "Are you all right? What happened to you? We turned around and you weren't *any*where—"

"Where's Flak?" Hunt put down his shopping bag, saw the alarm on a chest by the door, replaced it on the door's knob. When he was done, Mino still hadn't answered, just stood watching him. "Well?" He took his shopping bag to the coffee table, sinking down on the couch.

Mino followed. "He went back out to look for you." Hunt detected resentment. "Told me to stay here in case you showed. We didn't know *what* the fuck—whether to drag the river or call the Russian Embassy." He sat on the table, staring at Hunt reproachfully.

"Was that Flak on the phone?"

"No, sir, it wasn't. I'm about up to here"—Mino indicated with his hand a point at eye level— "with everybody treating me like the weak sister. I'm as good as anybody working at what I do—logistics, backup, that shit. So I laid into him about it and we got the work load split up right. That was a friend of mine from this executive helicopter service..... I can get us a chopper on an hour's notice, no questions asked—the guy owes me one: I pulled his ass off the hottest landing zone in—well, in wherever. Got him aboard without a hitch in heavy incomings, but while he was chugging his first beer, I lost half of one skid and most of the other. That was the only time I ever scrubbed a chopper." He grinned bleakly. "So we're cool if by air."

"Where's your stuff?" Hunt put his feet up on the table, laced his fingers behind his neck.

"Aw, Cory...it got pretty heavy when we found out you split. We had a sort of unpleasant discussion. You've got Flak—that is—I've never seen him like this; he's real insulted that you don't trust him, says it's an 'aspersion' on his chops—on his professionalism.... Anyway, we argued some and did sort of a minimal job in that store we were in, in case you were around there somewheres, then came right back here...." His mouth twitched in disgust. "He takes it real personal when you pull shit, sir."

"What time did you get back here?"

"About noon, I guess. I did get *some* stuff, Cory. Do you want to see it?"

"Yeah, I'd better. Have you had lunch?"

"I ordered sandwiches for everybody about ten minutes ago—thinking positive. Flak's pride ain't my problem, but I'd sure feel better if you'd tell me you're not going to go disappearing like that again, or give us some sort of procedure to follow when you do." As he spoke, he got up and fetched a Bloomingdale's bag from behind the couch and began dumping the contents on the table. When he had shown Hunt his purchases, he said, "What'd *you* get, Cory?"

The first thing Hunt showed him, unzipping his jacket, was the

Security Six. "I don't want this, you're welcome to it. I took it off an outboard observer. But remember, it's a government issue, and you wouldn't want to flash it around the Moraleses without giving an explanation."

"So you did have trouble." Mino took the revolver, flipped open the cylinder, snapped it shut, put it down. "No, sir, I don't want it, for that reason. Flak might, though.... You don't want to talk about it?"

"It's not important beyond demonstrating that we're not alone out here. This sort of unsolicited aid is going to blow us if it continues. I was rough enough on that guy to make sure that his superiors are going to find out what happened—he's lost weapons, face, and credibility. What's more important, nobody's going to send any more of his type out to ask me if I won't reconsider, or if I'm really serious, as they would have if I just talked it over with him and sent him home to try to convince his desk that it might be better to play ball with me. Could be I've solved the problem, but don't count on it."

"Can't count on much, these days."

"Flak hurt your feelings?"

"Ten years hangin' out with a guy and you find out you never really knew him? You might say so, sir. *I* got him this gig; he wasn't doin' shit, just getting fat and lazy, and he's bossing me around like I'm his personal property."

"Sorry. It's that way every once in a while, but you ought to be glad you're learning this particular lesson the easy way."

"This is easy?"

"Compared to some."

"Sir—Cory, did you really ditch us intentionally?"

"I had to do some things alone, yes. But I didn't realize it would stop you two in your tracks."

"Naw—that's not so. I got the one expensive thing—" He rooted through his jumbled purchases and showed Hunt a pair of leather jeans. "Can you tell me where the guy with the wheelgun was dispatched from? We've been pretty careful. I'd like to know how they found us."

"You were asleep when we ID'd the follow car. They were on us at Hanscom. ISA is Innotech's overt partner—they're sharing the take on this."

"Fuckers.... You *disarmed* an ISA—oh, shit.... I suppose it don't matter none. I'm beginning to *feel* like a fugitive, though."

"It'll help your verisimilitude."

"Yeah, I bet.... My what?"

Hunt, chuckling, uncrossed his legs and stood up. "Let's get rid of what we can of the clothes we brought from Zürich that might be signatures."

"Flak'll never give up his Kevlar-lined down vest," Mino warned, "but I ain't got nothin' I care much about.... Tell me about the lady, Dania. I usually remember fluffs...."

Hunt told him Dania was Austro-Italian, and hardly a "fluff."

Flak and the sandwiches arrived at approximately the same time, announced by the doorknob alarm.

When the waiter had left, Flak—who until then had leaned, fists on hips, against the chest by the parlor door, unresponsive to their greetings—said, "You cocksucker. I don't know if I'm relieved or disappointed." He let his clutch of shopping bags drop with a thud and stormed away toward one of the bedrooms. Almost instantly, two doors slammed in quick succession and Hunt heard the radio turned off and the shower begin to run.

Mino flashed him a mock grin and said maybe they'd better go ahead and eat.

Hunt agreed but, instead of sitting down, went over to Flak's discarded purchases and looked through them. The operative had done a thorough job, but he'd done it in such a way that Hunt wasn't pleased by what he saw: Chinos from Gucci shouldn't have been part of a struggling young asset's vocabulary; the person who made these buys understood money, had no qualms about spending it, as the affluent say, "wisely and well." Flak had bought a black one-and-a-half-inch Dunhill belt with a gold dragon buckle—Hunt tried to envision it strung with Flak's scabbard and clips. The younger asset had even thought to buy an American-currency-size wallet. As he examined Flak's things, he realized the "pilot" had done an impeccable job. He wished it had not been. He really did like Flak.

They did not speak to each other before Hunt went to bed. He was content to let Mino deal with his partner. He drew the blackout curtains and set an alarm on his bedroom's doorknob, took the hottest shower he could bear, and asked the operator to wake him at 9:00 P.M. Then, Commander wedged securely between the headboard and his pillow, staring into the almost-dark, an ashtray balanced on his naked chest with a lit cigarette in it, he dialed nine and a number.

An accented female voice answered, telling him he had reached "Nirvana." He said, "Angel Morales, please." She asked his name. He replied, "Cordell Hunt." She said Angel was out of town. He asked if Dania was in. "Not at the moment," the woman answered. He knew better than to ask when they would return: Basic security precluded responding to such a question. "Will you give them this number?" He recited his hotel and extension numbers. "I'll be here until eight-thirty or nine."

He hung up, not concerned about taps—the call had been short and it was too soon for Innotech or ISA to have arranged a line-in to his room. Tomorrow, however, he would have to make his calls from outside or use Flak's tap-free attaché system. Now, all he had to do was manage to get some sleep. Short of blowing up the hotel, coming in the windows, or poisoning the ventilation system, his enemies couldn't get to him. He was safe enough— from everything but dreams.

And they were horrid.

When the phone rang, he felt for it blindly. The room was pitch black but for a red pulse in sync with the ringing: warning flashes? He couldn't remember whose or where or why...

He fumbled the receiver against his ear, saying hoarsely, "*Yeb tvoyu matz*" before he realized he was speaking Russian; added in English, "This better be good," then remembered: It was probably his wake-up call.

A silence stretched; punctuated by breathing he could barely hear. He cleared his throat, said "Yes?" impatiently, and was about to put down the phone when a woman's voice spoke: "It *is* you."

He got up, groped for a cigarette in the dark, lit it. "Hello there. I've got to talk to you. I'm in deep shit, though. Will you see me?"

"Fuck *your* mother." Her laugh was throaty as she translated the Russian epithet with which he had answered the phone. "I *thought* it was you, in the Baur Au Lac. You are lodging at this number?"

"I'll meet you anywhere you say, anytime. I've got two people with me, but I'll come alone if you like. I need help. I've got nobody else to turn to…but you've gathered that by now." '

"Alone in your hotel's bar, then? Forty minutes?"

"Yes, fine. Thank you."

"Perhaps. *Ciao.*"

Click.

He reached and with his thumb pressed the phone's button down, releasing it in time to heard a second *click*.

In the Windjammer's bar, thirty minutes later, he took a strategic table, ordered a draft though he wanted coffee, and settled down to wait. Flak would probably grant him a few minutes' grace before drifting in to get a look at her. They had not discussed it—the second bedroom remained dark and silent until he left—but the "pilot" who might be code-named "Darling" had been superbly trained. He wondered where Flak had gone after depositing Mino at the hotel, what the younger operative had needed time alone to do.

Then he shelved it; he would find out soon enough. He was thankful he'd done his homework on the Moraleses when first he had arrived in Morocco, dazed and ill and consumed with the need to set up fallbacks and bailouts; the Moraleses had made it onto his list under the heading "worst-case." He found that amusing, buoyed with sleep and adrenaline and the slithering excitation he always felt in his gut at the beginning of a high-stakes encounter. He looked the part: Sporting nearly two weeks' growth of beard, which could not mask the stamp the Lubyanka had left on him, he wouldn't have to fake anything this time—legend and truth were becoming one.

When she appeared in the doorway, he left his seat and went to meet her. Fleetingly, he regretted not having dressed to her standard, but he needed to be prepared to leave with only what he had on: leather jacket, Commander, gray sweater over dark shirt, workbelt laced with necessities, bootknife at his ankle, money in his jeans.

The maître d', roused to action by the striking woman in fox and silk, was fawning over her. He had helped her off with her jacket by the time Hunt reached them. Hunt took it, smiled into the creamy oval face shielded with tinted glasses, brushed her cheek with his in the *de rigueur* greeting of her class, and escorted her decorously to his table, trying not to be thrown by the naked arm he was holding gently, or the gold-thread tank top that barely restrained her breasts, or the soft chestnut hair feathering her shoulders and curling close about her neck. If she was carrying, it would have to be under the cat's-cradle cinch around her waist, or down where her tiger silk pants tucked into calf-high boots.

He pulled out a chair for her; she sat where he wanted her; he went around and took his place, facing the door. They had not exchanged more than inanities: "You look wonderful." "I wish I could say the same." "This way—watch your step." "Thank you." "Thank *you* for coming."

"Drink?" he now asked while she took off her glasses and leaned forward, toying with them, giving him a good look at her décolletage. She smelled marvelous.

"Just a sip of your beer," she answered. There was no one at the tables on their right or left. She licked her lips with a pointed tongue, eyeing him directly over the beer's froth. "I can't stay long. I've a previous engagement. How may we help you?"

He ducked his head slightly, smiling just a bit. "All right, then ... I need to talk to Angel. I'm looking for work. I thought we might be able to overcome the bad blood between us and hash out something, I'm so desperate—" He shook his head, waved one hand despairingly, sat back. Behind her, he saw Flak and Mino amble in, sight them, negotiate with the maître d' for the table of their choice.

"That's impossible, at the moment—Angel is out of the country. But he's often expressed regret about what happened in Colombia—you weren't the only one who suffered from ... difficulties. We tried several times to reach you thereafter. Your security is very good—so good one wonders how you manage to keep busy."

What the fuck?

But she continued: "Wasn't that John Shy I saw you with in Zürich? Even the dead shouldn't have to consort with such a devil."

"You must have heard the shot, then."

"I heard something."

"You heard a shot. I killed one of Shy's goons who leaned on me too hard. Triage set me up in Afghanistan as a giveaway, blew me far and wide, let me take the fall by myself. Then when I almost had things back together in Morocco, Innotech came along and scooped me off the street, killed a friend of mine and passed him off as me, shipped me to Zürich under physical restraint, and started to interrogate me. After what I'd just come out of, that was a little difficult for me to handle."

"So you were their prisoner when I saw you? Yes, that makes good sense. They are done with you now?"

He nodded. "You're right, *that* doesn't make good sense. When they're done with me, they'll scratch me, of course—I don't exist anyway, so it's no problem. They sent me out with two backups— they're both promising—to find out who was behind better than a year's worth of covert and overt harassment directed at Innotech: killings, bombs, publicity-drawing incidents of every sort. They think they've got me in a position where I have to follow orders, and those orders led me to you: I'm here on their sufferance, their credit cards, their operation— Is this straight enough for you?"

She had stiffened; now she sat back. "Why are you telling me this?"

"Because I've managed to turn the two backups. I've only got a little bit of time before Shy scopes it and pulls the plug. I couldn't care less about who blew holes in Innotech's research labs, but I do care wholeheartedly about my own butt. To that end, I pointed them in your direction—they would have come up with your name sooner or later, anyhow—because I can't think of anyone else who'd lift a finger to help me. And from the way they've treated me and the amount of trouble they went through to put me in a position where I couldn't go to any agency or legitimate for help, they've got something very naughty to hide. If I can find out what it is, I've got a chance to checkmate them. Otherwise, I'll settle for fucking them as royally as I can manage in what time I've got left."

"Which is not, you think, very long?"

"Not if you two won't take me on, it isn't. I'll run out of cash by the end of this week. By then I have to have something lined up."

"You expect me to believe you?"

He shrugged. "It saves time to start with the truth. I lost my taste for question-and-answer in the Lubyanka. Why would I tell you a horror story like this if it weren't so? At least I've warned you; I owe you that much." He pushed back his chair.

"Wait." Her long-fingered hand reached out to him. He sat

back down. "How is it they sent you out with only two baby-sitters and so much freedom? How can they be sure you'll follow orders? You're not famous for it."

"I had one friend in Marrakech; when things got hairy in Rabat, I moved down there and lived in with this freedom fighter—a lady, she had a safe house...the usual sort of downtime entanglement. They picked her up and brought her to Zürich, let me see her, took her into deep custody. They've had her in a box ever since. They think they've got some strong leverage."

"And you? What do you think?"

"I think I won't be able to think about anything at all if I'm dead."

She frowned. "Cory, things have changed—our business has changed, our methodology has changed. We no longer quibble over nationality or ideology. We have no...we *play*—this is the term, yes?—no favorites. We take what is offered us. If you were to come aboard you, too, would have to put away many old prejudices."

"Are you asking me whether I'd work for capitalists? Or whether I'd work for ComBloc? Or just whether I've come to despise the Soviets more than I despise the rest?"

"I am asking whether you're ready, and willing, to put aside all vendettas—perhaps even revenge on Innotech, I can't say—and operate merely on a piecework basis."

"That's what I want."

"*Bene.* And your compatriots?"

"They want to be big bad free-lancers when they grow up."

"You trust them?"

"Don't worry, my mind's still in working order, whatever you may have heard. No, I don't trust them—and, yes, I've had to trust them with my life: I'm here, and as far as I can tell, I'm alive. I can lose them in twenty minutes if I have to, but they're both accredited jet and chopper pilots, reasonably mercenary, familiar with basic tradecraft. It's nice to know who's behind you when you're walking down the street, if you're me these days."

She reached out and touched the back of his hand, running her finger along it. "I'll consider your proposition. I'd like to say more, but I can't...." She rubbed the side of her delicate, aquiline nose, an old gesture he recalled, and smiled mischievously. "I was sorry to hear of your misfortune, angry for your sake at the Americans; expediency is their front-line instrument of foreign policy of late."

"Always has been," he replied, and the bitterness they both heard there was real. "Will you let me know one way or the other?"

"*Certainement.* I won't be back in New York until Friday evening. Perhaps if I can say yes to you, you'll take me to dinner?"

"On Innotech? My pleasure." He stood up while she collected herself, pulled back her chair, escorted her to the lobby, where a large, bearded man waited discreetly, ignoring Flak and Mino's concerted attempts to ignore him. "If I'm not still here, you can table the matter. I won't be needing any help."

She turned, seemingly impulsively, and placed her hands on his chest, running them slowly up until her fingers were at the nape of his neck. "It is sad to see you so weary, so worn. I never thought I'd see it." She pulled his head down to her, and the kiss her lips deposited on his was more heartfelt than necessary for cover. He returned it: Though his mind was consternated, his body understood perfectly what kind of tradecraft was involved. "No more talk of final solutions now, my old friend. If nothing more, we'll try to see you back to health." She tapped him on the nose with a manicured nail—"*Ciao,*"—released him, slipped into the coat Hunt held out, and was gone.

He stood watching until Blackbeard had followed, opened a navy limo's door at the curb, and the car drove away.

After extending his room occupancy through Saturday, he went directly to his suite, called Gallagher's and made a reservation for three at ten, and waited for Flak and Mino to show. He couldn't make any sense out of her—she was reacting all wrong in the clinches. Had they *known* he would call them? Did Angel *want* her to lure him aboard? Had he just set the date for his own execution?

He tabled supposition; it never did any good, just cluttered up his mind, which needed to be free to record minutiae without bias for later analysis.

He located the pad on which Mino had taken notes earlier, tore off the second sheet, raised a negative imprint with a soft pencil lead. It was unenlightening, merely numbers. He called one, found he'd reached a commercial helicopter service, hung up.

When Flak and Mino came racing down the hall, laughing and loud in their horseplay, he swung open the door and glowered at them. He had been pacing back and forth in the suite for twenty minutes, wondering whether they were in trouble, wishing he had coffee, wishing he had a joint, wishing he knew what he was doing, but exhilarated all the same.

There was nothing quite like the feeling he got from a go at its beginning. Despite the occasional twinge in his back and his post-Lubyanka doubts, he had set things in motion; his operation was on line. Dressing down the two assets for rowdiness, his heart wasn't in it. He didn't probe Flak about "Darling" or ask what had become of the .357 he had taken from the ISA operative. He couldn't even keep a straight face with them, and when they walked out of the lobby to catch a cab ten minutes later, all three were grinning from ear to ear.

Over what Cordell Hunt was willing to wager were still the best steaks in New York, they exulted en masse. "You didn't tell me she was *beau*tiful." Mino stabbed in Hunt's direction with a forkful of USDA prime. "She can point those thirty-eights at me any ol' time."

Flak was admiring, eager to share in Hunt's triumph: He would take the car downtown tomorrow morning and leave it at some outdoor lot. Hunt saw no sign of this afternoon's resentment, just honest professionalism, the right shadow of concern. Perhaps he was wrong about Flak's loyalties, perhaps the asset was exactly what he proclaimed. On the surface of it, Hunt had as much reason to suspect Mino of being somebody's double as he did Flak.

"Well, sir, here's to Friday; long may we wave." They toasted—Hunt, as he had in the Windjammer, nursing one beer to accommodate convention. Flak drained his glass and leaned back, rubbing his flat belly, saying that the only thing he needed to make it a perfect evening was word that he, too, was "going to get to go inside."

It was whim that prompted Hunt to turn on his bedroom's television when they got back; the Reuters printface news scrolled upward, silent, unnoticed by him until Flak came in, asking if Cory wouldn't mind "running the take down to me one more time, in case I missed anything in what she said."

Knowing Flak, that was not the reason, but Hunt sat down on his bed, stretched out, and began to reiterate the specifics of his conversation with Morales to which he felt Flak should be privy. He hadn't mentioned to Flak or Mino that he had alerted Dania to the exact nature of his arrangement with John Shy—or what he thought the warmth of his reception might indicate, beyond warning them to repeat nothing he had told them about his Colombian penetration of Angel's column.

The soundless TV screen made the room's walls seem to flicker. Hunt watched the asset who watched the bulletins on the screen, who nodded occasionally, who had not yet brought up the purpose of his visit, and trailed off: "That's it, I guess."

"Cory," said Flak, his face turned away, his shoulders hunched, "I'm sorry about today. I don't know what got into me—too much blow, maybe. I'm going to lay off for the duration, unless you want me to score again?" He turned his head so that he could see Hunt out of the corner of one eye.

"No offense taken. You had a right to be angry and a right to be worried. And you're correct once again: We ought to stay as straight as we can manage. It's going to be very touchy."

"I was unprofessional, though."

"Only if you're not sincere. Let's drop it. Nothing's a problem unless it creates problems."

"Mino showed me that low-signature Ruger. I didn't think they still made them."

"The machining's getting better."

"I noticed that. I think we ought to dispose of it."

"So do I. I'm glad you agree. We'll—"

"Oh, no—Cory, look at—"

But Hunt was already reading the bulletin printed out across the screen's blue background. It stated tersely: "Intelligence sources revealed late today that internationalist and former NATO southern commander Jackson Fowler remains in critical condition tonight, the victim of an assassination attempt early this morning outside his home in Mons, Belgium. Sources report that two unexploded Soviet grenades were found...."

"Why the fuck would they put that on the goddamned *wire?*" Flak muttered, aghast.

"Because they wanted somebody outside, somebody without access to normal back channels, to know about it."

Flak twisted about and they stared at one another, neither willing to suggest who that "somebody" might be.

Chapter 12

WHEN he realized how completely he'd been had, John Shy went to his high-security "cottage" on the Zürichsee's most exclusive stretch of shore to pick up his two-suiter and Grover, the indoor guard dog. Michele was already gone and she'd taken as little as he. What the hell did they think they needed all this stuff for? When had they talked each other into needing it? Now that they'd admitted to no longer needing one another, everything they had was tainted.

He wasn't going to sell any of it, though; he wasn't going to close down the house; he wasn't going to make a single thing easier for her: No matter the difficulties, she had no right to throw up her hands and flounce off to sulk in the States.

Moving through the empty rooms, he thought he ought to send her the silk Aubussons and room-size Tabriz hunting rugs, ongoing bones of contention because of their cost and his dogs. It would be nice to be able to spill something or forget to wipe his feet.

Flemish paintings he'd never liked glowed in the morning light, fat-faced and vacant-eyed like his Germanic servants, in hiding somewhere (their only real skill). He knew they were there, though he couldn't find a one of them, nursing their hereditary gloom and hoping to avoid his anger or, worse, word of their termination. He wasn't going to give them the satisfaction of making him shout. He didn't intend to lay them off. He had no special instructions; they knew the drill: Accept no deliveries, give out no information.

Grover was transported into Doberman ecstasy at the very thought of riding in the Mondial. Grover was his bottom line, he supposed: He didn't have to wonder where the dog's loyalties lay.

He pulled out of his driveway in a shower of bluestone and followed the lake's curves. He was going to his office. He'd clean out his desk, mothball what projects he could, hand Hubble those that couldn't wait. Then he was going to New York to straighten out Dropout's mess.

His mess, he admitted, as the dog won out and he opened its window; he'd rather be cold than driven to distraction by Grover's whining. A drunk in a dilapidated Renault barred his way; he wrenched the Mondial out into the passing lane and almost succeeded in running the weaving car off the road. The drunk, seeing his American vanity plate—STEALTH—shook a fist at him. Shy hardly noticed. Jack Fowler really must have thought he was dying, to give Shy the key to that drawer. In it was proof of how shabbily Jack had treated him. But Fowler had gotten all he was going to get from John Shy. "Win this one for me" meant something entirely different now that he knew Fowler hadn't respected his confidence.

Shy's Triage team had brought in the German boy Flak had wanted to tap, who hung out at the Bazillus and boasted of his exploits, who dressed like a West German "Popper" who'd gotten tired of beating up long-haired Greens, and who thought he was ready to play in the big leagues. In a tunnel behind and under the Bazillus's bar, which led to the street and which the revolutionaries used for meetings, he had airily confessed to Fowler's "execution." When Shy had arrived at Triage's facility, the youth explained that a "revolutionary court" had tried and sentenced the capitalist-imperialist mass murderer—Shy must try to understand. When gently pressed, the youth, reassured that matters would get no more difficult now that someone of Shy's stature was present, overconfident under the umbrella of his father's diplomatic immunity, implicated the militant "revolutionary cells," Libya, Fatah, and the Easter Bunny. After all, the towheaded youth had smirked, they would have to take his word for it— these were not the Dark Ages, Shy was not Torquemada, *he* was not suspected of Nazi war crimes. His smug inference, that all good Aryans must stick together in the face of this effluence of inferior bloodlines, was intolerable.

Subsequently, John Shy had gotten everything the young man had to give—up to and including a positive ID on the suborned stableboy who had helped the People's Crusaders for Peace do their "duty"—in three hours, the savagery of which had his Triage people treading softly and grinning at each other, offering to give him "five" when he hobbled out into the hall for a drink of water to wash down the pain-killers for his ankle.

The take was pathetically inadequate considering the suffering the kid was willing to endure to withhold it. Shy wouldn't have gone to dinner with people he knew as little about as those the youth was risking his health to protect. Convinced that he was dealing with a misguided adolescent rather than a budding ideologue, Shy had called the boy's father, ready to enter into a "difficult but frank discussion of the PCP's" and found the man didn't even know the acronym, much less that his son was a charter member of the "People's Crusaders for Peace." Shy detailed its membership, its manipulation, its eventual fate. He'd never been as heavy-handed in so delicate a situation. In fact, he'd been out for blood. Offering to send one of the unexploded, camouflaged, Soviet-made mines over for the father's inspection had put the advantage squarely in his court: Blowing up empty buildings on weekends was one thing; blowing off a man's foot was quite another.

So in a way he'd shed some of the blood he craved: Money was blood to the internationalists. By evening, lots of them knew who the PCP's were and what the letters stood for. Money was about to change hands because of them: damages totaling in the millions from the three Innotech EO's, most of it in the guise of arms sales and massive security contracts, the rest in intelligence oversight. Innotech could now command intelligence-sharing in four Western European nations, in America, and Japan, on a scale formerly reserved to such giants as CIA. The PCP's were on probation, and not in custody, because of Shy's marathon negotiation. The other parents had been informed; the costs were shared out; an understanding was reached that reparations as agreed covered only *past* misdeeds. If there were a future incident, the young scions who numbered among the brightest stars of the next generation's diplomatic community were going to shine their lights in various and assorted jails.

He was not very popular in his accustomed circles these days— certain customers were distressed.

But he had "won it" for Jack Fowler, and in so doing he had won a big one for Sid Cannard. It would be awfully nice not to have to go begging for information.

In fact, he had more information than he knew what to do with: He had Jack Fowler's precious "Cosmic" security file on Martinova, Innotech, Beth and Sid Cannard, himself, Dropout, somebody else code-named "Darling," Two Can Play, the price of gold in next year's market, and so much international trivia that only a madman or a genius could have read that batch of special cases and come up with Jack Fowler's equation: *Soviet war on Innotech equals Innotech war on Innotech*. It might had read, "Jack Fowler's war on Innotech," for all the sense Shy could make of it.

Shy couldn't remember where he had originally heard the story about CIA being paralyzed by a pair of defectors; Fowler had mentioned it during their initial meeting at the chalet: The first spent years in a safe house naming double agents and traitors in the field and at Langley; the second spent almost as long an interval, concurrently, incriminating everyone who was left and swearing the first defector was a provocation, feeding false information into CIA's counterespionage group to obsess it into inefficacy. Whichever one was lying, the two did their job.

Percy Hunt had once told Shy that the beauty of a good deception was that it only became visible if you looked at it sidelong:

"If you look at it straight on, boy, it disappears, dissolves into the natural chaos of random events."

Jack Fowler wasn't a genius. "Truth be known, Grove, Jack's not any smarter than I am. You believe that, don't you? Good dog. If this crap doesn't make any sense to me, then maybe it doesn't make any sense."

Innotech war on Innotech, Shy could have bought, maybe. But Soviet war on Innotech helped along by an in-house spoiler? At that moment the events under scrutiny seemed to Shy likely to fall into three distinct, related, but *not* coordinated, groups: the customers' efforts to keep tabs on Two Can Play and, later, Dropout; Innotech/Triage's attempts to cover up a possible long-term leak; Soviet retaliation.

When he got to his office, he was going to meet Sid Cannard at the now-familiar wall. This time he was going in armed, fresh coup in hand: The resolution of the EO's in so profitable a manner was bound to give him good leverage, so long as he was ready to apply it.

He understood why Fowler had urged him to resign, and he almost agreed with him: If Innotech was going to take a fall on this one, Shy needn't go with it. And the sheer amount of data Jack Fowler had on everything, from Sid Cannard's family to Shy's own performance in Sid's European shop, said that if a fall was in order, to save face for the community or to placate special interests, Innotech had been chosen for the honor. It was nice to know Jack and the interests he represented considered John Shy worth saving, but it was not comforting. If he decided to resign, it could not be before he brought Dropout's team back in: Without him to protect them, Innotech would clear their decks with full auto fire so fast they wouldn't get a chance to hit the ground before the incriminating evidence was rushed away.

He had gotten a positive ID on Dania Morales' photo from the German boy, but not Angel's. Normally, he would have passed the data on to Dropout, but Cordell Hunt was by all accounts concertedly out of touch with everyone and everything meant to protect and support him. This Thursday morning, Hunt's paranoia seemed like cautious optimism. Shy hoped that when he had finished "briefing" Sid Cannard, he would feel differently, but he did not expect a miracle.

He had arranged a judicious leak to apprise the team—"The Dropouts," Triage was calling them, since there were no paper work, no new file, hence no op or individual code names more recent that the SWA/2CP (Southwest Asia/Two Can Play) DROP-OUT cryptonym to refer to; everything was by mouth only, face-to-face. He hadn't instituted security like this since the Soviets and Americans nearly went to war in November of . . . seventy-three; he pinned the date and swung on to the Bahnhofstrasse, waved to the lady traffic cop in her little round podium at his intersection, and pulled up to Innotech's main gate.

Parking in his slot by the executive elevator in Innotech's underground garage, he reflected on that object lesson, culminating in the events of November 24, 1973, which had convinced him for all time that "cutouts" like Innotech/Triage were necessary: It was becoming altogether too commonplace for great powers to find themselves maneuvered by arms-supply contract provisions right up to the front lines; you had to resupply the clients' weaponry and provide replacement parts, sometimes by air-dropping material into war zones; you had your supply ships at risk in contested waterways; you even, on occasion, ended up with your personnel involved—advisers, mechanics, technical people. If a great power delayed in providing material at crucial moments, or because it could not approve of a client's objectives, a whole new raft of politico-military difficulties cropped up.

Because of the buffer nature of the independents, they enjoyed a certain degree of immunity—or had up until Innotech had mounted an operation aimed at the Soviet Union, a subtle and long-term counterdeception to alter world opinion. Called "Two Can Play," it utilized every known technique of espionage and covert action to ensure that the Soviets were going to be so busy maintaining internal order that they wouldn't have time for any more expanionist schemes.

The European Economic Community (EEC) and the United States were fed up with carrying ComBloc's debt. It was bad enough that, in the deceptive atmosphere of detente, the loans had been floated—everyone felt foolish to have been taken in, now that the Soviets were on the verge of default and holding out the natural-gas pipeline as a combination carrot and stick: The Western European powers' one chance to recoup and reduce their depen-

dence on foreign oil had been taken while cognizant that all the
valves would be operated from the Soviet side. Meanwhile, a dozen
Soviet client states paid only the interest on trillions in loans;
worldwide inflation and unemployment were the result. To have
suffered for peace might have been noble; to loan money to someone and find he has used it to upgrade his offensive nuclear
capability—that you have paid for the missiles he deploys on your
borders—was an insupportable error: The free world was increasingly reluctant to be the Soviets' dupe.

America's first executive, unbeknown to any but his most trusted
intelligence advisers, had envisioned Two Can Play. Together with
certain other NATO signatories—itself continually embattled and
imperiled by Soviet destablization campaigns, of which the pipeline was merely the latest—he had decided that some operational
facets were too sensitive to be handled by any government's agencies or working groups directly. Innotech had gotten the lion's
share of the paramilitary and fieldwork.

Everyone was agreed that there was no other recourse: Calling
ComBloc's loans would trigger a global depression. Something,
however, must be done to curb Soviet adventurism worldwide.
"Most pertinently," the American had written to Sid Cannard on
"Aboard *Air Force One*" letterhead, "I don't want those sons of
bitches to have enough free time to hatch up any more plots to
annex the free world. I want them too busy at home to run amok."

Everything would have been fine, if there hadn't been somebody
inside Innotech who knew what was going on almost from the
plan's inception. The penetration had to be somebody lofty: Until
Dropout, John Shy hadn't had better than a hazy awareness of
Two Can Play's existence; it was played out in little compartmentalized gambits—component by component, a juggernaut was
being built, the whole of which none of the operatives or controls
involved should have been able to extrapolate from their positions
among myriad other parts. Like blind men encountering ele-
phants, incomprehension should have been a certainty.

It hadn't been. He got awkwardly out of the car, mindful of his
Ace-bandaged ankle, and Grover tornadoed after him. "Cool," he
warned the dog, and training reasserted itself: Grover trotted
docilely at his heels.

He tried to determine—riding up to the top floor in the elevator, Grover so excited he shivered with the effort it took to obey Shy's command—what he could and couldn't tell Sid Cannard.

An hour and twenty minutes later, facing Innotech's director in Sid's seldom-used penthouse suite of offices, he found himself wishing he could unload the whole of it. He told Sid that the attempted handover of Hunt on the road to the chalet was just that: a hardballing stunt stage-managed by the clients, who, in view of their suspicions that Innotech was penetrated, were beside themselves with distress that Innotech was unilaterally deciding Hunt's fate. Darling's report to his code-designated superior made that clear. He also told Cannard that in his opinion it was best to keep an open mind, still, as to Darling's provenance—he might be ISA, or he might be from one of the customers' shops.

"But you think he's Jack's?"

"Right now, it looks a little more likely than not. I'm sorry, Sid, that I didn't realize how serious this whole thing was—but then, you could have told me. You didn't have to play me like a civilian."

"And you didn't have to assume I might be the enemy." Sid Cannard sat behind his desk, pipe in hand, in an old leather chair before a wall of windows, a skeet-shooting jacket draped over his shoulders. He looked tired and troubled, but his pink cheeks were freshly shaved and his wickedly perspicacious eyes sparkled. "You could have come back to me with your suspicions—after all, I elucidated mine to you when you came in from Morocco."

"I realize that now, Sid."

"But you thought *I* was your penetration agent, obviously. Do you still think that?"

Shy took a deep breath. "I don't know, Sid. Nearly everything you suggested to me has turned out to be true."

"Now you understand why I was distressed about Fowler getting a subscription—you *think*. I'll tell you one more thing: You don't have it yet. And I can't tell you what I suspect to be true, because I don't *want* it to be true, and I can't afford to color your perceptions at this moment, in case fortune smiles and I turn out to be mistaken. I wanted to keep this in the family. With Jack down, perhaps, we'll have a chance at recovering our clandestine edge. I want you to finish your investigation as soon as possible—the EO's have reached closure, finally. Let me congratulate you on that—the intelligence benefits we received are no small advan-

tage. I always anticipate results from you, but this time you have
exceeded my expectations."

"I can't shut down my fieldwork."

"Why not?" The old man took his pipe from his mouth and
stared at Shy.

"Don't you want the leak plugged? Don't you want the penetration?"

"You're not going to find the culprit through Dropout."

"That has to be your personal opinion."

"John, I was sorry to hear about Michele's decision. I know you
mentioned that there was a problem, but I never imagined one
so grave...."

"It's not grave; it's over. It was grave three or four years ago.
Now it's just overdue. There's a point, at least for me, when everything I've been discounting or ignoring or bearing with in human
interactions becomes insupportable—beyond that point, I don't
want anything from subsequent events, unless it is to 'reach closure.'"

"My, my! We are forceful this morning. Am I supposed to be
frightened?"

"Only if you're the bad guy."

"It's a good thing you are irreplaceable, by current standards.
Don't presume to chastise me. I still pay your salary. I can decide
that having you independently verify my suspicions is a good use
of Innotech money. And I can decide that funding Dropout's
rehabilitation is not. Bring in some hard data that will convince
me he's worth keeping in ordnance by next week, or scrub him."

"You mean, scrub the go."

Cannard sighed feelingly. "No comment."

Shy stood up, dry-mouthed. "Sid, I don't think you're looking
at this objectively. Whatever was between Beth and Dropout isn't
my business or yours, but ever since the party you've been actually
obstructive. That doesn't help my perception of what your interest
in this might be—you gave me carte blanche, and as far as I'm
concerned I've got it as long as I'm on staff here. I can't work in
a compromised situation." He thought, "*Oh, Jesus, I shouldn't do
this, not yet;* but he said, "So if you like, you can have my resignation.
Of course—"

"Then it would be clear that I'm the bad guy. To you. For now.

Have you had Beth analyze your urine lately, John? You're acting like a paranoid. I'm not going to obstruct you; I won't force closure; I won't even try to keep you quiet if you decide to run over to Fowler's people or whomever you feel might be more sympathetic. Do you know why? Because no one is going to be any more sympathetic; for once, everyone is in the same boat—every one of the agencies apprised, the governments involved. At midlevel, nobody will know what you're talking about. At the top, the various deputy directors and their counterparts will want to do to you what they wanted to do—still want to do—to Dropout. Two Can Play doesn't exist. No one who knows much about it can exist outside the team structure. That is why I tried to keep you as ignorant as possible for as long as possible—I know how idealistic you are, and I value that quality in you. But now we are beyond the point where you can walk away. You may have trouble adapting to that, but it's the truth."

Shy stood before Sid's desk, touching things absently: a Baccarat ashtray, a moon rock, a little brassbound clock.

After giving Shy time to respond, Sid Cannard continued. "I've made some errors in judgment because, as lacking in originality as I risk sounding, you're like the son I wish I'd had. Can you entertain the notion that I didn't realize you and I would see the bounds of our own relationship tested during this most delicate of times? John, look at me."

Shy did.

"For whatever good it may do, you *can* count on my support. Remember that—you may find you have no option but to trust someone. And events themselves will prove that I am, still, that someone." He lit his pipe, smiled avuncularly. "You are going to New York, you said. When?"

"Now. I've got to go now. I've got Hubble on top of things here."

Cannard sat forward, extending his hand. "Well, have a good trip. You know how to reach me."

Shy grasped it. "Thank you, Sid."

"I'll be there myself in ten days or so. I hope you'll be back by then. I hope Beth will be back by then."

"Sid? I was going to ask you where she's been."

Cannard shuddered in mock terror. "She's at better stores

throughout Manhattan—shopping, heaven help me. She only shops when she's depressed, but she does it with a vengeance. Perhaps you'd look her up—she's at my place on lower Fifth—and see if you can put her in better spirits? Save me a frightful lot of money if you should."

He mumbled that he would be sure to, and made his way out to where Grover held the world at bay beyond Sid's portal. The secretary could not hide her relief to see them go.

He drove to the airport—he was taking his car to the States, an expensive but necessary piece of baggage. On the way there, he wondered what worried him most: Sid's continuing to play cat and mouse with him, or the fact that Beth was in New York and Sid wanted him to "look her up."

Chapter
13

AS dusk's patina settled over New York and through it a fairyland of lights began the long night's burn, Dania Morales padded from her wet room, naked but for a turban of toweling about her head, to call Cordell Hunt.

Her bedroom facing the park was at its best at this hour, washed in the magnificent changing shades of sky. She paused at the window, watching the placid swirl of headlights below. She had so much to lose; what she had was priceless; what she had learned must be worth something. She turned and surveyed her lair, taupe and night blues and lavender in sunset, its avant-garde furnishings pure in their lines: lacquer chairs and low bed hung with lamé and swathed in satin. She went and lay, still nude, among its cushions, curled up around the telephone.

She felt like a teen-ager, filled with a sense of danger, of delicious risk. She could not simply have Cordell Hunt killed—another would come, and another. She must solve the problem he represented, direct suspicion elsewhere, if that was still possible, bring matters to some acceptable conclusion, if one existed.

Since Wednesday she'd thought of little else, but she had decided upon nothing, no course of action beyond meeting with him again.

The local Soviet resident had had little enlightening to say about him or Innotech, had offered her vodka and assistance and played dumb.

The woman whose accentless voice she had come to know so well had called about the final gambit in their long project. Under duress, she had confirmed all that Cordell Hunt had said, but had offered no suggestions: It was Dania's problem, her tone had clearly indicated, as was the fact that one of the PCP's had confessed all to Innotech's regional director. The amount paid to Dania assured the woman of Dania's silence; the client was unconcerned, whoever she was, with Dania's troubles beyond ensuring that her outstanding contract would be fulfilled.

Dania had done her setup work in Maryland and flown back early. There was no use in pretending she had her mind on business. Diehl had stayed down there, smoothing out the inevitable rough edges. His advice had been to eliminate Cordell Hunt and any number of successors. He, too, thought there was too much at risk.

She had her own secrets to protect. Anyone who could do what Cordell Hunt had done—walk in and tell her flatly he was an agent of Innotech sent to destroy her and expect her to be able to see beyond the threat, to the value of the man choosing not to make it—any such man could unearth her secret. This she could not allow.

He is like Angel, she thought. Angel thought like that, moved like that, inscrutably and coldly valiant, full of righteousness and rage. There were not many like him in the world. She had made do with less often enough. Angel would want her to use Hunt, not destroy him.

She nodded to herself, stroking upward with her palm along her flat belly, one leg bent at the knee. She put the phone on her stomach and stared at the canopy above her head. Clarity emerged: She must not let him find out her secrets until she knew his—she must not allow matters to devolve to the point where she had to kill him or he must kill her.

For Angel Morales was dead; and Cordell Hunt, along with the rest of the world, must never find it out. So long as Angel was alive in the minds of their friends and foes, she was shielded by his aura. She drew power from his legend. Without it, she would be vulnerable, though for five years it had been she who carried out a multitude of exploits in his name, to glorify and perpetuate his experientialized philosophy of participatory freedom: A man deserves only what freedom he is willing to preserve.

Only Diehl knew. Diehl had been with her when they pulled Angel's steaming body from the wreckage of his bullet-riddled Cessna. Angel had made it back to base camp but died at the Cessna's controls during landing approach. The plane had cartwheeled along the runway before bursting into flames. She had managed to convince Diehl that some events were too terrible to be allowed to occur. They had acted in Angel's stead ever since and become wealthy, the former bodyguard and his employer. Diehl would do what Dania told him to do, as he always had done. But this time she could depend upon no surrogate—whatever was to be done, she must do it herself.

And in her way, she was ready. She had planned the evening, so far as was possible. It remained only to secure his agreement. She picked up the phone and listened to the little song the push buttons made; on her bedside table, a green light appeared on the phone analyzer's face. Around her, the last wisps of dusk faded and she lay in semidarkness with just the light from the skyline and the oscilloscope and digital readout on the CCS TA 2000 telephone analyzer to see by.

The desk connected her to the suite she identified by its number. Her neck tensed; a mild headache began to creep up toward her left ear, where the phone was cradled. It rang three times, and ceased. A voice said, "Yo? . . . Hello?"

It was not Hunt. She remembered the two of whom he had spoken. But he had not given her his work name; she didn't know how much they knew. She thought quickly, then said, "Good evening, is Scratch—"

"Oh, yeah. Sure thing. Hold on, okay? Okay?"

"Yes, fine."

She listened to distant voices, far from the receiver on the other end of the line. She found she was trembling, and she fluffed her damp pubic hair, smiling at her unaccustomed nervousness: Was this a bad time? She had told him she would call...

The receiver on the other end must have fallen; a new voice said, "Yes?"

"Cory."

"Yes. I was in the shower..." His tone changed perceptibly as he spoke; some previous irritation fled.

"So was I." *Inane twat,* she scolded herself. "I returned early. Are you..." *Say it!* "...free this evening?"

"I've been waiting for your call," he assured her, perhaps amused. "Shall we make an evening of it?"

The others. She was prepared. "I thought you might wish to talk privately. Perhaps you should come along as soon as is convenient, alone. Your friends, if they are the young Apollo and Hermes whom I saw stalking us in the bar, might drop by about nine. By then the dinner companions I have in mind for them will have arrived. Is that suitable?"

"I'll have to ask 'Apollo' and 'Hermes,' here. Hold on." Without palming the phone, he asked them if they would be amenable to "dinner and dates, or vice versa," then relayed their assent. "I'll be by in a while," he promised with the necessary ambiguity of tradecraft, and said adieu.

Fifteen minutes later, a sheer navy and gold-lamé striped robe belted about her, she still hadn't decided what to wear. She unwound the towel from her head and brushed out her hair, letting nature style it, then went to the kitchen and checked the food the staff had prepared. All were dismissed now; no one would be there to distress him. It was enough that she'd set the encounter on her own turf. She'd noted the caution that her proposal, and even oblique references to its specifics, had evoked in him.

She must remember how to ease such a one; it had been a long time since she'd needed to do so. She wandered from room to room, turning on lights and adjusting them to convivial dimness. In the living room, before its corporate suite's international decor, she paused and took stock of the great marble hearth, the fifth-century Athenian torsos, the Chinese bronzes. The fireplace reputedly worked; she'd never utilized it. It was not a room for him to see yet. She closed it off, along with her office and the secretary's. She left the study, with its gun cases, open; it was small and not so decorated, a private room where traces of Angel still lingered in the comfortable leather divans and the rough Spanish woods, heavy and carved. In the dining room, the domestics had done nicely; all she had to do was turn the oven on, if he would agree to an evening "in."

They buzzed her from the lobby; she bade them admit him, and stood by the kitchen video intercom, heart pounding and throat dry like a young girl's. *This is wonderful,* she thought, and still did not run into her bedroom to change. It was too late, really. She had first better let him in, get him settled. Her tongue darted out, caught a curl brushing her cheek, played with it. She felt naughty and exceedingly optimistic.

The chimes sounded; she went to the door, opened it. *"Per bene,"* she approved, appraising him, his quiet, casual dress, his carefully trimmed young beard, his sheltered eyes behind dark glasses.

He took the glasses off and said, "I'm too early?" looking her over frankly, his mouth pulled in slightly at one corner.

"Come in, please. I lost track of the time." As she had not been before, she was conscious of the robe's transparency, and her own, though she had not meant it.

He stepped in and closed the door, leaned against it, his eyes no more readable than they had been behind the sunglasses. "Are you alone?"

"Yes." She backed away from him, not wanting to compound her error by exposing her backside. "Please, take off your coat and look around. I'll just change and—"

"Not on my account, don't. It's just that I haven't been greeted by many temptresses lately; cutbacks, you know, in the Soviet prison system." He slipped off his jacket and held it out to her, revealing an LW Commander, suspended, barrel up, from a harness over his gray sweater; clips were strung on his belt. She came forward to take the jacket and hang it, and he moved in close behind her.

"On second thought, maybe you'd better go put on a sweatshirt or something; I'm not going to be able to think too clearly this way—unless that's what you've got in mind." His hands went around her waist as she reached for a hanger, slid upward and cupped her breasts. As if nothing at all were happening, she straightened his jacket on the hanger, then leaned back against him.

He put his mouth to her ear: "We can't do this, this is crazy. Angel will kill us both. Dear God..." He kissed her throat and ran one hand down her belly, parting her robe. "...Say something. Say no, if you've got any more sense than I have."

She turned her head and caught his lower lip between her teeth, twisting in his embrace, pressing against him, letting her body speak and lips act. After a long kiss that sent flame throughout her, she determined there was still too much suspicion in him, and arched backward. "I can't—"

He let her go, slapping her bottom. "Go get dressed then. I'll wait."

"—see any reason to fear the consequences of this," she continued, reproachfully. "We are both adults. Come with me while I change. We'll talk our business through, and"—she shrugged, preceding him down the deeply carpeted hallway to her bedroom—"when you are content, we'll see what develops."

She heard his harsh chuckle. "You've got my full attention, that's for sure."

He whistled through his teeth when he saw her bedroom, and avoided the bed, straddling one of the lacquer chairs, his chin propped on its back over folded arms. "Angel certainly has gotten loose these last few years. He used to bomb places like this on principle." She heard the thickness in his voice, felt his eyes on her. She recalled, like a distant dream, what she had wanted to accomplish with him tonight. Now she wanted only to disarm him, to strip him, to let the coldness of him quench the burning in her flesh.

She said, "Cory, this is madness." She let her robe fall away and went to stand before his chair. "Shall we pretend we do not feel? My relationship with Angel is...spiritual." He looked up at her; she touched his face. He said nothing.

She sighed and knelt down beside his chair. "I didn't know—who could know—that I'd feel this way. I'll make certain Angel understands."

"Great, he'll blow my dick off with understanding."

"I used to fantasize, in Bogotá, about us. ... Of course, then, it was impossible. Now, as I have said, my husband and I maintain a spiritual bond; we do not lie in carnal embrace anymore."

"You're telling me *you're* celibate?" But he unclipped his holster's strap and shrugged out of it.

She laughed lightly—"Something like, that,"—and leaned forward to help him with his belt. "Our problems are many, but Angel's jealousy will not be one of them."

Then his hand grasped hers. "I'm out of practice; I'm not promising anything." He got up from the chair and stripped down quickly; she saw that his ribs could yet be counted, and she saw scars that were not from shrapnel, and some that were.

This man needed healing; her heart ached for him, for the months of torture his body showed. Had they used electric shocks on his genitals? Was he afraid he couldn't perform? She could not ask, only make sure that failure was no part of what the evening held in store for him. Still kneeling, she embraced his thighs, as Angel had liked her to do, and began slowly to kiss her way upward.

She felt him trembling as he strove to stand perfectly still, then she had reached his groin and he wound his fingers in her hair and pulled her up. Full length, they stood, simply touching, and she could not control her breathing, while he said, "Shit, I can't take too much of this," and gathered her up in his arms, lifting her legs from the floor. Held that way, arms clasped about his neck, she realized that he was not lacking in strength, but had lost the layer of protective fat that big men tend to carry. He laid her lightly on her pillows and sat beside her, his feet on the floor. He smiled at the TA 2000, seemingly, and just stroked her, saying nothing, looking at her with his armored eyes until she reached for him.

Then he slipped away, got his gun, and brought it to the bedside table with a grimace and an eloquent hand motion—he was what he was, she must understand.

She pulled him down to her by the hair and whispered in his ear, "Mount me. We will set an endurance record some other time."

"My pleasure," he whispered back, and spread her legs gently. He was atop her only a few moments when sweat broke out on

his forehead and she saw him blanch. He grunted and rolled them
both over so that she was on top, saying, "Easy, take it easy now,
nice and slow—*don't* move."

"*Comienzen fuego.*" Commence firing, she breathed in Spanish.
"We have all night to spend; we can indulge ourselves." And she
began, with her vaginal muscles, to bring him along. It took very
little, and his hands squeezing her buttocks returned the favor,
so that she forgot to be concerned about his faring, and drove
her own pleasure home.

They lay a time in silence, her sweat drying with his. When he
shifted, she would have rolled off him, but he said, "No, stay.
Dania, you're—we're ... What the fuck are we going to do now?"

"Ssh." Then: "It's up to you. As little, or as much, as you want
of me; as much help as I can be to you ... What I have is yours."

"Angel—"

"What *we* have is yours. It is decided." Then she did roll off
him. "Do you mind if I smoke?" She couldn't lie to him with him
inside her. She didn't want to lie to him. He had been right, they
were courting disaster. She hadn't had sex like this since the early
days with Angel.

"Only if you'll give me one, too."

"What? Oh, cigarettes. Surely." She took a pack out of her
drawer and he took them, and her lighter, lit two while she found
an ashtray, took the ashtray from her and put it on the line of
dark straight hair running down his belly to his groin. "Here."
He patted the pillow beside him; she nestled down in the crook
of his arm.

He put his arm around her neck and tickled one of her nipples
with his finger. She noted the fresh scars. "Did they hurt you
much, the Soviets?"

He snorted softly, but she felt him tense. "I tried to kill myself,
get them mad enough to kill me. When I finally gave up and tried
to cooperate with them, they were sure I'd just gotten my second
wind and was trotting out some new deception. It would have
been funny if it didn't hurt so much—nobody would take my
surrender, they were so sure I was some goddamned superspy."

"I'm sorry."

"Me, too. Most of me is in working order, at least a good deal
of the time, so I guess I can't complain."

All agents need handlers, she thought. *He is no exception. I can run him and win with him, and even help him.* She said, "Now you must tell me what you have and what you need, so that we can settle on a strategy before your friends arrive. I want, for safety's sake, to be able to see for myself their reaction to what we propose."

"All right. I've got the two assets you're going to meet—Flak and Mino; I've got Innotech thinking I'm their boy; I've got a time limit, though I don't know exactly how long, before the end of which I've got to have at least opened negotiations with Angel. Immediately, I need some take to feed Innotech until I figure out a way to get out from under them. Or I need a quick exit—a nice eighteen-month tour somewhere on hazard pay..."

"Even you must know you're not fit enough for that—look at you." She ran her hand over his prominent ribs. "But your serious proposal—this is intriguing. You want to be *my* double, feeding spurious information back to your Innotech handler, if I don't misunderstand you. But how could it work?"

"Look...John Shy's orders were open: Find some way to stop the attacks on Innotech. If you're done harassing them for whom-ever, perhaps you two would consider a preemptive bid—a re-tainer *not* to operate against them. It would take time to try to negotiate something like that—time is what we all need. You must be aware—as Angel will be when you tell him what I've said—that if I fail, or seem to have failed, somebody else will take over where I've left off. You've got problems to solve with Innotech as well as I do. I'm not asking you to compromise any sources, or even to put me in the picture as to what's going on here, but I've got to convince you I'm right—that our interests have effectively converged, and that *both* our interests will be served by making it seem that I've succeeded in convincing Angel that Innotech is a better friend than foe. They've given me a quarter-million Swiss francs on account, that much again is promised me on delivery, so they're concerned enough to risk at least half that amount—I don't think they expect to pay out the rest. But they didn't argue when I named a figure—*that* means they're pretty damned de-termined..."

"What is it you are expected to deliver? Our bodies?" She had pulled away from him in spite of herself.

"They'd like that, of course. But they'll settle for information,

I think. I've been as careful as I know how to be. I took that suite so that I wouldn't have to be running back and forth *to* here. I don't think they know exactly where you are, though I had to let them keep tabs on me or risk their deciding I'd turned on them. I've refused standard backup and reporting procedures—just in case we worked something out—but they're around, make no mistake."

She pulled up her knees, encircling them with her arms. He put a hand on her flank. She said, "I'm not sure I have any information which would be helpful."

"What?"

"This particular client is exceedingly security-conscious. A woman calls me; perhaps she is a cutout, perhaps a principal— she has no accent whatsoever. Whatever she is, whomever she represents, I have never met her. The moneys arrive in my Geneva account as agreed once the work is completed. I know no more than that. Is it enough?"

"For now, if you let me relay that information, it will have to be. Since what's been going on is not your personal vendetta, I can start by confirming that. But if you've got another project on line for her—against Innotech…"

"I don't know, Cory, what to do, how far I can trust you. As the Americans say, you are more than just another pretty face, this is clear. What Angel will think, I cannot be certain. But I will tell you that we are aware how much you risked, coming to us with this. In the beginning we had no idea these piecemeal actions were to be part of a radical campaign. We had no desire to anger Innotech. We do not vie with them for clients. It is simply money."

"Speaking of which, have you anything at all on the boards for me to hook in to? I've got bills to pay and those two assets to keep busy."

She got up abruptly. "I must wash up. Come, you haven't seen the wet room." She slid across him, and his hands were reluctant to lose contact. He followed, saying nothing at all about the black and silver playroom of matte Italian tile with its computerized "enviroment" that produced anything from sauna steam to "summer rain," and its Jacuzzi and its wall-mounted Universal weight-trainer. He merely crossed his arms and waited for her answer.

It had been a long time since a man had stood there, unconcerned, while she cleansed herself. She was cold now with uncertainty. Her flesh crawled. Who could say what was true and what was disinformation, what he meant and what he only needed her to think he meant? If he was sincere, she knew she could solve both their problems. She said, "I have a project in the works. It is—she took a deep breath under motionless scrutiny—"—a final gambit for the client in whom you are interested.... Oh, Cory, I don't know—"

"Trust me, I won't let you take a fall on my account. Let me on board; you don't know anything more than what I told you the other night; you can't be responsible for my unilateral or treacherous action. At worst, you can say you were taken in by my deception. Whatever happens, you'll be all right. As for me, I'm here to infiltrate you; I have to show some signs of success. If you let me tell them that there's one more leg to the go, not only will you help me, you'll help yourself: if I'm in midpenetration, they won't bother your operation—it's too early. The first go in an infiltration is traditionally a gift to the operative; if they even try to overview it, they'll be risking the bona fides they're trying to give me. So you'll have carte blanche. My assets will be working. I'll take whatever the standard pay scale is in your shop. Nobody loses, not even Innotech—yet. What do you say?"

"It is frightening even to consider that you might, after all, be my enemy."

"I've been thinking the same thing about you." He turned away and disappeared behind a partition of tile. She heard water; he was using the toilet.

She said, "Then, we will work toward trust on both sides. As ex-Triage/Innotech personnel engaged in a penetration, could you provide me with some technical information: the electrooptical surveillance specs for a house in Maryland that Triage wired? It is the only weak spot, the only pertinent information we are still lacking."

She heard his chuckle. "They'd have to give it to us. Flak would be the way to go. He's putatively my handler in the field. I've kept him away from them, but we'll see what he says. If he's straight up, it shouldn't be a problem. If he's not, I need to know about it." He emerged from behind the partition; she could see him in the mirror. He came up and put his hands around her waist, nuzzling her hair. "I've got to tell you, I feel like I've been given a new lease on life. However this turns out—thank you."

She leaned back against him, watching them both in the mirror. "Don't thank me yet, Cory. Certainly not until morning—you must stay the night."

"I can't." He let her go and muttered something about "getting dressed, it's late."

She reached out to stop him. "Why not? You have an obligation to build my confidence, if only for appearance's sake. I cannot let it be known that I am the 'pushover.'"

He avoided her reach, twisting away, retreating. From the bedroom proper, she heard: "I can't. I don't sleep well."

She followed in time to see him bend carefully, back straight, to retrieve his briefs and clothing from the floor. "You're joking. Is it me? Or is it your young friends?"

"I wish I were." He grunted, straightened up, threw his clothes to her bed and went there, sat beside them. "I have nightmares; sometimes I get noisy; sometimes I wake up and don't know where I am.... I just can't. I'd drive you nuts."

"I, too, have nightmares," she admitted, blinking back tears. "Sometimes the same one, over and over again. And I wake, some nights, weeping. So perhaps together we will not have bad dreams, or, having them, at least there will be someone to hold until the worst moments pass."

He said, "Yeah. Okay, it's worth a try," very low. "Do you want to tell me what the go is you've got on?"

"We prevent a handover, retrieve the item which is the subject of the meeting—it's something small enough to fit in a nine-by-twelve folder. And that is all, at this moment, I can tell you."

"Fair enough."

"And you, may I ask you an inappropriate question? I have answered enough of them."

He nodded, standing to fasten his pants.

"You said when last we met that Innotech's leverage on you was in the person of a woman whom they hold. How does she fit in to what you've proposed?"

"I don't know, yet. Maybe not at all. I can only do my best. I sent a quarter of my first Innotech payment to her ... shop, I guess we could call it. If they're smart, they'll use it to buy her way out. She's got more friends than I do. If they don't help her, I'll have to try to get her out of the mess I got her into—then I can walk away. If that sounds callous, I'm sorry."

"No, you're not."

"You're right, I'm not. So I'm not going to apologize for anything else. I'm a professional expedientist." He shrugged, sat back down, and slipped on his socks. "Where would you like to go to eat? I owe you the best dinner this town has to offer."

"Will you eat in? Everything is prepared, in case you agreed."

He laughed a boyish laugh she had not heard before. "You win. I'm outflanked again."

Waiting for Flak and Mino, they had played "Was this your go?" He had asked her if they had been involved in the SDS bombing, in 1970, of the Center for International Affairs housed in Harvard's Semitic Museum, and she had admitted they had a "hand" in it. She had asked him about the PLO moderate shot outside their Vienna office, and he'd agreed that it was "my signature, all right." They came down the years and stopped at the time they "joined forces" as if by mutual agreement.

He was sure by then that she didn't know he had turned on them during the Bogotá kidnapping's final stages. The only way that could have happened was if Angel hadn't mentioned it; and the only circumstances Hunt could envision that would allow for such an oversight were those in which Angel never made it home— or came home with a bullet in his brain. Angel Morales either was dead or had suffered a wound trauma with amnesia as a complication. He couldn't quite believe the "or." Any wound severe enough to cause discrete amnesia shouldn't have been treatable in the Brazilian bivouac's first-aid tent. His team had covered every hospital facility and internist known to be sympathetic to the rebels, expecting to pick up at least one or two that way. And there had been three or four others who escaped with him—none of them pilots. Hunt had personally taken out the other two capable of flying a plane.

Then none of them had gotten home. Or only Angel had survived, but lost his memory in some way that did not entail a bullet in his brain. Hysterical amnesia? He didn't believe it. It didn't feel right. So she was lying.

The reasons for perpetuating Angel's legend were obvious

enough. But who was running the shop? A very successful, international shop, at that—there had to be someone mastermind-
ing things. He kept trying to fit a damaged but cognizant Angel
into the picture, maybe paralyzed, writing out his orders with a
pencil held between his teeth.... No way. He couldn't be making
a deal with a guy he'd hurt that badly. He remembered there had
really been a man with her in the Baur Au Lac; the records said
they traveled as Mr. and Mrs. Diehl. Dania hadn't mentioned any
"Diehl": Was "Diehl" Angel's work name? He looked at her. No
one was running this shop without her. Maybe it *was* her show:
no Angel; a real Diehl, somewhere, just muscle.

There was no reason it couldn't be true. But he wanted it to be
true. He didn't want there to be an Angel Morales at this juncture.
So he kept discounting it. It was much more likely, he told himself,
"helping" her turn on the oven and put a bowl of chopped raw
onions on the dining-room table, that Angel was just waiting for
his moment—that she was playing her part in their revenge upon
him for all the harm he'd caused them. They wanted him to think
Angel was dead, of course. It was the perfect out for everyone
involved.

But it was hard to imagine Angel Morales putting up with this
show of opulence and corporate-level power. The hand-painted
porcelain and the silver beside and above each plate were anything
but modest. The goblets had angels' heads sculpted into their
stems and wings cut into their bowls. The table beneath them was
covered in appliquéd linen. He figured, absently, that he must be
looking at nearly a thousand American dollars in tableware per
diner. It was all as upscale as could be, and fanciful, the sort of
frivolous largesse only a woman could do well—or a gay designer.
Austere Angel used to balk at replacing tin-and-enamel cups when
they chipped.

"Dania," he said, "are you two separated—officially, I mean?
Is it business only? I really would feel better if I could talk to
him."

"Yes, we are separated. And no, you cannot talk to him. He is
nowhere he can be reached." The tone said she would answer no
further questions about him. Her downcast eyes and taut shoulders said that he'd hit the same nerve once too often.

He was regretting having asked when she came up behind him,
tugged on the strap of his harness, and reproved that even Angel

"does not go armed in this house. Come with me." She wiped her hands and took off the apron she had on over her long, loose, v-necked cashmere sweater. Beneath it, she wore nothing; her tanned legs, below the white sweater's end at midthigh, were long and shapely. In her "wet room," he had seen no sign of a resident male, yet the sweater, reaching almost to her knees, was a man's.

The room she took him to, past three closed doors whose alarms were activated, made him caution himself: Best not to let wishing blind him to truth. Here was Angel: Winchester elephant guns and custom Purdeys; Czech Skorpions and Kalashnikovs; a fifteen-shot 9mm Beretta 92S and a Walther PPK. There were, less obviously displayed, phosphorous and fragmentation grenades, stun grenades, tear-gas canisters, and Soviet nasties: bullet pens and poison dispensers of a dozen sorts.

The ash book walls were filled with treatises and journals: Kant, Marx, Lenin, Marighella, Qaddafi, Leibniz, Churchill—everything from *On War* by Clauswitz to Marshal Sokolovsky's *Voyennaya Strategiya (Military Strategy)*. The journals ranged, in English, from the hardware, hard-data purveyors like *Jane's Defence Weekly*, *Defense Electronics* and *Aviation Week* to the opinion-mongers such as *International Security*, *Foreign Policy* and *Foreign Affairs*. The French, German, Russian, and Spanish collection mirrored his interests: lots of publications from the Soviets' United States and Canada Institute, radical leftist efforts like *Covert Action* and *CounterSpy*. Somebody was doing a bit of technical reading in addition. He saw a number of defense-community in-house publications on specific systems proposals.

"Knowing we are so well armed, can't you now put your gun away?" *Won't* you *trust* me?

"It would look funny to my people. I'm not that certain of them yet. I haven't taken them into my confidence—they're working blind. Anything can happen—I might have to protect *you* from them."

"We will tell them, too—house rules."

He could not give in, dared not disarm. Graciously, she accepted his excuses, saying she would "set a good example" by giving him a tour of her security system. It was quite impressive. He hadn't seen as much as he would have liked when the buzzer summoned them to ID Flak and Mino's "dates."

He caught himself thinking that if *he* had had a woman like

Dania to help him, he might have been able to put something like this together himself.

She didn't miss a move or a nuance; the women in the monitor were lovely young head-turners, and—Dania assured him—discreet. "Politically aware and realistic," she confided as they awaited the two ladies at the door.

"Operatives, you mean?"

"Professionals, yes. Neither of us can afford any wild cards tonight. They are on my payroll. If you like, I can direct them to extract information most subtly from your assets—the one you worry over, he is 'Flak'?—or simply to engage them in harmless activity, or tell them nothing and let your agents fare as best they may."

"I'd prefer to keep it loose—tell them they're all in the same business and leave it at that."

"As you wish, Cory."

The door chimes sounded and at the same time the buzzer went off again. "Go tell the desk to admit your people." She smiled at him, tapping his nose. "And don't look so worried. As you say, we will 'keep it loose.'"

Hearing the tinkle of feminine laughter from the vestibule, in her kitchen he tried to separate his emotions from his reason as he told the Puerto Rican voice downstairs that these two were indeed invited guests. He'd made one crucial error in briefing Flak and Mino—he had told them too much when he'd told them about the Bogotá penetration. At the time, it had seemed the only fair and prudent thing to do. Now it made them liabilities, in possession of information that could incriminate him and blow the entire operation if Dania truly did *not* know what Hunt had done to her and Angel years ago. He'd warned them not to mention Bogotá when he came back from that first meeting with her. It would be enough, he hoped.

Shit. He went to join the others. It was too early to rule anything out. He had all night to interview her. They would see which one of them was better at what they both did well.

He just hoped Flak and Mino were perceptive enough to realize those two women were going to be pumping them for all they were worth.

As he had expected, Dania and her "friends" chatted by the

coat closet; he wasn't going to be able to get even a moment alone
with his assets before the starting gun went off. He had told them
what to do, how to dress, to come on guard and fully armed and
ready to walk away from base with only what they had on them.
Nobody could do any more than that. He couldn't let his affection
for them blur his objective. They wanted to play in the major
leagues. Now they were going to pass muster—or not—this evening, in the espionage game. He wished he had leaned harder on
tradecraft when he was training them, but he hadn't had time or
even the slightest inkling that he was going to play them the hard
way.

The two women were definitely better mousetraps: one sultry
with a long fall of black hair, a cream and jet greyhound of a girl
in a parachute-nylon jump suit and lizard cowboy boots—"Trish";
the other blonde with a Côte d'Azur tan, a sun-worshiping athlete
in a buttery suede dinner dress that left one shoulder bare and
impossibly high heels—"Liz." They were what in the trade one
called "sure shots."

He greeted them politely; the one with the heels stepped out
of them as Dania explained they would be dining "at home." You
could send women like this out as casually as a hunter dispatches
a retriever to bring in a duck. Flak and Mino weren't worth this
much trouble; Dania had these ladies on tap for something else,
and he was willing to bet he would be finding out that the "something" had to do with the operation she was mounting.

The chimes did not sound this time; they were playing at being
girls for him, taking turns at the peephole and giggling mischievously. The greyhound eyed him levelly as Dania opened the door,
remarking upon his Lebanese Christian T-shirt: "An unwinnable
war."

"My specialty," he admitted, wishing he'd put his sweater back
on. He was taking this whole thing too casually. He crossed his
arms.

Flak had his effects bag with him; Mino grinned from ear to
ear when he saw Hunt, and elbowed his companion: "Pay up,
sucker." Flak hushed him, gravely taking Dania's hand. "*Enchanté,
mademoiselle.*"

Hunt stepped in quickly before Flak could kiss Dania's hand or
Mino burst out laughing, took charge of the introductions, and

worried about what was going to happen when they took off their coats. He didn't even have to wait that long.

Flak, unshouldering the bag to give it to Hunt, said, "I'm being vibrated. These—" Something in his bag began to beep. "Damn, I thought I turned that off." The vibrator clipped on his belt was activated in the presence of a transmitter's field. "It's my nine o'clock alarm," he bluffed, and felt around in the bag. The beeping stopped. Everyone but Mino was watching.

Hunt, shaking his head, muttered, "Okay, sweetie, I hope you're ready for this," as he took Flak's jacket and hung it, hearing Trish's deep voice declare that *she* had shot herself in the left buttock the first time she had "had to draw fast from an FBI carry in a social situation."

Flak looked about slowly, as if in a dream, then approached her, saying, "I'll show you mine if you'll show me yours."

Hunt was sure then that only luck was going to get them through this unscathed.

Mino and Liz were already deep in conversation. "Mino, Dania tells me you're familiar with the new Bells. Have you had a chance to get your hands on a TiltRotor? Seems like my dream aircraft. We've got an XV-Fifteen TiltRotor coming on Monday—takes off like a helicopter and converts to a 345-mph airplane in twelve seconds. I *can't wait*. . . ." "Monday, you say? If we don't have any conflicts, I'd be real interested in getting some time in one of those myself. . . ." They disappeared down the carpeted corridor, leaving Dania and Cory facing one another, she holding Mino's jacket.

"Do you think that's fair?" he asked.

"I think that for Flak it was love at first sight. They should get to know one another. They'll be working together, after all."

"In Maryland?"

"Unless you've changed your mind." She hung Mino's jacket and came to him. "Cory, it is for the best. We shall test their loyalty. As you say, you can't be certain of them yet. With luck, you will become certain, and then have one less worry. That is what I have decided you need—you are carrying too great a load. Let me share it."

"I—don't know how. I'm going to have a little talk with Flak. He shouldn't have brought that electronic arsenal of his up here."

"*Niente*. It's nothing. I understand." She reached up to him, brought his head down to hers. "They're young, let them learn. You cannot save them from life."

"I never told you Mino was familiar with Bells."

"An American pilot, jet and helicopter, you said." She pursed her lips. "Now, you don't drink, is this still so? Do you mind if they do? And recreational drugs, shall I offer them? Or not? We"—she locked her fingers at the nape of his neck and on tiptoe leaned against him—"have been so busy with ourselves, we have both forgotten our basics. And we are host and hostess, after all."

He gave in, gave up, kissed her, knowing he had better stick close to his honest emotions—they were obvious enough, and appropriate enough, and he was floundering trying to anticipate her attempts to anticipate him.

Their little party reconvened in the gun room. To get there, he had to pass the three locked and computer-armed doors. Before he left here, he was going to see what was behind each one, and finish his tour of her security system.

Once they had settled on the divans with their drinks and Flak shook a joint from his cigarette pack, Hunt excused himself to make a cup of coffee with the miniature brass espresso machine he'd seen in the kitchen. He was too tense to sit there and spoil all their fun. Dania wondered if he could manage by himself; he assured her he could.

Flak came ambling in a few minutes later, holding out something shiny like a chrome flatworm. "Don't talk to me now," Hunt warned, not wanting to say even that much, took his cup and said, "Come on."

Flak put the strip of metal tape back in his pocket and accompanied him. "It's okay, boss. We're having a great time. They're super. *She's* super. Thanks for letting us come." Dissembling. Hunt wasn't in the mood.

"What was that 'pay up, sucker' about?"

"Uh—we had a bet, whether you'd fuck her first or later. Mino figured, since you went out with your holster over a sweater and now you're down to your undershirt... Is he right?"

"Maybe. How much was the bet, and who pays whom?"

"Five bills, sir. And if you did, I lose. I didn't think you'd risk it—"

"You'd better pay him. It's a good lesson for you to learn. Sometimes you do what's expected of you, even when it happens to be something like that."

It was Dania, a few minutes later, who broached business, saying that Cory and she had "agreed upon a joint endeavor."

Everyone voiced their pleasure at that revelation; when she made it clear that the women were part of the operation, Mino whooped and Flak, his eyes on Hunt and slitted, put his arm around the greyhound's shoulder and whispered in her ear.

"Don't start counting chickens, gentlemen." Hunt took over. "We have to buy in. We've got to come up with the security specs for a system Triage put into the Maryland house in question: intrusion-detection systems—microwave, laser, seismic, seismic/magnetic—closed circuit television, computer locks, peripheral lighting, the whole shooting match. So, Flak, it's up to you whether this is a social one-night stand or the beginning of a business arrangement. Can you get us that information?"

Flak was still as a statue; his girl peered up at him. He took his arm from her shoulder and stretched it out straight on the sofa's back. "I . . . How much is it going to be worth to us to get it? Who are—"

"Flak, yes or no." Hunt cut him off.

"Yes, *sir*. How soon do you need it? I know somebody, but I can't get to him on the weekend."

"Dania?"

"Early next week will be satisfactory. The sooner is better, of course."

"Of course," Flak echoed, face white and interrogatory stare still fixed on Hunt.

"Shit—excuse me, Liz—*I* can get it if he can't. Hey, Cory, they've got a TiltRotor. Even at treetop level to underfly radar, it's a cinch. Our part, anyway." Mino grinned at the blonde, who crossed her tanned legs. "You've got to excuse Flak, he's nervous—we're way out on a limb here, maybe in over our heads. It's not every day you switch horses—"

"Don't put words in my mouth. I'm concerned that I don't know what's going on and I'm already on the spot. If I'm on somebody's payroll other than yours, boss"—Flak spoke to Cory now—"I've got a right to know about it."

Hunt could have shot him dead. He said, "In another minute—"

Dania, who had been decorously far from him, on the divan's opposite end, broke in, simultaneously moving into a reclining position, her head close to Hunt's lap. "We will tell you all you need to know, Flak, when the time is right. But your question is valid. Your allegiance remains where it has been all along. I have hired Cory, and whatever arrangements he has made, or will make, with you and your friend are between you three. Does that ease your mind?"

"I wouldn't say so. But at least I know where I stand. That'll have to do, for—"

A beeper went off somewhere. "I was sure I turned that off," Flak mumbled, rising.

Dania rose, too. "That's our dinner bell. Come, Cory, let us serve the feast."

He had to go with her. In the kitchen she said, "They're cautious, but they should be. They love you—you didn't tell me that."

"I told you I'd turned them. How did you think I managed it, with promises of wealth beyond their wildest dreams? What can I tell them about their money?"

She named a price; he agreed—it was neither too much nor too little—and told her he was going to have to speak to Flak privately. She smiled at him, shaking her head. "You worry too much about me, Ifrit. Talk to him. Ease your soul."

He collared Flak and took him into Dania's wet room, closed the doors, ran the taps full. "Let's see the tape."

"Like you said, not now. It can wait until we go back to the hotel; I'm sorry I showed it to you."

"I'm staying here tonight."

"Christ, Cory, don't push me like this. I come in and you're making yourself right at home...what am I supposed to think? What's her husband going to think?"

"You're supposed to be smart enough to think that I got lucky, and sophisticated enough to realize that he'll think what she wants him to think. If you're not up to this, you can still bow out. No hard feelings. Mino and I can handle it alone if we have to."

Without a word, Flak handed him the chrome-colored Dymo marker tape. It had a series of numbers on it. "It's from an emergency fallback plan I don't think you heard about: If we lost contact...the dead drop was to be Shy's car—you know, the Stealth Mondial. Well, it's parked outside the hotel. I walked by like I was supposed to, and this was taped on the door handle, like it was supposed to be. Now from here on, it gets tricky. I have to respond within three hours if I want to leave a message. Otherwise, I've got to call this number at nine tomorrow morning."

"You haven't called yet, or left a message yet?"

"Would I do that without talking to you?"

"Good enough. Call. You've got a request to make—we need that data."

"But what do I tell him?"

"Well, unless you blew it back there with your worried-amateur act, you can tell him we're in and we're rolling and to keep his nose out of it. As a matter of fact, get some more numbers from him; it'd suit me if he'd start sitting by the phone. I'm going to want to brief him sometime between now and next Wednesday— verbally, someplace safe. See what you can set up."

He saw the tension drain from the asset, his color return. "Thanks, sir. Thanks a lot."

"Any time, Flak. Let's go eat."

Flak turned off the taps. "Cory? Is it okay to mix it up with those ladies?"

"Fine with me. Just remember they're probably smarter than you are."

Flak smiled disarmingly. "Yes, sir. I'll keep it in mind. And—"

"*Yes*, Flak. This is terrible procedure—we're being most conspicuous."

"I know, sir. It won't happen again. But I just thought you'd like to know—Fowler's going to be okay. I bought a paper, and it says he's doing nicely."

"You still don't understand, do you? I can't be—*we* can't be concerned with that right now."

The dinner was reminiscent of Angel's taste only in the Panamanian chili, served midway through with corn and raw onions. Mino, looking at the array of silverware before him, caught Hunt's eye quizzically. Cory indicated that Mino should do as he did, picking up the outside fork and dealing unequivocally with the asparagus in puff pastry topped with orange sauce that Dania served with the first wine. Each woman served a course; each man cleared a course. When they had come down to salad, coffee, and desserts, he and Dania dawdled in the kitchen, surveying the havoc of dishes and sherbets and glasses the elaborate dinner had produced. Mino and Flak had drunk deeply of all three wines and were talking of taking the athlete and the greyhound dancing. Hunt would be relieved to see them go.

"You can't eat like this all the time. You'd get fat and sickly."

"No, but I wanted it to be special for you. You hardly ate."

"I ate the chili. I remember you used to make it—what, twenty quarts at a time?"

She pushed down on the espresso maker's handle; steam hissed and gurgled. "At the least, I think we've succeeded in broadening your friends' horizons. I wanted you to be impressed, when I planned the menu; now I want you to be...proud of what we have here."

"You're going too fast for me."

"I don't think so."

She offered him his coffee: "To keep you going while I ready the rest."

He reached for her instead. "I wish they'd leave."

She giggled, pushing him away. "They will, be patient. I have it well in hand."

And she did. In less than an hour, the ladies were being helped into their coats while Hunt tried to decide what among the remnants of the meal was worth saving.

He came out of the kitchen just in time to hear Flak asking Dania for her phone number: "I don't mean to be forward, Mrs. Morales, but I'd like to make sure we can get in touch with each other in case—in case you need me." Hunt slipped back a few steps, flattened himself against the wall. Flak's voice was low, conspiratorial. "He says he's staying the night. Ma'am, I don't mean any offense, but I've been sort of taking care of him; he's been through a pretty rough time. He's...sometimes he loses track of things—people, places. Not often, but *some*times.... If anything happens like that, it's always at night. If— Aw, *damn* it: If he holds you at gunpoint or anything, don't freak, just talk him back. You know, let him know where he is, that everything's okay. Or call me and I'll come right over. I haven't been more than a room away from him ever since we brought him in from Marrakech. I hate to leave him where somebody might not understand what—"

"Flak, you're very sweet. I'll take good care of him, don't worry. I have seen men much worse. It is...one of the occupational hazards of his profession. Go have a splendid evening. Here. Call any time before two, if you wish. To say goodnight."

"Great. Thanks. Hey—don't tell him I said anything, okay?"

"I wouldn't think of it. Goodnight— Oh, Cory, say goodnight to our guests. I was on my way to fetch you."

"Goodnight, Flak, don't forget your effects bag."

When they had gone, he asked to see the rooms she had kept closed. She agreed to open them, but she kept looking at him askance. Finally she said, "Your young friend meant no harm. I find his concern charming."

"Yeah, wonderful. 'Here's this basket case, be careful with him.'"

"Cory, that *is* unfair. He's an agent; he was simply setting up his own line of communication. I thought he did it very well— he was more than a little drunk."

"He should have asked me."

"Perhaps, but wouldn't you then have had to ask me? Your doubts about him are increasingly grave, is this so? Or did he unwittingly hurt your feelings, and you're punishing him? It's not prudent to punish loyalty."

She tapped out a combination on the digital keyboard, switchplate-size, beside the first door: "D-A-N-I-A," she explained, "the numerical values of the letters of my name plus three: This is this month's master code. It will open any of these."

He realized that she had finished playing house—for now. She, too, must have questions.

Then he stood in the middle of the war room and felt uncomfortable.

Dania was saying, walking ahead, "I want you to have the run of the place. If there's anything here you don't understand..." She trailed off, peered over her shoulder, came back, and slid her arm through his. "Now, this is what we show the world, Cory; it is meant to dazzle, but not to dazzle you." She led him past the conference table and the wall of Lucite overlay maps and light-studded ceiling and racked electronics with computer consoles nestled beneath. "Back here"—she took him through a rosewood door—"is the business end."

All the room surveillance and alarm systems and troubleshooting devices—from those that detected explosive vapors to those that pinpointed the locations where security had been breached—were gathered together. A screen under the motion-sensor system had frozen its last videotape frame of Dania and him entering the restricted area. The phone links included database, computer time sharing, satellite-bounced long-distance, and what seemed to be an illicit buy-in to somebody's corporate trunk line. Each system had its own tap monitors, header monitors, and provisions for transmitting written reports across telephone lines.

"This looks like the Triage system they had where they boxed me for debriefing—Innotech, I mean."

"A former employee of theirs is responsible, I believe. I feel it is important you realize we are secure—you're safe here. You can afford to relax."

"I felt safe in Afghanistan. How many people work here—not your payroll, just who's going to show up here tomorrow morning, and at what ungodly hour?"

"Tomorrow is Saturday. Only the couple who take care of the house, and I told them not to come until noon. They won't bother you; they are invisible and invincible—they create order amid my chaos."

"Let's get out of here." He rewound the cassette with their images, erased it, set the unit to rearm after a five-minute delay, checked to see that no other machine was recording, and ushered her through into the hall. "Phew. Is the rest like that?"

"No. Cory, what's wrong?"

"Nothing. Three plus the letters of your name, you said? Let's see...that's seven, four, seventeen, twelve, four." The red light beneath the little wall-mounted push buttons disappeared, a green one came on. "My office, quite free of gadgetry, as you see. None of the private rooms we use has any surveillance, only counter-surveillance. But in the business world, I have found people's memories hazy, on occasion, as to the exact wording of agreements they have made. In a situation like mine, where verbal contracts are binding, it is well to store referential data."

"You wouldn't have tapes of your conversations with—" He stopped, seeing from her face that it was too early, changed direction "me? Of me calling here, even, and leaving my name? I was betting you wouldn't keep tapes—they can fall into the wrong hands. Will you destroy anything you've got on me?"

She said she would be glad to do so, and took him into her secretary's office, where his initial call would have been logged. Her return call, she assured him, had been made on her bedroom line, which was never monitored.

He must be careful. His body was giving him a lot of static, responding to hers; she had had him playing house, and he had liked it; even after seeing her security system, the greater part of him still wanted, most of all, to get her back into bed. The analyst in him was concurring; right now, there was no more prudent move.

But she, too, was maneuvering: She took him through the secretary's office and a door beyond, which shielded two additional bedrooms from view. "These have their own exit; one can come and go and not disturb the rest of the house."

"For friends in need?"

She nodded. "Everyone has to drop out of sight now and again." She leaned against the spare bedroom's doorframe; her hip brushed his. "Cory, will you move your team in here? Until the operation is over?"

"No."

"Will you stay, yourself, until then? I know you have many questions; if I'm to answer them, you must show good faith. I can't give you specifics at the depth you would prefer if you won't live in—"

"Standard procedure, I know. Yes, surely, which of these rooms?"

She turned, leaning against the frame, impish. "No, no. You I must watch more closely...."

He gathered her against him. "This closely?"

"At least this closely. Have you never dreamed of being kept by a beautiful woman? I won't be as hard on you as either the Soviets or your Innotech hosts."

Chapter 14

FLAK had brought the car and Hunt went down to meet him. Their rendezvous with John Shy had been set for 2200 hours, somewhere in Central Park this Sunday evening. Much more complex meets had been suggested, but Hunt had refused to dress up like a towing firm's representative or a mechanic, or sidle into Shy's favorite sushi bar or whisper together in consecutive seats at the Met or sit like an NRA target in the UN's public gallery while Shy debriefed him. Innotech on Madison was out of the question; fitting rooms or men's rooms in posh department stores or restaurants occluded his escape routes, not to mention his sight pictures: He wanted a clear field of view and the minimum possible cover for uninvited guests. "Just tell him to park along the inner drive somewhere and open his hood," Hunt had told Flak, not bothering to hide his exasperation.

Now, coming out onto the wide, open sidewalk in front of the Essex Towers where Flak waited, he said, "Got the jumper cables?" Mino was off somewhere with the athlete, boning up for his maiden flight tomorrow in the TiltRotor.

"Yes, sir, sure do. I hope he's got those schematics for us—I don't like to think how it's going to go if he won't let us have them." Flak, walking backward toward the car, craned his neck upward. "Bet she's watching—"

Hunt had been playing civilian all weekend with Morales, who felt safe enough to suggest they walk through the country-starved crowds who thronged the park in spite of a cold snap that made him wish he'd kept the expedition parka. He had his hands in his pockets; in moments, despite gloves and his daily improving condition, they had gone stiff with cold.

He saw men emerge from the Essex House, on his right; from the New York Athletic Club, on his left; from two cars pulling up to block the Wagoneer's exit—one abreast, one behind. From a parked car in front, a familiar, bulky figure in a European storm coat emerged.

Hunt said, "I hope she is," and Flak, hearing his tone, seeing him shake loose the Detonics from his pocket, spun about, saying, "Good fucking Christ!" and, facing Hunt once more, held out his hands wide: "Don't shoot, sir. Just hold on, he only wants to talk to you—"

It was farther back to the Towers' door than he could make, with no cover, and he heard somebody behind him. The Detonics was going to be very noisy; he took careful aim around Flak's outstretched arms and squeezed one off as Flak realized what he was going to do and lunged for the gun Hunt had to hold high and away from his body to avoid hitting Flak. The asset's hand chopped down at Hunt's wrist as the report sounded and the muzzle recoiled upward.

Hunt saw the other men running toward him, Helms clutch his shoulder. But Flak was in his way. "Sorry, sir, but you've got to listen—" A desperate face, imploring and concerned, came close.

He was surprised that he wasn't going to simply shoot Flak even as the Detonics snapped out, seemingly of its own accord, barrel hitting the younger man across the temple, and Flak dropped to his knees, huddled in pain.

But by then three of the suits were behind him, and Helms, black blood streaming over his hand in the streetlight, suggested they disarm him. Hunt, Detonics in close to his hip, said generally, "Touch me and I'll splatter your boss so far and wide, somebody's gonna have a lot of explaining to do. Okay, officer, what's the message?"

The man whose voice was raspy and quiet stepped around Flak, who had his head between his knees and occasionally tried to raise it. "We think you ought to walk, Dropout. We insist on it." Now Helms was very close; they had never, Hunt realized, spoken before—they had not had to.

"Who's we?"

Helms took his hand away from his shoulder. Hunt could see the pain, discounted, in the man's eyes, and the tremors that ran across his body, shaking clean-shaven jowls. "Come on, Hunt, everybody here knows the score. Why the fuck did you blow the handover?"

"Why not? I don't know you. Which is it, ISA or DIA?" He didn't really care whether it was ISA or the Defense Intelligence Agency who'd sicced Helms on him; he was stalling, giving Helms time to reconsider. "Or is it just sour grapes?"

"Jesus, I'm gonna take your ass in; you're too crazy to run around loose. You're going to *argue* with me about who's who? Try and remember, fella, who and where you are."

"Tell me about it, or you'll be debriefing to the coroner."

Hunt squeezed off another unsilenced round from the Detonics, high enough that in the mile or so of the bullet's travel potential, it wouldn't take down some civilian along the way.

Helms gave a hand signal and Hunt broke for the Towers' door behind him, shooting a startled agent, just reaching for his own gun, between the eyes.

Somebody tackled him from behind. He hit the pavement hard, trying to break his fall with his elbows. The wind knocked out of him, he kicked, twisting, hoping to shake loose his assailant: They really did want him alive if they were willing to risk this overt scene. Helms was cursing; Hunt heard "...not worth it. Get that body into the car" as he pulled himself in tight, cradling the Detonics against his chest. He was setting up for a shot under his arm or over his shoulder at the man holding him down when something caught him in the kidneys and lights exploded in the back of his head. Helms's voice was close to his ear but distant as he told somebody to "go ahead and do a little damage, he's one son of a bitch that deserves it. He's got some shrapnel next to his spine." Now louder: "Dropout? Hey, Dropout, can you hear me? Maybe you'll walk away from this one, spook, or maybe you'll have to crawl. One way or another, here's a little something from all the boys in Defense—"

And then Hunt truly couldn't hear him. Agony lanced up his back and blows rained down on him. He curled up, rolled away as he had learned to do in the Lubyanka, not even remembering the pistol he held, unable to see beyond the pain, and knew he was going to lose consciousness. He heard faraway shouting and suddenly there were no more blows, no one around him, just the sounds of running feet and slamming doors and his own breathing. His shoulder felt sprained and he couldn't remember how that might have happened. The pain ebbed and left him with the taste of blood in his mouth, seeping from between his teeth. He spat and wiped his lips, beginning to feel the cold sidewalk under him as black shoes came into his swimming field of view.

Uniformed arms helped him up; he saw the street and on it there remained only Flak, being helped up by an Essex security officer, and spatter-stars of brown blood on the sidewalk. The security men weren't sure who the bad guys were. Hunt showed the ISA ID he had taken from the Frenchman—it had no photo. "Listen, this is what's called an 'interagency squabble'—TTS, if you get my drift." The elder told the younger that TTS meant "Top, Top Secret" and wasn't he glad they hadn't called 911?

"But somebody's fuckin' dead!" said the younger guard, helping Flak take slow, uncertain steps. "I *saw* the back of his head come off." Over by the building was a smattering of cranial tissue and an abstract of blood. "What's International Security Agency, anyway?"

Flak, hand to his temple, was beginning to come out of it. "DoD— Department of Defense, it's okay. I'm all right. You can't say anything—you didn't see anything. If you do, you'll just lose your jobs—maybe more. Those guys are military intelligence types—nobody fucks with them and walks away happy. Believe me, I've been there. The best thing is to just forget it."

"But what am I going to say about the shots?"

"Firecrackers, backfires—I don't know." Flak stood alone, not taking his hand away from his temple. "Where are you guys from, the hotel or the Towers?"

"The hotel." While the other three spoke, Hunt walked around picking up spent brass.

"Good enough. I'll have something for you tomorrow—sort of hazard pay. Okay?"

The older one jumped in, saying that would be fine and it was nice to know Flak was "staying with us—in case something else comes up." He grinned at the younger guard and offered to buy him a drink when his shift was done.

As Flak and Hunt got into the Wagoneer and pulled away from the curb, Hunt saw the young guard bending over the polished brass fixture protruding from the building to give up his last meal.

"Sure you can drive?" Hunt asked.

"Yep."

"Well, congratulations. That's as bad a job as I've ever seen. The hotel security is alerted; you can bet they know your suite number now, if they didn't before. You've probably put this whole op in the dumper, Darling. You want to tell me about it or you want to die here and now?" His back still hurt severely, but the stabbing pains were diminishing. "Because *no*body is taking me *any*where, to ask me *any* sort of questions, ever again—not coercively, or politely, or any way at all while I'm alive. Copy, Mr. Whoever-the-fuck?"

"What? You think that—" Flak wrenched the wheel and tires screeched as he cut across a lane of traffic and parked. Tears were streaming from his eyes. He leaned his head back and said, "Christ, it feels like my brain is on fire. You drive, sir. You want me out of the car, I'll go. Out of your life, that's fine, too. If you don't trust me by now, you never will." He looked sideways at Hunt, saw the Detonics pointed at him. "Is that one muzzle or two? I think I've got a concussion. I just didn't want you to kill anybody, Cory. I don't know who you think I am, or what you think I'm doing, but *I* didn't know that was going to happen. If I didn't care…" He put his head in his hands and Hunt saw that his shoulders were actually shaking. From between them, muffled, he heard "I goddamned put myself between you and incoming fire. I would've gone down for you, taken a hit for you, and I didn't even think twice about it.…"

Hunt sat watching until Flak raised his head and turned it. A hematoma the size of a Ping-Pong ball was raised on his temple. They stared at each other. "You didn't even—sir—Cory, man, that's Defense Intelligence, Helms and those. Nobody can control DIA, you know that—all those little fucking army, air, and naval intelligence units.…I don't think Shy knows about this. He couldn't have. I didn't. They're getting antsy. Maybe we're messing up their game plan; maybe it's just personal—you and Helms and all, plus how many guys they lost because of you. But no matter what, you don't want to kill cousins—"

"I just did." Hunt extracted the Detonics's half-empty clip, replaced it with a full magazine from his belt. "It doesn't matter who dispatched them when better than half a dozen guys come at you from nowhere. If they'd had an executive action order, we'd both be dead now. Next time they'll come prepared. You've got to be ready for that."

"You're ISA, sir?"

Hunt laughed softly, and felt tenderness where his jaw had hit the pavement. "I took that card from the guy who had the Ruger."

"But Fowler—" Flak stopped, shook his head. "If you're going to shoot me, sir, shoot me. Otherwise put the gun away and we'll make the meet—barely."

Hunt watched him. He hurt and he didn't know what to think. But the same was true for the other asset. "I think you and I are due for a cards-down discussion."

"Okay, sir, whenever you say. Like you said, I'm not going to be a lot of use from here on in—"

"I didn't say that. Slide over."

Hunt climbed over him and took the wheel. "Let's see your head." Hunt tsked. "Well, you're lucky I like you enough to remember it when the adrenaline starts pumping. If your vision doesn't clear in a couple of hours, or if you get sick to your stomach or real sleepy or suddenly the world looks unfamiliar, we'll have a doctor scan you for internal bleeding. Otherwise, you'll be okay."

"Are we really fucked at the hotel?"

"No, quite the contrary. We used to get Special-Agent cards—you know, FBI—for domestic travel and we'd show 'em to the airport guards so we could carry on board. They're glad to help you, and glad to have you—makes them feel that they're really professionals, part of the covert community. Any of those guys would give his right arm to be where you are. You did *that* just right." He pulled away from the curb and began looking for a place to turn around.

Flak gave him cogent directions, then: "Are we going to tell Shy? If you don't want to, just let me know in advance."

"Yeah, you don't want him to know, either, I bet. But one look at you and he'll scope that something happened." He rubbed his own jaw, his face, looked in the rearview mirror and desultorily ran his fingers through his hair—he might feel bad, but he looked good, if you weren't looking close enough to see the blood matted in his whiskers. "I don't know, let me think about it. . . . Or be vague, don't volunteer, follow my lead. Maybe he *does* know about it. *Some*body thinks you can handle it from here on your own, or they wouldn't be trying to pull me out of the picture."

"No, sir, it couldn't be—"

"*Yes, sir*, it sure as hell could be. And maybe Shy's decided he doesn't want to take the weight all by himself. This isn't counter-terrorism anymore—maybe it never was. I haven't had time to talk to you about what I think is happening, but you can bet Shy's been rethinking *his* alternatives. I've gotten this close before, and had somebody waltz in and pull me off. Sometimes they're polite and straightforward, sometimes they just arrange a nice little ac-cident for you, and by the time you're out of the hospital or picked up out of the desert or whatever they've fixed up to skew you, the op's over and everybody has shit-eating grins. But they never admit it was part of their scenario that you be put out of action.

"So for your own sake, be careful. John Shy's nobody's friend. He's a dedicated analyst, and analysts don't think about blood and pain—they think about reports with nice red borders and how hip they're going to look at intelligence board meetings and how things will affect their 'career performance.' In other words, a man like that will do any damn thing at all not to have a black mark on his record—his six-figure income depends on it. Keep it in mind."

Shy's Mondial was up on the grass off the park drive near the Sheep Meadow, hood up, flare behind, interior light on. A large red and brown Doberman sat in the driver's seat.

Hunt pulled up beside it, offering deadpan to lend a hand. When Shy, on the meadow side of the car, leaning on its front fender, gave the "clear" signal, Hunt pulled the Wagoneer up onto the grass so that the cars were nose-to-nose. "Stay on the street side and keep your head out of the light and you'll never have to say a word," Hunt cautioned Flak, wondering who was playing whom for what kind of fool.

"Hello, Cord," said Shy, his graying temples silver in the underhood light of the Mondial. Flak sauntered up with the jumper cables. "Flak tells me you want to murder some diplomats in Maryland."

"I don't want to do any such thing, but that's worst-case for this part. A House of Saud type owns the place in question; the two are a Soviet and an unidentified. 'Prevent a handover' can mean anything. Have you got the schematics?"

"Right there." Shy pointed to a magnetized case stuck to the inside of the hood, about the size of a paperback book. "Microfiche, is that suitable?"

Hunt took it. His head was beginning to ache. "Fine. Thanks. This is going to take at least another week or two. Angel's abroad; his wife's not real communicative—she doesn't seem to know much about the nuts and bolts of his business. Once we pass this test, we'll be in better shape. But they're not the culprits, they're just hired hands. You still want to retain and/or kill them? I offered a preemptive bid."

"What did they say?"

"They're thinking about it."

"I'll think about it, too. But I'd hate to have this particular Saudi involved, even indirectly ... there's nowhere else?"

"It's hardly my scenario. Your people are all over me. One more gun pointed my way by people who are supposed to be friendlies and I'm going to start putting down out of hand anybody who even looks suspicious."

"Let's not get emotional. Are you all right? You seem terribly wired."

"You know what they say about living in a terrorist environment—you've got to be able to leave it every once in a while for R&R. This ain't Hawaii."

"Yes, well…I have some news for you. I picked up a PCP 'spokesperson' who identified Dania but not Angel Morales. However, if you say Angel was in Europe when Fowler's misfortune occurred, maybe the kid had more gumption than we—"

"I don't know where he was. He wasn't here, or so she said. I haven't seen him yet. They don't trust me enough yet, and I don't blame them. I'll have to stick close to her—"

"Yes, Flak told me you moved in with her, lock, stock, and armory. I'm not going to ask if you think that was wise, but remember—if you get into trouble your own people can't extricate you from, *I* can't get you out." Shy leaned forward; Hunt followed suit. Flak attached the jumper cables to the Mondial's battery and went to sit in the Wagoneer. "There's someone named 'Darling' in this, and he's not mine—he's been reporting to Fowler, but I think he belongs to the—"

"Customers. I know. Thanks for the warning." Hunt leaned back and glanced at Flak, spoke to Shy: "Can we sit in the car with that dog there?"

"It's my dog."

They both sat in the Mondial once the dog had scrambled into the 2 + 2's rear seat. "Anything on this 'Diehl'?"

"Not beyond what you already know."

"How are you going to feel about me if I bring you news you won't like?" Hunt said carefully. "My only interest in this is survival. I don't want to find out something you'll then have to kill me for knowing. Give me a pullback point."

"I can't. We've got to go all the way. As for your position, it will probably be no different. I thought this would happen."

"Yeah, I figured. You've known all along what I'm supposed to find out, is that it?"

"Not exactly. When Fowler thought he was dying, he gave me access to some of his sources. Between that and what Sid's said since, I'm pretty uncomfortable, but I'm sticking it out. No one's going to silence me; there, I *can* protect you."

"Even if the name I come back with is Cannard? Tell me another one. You want to play chicken with Ivan over technology transfer, that's your business. There's a woman or two in this—people are going to get hurt. I just shot somebody—"

"Don't tell me your troubles, Cord. You're paid to deal with them. Just bring me data, Dropout—no regrets, no speculations. I've enough of my own. We're both going to find out some things we might not like to know. What else is new?"

"DIA's new, as far as I'm concerned."

"Your fraternity brothers? I'm sure they're trying to keep it low-profile. Jack was holding them off for a while. But he's not ambulatory yet. Just do the best you can."

"I don't know ... somebody's telling me in no uncertain terms to walk away. They don't seem to think they have to be polite about it, either. There's something here somebody doesn't want me—or you—to find out. You ought to have a talk with a couple of those somebodies—ISA, DIA, State, or whomever—"

"Believe me, you're wrong in thinking anyone expects to be able to stop this now. It's just confirmation at this point. I'll be staying at Sid's co-op downtown; Beth's here. If you've only got one phone call, you can ring me there in an emergency."

"That's not funny."

"It wasn't meant to be. How are the pilots?"

"Oh, great. They're having a ball. Don't know what I'd do without them." Shy turned the Mondial's key and the lights on the Wagoneer dimmed. "See you," Hunt promised, and got out to disengage the jumper cables, asking, finally, "How's Martinova?"

"Full of surprises."

Cordell Hunt, choking off a response, slammed the door as the Doberman, all teeth and speed, catapulted itself into the front seat he had just vacated.

When Hunt got back into the Wagoneer, jumper cables in hand, Flak, elbow propped on the wheel and chin on fist, said, "So? Did you blow me?"

"Not yet."

"What did he say?"

"Drive, or I will. He *didn't* say that Innotech is racing I-don't-know-how-many other agencies to apprehend some in-house spoiler, or that Innotech's prime concern is to clear its decks before a competitor gets hold of the person or thing in question. Understand? You and I, as Innotech agents, are expected to beat any and all comers to this honeypot. Anyone who gets it before we do owns Innotech henceforth, R&D, clandestine courier service, satellite links, the whole unsightly mess."

"He said that?" Flak wheeled the car onto the street and accelerated. "Where to?"

"Back to the hotel, and—shit, no, *I'm* saying that. What he said is to take out anybody who gets in our way—whether we're messing up God's own go, no matter whose fingers are in the pie—without coming to him for additional help or even moral support. He doesn't want to hear about it. And with that as a given, what else is there to think?"

"Damned if I know. What did he say about—"

"Hold it. I'm still deciding what I'm going to do about you."

"Me?"

"You. We might make our own little deal, depending on where you're from and what you want out of this. Why don't you begin by telling me what acronym starts your particular alphabet."

"Oh, boy. Kori"—Flak took a deep breath and expelled it—"I just . . . *can't.*"

"Unless you want to be either real dead or all alone wondering where everybody went, you can't do anything else."

Flak headed the car out of the park. Hunt let him think. Presently he pulled over, parked opposite the hotel, sat catty-corner facing Hunt, lit by the spill of a streetlight. Hunt couldn't blame him—driving would put him at a disadvantage if push came to shove. Eventually, Flak shook his head. "I don't *believe* I've screwed up like this—those DIA bastards . . ."

"Okay, Cory." He held out his hand. "My name is Fletcher Godwin. I've been on this a long while." Hunt didn't shake with him; Flak let his hand drop. "I haven't been lying to you, or fucking you over in any way. I asked for this assignment—fought for it. It's *my* chance at the big time. When you went to Triage, Defense started prepping some guys to maybe follow things up. I studied you a whole lot. I was the right type; they knew I had an in through Mino—all back-burner stuff. Then the shit hit the fan and they activated me. I've been inside since Triage gave you to the Soviets, and my orders were to see what I could do to help, what I could find out . . . you know how they are, so damn cautious. My initial shot was to try to get you away from Innotech/Triage when they picked you up—the handover in the Albis: That was

DIA's idea of a real good time . . . it wasn't supposed to be hard-ball."

"Fowler?"

"Later I started hearing his name, not at first. Fowler loves your ass; so do some other people. I know how it looks, but I'm proof that we—that the government—didn't just throw you away."

"No, you're not. You're proof that when Triage ran me, some-body wanted to know how come, how fast, and how far."

"Yeah, that, too—*then*. Look, Cory, the end of a whole lot of maneuvering is that I'm reporting to Jack Fowler; Shy thinks I'm his—I'm reporting to him, too; I came out of the Agency by special request of the Joint Chiefs, because I was capable of working solo, and because they'd turned over every rock in the community looking for somebody with the right profile—somebody who could get next to you. . . . I've been flipped so many times that I'm sick to my stomach, but I haven't turned in a straight-ahead report since we left Zürich. I don't know *what* that makes me, but what's happened to you is going to happen to me if I don't watch out. You're seven years older than I am, according to your file, and your credentials were fucking impeccable. I couldn't *believe* the way Helms treated you back there; I can't be a party to that kind of shit. At this point, I can't honestly recommend anybody's shop— they're all looking alike to me. I've got vertigo of the integrity or something." He stopped, looked disgusted, spread his hands, let them fall.

Hunt said, "I believe it's called a 'crisis of confidence.'"

"Sir, I'm not much better than I've been pretending to be— maybe just a little. But now it looks to me like you're about to double for Morales—that this isn't any legend or fabrication. Mino and I have been talking it over—what's going on, what's likely to happen—and we'd like to volunteer for real . . . *be* your backups; play it your way; get Martinova out from under. I know we could do it together, sir. . . . I'm taking an awful chance. For all I know, *you* might be reporting to—"

"I said cards down. Initially, someone suggested I take the Triage gig. I figure my responsibility ended when they let me go down by my lonesome. I am, and intend to remain, a free agent. As for you and Mino, I'll give you the benefit of the doubt. Let's go pack you up. You two are moving into Dania's place with me."

Now that he had a check on Flak Fletcher Darling Godwin, he didn't have to worry that Flak would purposely blow him to Morales using what he knew of the Bogotá penetration: Flak wouldn't risk the consequences of being unmasked to John Shy; as the asset had said, if he wasn't careful, he was going to end up like Hunt.

Dania's face when she opened her door answered the first of his questions: She had seen or heard something. He went into gear, kissing her pale brow, forcing her backward as he hurried Flak inside. Both of them carried hard cases. "I hope you meant it, what you said about letting them stay here."

"Cory, you are hurt. What happened? Who were they?" Her voice was very soft, but clipped. "Come this way. You, too, Flak."

In her kitchen Hunt answered: "DIA types. I told you I was hot. I shouldn't even be here." He pulled out the Detonics and put it on the table. "I've got to make this gun disappear."

"Yes, I know," she soothed, "I saw." She was feeling his head; he winced when she touched a bump he hadn't noticed. "Sit on the table, both of you." From the refrigerator she took cold packs filled with blue viscous fluid and came toward them, wrapping the packs in clean dish towels. "Hold this against it, Flak—gently."

Flak grunted when the cold pack touched his temple. Dania was gone, the gun with her. Hunt heard voices from another room. They looked at each other, nonplussed, then Hunt shook his head "no," leaned back against the white-tiled wall, and closed his eyes, his cold pack propped between the wall and the back of his head. He had thought about leaving the Detonics in the Wagoneer, now on its way to the Essex garage, but kept it for this eventuality. Op guns came and went, but if he could help it, he wasn't using his Commander on this go. He'd have to come up with another sterile piece, but he couldn't risk her thinking he dared hold on to the Detonics.

When she came back in, she had a medikit. "Oh, no," he said, looking at the antiseptic.

"For your chin, coward." He let her wash and dress his superficial wound. "I knew you should not have gone alone—"

"We got your data," Flak said huffily. "Who's here? I heard somebody."

"Diehl. He will discard the firearm and come right back. Your eyes, Flak, do they focus?"

"Yeah, I'm okay. My stuff—"

Hunt broke in: "It *is* still all right that they stay? Or are you all filled up?" *Diehl.* "I'm keeping the suite booked for cover. If it's inconvenient—"

"It is fine. I'm pleased to have them. But from now on, Cory, you must listen to my advice. I know when trouble brews—I can *feel* it in my bones. When Flak's friend requested this evening meeting so soon—"

"It wasn't them, it was just an old enemy out to even a score. Run the data. I'm betting my life that it's good." He held out the case to her. She put down the soapy washcloth, rubbing her hands on her blue-jeaned thighs, then took it. "And I've got to go downtown tomorrow—you're welcome to come, but I can't have a battalion behind me wherever I go. I've got a man to see about a job; life doesn't stop because some asshole takes it into his head to give you a hard time. They won't be back; he's got enough explaining to do—he got one of his people killed on a personal vendetta. But that doesn't mean every agency in town isn't hoping I'll walk into their hands or their offices.... Are you *sure* you want me here, Dania? The only place I'm safe is—"

"With me. Hush. Let's find you another side arm. Flak, call Trish, if you feel up to it—she was concerned. She's not due here for another hour, so you may catch her at home." She handed Flak an open address book. "We'll be in the study. Don't worry about your belongings—Cory and I will take care of them."

He was cold, chilled from the packs, and trembling slightly. He let her lead him into the study, saw her hesitate over one of the gun cases, went and put an arm around her. "Dania, you don't have to do this. I can manage with what I've got."

"I've never wanted to...disturb these...before. You *are* good for me, Cory. It's healthy." She unlocked the case, stepped aside. "Choose."

He said, truthfully, "There's nothing there I'd want to use once and throw away. Besides, I've got this." He tapped his shoulder harness. "And that means I'm sticking to forty-five acp. Get me another Detonics or a Safari Arms Enforcer, sterilized, or I might as well forget about a backup gun." He looked regretfully at Angel's Beretta 92S. He didn't want one of Angel Morales' guns, but he was certain now that Angel wasn't going to come around and ask for it back: This was a night for blowing covers.

She sighed, "Men," reached in, took out the tiny Walther PPK, handed it to him.

"No, really. Don't complicate my life. I don't want to carry two calibers—I had the Detonics modified so it would feed from my Commander's clips in a pinch. I really do like to keep it simple. All I'd need is to forget which clips are which in the middle of a fire fight. If you want to do something for me, let me listen to the tapes you've got of the female client—maybe I can make an audio ID."

"Ah, Cory—always the edge. Very well, come with me, and we shall both do a little intelligence work." She replaced the PPK, locked the case, and led the way into her communications center, saying as she went, "You do not want one of Angel's guns, is that it?"

"You got it," he admitted—and took a chance: "God knows how long it's been since any of those have been fired."

She had activated a computer terminal, which was giving her a call-by-call index of incomings. She said, "Here, and here," and jotted down two numbers, tore off a sheet of paper, sent him to the tape library to match the numbers with the corresponding cassettes.

By the time he'd located them, she had turned to a microfiche viewer and was adjusting its focus. Hunt, unconcerned, was looking for a headset, the first cassette already loaded in one of the racked machines, when a beep sounded. "This is very good, Cory," she said, leaning over to flip a switch that caused a monitor to blossom with a view of the front door: A bearded man was just extracting his key from the lock. "Diehl. I must go introduce Flak to him. Will you join me?"

He left with her—he had no alternative—one cassette still loaded, the other in his back pocket. "What's the situation with Diehl? I need to know where I stand, what the pecking order is."

Walking beside him, her hand touched his hip, slid along his waist. "He is our right hand, my bodyguard when I feel the need of one. You know he's been on-site in Maryland, so you know we use him as a column commander. What are you asking?"

"Whether there's going to be any confusion as to who's sleeping where—or any resentment I'm going to have to deal with."

"I would have sent him with you tonight, and then you wouldn't have had questions. I trust him implicitly—his ability, his discretion, his professionalism. He has been with us a long time—he'll treat you as my honored guest, how else?"

"You don't understand—is he running Maryland, or am I?"

"It has been his from the beginning, Cory. You and I don't have to risk our lives in the field—you must get used to that."

He didn't like that one bit. "I'm not taking blind orders from anybody, and I'm not taking money for something I'm not really going to do. Everybody wants to put me out to pasture. It's fucking insulting."

That stopped her in the hall. She put her other arm around his waist, leaning back with her pelvis braced against his. "Hush, Ifrit. You've suffered a blow to the head, perhaps a severe one, so I will forgive your suspicions." He let her kiss him and thought that he could deal with Diehl when the time came.

The big black-bearded man was lounging in the gun room with Flak, a leg crooked over one leather divan's arm. They both had bottles of Moosehead in their hands and grins on their faces.

Flak held out a joint: "Trish is on her way..."

By then Diehl was up and lumbering over to them, one hamlike hand extended in greeting, the other in plain view on his spare-tired hip next to a holstered Beretta. Hunt guessed he weighed two-fifty; the blue-eyed German had at least two inches on him in height, as well as a longer reach and eighty pounds more weight to throw around.

The precariousness of his position in that room at that moment sent his pulse rate skyrocketing, and he knew his hand would be shaking when he held it out from the way his mouth felt. Diehl welcomed Hunt into their "little family" in Arabic, and Hunt responded in English, saying he'd heard good things about Diehl from Dania.

The hand he had shaken was cool and dry as the eyes that assessed him openly. Diehl said, "You are the lucky one; perhaps you will bring your luck to us. We need all we can get. I know you by reputation. A shame about the little barker"—he meant the Detonics—"but from what I saw, nothing less would be appropriate. Have you many such acquaintances?"

Hunt, unreasoningly, was near tears. "I've got to sit down. I took a good clout on the skull tonight, and it's not my first."

He did that, and Diehl sat next to Flak, thick legs spread wide in suit pants, his conservative tie dangling between them. "We are working together, yes? Dania said there was a chance of it."

She spoke for the first time; he had almost forgotten her; both she and Flak were watching so carefully, they might have been taking notes. "They have brought the plans of the target security system. It looked marvelous to me—everything you might need. Take a look when you have a moment."

"I don't need to look. I have been talking to this electronic wizard of yours, and I am like a boy climbing his first mountain: I have seen the pinnacle, the rest is merely putting one foot before the other. I remember when they taught only wine tasting and gentlemanly behavior in and out of bed at intelligence schools."

Only in the Middle East and in ComBloc, Hunt thought. He really would like to put this guy down before he had trouble with him, because he *was* going to have trouble with him. Instead, he made friends with him, asking about a suitable replacement for the Detonics: "I've got no connection in the States for sterile handguns. I could pay—"

"If Dania pleases, I can get you whatever you want, tonight. Yes? Then if you will excuse me . . . I'll look at the 'fiche on the way out, madonna. Coming, my friend?" He looked quizzically at Hunt: "What shall I call you?"

"Cory. Or 'Scratch' is okay."

"Not 'Abu Ifrit'? We used to curse you in that name in the Lebanon."

"I figured we might have crossed paths once or twice." Hunt levered himself up and the jerkiness of his motions was no sham. He had to stand very still for a moment or he was going to fall flat on his face. He hoped it didn't look as if he were staging some convenient play. He felt Dania's arm before he saw her beside him, covering for his indisposition by whispering in his ear. "Thanks," he whispered back, and went off with Diehl toward the communications center.

Hunt told him how he wanted the Detonics set up and handed him the half-empty clip from his belt as a sample of what he meant by "interchangeable" magazines; they agreed that the longer Commander magazine could protrude from the shallower Detonics well. Hunt went through the motions almost without thinking. It was always the same: They had to establish a working relationship based on the no-trust, no-fault givens of tradecraft. He couldn't have been less prepared when Diehl said, "Cory Hunt, what part do you see for yourself in this?"

"I don't know. You tell me. Maryland's your baby."

"And Dania is yours? Angel is liberal—the new morality—but I...I am loyal like a—"

"Unless you're fucking her yourself, I think you're out-of-bounds."

"I see." He knitted his brows gravely. "I thought as much." He crossed massive arms, frowned, then suddenly his face split in a beaming smile and he unwound his hands, clapping Hunt upon the shoulder. "Good! Good, I think." He laughed loudly. "I shall take good care of you, too, then—Ifrit. Next time, when you crave a street fight, invite me along. If you make Dania happy, that is enough for me."

And he left Hunt there, saying he was off to look over the microfiche and then to get the pistol.

Hunt was leaning back against the wall, eyes closed, just resting where he was, too enervated even to move, when he smelled coffee and opened his eyes to see Dania, impish and coy, holding a cup and blowing the steam his way. "Ah...Come, come. Come with me or you'll not have it." She began walking backward, toward the bedroom. "Come—"

"I have to help Flak get settled. Give that to me."

"You are going to lie down and be ministered to, thoroughly, by me. When Trish comes, she can see to Flak. We have division of labor—and love."

"Sorry, I've got work to do." He pushed away from the wall and started to move off in the opposite direction, toward the communications center where Diehl had gone.

She came after him. "Cory? Cory, what is it?" Her eyes sparkled as she touched his arm, holding out the cup, whose contents slopped over into its saucer.

He took it, paused, said, "You *watched* that whole little drama on the street and didn't try to help me. You set me up to take a back seat to somebody I don't know anything about—to risk my people's lives, my own life, on him. *He's* got the balls to ask me whether we're sleeping together and exactly how much of this I expect to cut myself in for the minute you spring him on me from out of nowhere just after—*not before*—I get you the crucial intelligence on which this whole operation rests. And you want to know what's wrong? Honey, I'm just not sure where it is you're coming from, and that makes me real nervous."

He was rewarded by honest tears. He sipped his espresso, watching her weep silently. She had even fired a lemon peel over it. He felt despicable, but she said, "You—can't mean this. Diehl was arriving as you departed—I was *so* worried. You must *not* take chances like this again—too many others are involved."

"I can't follow orders, you said that yourself. You've been telling me you were going to lay this thing out for me, now you say you're not. Whose setup is this—yours, or Diehl's, or Angel's? Or is it some triumvirate into which I can never hope to fit? I don't like that guy telling me that it's fine with him if I make you happy—he'll protect me. I'm nobody's gigolo. The only whoring I do is the operational sort."

She took a step toward him, shaking her head, wordless, her lips puffy and her nose reddening. He held the cup between them. "It's him or me: Either you have a talk with him or you're going to lose me and I'll call us even—the security specs for a really spectacular weekend. Whatever your motives, I've felt better here with you than I have for years."

"I will— Oh, Cory, *caro*... Diehl didn't mean that. I'll talk to him. Please..." She laughed thickly, drew herself up, wiped her eyes. "Tomorrow we'll hold a strategy conference; then you'll know—"

"I told you, tomorrow I've got things to do. I've bailouts to set up." He was pushing her hard; he didn't want to blow it—he was so close.

Right then Diehl came into view. He let the big man see what was going on and watched him turn around and head back the way he had come; he could exit through the rear bedrooms. Hunt mentally gave Diehl one point for social awareness.

Then he let her escort him into the communications center and wait, massaging his neck, while he listened to the client's voice. He ran the two tapes three times each. He knew she must have more tape on this client—there were no specific details in what he heard, just oblique activation orders and drop confirmations and money talk.

When he took off his headset, he swiveled the chair around and pulled Dania down onto his lap. She had regained her composure; it was time for him to lose his. "I'm jumpy. I don't feel as well as I might. If your offer's still good, I'm more than ready to be ministered to."

Dania kissed him in response. "Nothing?" she guessed, reaching over to rewind the cassette.

"I'll have to listen to them some more. It's either a very sophisticated electronic voice-masking device, or it's Beth Cannard."

Chapter 15

WHEN John Shy saw Cordell Hunt walk into the party at the United Arab Emirates Mission with Dania Morales on his arm, he spilled his drink. The affair was invitation-only, a welcoming bash for the PLO's new permanent observer to the UN, and high-security because the guest of honor's predecessor had died in a car bombing in Beirut only three weeks before.

Beth Cannard scolded, "John! You really can't hold your liquor anymore." She took the champagne flute away from him. "You've had enough."

He drifted away from Beth, engaged in animated but useless

debate with a pinstriped PLO moderate about the possibilities of
drawing a line that would legally separate the terrorists from the
freedom fighters. It was an exercise in futility he had been unwilling to enter into previously. Now his own particular harpy/
terrorist/freedom fighter/rogue agent was about to pin him to the
wall.

It bothered him—beyond Hunt's disregard of caution and
tradecraft—how comfortable the asset looked in this milieu, im-
maculate in a good dark suit with the magnificent Morales woman
cleaving to him, devastating in a little black evening suit and raptly
attentive.

He made his way toward them, among the berobed Saudis and
the occidental women they tended to collect as warm-blooded
souvenirs. He had been invited to a Florida harem. He wondered
what the nightly news might make of that.

Hunt let his hand slide provocatively off the Morales woman's
high rump and came to meet him. "Hi there. I thought you might
be here tonight. Beth Cannard's definitely part of our problem.
I need to know how much, if anything, you've told her. If she's
been getting updates from you on this go, it's off. I'm hoping to
alter some of the details of the op in progress. Don't concern
yourself, whatever you hear, until you hear from me. What's at
stake here, laser battle stations?"

"*Shut up!*" Shy hissed. Beth was almost certainly implicated;
Dropout was overtly chatting with him, hands in his pockets and
about as casual as a cruise missile, where half the UN's KGB agents
and the revolutionary movers of the "progressive" Gulf Cooperation Council could see them: Hunt was up to his old tricks. "Let's
go relieve ourselves," Shy suggested.

"Don't worry, I'm here as Dania's escort; she's got an invitation.
We're here to make sure Beth doesn't leave early—Flak and Mino
are downtown bugging Sid's co-op. I need two hours, and I need
to know you haven't been disseminating to Beth."

"I haven't." An Omani murmured a greeting in passing. Shy
reached out and fingered Hunt's black/gray/gold Sulka tie. "Did
I buy you that?"

"Innotech is very understanding about the need to dress ap-
propriately."

"Not that understanding. Take it easy on my budget. I'll take
care of Beth."

"Then you ought to arm yourself. You know what the Ethiopians say: 'Kiss-kiss, bang-bang.'" From his pocket Hunt pulled his fist, extended it. Shy felt the little gun pressed into his hand. "It's an ISA scratch gun, silenced, sterile, and underpowered. If you have to use it, empty the whole load into your target's ear, or—"

"Enough. Now get out of here. I can't afford to be seen with you." Shy put the hand with the gun in it in his pants pocket.

"In this murderous crowd? You'll get a little respect. I know most of these radical Muslims from the days when Arafat was d/b/a 'Abu Jihad'—one thing they understand is firepower."

Firepower. Dear God. "Dropout—Grover! My dog. What—"

"Listen, case officer, your pooch is the least of my worries. Right now he's tripping his doggie brains out on B-Z. Look, I've got to go scare some of these spooks and spookettes. I'll keep in touch. If Morales buttonholes you, make them some kind of preemptive offer, even if you don't mean it. Things are going to grind to a halt abruptly if you don't play along."

And he was gone, sidling through the crowd of Gulf potentates, Middle East marauders, and Soviets, shaking hands, stopping to smile and nod. Shy saw him put an arm companionably around one of their Omani hosts, laugh softly, let himself be introduced to the local "resident," the Soviet's New York chief of station.

When Shy had come to Innotech, he had accepted the need to deal evenhandedly with the progressives, the revolutionaries, and the Soviet-leaning Gulf states. Anti-Western Muslims were so for a reason, and that reason was simple: modernization and the upheavals it was causing. The Soviets termed this inevitability "technological neocolonialism" and mounted indirect, incremental "vector" strategies to minimize their own cultural differences with the Muslim states and maximize the West's. Creeping Soviet subversion and intervention of the most covertly staged sort was the USSR's stick; freedom from the decadent West's hegemony over technology transfer was its carrot. Russia's indigenous Muslims were the perfect agents; the land borders in question were uncontrollable. The fate of Afghanistan and the resurrection of Iran as a revolutionary state were object lessons. No one doubted or denied in private Russia's indirect involvement in Muslim revolutions, but various kingdoms and emirates took note: It was better to lean toward the Soviets than be deposed by them.

Internationalist "second-source" corporations like Innotech, to maintain nonalignment, must deal with everyone. But John Shy, an old ComBloc hand, didn't like it. His personal interest in Innotech's development was that it supply an alternative to direct importation—by its multinationality, help the United States, bound to forty treaty partners by conflicting arms-purchasing agreements that more often than not put U.S. defense procurers at the tail end of her own line of priority customers—and reduce her dependence on untrustworthy third-world suppliers of titanium, molybdenum, manganese, vanadium, and European purveyors of engineering talent, specialty glasses, and ball bearings.

Lacking a twenty-year plan such as France's or Germany's to reestablish the independence of America's defense community, stymied at every turn by politicians and shortsighted procurement policies that favored the primary contractors who could afford the low-bidding buy-in system, Defense and CIA jointly had expended the seed money to establish Innotech's "independence." But no one had ever anticipated that the fallback supplier role Innotech must play to avoid being tainted by its provenance would become so important, so profitable, or so difficult. The information the Innotech/Triage shops collected more than justified their existence; only in moments of crisis—such as that which had generated Two Can Play—was that independence compromised.

If Beth Cannard *was* involved in some gambit with the Soviets, then her father's hints and innuendos and desperately clandestine behavior made sense. Innotech was Sid's baby, but so was Beth. A younger, stronger man would have acted sooner, more unilaterally; Sid Cannard had found one to do it for him—John Shy. No wonder they'd sent him down to Morocco by way of Gabon to haul in Dropout while Beth's operation went down; no wonder there hadn't been a single EO-related casualty or any concerted attempt, beyond his own, to find out what was going on; no wonder Sid was acting as if he were somebody's penetration agent himself: It must be a terrible thing to find out your kid is working for the competition. He recalled Sid's wistful plea, when last they met, to "keep this in the family." The worst part, for the old man, would have been the long interval of unconfirmed suspicion. At the outset, when Shy had gotten off the Falcon in Zürich and into Sid's waiting limousine, Sid had said, "Someday you shall know true agony: the problems of one's child that neither money nor ingenuity can solve."

All this time, he had thought Sid was covering his own tracks—covering his own initiative, in which Beth was only peripherally involved as an accomplice, witting or unwitting. Jack Fowler had thought so, too. Fowler's "Cosmic" file had contained the minutes of an affair Beth Cannard had had with one of those thirty-seven-year-old exchange students the KGB sends to the West as doctoral candidates to loot the universities of technological wealth. When the agent was pulled out of place, Sid Cannard went through endless arbitration to try to expedite the boyfriend's emigration. Officially, the agent had become a "refusnik"—a Jew who has been denied the right to leave Russia—since his cover was that of a Soviet Jew. Beth Cannard had tried to marry him in absentia to pressure the Soviets into releasing him, but since the agent was neither Jewish nor in love, it was to no avail.

The report affirmed that the agent had gotten a great deal of take through Beth during the time he was assigned to America—and postulated that afterward their relationship and the exchange of information continued, but whether it was giveaway take (useless and disinforming, or useful but not crucial), the estimate boys couldn't say. They did say that sources in the Presidium reported comrades rolling in the aisles over the intelligence coup, but that would have been par for the course if Sid was trying to make the entangled KGB asset into a double or an unwitting provocation agent who was getting bad take meant to gum up the workings of the Central Committee. So nothing had been said, nothing had been done—not by Jack Fowler or by Sid himself, who was the only one who would have known whether something *had* to be done.

If Beth wasn't working for or confiding in her father, Sid Cannard's distress made perfect sense. If Shy had been Cannard, he would have been equally slow to point an incriminatory finger: One would want to be damn sure before one acted. Spies could still be executed. Nothing could be made public, especially Innotech's clandestine and special relationship to Defense and CIA. The interests still clamoring to wash away Dropout's memories with 2–4 pyrolo for the crime of having spent six months talking to the Komitat Gosudarstvennoy Bezopasnosti about how much he *didn't* know of Innotech/Triage would have apoplexy if they found out Innotech's director's daughter was routinely passing on goodies to the Soviets.

A hand was waved before Shy's eyes: "Good evening? Am I intruding?"

He let his gaze focus on Dania Morales, sloe-eyed and self-possessed, reminding him that they had met briefly in the corridor of the Baur Au Lac.

"Where?" he teased, stalling for time, and she pouted fetchingly. As when Hunt had cornered him, he could feel the hawks' eyes upon him. If there were any innocents in New York's diplomatic community, they weren't here tonight: Half the Arabs were personae non gratae, Libyans and Palestinians and Iranians under Saudi diplomatic covers. Fully a quarter were representatives of the (conservatively) five-thousand-strong spy contingent the Soviets floated out of the UN and subordinate missions, complete with ID cards from the nonexistent "UN Intelligence Agency." The last quarter seemed to be the defenders, his old friends from the Agency and State and DIA and ISA, DoD's own ferocious little shop, plus the independent contractors, among which the Moraleses were preeminent in Western circles now that the Jackal was penned in Libya and the Germans were down for the count.

She was astoundingly attractive; calculatedly conservative in her little black Galanos suit (the double of which he had dissuaded Beth from buying only yesterday for Sid's sake), a gunmetal silk chiffon blouse with a high neck meant to accommodate Muslim convention, black silk stockings, and Chanel pumps. She slid an unpolished, manicured fingernail along a string of black pearls, her only jewelry. Dressed for business, prepared to deal and be dealt with by men of chauvinistic prejudice, she was deadly: He couldn't think of a thing to say. He remembered having the same reaction to her during their previous encounter. Flak had reported that she was merely Angel's private secretary, a "live drop." She took the orders and the messages, and her husband interpreted and executed them. As he floundered, speechless, she came to his rescue, slipping a hand through the crook of his arm. "We must revenge ourselves," she advised him. "Look at them."

He followed her gaze and saw Cordell Hunt with Beth and some Arabs in traditional garb. He should have been able to tell which faction they represented by their headgear, but never could remember even the names of the damn things. Ah, yes, the double cord was the *aghal* and the cloth was the *ghutra*. That was the extent of his working knowledge. Despite his knowledge gap, he was here because Triage had just finished training and equipping the Oman national guard. He said to Dania, "That man is ruining my life," then regretted it, but had to continue: "My wife left me because of him."

"Surely not *just* because of him," she replied wickedly, taking all in stride. "We have some business to discuss, he tells me."

"I had hoped to talk to your husband. I want to arrange a cease-fire."

"You must talk to me, then. It is my specialty—putting things back together after men have torn them asunder."

"Yes, well . . . I don't want to discuss details, certainly not here. Can we meet privately?"

She raised an eyebrow, manicured and perfect. "At the moment, that would not be wise. Once more you have caught me in an indiscretion; I mustn't compound it. You kept my secret, from Zürich?"

He thought back—the man in her room. "Yes, of course. Why don't you call my office with a ball-park figure and we'll take it from there?"

"For a cessation of hostilities? On a yearly basis? With options? Or something shorter in term?"

He shifted to face her squarely. He hadn't known what to expect, but certainly not her quiet amusement. "Whatever proposal you think might be workable—that your husband would be disposed to accept. I don't need any more PCP's in my life. Neither does Jack Fowler."

She didn't even blink. "Ah, yes, the naughty children. Control over such groups is nominal, you must realize. Not even their Soviet suppliers can do more than suggest obliquely who are the enemies of the revolutionary states they are bound by their own charter to support. Dupes are easy to come by, impossible to control. As in the case of the Western European peace movement into which so much KGB money is funneled, one can merely prompt. Any person so foolish as to adopt an ideology as personal philosophy or to follow a politician who wears a uniform, we feel, deserves to learn by doing. So, I am afraid, I can't help you with the PCP's."

She unlinked their arms, smiling politely. There was something dispassionate about her eyes; like Dropout's, they seemed to be shields, opaque windows. But he must not shut down the possibility of negotiation. He said, "I just wanted you to be aware that I know of your involvement."

"I never doubted it. Give me your card, if we have something to talk about. I must rescue my friend from your friend, even if you will not help me...."

He fumbled in his pocket, feeling the little Ruger there, fished out his card case, wrote his New York numbers on the back of one, and, handing it to her, said that he was more than willing to help her separate those two: "Even if I didn't agree with you that they shouldn't be alone together, I'm categorically incapable of refusing to aid a lady in distress."

He knew he was botching it; he didn't want to think about how badly or how completely, or what Dania Morales was doing to Cordell Hunt's perspective and priorities. He merely followed in the cloud of her perfume, across the room, thinking out of context that he should have realized, when Fowler took a hit, that only Beth or her father could have targeted Jack for this beautiful succubus.

The Soviet resident cut a path through the crowd to interdict them, prowlike nose and bushy eyebrows and custom-tailored suit over ponderous limbs making him look like a radar-rigged spy trawler. He pressed Dania's hand to his Slavic lips, kissed both of Shy's cheeks. While enfolded in the second secretary's bear hug, he heard the man's cynical whisper: "It says something either very good or very bad about both democratic and Communist systems that this man could be here tonight." Shy had no doubt which man the New York resident meant. He hoped to hell the Soviet wasn't going to give him a hard time; he, too, had sacrificed anonymity for power. He whispered back that Innotech could hardly be considered a democracy and that Cordell Hunt was no longer a citizen of the United States, and stepped backward, out of the resident's embrace.

"This," the huge Slav rumbled, "*he* says, also." The man's fat-swathed eyes gleamed. Then he emitted a gusting, theatrical sigh.

"I crave the old days, when your country and mine waged a simple war, a war of minds, of wit, of the elite. Now"—he pawed the air, a palm up, indicating the crowd of guests—"we deal with pigs, fanatics, and assassins. You know, in my country it is said that if a dancer is clumsy, even his balls get in the way." He thrust his head toward Dania suddenly: "A good revisionist like yourself, consorting with these mongrel technologists." He cocked his head at Shy: "Life is not simple anymore, and neither of you remembers what my people know: The fox will work for low wages if you let him guard the henhouse." He straightened up, shook his thick finger at Shy, as Dania said the days of the dueling superpowers were over, the resident must simply get used to it, and she for one was glad that this was so.

Shy thought she was harsh, but the Russian burst out laughing and called her "dash"—he thought it meant "darling" in Albanian—and they made a luncheon date before she turned away, excusing herself and Shy.

"Don't look so pale," she chided, brushing the tip of her nose with her finger. "Old Grechko has a right to be curious—we have a long-standing...knowledge...of each other. Sometimes we collaborate, sometimes we find we have a mutuality of interest—as you and I may yet discover. And in my friend, they may have some vested interest, although I've asked Grechko and he insists they do not."

"Cord says that, too—that there's only armed neutrality."

"We shall discover," said Dania Morales as casually as some other woman might discuss the sleeping habits of a fellow partygoer, "the truth, in good time. I think he wouldn't have spoken to him here if there were anything to conceal."

"My thought exactly," Shy heard himself saying as Dania shepherded him up to Beth and Hunt. Shy began to introduce them: "Beth Cannard, I'd like you to meet—"

Hunt interrupted, asking Shy for the time, and, hearing it, excusing himself: "We've got to leave. Goodnight, Beth, Shy. Pleasant dreams," and spirited Dania Morales away.

"Well," Beth said, her hand at her throat, toying with her Lalaounis torque. "It's nice to see that *someone* can afford to dress properly these days."

"Come on, Beth. Now who is it that can't hold her liquor?" He had talked her into "settling" for the green Halston tunic and skirt she had on, in itself more an investment than a piece of clothing. At that moment it was hard to believe this self-centered woman was capable of thinking about more than what would enhance her next seduction: This evening, if only by default and Hunt's absence, that was him. "You look elegant and understated, which is exactly how I wanted you to look. You know how parochial these Arabs are."

"Who is she? It looks a match made in hell to me." She was angry, piqued, jealous—or frightened, perhaps. He made placatory remarks, hoping to draw her out, unwilling to tell her Dania Morales' name if she truly didn't know it. After a time, she seemed calmer; the color in her cheeks was once again merely that of makeup. She asked him what he would think of "getting out of here? These things are so dreadfully boring. Some of us have been talking about reconvening in the Mayfair. Le Cirque would suit me, this evening."

He agreed hastily. His heart had stopped when she had expressed a wish to leave; he couldn't take her home. Still, he hated the society crowd's New York watering holes, and Le Cirque most of all—his name in the tattle columns was all he needed.

When he was getting her coat, she brought up Hunt again: "How is he doing? He's certainly looking well. And the Dragon Lady with the unlimited bank account? You didn't answer me before. Who was she? You seemed quite taken with her, as if you'd lost her and just found her again. Is she part of his work load, or his rehabilitation?"

"I don't know, Beth—I really don't know. I ran across her in Zürich once, and I believe he's known her for quite some time. I forgot her name, but she knows mine, so I couldn't ask it. When the Soviet resident came over, I was hoping he'd call her by name, but he just called her *dash*—that's darling, isn't it? So you see, I'm as much in the dark as you—"

"John, what's the matter with you? Are you upset? Don't let Scratch get under your skin—he's 'more himself,' he says, which means, as I warned you, that he's operationally stimulated, full of chemical imbalances, and probably certifiably psychotic by this time. Maybe it *is* a match made in hell, or maybe in Moscow. Whatever it is, I'm not going to let them spoil *our* evening. I was being bitchy—I know you hate Le Cirque. And I know it's hard for you, not drinking the way you used to, but you can't let alcohol control your life. We needn't go out. Let's go home and I'll fix us something."

Dear God, I *am* going to fail, he thought. That bastard Hunt …"No, no, I'd just brood. I'll take you to Le Cirque and later you can make it worth my while." He summoned up what he hoped was a serviceable leer. If she was playing him, she was doing a damned good job of it. Women had such an advantage in the intelligence game—natural deviousness coupled with inbred camouflage. He wished he could really go home, home to Zürich to sit by his window and run war-game scenarios on his computers—his way of burying his head in the sand.

No such easy out was going to be forthcoming. He escorted Beth, with something like real compassion, toward the door. If she was the fox everyone's hounds were running to a standstill, she didn't have much time left. And if what he had learned tonight from Hunt was true, then that inept affair with a clever *mokrie dela* boy on what amounted to token duty had really made her into an enemy agent. It was such a textbook case of agent acquisition, he still didn't want to believe it. But not believing it meant that he had to discount Hunt's estimate, Jack Fowler's data, Sid Cannard's morose innuendos, and even the statement Beth had just made: "Maybe it *is* a match made in hell, or maybe in Moscow." And he just couldn't. That was a solid attempt at misdirection, based on information she shouldn't have been able to bring to bear, unless she knew Dania Morales.

He tried to keep up his end of the conversation, but did a bad job of it. He wasn't a field operator. He liked to have plenty of time to mull things over before he acted. Getting into his car, when finally it was brought up in a screech of tires, he felt the little gun Hunt had given him; if she put her hand on his thigh, as she sometimes did when he was driving, she was going to feel it there. He shouldn't have taken it. He vaguely remembered who else was coming with them—those there waiting for their cars: two Americans, an Englishman and his Egyptian wife, a French couple or two. He could handle that crowd. He'd make sure to. He was worried about Grover: B-Z was unpredictable; the dog would probably be crouched in a corner, terrified of its own shadow, but could have had an aggressive reaction, in which case he didn't know what he might find when he unlocked the co-op's door.

Whatever he found, he'd better have a likely explanation ready. He'd work on it during dinner. He had to get through this evening without making any irrevocable errors. Then he had to get in touch with Sid. He needed to find out how much Sid really knew, and what the old spymaster had up his sleeve in the way of solutions, compromises, conciliatory gestures. Maybe they could work something out, for Beth's sake and all of theirs. He'd have to hear what Sid had to say before he could decide how far he was willing to go to win this one for himself.

Hunt thought, *This is impossible* as he began to make love to Dania an hour after leaving the UAE reception. *I'm going to take a fall over this one, she's setting me up and I'm letting her—I haven't even got enough sense to be nervous.* But he knew better—this was his mid-op, deadly calm. Her breasts became the center of his world for a time, but even with her legs wrapped around him, he couldn't forget the mind flexing that malleable body under his, the danger she represented. He had never played at love so hard.

She even knew when his stamina was flagging, and she chose that moment to whisper, "Cory, please, oh, please, do not betray me."

"I couldn't." He licked the sweat between her breasts. "Not now."

"It is so..."—tears leaked from her tight-shut eyes—"...frightening, to want you—so much.... It, us... I—"

"Shush." He judged her heat, and his own, let a few seconds pass. "Now?"

He thought she said "Please." She shuddered under him; he held back, taking her as far as he thought she could go, but when he let himself explode inside her, he found she had saved something for that moment. Then it was too late for technique, and he spent all his reserves in a world of color and rhythm during which he could not have moved to defend himself had the entire PLO come bursting through her door.

This time it was she who said "Stay" when he came to his senses and reached out for a cigarette in the green light of the TA 2000 by her bed.

But he did not; his back was warning him. He rolled aside and stretched out flat, fumbling with cigarettes and lighter and ashtray and hoping he wasn't going to black out or start to shake. She rubbed his solar plexus. "You are cold."

Pulling the satin quilt over them, she fit herself close. "Your part," she began throatily, "in the coming operation—and mine—need not be strenuous. I told you, we no longer have to risk life and limb in the field."

"How so? You don't call this strenuous?"

"Beast! Be serious."

"I am. If I can't keep my hands off you, there won't be anything left of us by Thursday, let alone the weekend or whenever. This is ridiculous. We're supposed to be professionals. I'm not used to being the abject slave of my own dick. Where were you when I thought—never mind, it's too late now anyway."

"When you thought what?"

"When I thought about quitting—you know, home and family and a desk job: the over-thirty blues."

"Ah, I understand. but it's not too late if—if you choose"—she propped herself up on one elbow—"not to destroy what we could have together. Cory ... I thought until last Wednesday I had everything I needed. Now, in one week's time, I no longer think so....Oh, *caro*, you are so...you *do* so need help—but I think you don't know it, or you don't care."

"Angel's dead, isn't he?"

She took a deep breath. "My love for him is dead tonight, a thing I never thought I'd be able to say. If it were so, what would the consequences be?"

Here goes, he thought. "I suppose it would mean we might be able to risk some...long shots...stay together, if we can survive it, long enough to put the Innotech problem to bed, and take it from there."

But she didn't bite. She said, "*We* don't have to involve ourselves in the Maryland go. Diehl is down there with Trish and Liz and the house schematics; it's enough without us. We could go to the Côte d'Azur and wait. I have a place, a safe one...."

"I told you I can't take money for something I didn't do. I'll have money of my own after I bring in Shy's op. With that and what I'll earn from you, and the little bit I've been putting away, I could consider something longer-term. You've got to realize that to somebody who has as little as I do, this much wealth can be pretty daunting. Self-respect is something I've been known to fight to keep."

"So, then, how can I help you bring in Shy's op? You talked to him at the reception. What did he say?"

"He wants me to ID the person who's been contracting these hits. Then I can collect my pay. If it's not Beth, I've got to look further. The tap should help, if she's somebody's cutout. After seeing us together there this evening, she'll be plenty spooked."

"And the woman they have? The Afghan?"

"If the nine-by-twelve envelope involved in this go is what I think it is, and I can get my hands on it, I'll be able to trade it for her freedom."

"Cory! How can you ask such a thing of me? I can't—what *is* the phrase?—double-cross a client."

"I'm not asking you to do any such thing. I can set it up lots of ways. Want to hear them? I could grab the hard evidence; I could hip Innotech or the courier, whoever it turns out to be; I—"

"Cory, let me think about this." He reached over to her and she turned her lips into his hand, kissing his fingers: "Is it these hands, then, or your eyes that take away my common sense and leave me a naked fool? If only I could trust you..."

"Yeah, that's the problem, all right. We've both got it, and it's a bitch. Excuse me, I've got to piss."

She came in and he could feel her watching him from the wet room's door. "You're coming back to bed?"

He realized then that she thought he'd leave; he hadn't suspected she might be that vulnerable; he hadn't, truly, believed her. She *was* moving too fast for him.

'As if reading his mind, she said, "Cory, it's unfair—we have so little time. Sometimes I think I shall be reduced to a single alternative to prove my sincerity, and I just...can't. But otherwise I'll spend the whole time lying to you, and for that I'm simply not strong enough...."

He nodded, back still turned, finished what he was doing, then went and held her while she told him, in a whisper, that he mustn't betray her, for "Angel must remain alive in spirit, whatever happens. Promise me."

She was crying and he promised that he'd never turn on her and took her back to bed. She talked about her fears now—he wouldn't approve of her methods in Maryland; the chances they were taking; the weakness she'd shown by crumbling so completely before his interrogation. "What frightens me most is that I'm not afraid of you in my heart, *caro*, only in my mind. Are you so great a deceiver that I am wrong? Or is it true? Are we—" She hesitated, dragged on her cigarette so that her face was momentarily lit by its coal.

He didn't help her.

"Are we falling in love, despite everything?"

"Maybe because of everything," he answered, surprising himself. He could play it her way; he had a handle on it; he could step right into Angel Morales' shoes and the world would never know the difference—or he could bring in his op, betray her and air-drop with Martinova back into Kandahar, fight his war, his way. He didn't know, that evening, what he was going to do.

But his response had satisfied her. He cuddled with her, smelling her hair, feeling his heart pound with confusion and doubts. He had never played for stakes like these. He ran his hand over her supple thighs, wishing his life were not such an irretrievable mess. Somehow, he dozed off, holding her. He woke sometime later with her lips at his throat and he was not disoriented; he knew right where he was.

She had brought them tea and biscuits, and she was tentative: "I can't waste the night, our night, sleeping. Are you angry?"

"No, I'm lucky. Come here."

He was not twenty any longer; he dealt with her in short order and remarked that for the rest of the evening affection was all she could expect.

"How did you get started?" she asked from the crook of his arm, turned sideways with breath tickling his neck and a thigh thrown over him. "In intelligence work, I mean. When we met, you had just left Central Intelligence. How long were you their officer?"

He recalled the old lies, the old operation, and realized that he had been discounting certain major difficulties: Eventually she was going to deduce or discover that he had turned on her and Angel; that he had killed the man she loved. Flak or Mino could drop enough clues to allow her to put things together; Shy could outright implicate him. He wondered what she would think of him then.

He said, "God, that was centuries ago. My dad was chief of station in Tel Aviv and I had a summer job, straight errand-boy stuff. That was just after the Egyptian/German missile scandal, and Mossad's misreading of the data caused a shake-up, so that Amit, from Military Intelligence, took over Mossad from Isser Harel and all hell broke loose—deputies resigning, that sort of thing. Nobody sulks like an intelligence professional. Midway through, Ben-Gurion resigned. Files disappeared in Mossad—they weren't ready for an army takeover. Harel had a following like only an operational commander can put together—by September he was back in as intelligence overseer, but Amit was confirmed as head of Mossad.

"In the interim—July 2, I think it was—I was riding my bike through town and one of Harel's deputies came by in a car and sideswiped me—just enough so that he had to get out of his car. By the time my bike's fender was back in working order, I had an agent who was proposing that I be his contact—the old Mossad group wanted to keep their channels to CIA open and keep the militarists from closing down all the intelligence-sharing lines. I was too young at seventeen to be suspect.

"It was so covert, even I didn't understand what the deputy was really asking, but I did what he suggested. I took the first envelope to another officer in my dad's station, and made a deal with him to keep supplying take as long as Percy didn't find out. I was a perfect cutout—I didn't know the deputy's name, but he knew everything about me, including my indiscretions with certain daughters of Israel. It worked fine until my father found out about it. It was the only time he ever hit me, and he was right. But I didn't know it—when you're young and ignorant, you don't count your condition as a debit. I hit him back; gave him a black eye, I heard later. At the time, I was out of my head. Percy told me to get out of there before he killed me, and I took him at his word—ran off and joined the Israeli army as a grunt.

"They found me two weeks later, shipped me back to Tel Aviv

under guard. I thought Percy was going to send me back to the States—that was a fate worse than death to me in those days. But they put me back in place, and I've been doing pretty much the same thing ever since." Surprised at how long he'd talked, he admitted to himself that she was damn good, getting that much take from him.

"I, too, started early. Since we've worked so long and hard for others, it seems to me that we deserve some time for ourselves," she said dreamily, stretching. "Your tea will get cold. Here." He took it. "Did you ever arrive at the philosophical base you were seeking? I remember how you and Angel used to argue."

He shrugged, pretending it wasn't a loaded question. "Sort of. ...I don't talk about it. You can't if you've really got anything worthwhile. When I see something happening that's unequivocally worth fighting for—or against—I throw my weight where I think it should be. Otherwise, I'm still working all sides against the middle—we could do with a lot fewer political manipulators of all persuasions."

She snorted softly. "Now you sound like Angel—or me. In the important things, Cory, we agree."

"I wouldn't have helped those kids—the PCP's—you were with in the Baur Au Lac."

"Ah, ah, ah! Yes you would. They were going to blow up a nuclear power station. I diverted them to less disastrous amusements. Innotech was on the Soviet list of targets being circulated— you know, 'enemies of the revolution'—and the client wanted to take advantage of that fact to cover certain materiel transfers.... It wasn't an ideological action on our part. The Soviets were happy, having gotten an unexpected return on all that money they've been pumping into the West European peace movement; the client was happy; the PCP's..."

"Jack Fowler wasn't happy."

"I've told you, I only want to extricate myself from what has become a difficult position. There's no right or wrong side in our world, Cory: All freedom fighters are terrorists, all societies to some degree unfree. You've suffered from those who sit at the UN pretending to be able to take human rights from 'terrorists' while protecting 'freedom fighters.' *All* governments are totalitarian, equally reprehensible—"

"But you live in America?"

"Democracy has its problems: mediocrity, obsession, gullibility, waste...perhaps less problems than other systems, though. For me, since we almost never work here, it's been a safe and convenient base."

"But no more?"

"That, Cory, is up to you. If I can finish this contract and still consider myself safe here, we'll have an opportunity granted to few—we shall make abandoned dreams come true."

"We'll see what we can do," he promised, lethargic and content with her head on his belly and her dreams in his head.

She had lots of guts to even talk about dreams and safety after his encounter on Sunday with Helms, and hers tonight with Shy. When she asked him for his estimate of Shy's sincerity, he responded honestly that she'd have to submit a proposal before she found out "whether it's a negotiation or his chance to deliver an ultimatum. Corporate types often don't know the difference. He could be playing for time—don't forget that Beth's Sid Cannard's daughter, whether she's your 'client' or not."

"So"—Dania rolled over onto him—"you don't think he'd free your compatriot as part of a negotiated settlement with me?"

"I—" He pulled her head down and kissed her; then, holding her cheek against his, managed: "That's the nicest thing anybody's ever offered to do for me," but his voice was not behaving. "Shit. No, I don't think so. He doesn't have her. ISA does. I need take to bargain with, otherwise I'm going to end up storming some high-security holding facility, a forward base or ISA safe house—she could be anywhere by now. Unfortunately, I stuck my foot in my mouth on camera and promised her I'd get her out—they know I'm going to come after her."

"Then you can't." She sat up.

"Yeah, so it would seem. But I've got to do something. My boys say...Flak and Mino volunteered to help me with it. I'm fucked if I do and fucked if I don't. I've got too much guilt riding on this one. A friend of mine from SIS was blown away to give them a body to toe-tag 'Cordell Hunt'—I think I told you about it. This girl's not even of that caliber, just a revolutionary with soul but no cool. She'd rather have them think she's KGB than admit her NTS connections, so she's disinforming her way right into intensive interrogations. A couple weeks of psychedelics and truth drugs and you begin making up stuff to please them. There might not be anything left of her mind by now. Some people trade in their personalities—draw a blank, become a clean slate. Zero. Zip."

He got up abruptly, pulled on his jeans. He had switched to his Marrakech workbelt Monday morning, stripped the silencer from his Commander, seated it in its old SSS holster. In the belt itself was now the thirty-one thousand in cash he had picked up with his bailout documents Monday morning. He had missed her strategy conference, but it had been well worth it: A workable bailout meant that he wouldn't come up short, made the last move his, gave him the "edge" Dania had accused him of needing, without which he couldn't take high-stakes chances.

"Cory?"

"Flak and Mino ought to be here any minute." He buckled his belt, reached across her, reclaimed his Commander from its niche between his pillow and the headboard. He hadn't fired the Detonics Diehl had provided. He couldn't count on it until he'd checked it out. He settled the Commander on his hip.

"Cory, I will give it to you."

"What?" He raised his head.

She had come up on her knees. "The packet—the intelligence. I have thought it through. You are going to neutralize the client, yes?"

"Yes. No one's going to come back to you crying foul, not even Innotech. I'll steal it, I'll take the blame. It won't reflect on you—"

"Even if it did, if it's what you say, you'll have sufficient leverage to protect us. If it is not"—she shrugged fatalistically—"I'll pass it on when I am instructed to, or not, as you wish. Perhaps even if it's valueless, they could be made to think that it is not. But you must promise not to resort to force to free your friend. If we must extricate her, we shall find a group mounting an action against some suitable government—you say this is ISA—and they will include her release in their forthcoming list of justice demands. Do you agree?"

He sat down on the bed. "Why are you doing this?" He looked at his feet.

"I am selfish, I want you for myself—alive and well."

"I—" The buzzer rang, saving him. He grabbed his chance and bolted for the door, leaving her to dress with only his admission that he didn't know how to thank her.

He was home free.

All that remained was the easy part: getting in, out, leaving the targets dead or helpless and the specifics as confused as possible so that no one could piece it together. His relief was immense and immediate as he let Flak and Mino, unharmed and wild with suppressed excitement, in the door.

"Cool, Grover, *cool!*" Mino was crowing in an uncanny imitation of Flak's man-of-the-people diction. They both wore Triage baseball caps and jump suits and carried tool kits. "Cory, man, you should have seen how slick we were—"

Flak interrupted. "Excuse me, okay? I've just got to go hook the receiving end up, so we don't lose anything while we're congratulating ourselves." He was high-tensile, pale and squinting; his words came from between gritted teeth.

"Any problems I should know about?" As the asset came abreast of him, Hunt put a hand on Flak's arm.

"No, sir, if you're right about nothing being a problem that doesn't cause problems. That fucking hound bit me." He showed Hunt his forearm, wrapped in stained gauze. "I hope to hell he's had his rabies shots, or I'm going back over there and bite Shy. There's enough Colombian flake in there to put Beth away for twenty years on drug-importation charges. And...you think *this* one lives good? You should *see* that place. I don't think guys like us even have a chance in life; her type's got everything worth having sewn up.

"I had some technical difficulties, too—had to rewire all their countersurveillance so that the 'standby' lights and the 'on' lights were reversed. Before we did that, we had to give them something to find if the building super mentioned we were there and Shy didn't cover for us, so we went down into the basement and did a punch-block tap." He pulled a punch-block tool from his rear pocket. "So we've got a diversionary 'number-dialed' decoder in the basement, and she's got no countersurveillance at all, and what's left that's working is my best shot at undetectable transmissions...."

"But?"

"But, I don't know. I put some line analyzers and transmitters and phony tap-traps around to justify the service call. But the big stuff—if they run a check on their logic sequencer or anything technical, they'll figure this whole thing out. So there's about a twelve-hour half-life, I figure. If we don't get something by then, what we get might be bogus. Right now, with her counter-surveillance on, she's defeating it, but if she puts her system on standby…"

"It'll register all your surveillance gear."

"You got it, sir. Can I go hook in? Dania won't mind if I use her consoles, will—"

"Go ahead, go on. Come with me, Mino, you look like you could use a cup of coffee."

"And a meal and some sleepy-weed, sir. Flak's so damn nervy. We were supposed to get dinner, but he sat around waiting to see if they came in, if the lights went on, if nobody came out right away. Then we drove two blocks uptown, and turned everything in the car on to see if we were getting any signals. You know him, sir—he can't let anything go. He's never heard about fleeing the scene of the crime."

Hunt opened the refrigerator, bowed slightly: "Do your worst."

Mino rooted among the spoils of a raid Hunt and Dania had made on Zabar's delicatessen, piling paper cartons in the crook of his arm. "Hey, sir, did you get to talk to Dania about Liz and Trish, like I asked you?"

"No, I'm sorry, I will. But you have to realize that they're grown women, they've been doing this probably as long as you've been flying. Nobody's making them. We're the outsiders—we can't come in and say we don't like hanky-panky in our assaults, just straight-ahead shoot-'em-ups, if you please. As far as I know, we're just backup. But then, I missed the meeting.…"

"Yes, sir, that's right. They're making room for us, and under the circumstances, I like it just as well. It's Liz I'm thinking about."

"Think about running your end of it—*our* end of it. We might be bringing other people down on them—other agencies, anyone. We've got to do a lot of sweeping of the area, maybe for a couple of days before, and I need to keep all these different interests thinking like a team. You'll have to help me. Okay?"

"Okay, sir." Mino grinned, and brought his armload of food to the counter. "Anything you say." He opened a carton, wrinkled his nose. "Fish." He put the Scottish salmon aside and tried again, coming up with Westphalian ham, which he laid on raisin pumpernickel, followed by a layer of cream cheese and tomatoes vinaigrette. "That ought to do it," the pilot judged critically, and in the same breath: "Sir, we took a little of her blow—I mean, who wouldn't? For verisimilitude's sake, like you say—we had to make it look right. So I'm wired and maybe I'm mouthing off too much, but it really bothers me about these people. I mean, I like them, I really like them. I'd hate to see anything happen to Liz."

"They're counting on that. So am I. We'll be there to support them, Mino."

"For a minute, anyway." He looked up at Hunt, chewing ruminatively, a wad of sandwich puffing out his cheek. He swallowed. "Flak says this thing's out of control, that you're serious about... her, this... you know what I'm saying—that it's real. That so, sir?"

"You expect me to answer that? Here? Now?"

"Nope, but it's getting pretty real for me, too, if you know what I mean." He was turning away, rummaging in Dania's larder for a beer. "Beth, man... I can't understand it. She's *got* everything already. What could she want?"

Hunt, making himself an espresso, said over the gasp of steam, "More."

"More what?"

"It's not my business to worry about what, only who, where, when, and how."

Mino came close, taking off his Triage baseball cap and fingering it. "Flak told me you're taking us along when you go get Martinova. Liz says we aren't coming back here after Maryland. That so?"

Hunt got a lemon from the refrigerator, pared some peel, and lit the spray as he pinched it over his cup. It burst into flame.

"Doesn't that hurt your fingers?"

"Sometimes. But you can't do it any other way."

"Is there a message in that for me?"

"Maybe. It depends on the kind of work you do and the kind of decisions you make. If we come through Maryland intact, I'm going with Morales to her little hideaway on the Côte d'Azur. I'll lick my wounds and ready up for Martinova from there. But it's a big 'if,' and there's always plenty of skew factor in these things.

Maryland's not our go, so we don't have much say in minimizing risk. Given a one-hundred-percent survival rate, and nominal success, you'll have time to sort your options."

"Cory, I'm trying to tell you that if you decide to hang with this Nirvana bunch for real, I'd be—"

"Flaps up, tiger. You do what feels right to you. That's the only way—take the risks you figure you can afford to take, for whatever reasons matter to you, so if you go down, you'll understand why. But don't do what I do—I can afford to take any damn risk at all; I haven't a lot to lose."

"But plenty to gain." Mino grinned broadly. "It's going to be okay, sir. Honest. Just like making a training film."

"I hope that won't be what we're doing—making someone else's. But listen up, my friend. I've got lots of personal reasons to kick these particular asses. Whoever it is that's been hassling Innotech paved my way into the Lubyanka. John Shy's no real close friend of mine; he could turn on us in a minute. You're in danger because of me as long as you're doing this. You can't trust me. You can't trust Flak. You can't trust Liz."

"I can trust Flak. And I can trust you. Liz, that's different—boy-girl shit." He caught Hunt's gaze. "You know, Cory, you *can* count on me. *I* always knew you could cut it, when everybody was saying you couldn't, even Flak. So it's sort of similar for me, everyone always estimating me as the low-end, high-risk factor. I've scoped things, boss, and I'm right here with you."

"Yeah, I believe you are. All right. About the Falcon—"

"Glad you asked. The TiltRotor's got an effective one-way range of eight hundred and fifty miles, so getting to Hanscom's no problem. But we shouldn't file a flight plan until the last possible minute. As it is, we'll be convening a SWAT team invitational if Shy decides we're stealing his plane. And I've got to do a little research into uncontrolled fields with five-thousand-foot runways. Sometimes you find an abandoned one—"

"Liz talked to you about the Falcon?"

"I told her we had it, somehow. Then your—Mrs.—Dania, she asked me about it, about how I thought you'd feel about her asking you. Ain't women wonderful?" He shook out his curls, flattened from the cap. "So I said I'd ask you. So I'm asking you—you want to use it?"

"Just keep it on the back burner; have it gassed up and checked out. That's all the hint I want to give Shy right now as to what I've got in mind."

"Yeah. Did you hear he told Flak we couldn't use any of the fallbacks he gave us?" Mino fingered his jump suit's zipper. "He'll be ripshit when he finds out we wired his house. That Grover really took a fall. It's a shame to see a brave dog like that shivering and whining—"

"I told him. I saw him at the UAE reception, along with nearly the whole of the Gulf Criminal Council and assorted KGB and CIA types."

"I'd like to have seen that. Was Beth with him?"

"Oh, yeah. Dania—"

"I what?" she said from behind him. Mino said he'd best go check on Flak. Hunt said they all should.

In the doorway, Flak stopped them with a finger to his lips, then flipped a switch and voices filled the air: Beth's, John Shy's.

Shy was saying, "... call your father and get things straightened out before—"

Beth, in a strained voice, replied, "You do and I'll kill you, you sanctimonious bastard. I got myself into this and I'll see it through without any help or hindrance from you. None of you are any better than I—" Her pitch heightened.

Flak snapped off the audio, pushed his headset down so that it collared his neck, tilting his chair back on two legs as Dania objected she wanted to hear more. Pointing to a loaded cassette, he said, "You can listen to them argue to your heart's content. But I think it's clear enough—that bastard fucked us. He's going to make a deal with Sid Cannard. I was worried about this. Christ, Cory, what do we do?"

Hunt was conscious that Flak should have directed his question to Dania, whose op was in danger of being compromised, even as he responded, "Exactly what we were going to do before."

Dania stood on tiptoe and kissed him; he felt her palm run up his spine. "He's right, children. By the time Shy is mobilized to action, we'll be sunning ourselves on my patio, listening to waves slap the sand. Shy is not an operational commander if he would willingly give up the element of surprise."

"And you are?" Flak responded to her.

Hunt closed his eyes, existing in a distended moment where

only sounds mattered, until he heard Dania rejoin calmly that she was not, but Cory was, Flak must certainly agree, "*ultima.*"

Then he opened them and said, "Listen, there's no way of telling what he's trying to do from that. Maybe he's seen an angle in this for himself. If there are repercussions from the bugging, the fault is mine. But when you do this, you always hear stuff that can skew you—unrelated conversations that seem related, anything. Let Flak stay on the line and we'll analyze the night's take in the morning. Okay, Flak? Mino tells me you're probably not tired."

"Yes, sir." Flak's chair tipped down abruptly. He put the headset back on and sat hunched over, palms cupping the pads on his ears.

"Come on, people, let him work."

He headed for the kitchen to make Flak a sandwich. Dania took over when she saw what he had in mind, making up three plates. Mino took one in to Flak.

"Bed?" she said, putting their plates on trays and handing one to him.

She was shaken as he had not seen her since he had come in from the street encounter. "Wonderful," he replied, and, following her down the hall, "Don't worry—if she aborts your operation, you'll be in better shape than you are now."

"And the intelligence you say you need?"

"Oh, I'll get it. Or I'll get by without it."

Twice he woke that night, once slick with sweat and once bolt upright in bed. Both times she was holding him, and hushed him when he tried to apologize.

Chapter
16

ON Water Street, Krump Tower rises high over New York's Battery district and the East River. In its elevator, Flak searched through his keys; inserted one in the floor-selector panel; turned it to "on" so that when he pressed the button for the thirty-seventh floor, the sensor would respond and the elevator take him there; saw the button come alight; turned the key back to "off" and removed it from the lock.

This was his own eleventh-hour fallback. Fucking Hunt. There was going to be hell to pay. Right now the elevator cameras were shunting their signal to the station's monitors. When the doors opened and he stepped out into a river-view reception area of bronze and steel and rosewood, he was passing through an archway that was verifying his identity visually, reporting the heat signature of his weapons, sniffing him for chemical explosives, and collating that information with the fingerprint-identification system he had triggered by pressing the elevator's button and with whatever security notations existed in his file. If his had been for any reason an unauthorized print, he wouldn't have gotten this far; the elevator would have refused him entry by rejecting his instructions; automatic isolation, a further access control, would detain him in the hallway, now, if the fingerprint ID didn't match the microwave/infrared profile that scanners were comparing to his files; doors would automatically lock; heat or air-conditioning ducts would deliver incapacitants to subdue the intruder in the automatic isolation area. He was always relieved when the doors at the end of such halls opened in response to his "insert card, press plate, speak name, tap code" formula.

Beyond the inner rosewood door, the office was busy. A male receptionist looked up from his desk as Flak approached. "Well, if it isn't *point* 007."

"Cute. Give me an office for an hour," Flak said over the chatter of computer terminals. The man tapped his, chewed a stylus with a loud sucking noise, and at last said, "Negative. Sorry."

"It's lunch. Don't bullshit me, *puttana.* I'm taking a 'procedural liberty' just being here. A couple more won't ruin my day."

"Take a look," the man suggested. Flak went around behind him and glanced at the screen. "See?" the secretary wheedled. "We're full up, sir. *Sir? Sir!*"

Flak was already headed down the long partitioned hall. At the fifth door he came to, he stepped aside as someone came out with an armful of software, then he caught the door as it began to close and stepped inside. The man behind this particular desk was gray and distinguished-looking, fiftyish and pale. "How did *you* get— Ah, Darling, isn't it? What an unexpected—"

"Come on, cut the crap. I need to use the facilities. Go have lunch or something." Flak unzipped his jacket, took it off, threw it over the interviewee's chair before the desk.

"Look here, Godwin—"

"*You* look here." He put his hand on his hip, where his side arm was holstered. "I've been out there a long time and I've had a real *rough* time and I'm not feeling reasonable. You know who Helms is?"

The ISA control officer assured him he did.

"Well, if I see that asshole anywhere near my agent again, *I'm* going to blow his head to New Jersey. Talk to somebody at DIA. People with personal grudges don't belong in this business."

"I believe he's pulled two weeks' sick leave."

"Bullshit. I'm telling you, get out of here for a few minutes. There's no use in my talking to you, and you know it. I'd have shuttled down to D.C. if I had the time, but I don't." He was tempted to stick his snubby in the bureaucrat's face. "If you're smart, you'll go listen in on my call from some 'secure location.' But don't let me find out about it. If there are any uninvited guests at my party, I'm going to come back here and lay a load of lewisite in your ventilation system. Fucking ISA can't keep its nose out of this, DIA's breathing down my neck. It's like alphabet soup out there."

The controller's face reddened, but he stood up. "You can't just come in here and—"

"You want to throw me out? You want to sign a refuse-assistance order? If you're not out of here in ten seconds, I'm going back to the desk and fill out an interdepartmental memo, and you can have the pleasure of signing off on your own dismissal slip. Because if things blow up in our faces, that's what you'll have done. And you're at just the right level to take all the weight—not important enough to save, but ranked high enough that you ought to know better. Go on. *Disappear!*"

The man did, and Flak sank into the executive's yet-warm orthopedic chair, muttered counterthreats the other man had thrown out behind him lingering in the air. When the door had slammed, he punched up access blocks and hooked in to an international secure line. Getting Jack Fowler on the phone took a little more than ten minutes, but at least the delay gave him time to find and defeat the recording function on the executive's phone. They never learned. They thought the records would protect them if they were falsely accused of complicity or lack of cooperation. But things didn't work that way.

Jack's voice was clear and his diction unblurred by drugs or distance: "I thought I'd be hearing from you about now. How's it going?"

"It's not good news. How are you feeling, sir?"

The voice coming back to him was dry: "You think I can't stand the shock? How's our Dropout?"

"Salvageable. If our relatives don't take him out. We're awfully hot, sir. I put a tap on Shy's girlfriend's phone and it seems to me Innotech's going to be coming to you to make some sort of deal—"

"Where are you?"

"Water Street. It's okay, sort of—at least, you told me if I needed to—"

"Yes, yes. What else?"

"I'm trying to tell you. Our people are still too overt with their surveillance. Helms's guys tried to interdict us on the street—we scratched one and winged one. The client's passion seems to be a double cross; the drop zone is Turki-al-Faisal's place in Maryland, you know the one—"

"Saudi intelligence is in this?"

"Not knowingly, or wittingly. The Soviets' New York resident borrowed the guy's house key for the handover. From what I can make out, he's trying to buy his way West—use the take as defector's buy-in, and the contact is Agency. So it looks like all the stuff's been going in a big circle to Langley—" He heard a chuckle, stopped. "Did you *know* that, sir?"

"You're doing a remarkable job, Darling. What's the problem?"

"Sir, I can't imagine everybody's not going to have teams on-site. You know they can't resist that sort of coup. We're under the gun to prove to Nirvana that we're not trying to insert ourselves for just that reason—to take *them* out. The second-in-command there, name of Diehl, told me straight out that if he sees one indication that we're penetrations, he's going to consider it a personal affront." Again, Fowler chuckled. "Sir," Flak protested, "it's no laughing matter. Dropout wants to secure the package and trade it to you—to ISA—for Martinova, so that's perfect. But if there's a fucking army of intelligence types coming out of the bushes in Maryland, we might not get that far. If the types don't get us, the people we're with are going to take a dim view of us—there'll be no way to make them believe we weren't in on any attempt to interdict."

"You've convinced me. But it's a delicate matter. Just do the best you can."

"Now you sound like Shy. Give me your word you won't make a deal with Cannard that endangers my team?"

"That goes without saying. I'll try to do more, to make it clear to him that *I* shall consider it a personal affront if any of his apes touch a hair of your fair heads. What else?"

"What else? Oh, yeah...can I use my credentials if I have to? I may have to go straight up with Dropout. You know, he's still sharp. I'd like to be able to assure the Côte d'Azur landing—no welcoming committee, maybe even be able to divert to a base if things get tough enough."

"No. You stay within the bounds of your cover. If Dropout can hack it, so can you; no need to play truth or consequences with Nirvana. I need you as a trustee. No matter what *he* does, you be a good little independent. Make yourself indispensable. You've had plenty of practice."

"Yeah, sir, but—"

"Speak up, son, that's what we're doing—talking about it."

"Morales and the rest aren't any kind of insurgents. There's no net to roll up, no specific Soviet or radical tilt. Just those kids that mined your lawn and like that."

"Your prior orders stand so far as they go."

"Yes, sir."

"That sounded very grudging. Almost disgusted. Suggest an alternative then."

"How about *not* taking part in this handover? Staying out of the way and letting the various services take each other out on-site. I don't like the weather report. It's going to get very wet."

"*Then* you flash your credentials. That's what umbrellas are for. We need the edge this is going to give us. I want Sid Cannard."

"Yes, sir, you'll get him. If they don't get us first."

"That's up to you. It seems to me you asked for something challenging."

"That's true, sir. Next time, tell me to shut up."

When he had said goodbye and made his way to the street, he found Hunt sitting in the Wagoneer just outside by the curb.

"So? How's Jack?"

"He says he's right with us, sir. I guess we'll have to settle for that."

* * *

Dania Morales had no option but to keep her luncheon date with Grechko, the Soviet resident. One never knew enough about a target. She still knew no more than one could deduce from Grechko's overt embassy posting: He was not GRU (Glavnoye Razvedyvatelnoye Upravleniye—Chief Intelligence Directorate), though GRU agents, reporting to the Soviet General Staff, were commonly charged with strategic, tactical, and technological military intelligence collection as well as with industrial espionage and what was currently called "clandestine technology transfer." Nor was Grechko, like Hunt, a man "in black" or, as the Soviets say, "within the stones," a deep-cover operative or a specialist in executive action, guerrilla warfare, or black networks.

Grechko was just a man with problems. As a chief of station, he must report to his ambassador. Seven years in New York was a long time for a KGB colonel of Special Service II; they would pull him out, soon, to determine how much the decadence to which he had long been exposed had corrupted his stout Slavic soul. The First Chief Directorate of KGB, which oversaw all, had seen something it did not condone in Grechko—perhaps his credit-card receipts, perhaps something more damning. Or so Grechko thought he could make her believe.

But she knew better, from the client. And she knew Special Service II, which had grown so powerful that it virtually controlled GRU and Directorate S (the *mokrie dela*, or wet affairs, department), as she made it her business to know the workings of all counterintelligence services for and against whom she was likely to act.

It was a measure of the sensitivity of the situation that the Soviets' First (U.S. and Canada) Department had not exposed their own agent through a series of judicious leaks (as Cory Hunt had been exposed by the Americans, who were afraid to either claim him or disown him under the Chafee amendment, S. 391, or the corollary Agent Identities Act), discreetly ruining his career without admitting his provenance; nor had it dispatched a *mokrie dela* assassin to arrange for him a "heart attack," a ricin-induced flu, an unfortunate accident if poisons were considered too chancy.

None of this had happened. Instead, the client had called upon her to prevent the handover of certain delicate data and ensure that there would be "no further problem from that quarter." One tended to read that last as a call for executive action. One tended to assume, from what was given and what was withheld, that the Soviet wanted to defect before he was recalled to Moscow. One tended to sympathize.

But there was something to worry about, or the work would not have been contracted out: The Soviets were perfectly capable of, and temperamentally prone to, making their own hits. Cory had remarked upon this to her, cautiously, offhandedly, as he continually was careful to be. He offered no suggestions, cast no aspersions, asked no questions that might be construed as operational interrogation. He'd carefully stayed away from the strategy conference, not wanting, he later admitted, to lock horns with Diehl, to be forced to approve or disapprove, to "make anybody nervous." Now he was gone, down in Maryland with his two trainees and her soul.

She felt emptied, now that he had left. All the things she had worried about while he had been with her seemed petty and foolish. He had shared the take his young technician had gotten from the bugging with her; he'd told her the truth from the beginning. But no one did that anymore. And truth where lies were appropriate stirred suspicions. Diehl was upset, sure that Cory would bring his own troubles upon them, at the least: "After all, madonna, you do not need him or his people for this. Yet we must accommodate them. Why is that? Why not take him abroad and wait with him? When I have completed my mission, I will join you. No? He will not, you say? Then ask yourself why he is so insistent on risking his life, willing to undertake an unspecified action—it goes against such a man's nature to work blind, or to take direction. Do this, and tell me your conclusions."

Dania knew what Cory wanted—the packet, whatever it contained. But she could not tell Diehl, who was convinced that Dania was loveswept, though he was too loyal to say so; who was concerned but confident of his ability to deal with any threat Cordell Hunt might come to pose. And there was the subtler difficulty of Diehl's personal chagrin at being superseded, though Cory had gone out of his way to minimize discord.

If she had been able to ascertain that the resident had the packet with him in New York, she would have altered her tactics, taken the intelligence now, given up on the Maryland segment, with its concomitant difficulties of Saudi involvement and disaffection in her ranks.

The ladies had reported mixed results: Liz had succeeded in extracting a good deal of information from Mino, little of it pertinent, seemingly, beyond reaffirming his unswerving loyalty to his teammates; Trish had fared badly, in her own estimation, giving more than she got back from Flak. Flak, as Cory had warned, was the one to watch.

Also, as he had predicted, John Shy's offer to open negotiations had proved to be little more than a delaying action. Shy was formidable, an old hand who had started in the Office of Naval Intelligence, gone into Task Force 157, from there to an administrative post in the National Security Agency, then over to CIA's Directorate of Science and Technology, before he left to earn five times his Agency salary in the private sector as Innotech's Western European regional director.

If the client was (as Cory was certain and had nearly succeeded in convincing her at the UAE reception) Beth Cannard, daughter of Innotech's director and mistress of John Shy, and if Shy (as he himself had declared to Beth during the argument they had had while Flak listened and taped all that was said) was going to "see what could be done to salvage something from this abysmal mess," then what had seemed a straightforward action was becoming very complicated indeed.

Cory's dry reminder that Shy knew the taps were in place didn't ease her mind. She didn't understand why Shy would go to such lengths to force Beth Cannard to incriminate herself for the record, especially when that record was being taped at what he must consider an enemy location. All of that shouting and crying and recriminating and threatening she had heard might well have been for their benefit, but what she had been intended to construe from it, she still could not say: It was inconclusive.

If it were Cory's life Shy wanted, he could have had it in Zürich, in Marrakech, or any time since. Cory needed to look more squarely at his position, but she understood why he had not yet done so: Uppermost in his mind was survival; with no likelihood of it save serendipity, he saw things in a perspective that would allow him to keep fighting. She had seen it all before. This time she was determined to do more. To do that, she must make him realize the time had come for him to give up fieldwork. And this was very difficult: They always thought they could not; years of experience told them to keep moving, keep acting, keep the world

at bay. She had failed with Angel. She could not fail with Cordell
Hunt.

If Grechko could contemplate a new life under the auspices of
an American resettlement program despite the diminishingly small
chance of survival a Soviet had when he had betrayed the moth-
erland, she could see to Cory's needs, if he would let her. To that
end, she must extract from the Russian some additional intelligence, either during luncheon or after.

The restaurant Grechko had chosen was Chanterelle in SoHo,
American nouvelle cuisine served *prix fixe* in a narrow apricot
room dominated by an antique armoire and desk. Her feet made
no sound on the gray carpet; the Soviet sat midway back, pon-
derously chic in an Armani suit and gleaming crocodile shoes.
Dania doubted his CIA handler would be either willing or able
to allow the Russian to defect in the style to which he had become
accustomed. And for the first time in years, she doubted her own
prowess, not her ability to extract information or stage an action
but to see clearly ahead to end-game contingencies when, wherever she looked, all she saw was Cordell Hunt, leaning back against
the wall in her hallway as he had been that night he came in from
his sidewalk encounter, exhausted yet taut with the high-tensile
paranoia of a man forced to his limit of endurance and finding
that this time he could not push himself beyond it.

It was this harm the Soviets had done him, above and beyond
any lesser harm: They had shown him he could no longer tran-
scend himself, as the finest athletes, soldiers, and operatives must
be confident they could do. Angel had died before he came up
against the limits of his ability. She had no reference point from
which to deal with a man betrayed by his own humanity, unfor-
giving of his body's frailty or his mind's failure to endure all trials.
Though it was unfair to expect better, Cory Hunt, whose arms
bore traces of growths removed where chemical interrogation had
caused his very cells to revolt, and whose dreams found ways to
damn him for not doing what could not, in waking, be done,
harbored such deep and unremitting disappointment in his performance that several times she had wondered if he was seeking
only an acceptable way to die.

For that, she could blame Grechko, and all the Grechkos and
Shys and Cannards of this world, who risked nothing of their

persons yet passed on the lives and deaths of others routinely, in their businesslike cocoons of cost-effective considerations of performance and long-term gain. Angel had maintained that there were no innocents, only victims and perpetrators waiting to change places; that greed and envy had become codified in communism and disseminated by democracy; that social democracy and scientific socialism were merely old dogs pretending to new tricks, but that in actuality there existed but a single trick, common to all: deception for personal gain. And so, accepting the premise, the most straightforward behavior, the greatest degree of honesty that could be attained, was that of giving up all illusions of sanctimony, all pretense of ideology, all lip service to duty, honor, or morality beyond the personal sort to which Cordell Hunt occasionally alluded—which she feared he thought he had lost and could never regain.

The Grechkos were wiser for having no pretensions; they had nothing to lose; all behavior was to them acceptable, as long as it was survivable. And with that sad hypothesis, at this point in her life, she had come to agree—until Cory made her remember what it was like to feel. And, feeling, she was vulnerable as she had not been for five years. But she was also more dangerous: She would protect Cory, who wakened her sleeping soul, at any cost.

Grechko rose to greet her, and his extended hand allowed his Cartier cuff links to gleam in the nearly windowless restaurant's soft, pale light. There were perhaps fifteen tables, half of them occupied by others who chose to meet quietly where they would not be observed. She smiled and responded to him in Russian, endured a modicum of small talk, accepted graciously compliments on her appearance that she felt, today, she did not deserve, and deliberated as seriously with him over their choice of fried crab-meat balls, seafood sausage, or trout mousse as if they were counting theater MIRV's for NATO deployment.

One could order à la carte, he suggested wickedly, unbuttoning his suit so that his great gut rolled forth. She was thin, he said, too thin to suit him, too thin for one who enjoyed American perquisites.

She riposted that the American fat he was carrying around would come off quickly in Gorki. He sighed deeply and hailed the waitress, ordering them the trout mousse and poached oysters in wine for starters (since Dania steadfastly refused a drink and he already had his vodka), a spicy salmi of duck for him, and a steak cooked in marrow with Bordelaise sauce for her. As the waitress was leaving, Dania murmured that she would have coffee before the meal. The waitress did not bat an eye, but Grechko made a comment, to which she replied that caffeine has a dark side, that of feeling helpless and exhausted, and she must keep away its doldrums with more of the noxious drug.

They had a problem with the wine—he waggled a sausagelike finger at her—because she had ordered meat. She assured him she wouldn't tell a soul, and he should suit his wine to his duck. There was nothing worse than this sort of man in a restaurant; he must make up, at every meal, for all the dreadful Russian nights when meals had been at risk, for all the soured borscht in the Lubyanka's basement cafeteria, for black-market meat gone far beyond appropriate age. She understood; she remembered Angel's sortie as a guest lecturer at Lumumba; she would never forget the endless beans and couscous in Aden, the impossible hardship of the revolutionary training camps. But Grechko was worse than usual, using his meal as a tranquilizer, storing calories like a squirrel facing a long winter. At their last luncheon, by the pool in the Four Seasons, he had been moderate, saving himself for the dessert "cart," a towering siege engine of sugared delights. But the man's mien here was too forced; he was desperately jovial. She urged him to have another vodka, not in hopes of getting him drunk, but in hopes of making him relax enough to broach the subject of her interest.

After the first course had been cleared, she mentioned Cory, and his bushy eyebrows drew down. "*Dash*, I express surprise. Is this politic? I shall be forced to say things you will not like. I respect you; I trust you; please, we shall not talk about sad things today. Tomorrow, upon my new life I will be embarking. Tell me about the bodyguards, the beautiful ones, you have arranged for me. Tell me about the weather, my heart, or any other thing. If we speak of that one, we shall argue. I shall say you shouldn't be in the company of a traitor to all countries, a wolf on the rampage, a murderer and a whore. And then how shall we fare?"

"I mention him, Misha, only as a case in point. How do you think they will treat you, the Americans? Remember Golitsyn? Three years, or more, held incommunicado, left in a room in a hard chair for hours while his interrogators went out to lunch; day after day the questions, the cross-examinations, the manipulation, and the dread that it may never end. How can you be concerned about what your people have made of him without wondering what his will do to you?"

"The point? If there is one?"

"I do not want to see you into a worse life. That, frankly and honestly, is the point."

"The Americans are afraid to act boldly. And I bring them valuable information."

"What you have in your head?" She touched her temple. "You know the spoken word is never conclusive. You, among all sorts, know how horrible debriefings can be."

"Yes, yes. But Americans have no stomach for coercion. This is a civilized country, everyone affirms. And, too, I have done much already to ensure they understand my needs and value my loyalty. Your concern I appreciate, but it will not be for me as for the *mokrie dela* boy you took to your bosom."

"How can you know?" From his syntax, she was scoring points. But to speak so openly, to question so brazenly—it was difficult, and dangerous.

Yet he responded: "For nearly two years I have been arranging this. 'Stay, stay in place,' they kept saying. And this is very hard to do. 'Stay until you have something of fabulous value, something so magnificent in quality and so damaging in content that my superiors will allow any concessions you demand,' my case officer often said in those days. And it is *very* hard to stay and yet be gone in one's heart, to pass facsimiles of information, day after day, week after week, and always they are saying I must stay, they must have more, more. It is not good enough, it is never good enough.

"The chairman's health, the name of his successor, the replacement slated for old Chebrikov—these are the sorts of matters with which the Americans concern themselves. And AMORG— you know our trading company?—and the Mexican connection which we have established now that Aeroflot is not allowed to fly its planes into precious American airports. But I have no access— you know how it is: I run my *residentura*—my network—and pass what must be passed. Occasionally a chip or a schematic or a header-tap comes my way—these clever Americans have digitized their telephone system so that a child could monitor it. Or the name of a bought congressman or sympathetic physicist. But mostly, as always, it is who sleeps with whom or can be made to, who is a pederast, whose child takes drugs or who needs money.

"For this, the Americans do not need me. They know their own barrel of apples—which are rotten, which not. And half are, always, as *you* well know, rotten. But this time I have fortuitously come upon the source which is exceptional, the wellspring of all information which the Americans desire, and I have therefore come into the commissar's seat. They will grant me a fine living, a new life, every convenience."

"What have you got that could be so good? What can a station chief get but smut and dirty pictures? They are playing with you; a defector is good for headlines, then he is forgotten. When the *mokrie dela* come to kill him, it is quiet, the Americans are relieved of a burden, no one cares."

"You are ruining my lunch." The waitress was bringing the entrée. "Why are you doing this?" Grechko demanded, his voice half growl, half whine, when she'd gone.

"Because I'm concerned for you. They wouldn't give up an agent in place for a bit of gossip, a guidance-system prototype, or even the details of the Teflon-coated Stealth bomber. I've no wish to be party to your destruction. Are you certain that what you have is valuable? This valuable? That they think so? Or do they only wish to use you to mock the state? Would this be possible?"

"I have *said* it is good. It is not merely a list of comrades, illegals, those who are of this country or from the Cubans' Dirección General de Inteligencia. It is better."

"If it is good enough, perhaps you'd be wiser to let me agent it for you; sell what you have on the open market; retire to a neutral nation, a tropical island."

"Ah, so it is *this*. You already have me worrying, little *dash*, that you could not provide the ladies in question, or the transportation, or were yourself afraid, or turned against me by that assassin you paraded at the UAE reception. Is this what you do for him? Is he then your operative?"

"Something like that. He works."

"It is good that you tell me this. If revenge were in his heart, as some men would feel the need, then I should be worried about *your* intentions."

She smiled, and stretched lithely, letting Grechko, his lips slick with duck, get a good look at her breasts. "You need not worry about me, old friend. But you may help me, even if you will not let me see what it is you have to offer—"

"*Then* the Americans would descend upon me with their many agents and their electronic magic and I would never be safe. But tell me what information you require, and I will see what is possible. Perhaps you will not send me a bill if I can satisfy your request? This which we are doing can hardly be added to my station's expense account."

"Of the woman called Anastacia Martinova, I need intelligence. Some say she is a sheep from your fold."

Grechko took out his *Le Must* notepad and jotted with a Cross pen.

"And I would like to see what can be gotten of Cordell Hunt's debriefing in the Lubyanka. He, some still say, is also one of yours. And your warnings about him make me feel no better. So much protest that I am again wondering whose agent he might be. His case was handled by one—"

"Yes, I know. Chebrikov. It is a very famous and talked-about item in the back rooms. A failure of immense proportions, my *dash*." He shoveled duck into his mouth, chewed and swallowed. "You do not know the history?"

"Only what he has told me"—she spread her hands—"and you know I must discount some of that. Can you get me—"

"Only some. I have some. Chebrikov's death was so scandalous—"

"What did you say?"

"Oh, he did not tell you?"

"He doesn't know, I must assume."

The Russian, squinting so that his eyes disappeared behind sacs of fat, wiped his mouth with snowy, red-stained linen. Then he belched, behind the cloth. Then he agreed that, yes, this could be so. It was a Soviet matter, and Soviet security was, as she well knew, still the finest in the world.

"By tomorrow," she teased disbelievingly, "by your flight's departure?"

"Either by then or not at all. I, for one, have no expectation of returning to my office ever again after tomorrow."

"And your material, you have it on hand?"

"Now do not be too curious, Dania, for your own good. We have our ways, and I make best use of them. It will be at the Saudi's house when I am there. As I hope the ladies you have found for me will be. Tell me about them, as it is time for dessert. The triple crème here is paradisiacal, not to be missed."

Wondering where the wine had gone, where even in that massive body so much food could be stored, she allowed her steak to be cleared and salad to be placed before her. She thought him a fool and a weary one at that; a frightened little man somewhere inside that huge body who had fooled himself so long, he was believing his own fantasies. Unfortunately, he wasn't quite fool enough to let her know where the packet in dispute was, or what it contained.

She would find out soon enough. In forty-eight hours, she would know all she needed to know, perhaps even what Grechko was too canny to confirm or deny: whether the take with which he was buying his way into American arms actually did come to him under the auspices of Innotech's own Beth Cannard.

Chapter
17

"JUST like they say in the ad, sir, 'no other aircraft is as fuel-efficient or as quiet in both hover and cruise modes.... Missions that were never before considered feasible can now be accomplished because Bell's TiltRotor operates far beyond the range of a helicopter, hovering and landing where fixed-wing aircraft can't.'" Mino finished quoting the literature verbatim; flashed Hunt a grin, luminous in the cockpit's indicator spill; and began paraphrasing, his gaiety forced: "Just think what that's going to mean to *our* special operation, whether it's assault, search and rescue, evac, or whatever—"

Hunt pushed the night-sight goggles, which turned everything below green and bilious, up on his forehead and shook out a Camel. "Is the smoking lamp lit?"

"Yes, sir, if you want."

Flak was in the passenger compartment, jury-rigged to accommodate his monitoring equipment, checking signals from the kidnap-recovery beacons he had put on Dania, the tiny transmitters the athlete and the greyhound—Liz and Trish—wore around their necks as jewelry, and the remotes he had introduced into the Triage system protecting Turki-al-Faisal's Maryland hunt-country estate during a service call they had engendered Thursday evening by temporarily putting down the local power lines. Such calls were SOP after an outage to reset alarms and check for surge damage.

Diehl had "made room for them," all right. Hunt didn't blame the big man, either for taking advantage of their help or for trying to keep them out of the way. But his people were as aware as he that only if something went wrong were they going to be of any use. The hardest thing he knew how to do was stand around and wait for the worst to occur.

He slid down in his seat, using his palm as an ashtray, and stared into the 2100 dark pierced by the lit windows of a single house approximately a quarter-mile away. Dania was in there; they had let him think she wouldn't be, worried about what he might do or whom he might tell or the heat he might bring on-site. He hadn't seen her since Thursday morning, when he and Flak had left New York in the Wagoneer. Shy had precipitated a lot of unnecessary tension, stonewalling Dania and then disappearing back into his European shadows, never even bothering to return Flak's calls. Hunt had taken advantage of Flak's disquiet by getting him to call Fowler, but the advantage was small and the damage Shy had done to Flak and Mino's morale and Dania's faith in him, pulling out on them without a word, was much more significant. He wished she weren't in there, despite Diehl's presence on-site and the two other women with their thigh-holstered, Teflon-finished Enforcers and everyone's expectations that this was going to be an easy mission.

As he watched, a pair of headlights blossomed before the mansion and proceeded toward the gatepost at the head of the Saudi's drive. A dozen Saudis lived on the premises in outbuildings; twenty people had been invited to Grechko's farewell party. The Soviet agent wasn't expecting trouble, he just knew his tradecraft. No one was going to be able to cut out the courier before he or she reached the house. It was up to the greyhound and the athlete to finger the messenger or secure the packet when Grechko tried to hand it over to his CIA contact.

Dania shouldn't be involved in anything like this. This was espionage, pure and simple. He hoped she had taken her antidote pills and remembered to bring her amyl-nitrate ampules. The lady bodyguards had their Russian-made pen guns and even little poison pins tipped with radioactive thallium; any Soviet agent worth his salt was going to have much newer poisons, ricin and the politburo-knew-what. If it had been up to Hunt, he would have put the entire party to sleep with knockout gas, gone in, and carried out whom he chose and what he chose. You didn't finesse *mokrie dela* assassins, and he couldn't convince himself that in a situation like this one, where everyone knew too much, at least one Soviet from Grechko's shop hadn't gotten wind of the go in progress; *somebody* had counseled Beth Cannard, told her the take wasn't getting through. Soviets didn't take chances. There was a backup team or a fallback plan or some damn thing. And then there was Shy, and what his sudden withdrawal could mean—"Is that Dania's car?" he asked Mino, and pulled down the goggles, trying to get a make.

"I can't get you close enough to tell, sir, unless you're ready to escalate ... ?"

The car, which was leaving the party early, had gotten past the guards at the checkpoint. "Let's follow it awhile."

"Awright," Mino sighed, "but we're not *that* quiet." He wanted to stay where they were, circling the fifteen acres of fenced lowland. "We can't take this thing in too close until we don't care if they hear us—"

"I know, Mino. I just want to know where it's going. Do you want to talk about it?"

"About what, Cory?" He banked the TiltRotor almost imperceptibly. They were flying low to avoid popping up on any of the area flight watches; the locale was dotted with "restricted" and "prohibited" airspace, military installations and covert government training camps. But Hunt didn't think that was what was bothering his pilot. He didn't answer, just flicked an ash into his palm, crumpled it and let it fall, caressed the Mauser in a sling under the passenger-side window.

"Yeah, sir, sort of. . . . It's Liz, and Trish, too. I just hate to think of them doing stuff like this. I know it's their gig and all, but it's bitchin' me somethin' fierce."

There it was. "I've been having a good time watching them practice their draws from those thigh holsters. There's nothing like ladies in pretty dresses who know what they're doing and have all that primo equipment to do it with. But I know what you mean. I tried to scale things down; I don't have any authority; I couldn't make trouble. They want their piece, Mino." Liz and Trish were definitely on the most dangerous leg of this operation: seduction and/or executive action from the inside. "It's hard to stand by and let them take chances, especially if you care. . . ." Mino was entranced with the athlete; even Flak was worried about how deeply.

"Yeah, well—sir . . . you ever been in love?"

"Not that I'd admit to, beyond operational necessity." They had skirted the estate's perimeter and were banking low over the road. Hunt squinted through the goggles, recognized the plate number as a DPL, not Dania's, and the car as a limo, not her 380 SEC Mercedes, and motioned with his hand that Mino take the TiltRotor up.

"Not even with Martinova?"

"That's guilt, Mino. Sort of overemotional responsibility. Sometimes it's hard to tell the difference. When I talked to Diehl about making changes, I got a whole lot of resistance, even though with three extra people we could have done this without any kissy-face."

"I know you tried, sir. I'm not saying that. It's that she *wants* to do it—I mean, that's what they do. I can accept that. But it doesn't bother me so much that she might kill this guy as that she might suck his schlong first, 'line of duty' or not. Is that crazy?"

"Ah—no. I don't think so. It's natural, I guess. I told you this isn't any nice clean paramilitary outfit, Mino. If you don't like it, it just means you're of a finer ethical cloth than the rest of us—"

"No, sir, I'm not. I just don't see why they need to go through all this complex playacting if they're going to kill the guy afterward."

"Dania needs the tape, I think. To back off anybody with

thoughts of reprisal—KGB, Beth, CIA, whoever. That's what they wanted the Triage specs for: they're going to record the whole thing."

"Dania said that?"

"No, Mino, I'm guessing."

"This is real scary, sir. I'm glad you're here with us after all, and not down there with them."

"I'm glad, too, Mino. You two are my first concern right now. Net chiefs get real tired of sorting out pieces of their guys when they come home in bags. I promised myself I wouldn't do that anymore. If we have to go into action, it's going to get wet. You have to pump up for that eventuality: If they need us, they're *really* going to need us. But I'm betting they won't, that you won't have to do any more than fly, maybe hold this baby steady while Flak tries out his rappelling gear or that sling winch we've got. In fact, I'm so sure, I'd like to go aft awhile. Flak's going to have bad dreams if we're alone together too long." He patted the pilot on the shoulder, stooped over, and ducked into the cabin proper.

He had to get away from Mino. The young agent was right to be upset. It felt wrong. This whole thing felt so wrong to Hunt, his stomach was sour and he'd been having training dreams, a sure sign he wasn't prepared. His subconscious mind kept trying to tell him he'd skipped some steps, missed something, but it wouldn't tell him what.

"Hi there, cowboy." Flak had his headset down around his throat, a cigarette in one hand and a bottle of beer in the other, one leg up on his console. He nodded to Hunt, one corner of his mouth pulled in tight. Cory had been pushing Flak hard ever since the New York street scene, trying to get the asset to level with him. He had forced the bugging and the call to Fowler and prevailed upon Flak during the drive down here to share the take he'd gotten from Trish. Flak didn't like being run—but then, no one ever did. Blackmail once, blackmail twice: Once he'd dragged the confession out of him in the car by the park, Flak was his; each time the agent followed Cory's orders, he was digging himself in deeper.

Today Hunt had sent him into Washington to try to come up with a picture of Martinova from NTS or the Afghan Embassy; when that didn't work, he sent him to McLean; when Langley came up dry, they called it a day. Hunt hadn't really expected to get the picture, without which it was impossible, despite the requisite thirty thousand dollars Hunt had saved in cash, to purchase a passport from the Dominican or Costa Rican Embassy brokers; but he had been hopeful of cracking Flak open at last. He needed to know what the agent's orders were, and fast.

"Find any of those SWAT teams you're so worried about?"

Flak took a final drag on his Marlboro, dropped the stub in his half-finished beer. "You know I didn't. How's Mino?" The TiltRotor angled; Flak put out a hand to steady himself.

"In love, he says."

"Why not? Everything else has gone wrong. You want to hear any of this? We could go into the porno-cassette business when we get out of Leavenworth. Did you talk to him about it?"

"Not my business." Hunt perched on the side of the console, watching the younger man's face.

"The fuck not. They're Soviet contract agents, by default; this hit's being paid for in rubles."

"Did you ever notice how much the old FBI building in Washington and the Lubyanka on Dzerzhinsky Square look alike?" It bothered him, too, terribly, that Morales was acting as a KGB proxy. This sort of thing went on and on; nobody on the dispatching desk was ever going to consider the job done until everyone involved was silenced permanently. There was something much cleaner about the overt sort of revolutionary actions Angel had favored. This wasn't Hunt's sort of war; it hadn't been Angel's. He didn't mean to defend Dania to Flak, but he did: "She just wants to get out of this without reneging on her commitment. Nirvana didn't know what was going on when this started—Beth's that good."

"Well, that makes it all right then, doesn't it?" Flak shook his head, shot Hunt a disgusted look, and got up. "Sit in if you want; I've heard enough." He went forward, leaving Hunt alone with the little bank of racked receivers and recorders.

Hunt didn't try to stop him, but it wasn't long until the agent came back, ducking through the partition, sighing, "I give up."

"Good. Then maybe you'd care to tell me how we ended up in the middle of this internecine war."

Flak looked squarely at him and inclined his head. "The Agency would like Innotech/Triage back. Sid Cannard was a supergrade, one time. Nobody expected him to go off in his own direction.

It's pretty hairy, what with all the Two Can Play take being out-standing, and God-knows-what's in this packet. You wouldn't have been blown in Afghanistan but for Beth and Sid Cannard."

"The Two Can Play take—at least the parts of it concerned with fomenting civil war behind the Iron Curtain, if we can use an old misnomer—and arms transfer/materiel support aren't out-standing. I saw them in the Lubyanka. And I've known about Cannard for better than a year—from outside sources, then from Chebrikov. Nobody really cares if we give countermeasures to the Durrani Pushtuns; it's not going to neuter the Soviets the way Vietnam did America if they have to pull out—which they'll never do. Don't you see it yet, Flak? You can make a life's work out of becoming disillusioned or disaffected, or you can refuse to par-ticipate in what you can't condone and cut out ninety-five percent of the bullshit."

"That's easy for you to say. You don't believe in anything. I got into intelligence work because the overriding objectives, despite the occasional misjudgment, seemed clear-cut and ... honorable, I guess I'd have to say. I love my country. That sounds dumb, but—"

"First point: I believe in myself; *I'm* my country; I live in here." Hunt indicated his frame. "Second point: Overriding objectives ain't shit to a dead man. Third point: The country *I* loved doesn't return my affection; even if it did, America's not what it used to be. The Pushtuns talk about *pushtunwali*—the way of a man of the blood; honor and self-respect in that context make better sense than "overriding" anything ... and they talk about *zar, zan,* and *zamin*—gold, women, and land. Now, I haven't managed to ac-cumulate any of that last bunch, but I know they're right about *pushtunwali:* You avenge your dead and take care of your loved ones and hold on to your freedom."

"Yeah, maybe. Say I *was* sick and tired of these petty power plays and this blind self-centeredness. Where does that put me? You've just about turned me into a renegade as it stands, so I've got a right to ask: Where do we go from here?"

"That depends on you: what you told Fowler, whom you talked to this morning at Langley; what your orders are and whether you follow them. But if you interfere with me one more time like you did with Helms, I'm going to close down your options."

"I told Jack *we* did that. I didn't tell Langley anything; they could have given us that photo if they'd wanted to. Shy's cooking up some way to make sure none of us is going to tell *anybody* anything." Flak blinked rapidly. "Sir, I just don't see any options. You've got to play ball with *some*body; if we're out there by our lonesomes, we're as good as dead."

"You're as good as dead the minute you're born. You want me to tell you I'll take care of you? I can't. I couldn't even if I trusted you, which I don't. You said before if you weren't careful, you'd end up like me. If you do, you'll know it: You'll have quit wondering about who's on your side, quit making naïve assumptions. If you can find one person you can trust to stand with you despite any considerations of performance—whose perception of you transcends expediency—you'll be all right. If not, you've got to be better at staying alive. Don't worry about the Agency, or Fowler, or Shy or the Cannards. Worry about the next forty-eight hours, operationally. I shouldn't have had to drag these data out of you; you should have seen for yourself that if we're not working together, we're working against one another. All of this soul-searching is a long time too late."

"Don't make Mino into a fucking accessory to treason, murder, and what have you, *then* talk to me about should-have-dones. You shacking up with that Morales bitch is what's going to really screw us. Her old boyfriend there is just waiting for his chance; her husband's going to have us all for dinner once we get to the Côte d'Azur, Diehl says."

"I'm shaking in my boots." Hunt got up. "Sit down here and do what you're being paid to do."

He went forward, thinking he'd just about done it: Flak had a good fix on things; Hunt finally had a good fix on Flak. It was up to the asset, now, to figure out where optimum survivability lay.

"Sir, that's her now." Mino pointed to a car heading slowly away from the Saudi's estate. "She flashed her lights twice, high-lows."

Hunt slipped into his seat, more relieved than he wanted to be. At least Dania was out of harm's way. "Okay, let's cover her until she's back at the staging area."

Without a word, Mino obeyed. They were halfway there and bantering about what they were going to do on the Riviera when two cars pulled out from the bushes before hers, and another blocked the road from behind, too close, fore and aft, for her to get up speed to ram through.

Dania's Mercedes had no choice but to stop. "Mino, douse all your lights and put me right down there—hold steady at three hundred feet if you can." Hunt got out the Mauser, opened the side window, pulled off the goggles, settled the wood stock against his shoulder, and began watching through the sniperscope. He saw two men get out of the cars stopped sideways across the road directly in front of hers. He prayed she'd just sit in there; she had a class-six armored. Flak stuck his head through to tell them he was getting a mayday from Diehl in the Mercedes, bent down between the seats, got out the second Mauser from its case, and leaned over behind Mino to get the pilot's window open.

They saw the two men pouring something from a can around the car, one crouching down to affix something to a tire; saw the man fall; Diehl had taken a chance by opening the door enough to take a shot. "Landing lights, Mino."

The blinding glare stopped the action below for a moment, then they heard a bullet ping against their wing. Hunt wanted the guy with the can, who mustn't be allowed to light a match. Mino was cursing the shooter below; the sound of the rotors, through the open windows, obscured everything else until Flak's first report resounded in the cockpit and Hunt saw the man go down and the incendiaries burst into flame and Dania's door open. He took a bead on her, not shooting, just watching through the scope as she scrambled out, Diehl breaking out of the car in a leap at the same time.

More men were out of their cars now. "Lights out." Mino doused them, but Hunt had seen two men grab Dania as she sprinted for the woods. "Get me down there," he heard himself say. Flak's Mauser, loaded with Accelerators, barked three times and Mino swore he'd be deaf before this was over. Hunt, his arm steadied on the window frame, took careful aim at the green-white figures hustling Morales toward their cars while Flak reloaded.

Hunt got one, who dropped; he could see the blood splatter and Dania's open mouth. He went for the second, but some of the additionals pouring out of the third car were returning fire. Diehl hadn't made the woods. Hunt took his third shot while Mino, saying "Sorry, sirs, but I gotta," took evasive action. Hunt had hit one of the shooters who had Diehl pinned down in the light of the burning gas. It occurred to him that despite its armored gas tank, the Mercedes was going to blow any minute. Just then the remaining men broke for their cars, and he could count six. He got one more, but Dania was being hustled into the lead vehicle by then and he was empty; the Mausers took three in an integral magazine and one in the chamber. The Mercedes below exploded, showering metal and flame.

Mino was on the lead car without a word from Hunt. Flak said nothing; the pilot, bent forward, running lights off, felt around for Hunt's goggles, giving Flak as much room as he could: "Just like the Group Nine training film, Cory?"

"Yep," Hunt said, and leaned out the window until his shoulders and arms were free and his eyes tearing in the icy air that whipped him. The Star-tron scope was worth the money. He waited until Mino had them right on top of the speeding car in which Dania was being carried away. They had their headlights off, but he could see well enough in the green night sight; she was in the back with one guy; there were two more up front. He had reloaded with armor-piercing rounds that exploded .006 seconds after impact. He would have to be very careful.

The TiltRotor had no skids; Mino brought them in so low there was danger to the rotors from trees along the sides of the road. Flak was shooting behind them at the follow cars; Hunt wanted the driver first. Mino brought him alongside and he got his chance; he took the driver through the front window, the man beside him a half-second later as soon as the Mauser's muzzle came down. The car began to veer wildly along the road, the driver slumped over the wheel; the guy in the back was leaning over the seat, trying to get the corpse off the steering wheel. Hunt shot him and turned, wedged in the window, reloading from his jacket pocket, hoping to hell Mino didn't dump him out on the ground, to help Flak with the follow cars. He didn't know if Diehl was in the second car or not; he was past caring—they were just targets, little pop-ups he had to score. The second car fishtailed into the woods and burst into flame. Flak was back inside the cockpit, and Hunt, his ammo expended, followed.

The third car was slowing; Hunt hadn't even thought about the car Morales had been in since he had killed her abductors. Mino was already on it, taking them back there. Flak, muttering "The hell with this," got out his SAR and began strafing the third car. Hunt hoped Diehl wasn't in it as he topped off the Mauser and told Mino to put them down on the road, as close as he could.

"Yes, sir."

They came down on the white line, Flak still spitting rounds from the Galil into the third car, trying to get the gas tank.

Hunt was out of the TiltRotor and wondering if Flak was going to cover him or kill him before the TiltRotor's wheels had made contact. He sprinted toward the first car.

When he reached it, it was empty, but for the dead men. One door was open; he crashed around in the brush calling her name, wishing he'd brought the goggles, when she came flying into him, cut and breathing heavily. "Cory!"

"Let's go. *Run.*"

She ran beside him and he realized, suddenly, that he wasn't hearing any fire.

At the roadside he saw Flak, Diehl's arm slung over his shoulders, the big man limping, but moving. The TiltRotor's door was open and he boosted Dania up into it, then went to help Flak. Diehl was growling something; Hunt couldn't tell what. Blood was all over him. They heaved him up and in, and Hunt peered back into the darkness until Flak was safely aboard. He heard the round coming at him—a sharp report followed by the whisper a supersonic bullet makes, half a whistle, half a hum, as it splits the air—and jumped aside and up into the open hatch. It caught him in the calf and went on through; he could hear the impact as it hit the TiltRotor's metal. Then Flak pulled the door shut and shouted to Mino to get them out of there.

Dania, her black tuxedo bloody and torn, turned from Diehl, outstretched flat on the cabin's floor, and crawled toward him spitting something about "Innotech *fascisti,*" medikit in hand. He grabbed the kit from her and packed gauze into the entry and exit wounds; he could do it faster; he didn't need help; the wounds' diameters were already shrinking, traumatized flesh recovering from hydrostatic shock. There was a lot of incoming fire, everyone talking at once. He shouted over it: "Let's get those ladies out of there, now!"

Flak scrambled over to his console, headset held to one ear, then turned to Hunt: "Signal executed, sir."

The girls' vibrators would have warned them, unless they were naked; their watches had LED's that would glow red in that event. Dania, hands to Hunt's face, was trying to tell him it was all right, they were all right. He didn't believe her: gunshots, fireballs, exploding cars. The adversaries had been careful lest they damage the take they were after—only that had saved Dania and Diehl, not anything he or his team had done. Vehicles and bodies all over the place; they had a few minutes at best, to get out of the area. He pushed himself up, ignoring his calf wound; he'd have time to feel it later, and he knew himself: He would. Before then, he had to take the single advantage offered him: When there was surely going to be trouble, he always liked to pick the moment.

Passing Diehl, he hesitated. "Scratches," the big man shrugged off Hunt's question. Besides his thigh wound, a shot had grazed his bull's neck; his face had been lacerated diving through brambles in the woods. Diehl's eyes made Hunt unpleasant promises: All of this is your fault; you brought them down on us.

It was true. Hunt clapped the big man on the shoulder. Diehl's huge hand grasped his wrist. "Later, Cory Hunt, we will hear what you have to say."

Dania squeezed into the cockpit after Hunt, telling him not to mind Diehl. She had blood trickling down her face from a scalp wound. He touched her cheek, her lips with his fingers. "Be quiet. Mino, damage report?"

"We'll make it, Cory. Want to watch those pineapples though— remember to throw 'em out first if we start crashing." Mino had taken some of the grenades from Dania's apartment and, pulling their pins, placed them in glass jars. When dropped, the jars would shatter, freeing the handles of the grenades: It was five seconds from shatter to explosion. They had a half-dozen of the jars taped together, an effective homemade bomb. Hunt saw a spider-crack in the TiltRotor's windshield and heard Dania, right below him, kneeling between the seats, asking Mino where the bomb was. He told her; she went aft.

"Okay, sir?" The TiltRotor, without lights, sped through the darkness.

"Okay, Mino. Just like we drilled: down on the roof right over that widow's walk or whatever it is."

"Good fucking—" Another chopper, running without lights, almost collided with them. Only the greenish spill of its cockpit and Mino's instinct saved them. "I don't believe I'm alive. Sir, reach over there and flip that switch; we're set to monitor Langley."

Hunt did that. Mino had climbed higher. He could see four cars streaming, nose to tail, out of the estate: the Saudis, going to find out what the trouble was. They circled once, then descended, Langley's laconic traffic control giving no warning that Mino's altitude had drawn their attention, no indication of the other chopper's ID.

He went aft when Mino told him it was "go time," and saw Flak, belted up and ready to slide down to the roof. Dania had the winch, protruding out the door, under control, and waved him back. "Ifrit, don't worry—*I* will not betray *you*." Her hair was pulled back behind her ears, her eyes very bright. She had taken off her jacket and he could see under her white shirt a bulge beside the waistband holster, empty now, where her PPK should have been. He took the SAR Flak handed him, smeared camouflage black on his face, and cinched the belt with its pulley rings around his waist, lastly pulling on tight, fingerless gloves.

Then Mino was holding them steady and Flak braced himself in the doorway. Beyond him, Hunt could see the little white fence around the widow's walk. With luck, they wouldn't have to dodge any incomings; the Saudis would be busy down below, not expecting anything from the air.

Flak grabbed the rope and swung out beneath the winch, disappeared from view as Hunt braced next in the doorway, pushed out, slid down, landed hard, dropping to his knees on the roof, the Galil slung over his shoulder.

Then the two of them were jimmying the hatchlike trapdoor open, the sound of the TiltRotor above them in the darkness, waves of chopped air lashing them. "Okay, sir. That's got it."

Light cracked, a thin line, a bracket, a square. They heard shouting below and running, an Arabic warning to look above, look above.

The women were dashing up the stairs—one in bra and panties, the other fully dressed but for her shoes; both had their Enforcers out. Trish was in the lead, looking backward, taking an occasional shot; when she turned her head, he saw she had something in her mouth, clenched between her teeth. They scrambled back out of the way and pulled her through; behind her Hunt could see the staircase, Saudi heads in red-and-white *ghutras* popping up and falling back. "Get her up, Flak."

There was an emergency ladder that Dania was supposed to throw out if the women weren't injured; Flak left to steady the bottom of it. He heard an exterior report, then another, heard Flak curse. Liz, in her panties, was scrambling up the last flight. Hunt, flat on the roof, sighted down the Galil and began firing around her. He saw her shiver and blood blossom beneath her breasts. He turned three *ghutras* solid red and grabbed for her outstretched hand; in it were cassettes. He took them, stuffed them in his shirt, and reached for her arm, but the athlete was faltering, her other hand between her breasts, covered with blood. "Come on, girl," he urged. He saw her dilated pupils and knew she was in trouble, grabbed her under the arms, the Galil discarded, as she began to stumble on the last steps.

He dragged her through and yelled to Flak, who slammed the trapdoor shut and stood on it. "Aw, Christ. We'll need the winch."

"No, just cover me. We don't have time." He looped his rope around her, under her arms.

He hoisted her on his shoulder, talking to her, asking her if she could hold on to his neck, if she could just hold on. She said she could. He began to climb with her, feeling the blood seep through his shirt, the weight of her, feeling her slip, go limp, come back to life just as he thought he was going to lose her, or fall himself.

The ladder began to sway as Flak turned away to jam the crowbar into the trapdoor's hasp, then steadied again. One foot after the other, he told himself; she was heavy and her breath was too loud and she thought he was Mino. He didn't argue about it, just got her up where Dania and Trish could see her. "Diehl, get Diehl." He and Diehl got the failing girl inside just as Flak started climbing. The ladder blew wildly. Hunt closed his eyes and hung on. Mino was lifting the TiltRotor away from the roof.

He heard Flak cursing below as he scrambled inside, turned in the doorway, grabbed the third Galil Dania was holding, and crouched there, covering Flak, who had shouldered Hunt's SAR.

The asset had only three rungs to go when the trapdoor burst open and the Saudi guards opened fire, silhouetted in the square of light. He saw Flak shiver and he began to pick them off, jammed between the doorframe and the others waiting to help Flak inside. He got two with placed shots and saw Flak's hand reach the door-well, then opened up, full auto fire, and cleared the trapdoor.

Dania, who had been crouched over Liz, bolted for the cockpit. Trish touched him, wanting him to get out of the doorway. He stayed there, oblivious; even with him in position, they were going to be able to get Flak inside.

The house was dwindling below. The rounds from the shooters on the ground couldn't reach them; only a ground-to-air missile or another chopper could stop them. When Flak was in, Hunt inched back from the doorway and let Trish retract the winch and the ladder, pull the door shut; the noise lessened.

His shot leg was cramped and burning; he sat down, knees up, the Galil's hot barrel against his cheek, and looked around.

Flak had taken a bloody hit; Dania was pulling down his pants while he objected in a strained voice that he'd been shot in the ass before; not to worry about him, just patch him up quick so he could "relieve Mino, he'll never fucking forgive me."

Hunt put aside the Galil and maneuvered through the litter of guns and equipment to where Liz lay, a makeshift bandage stain-ing red and her breath gurgling. "Great." He got up, sat back down, took the girl's hand. It was too low to have hit her lungs, but he thought it might have punctured her spleen. She was slick with sweat and there was blood coming out of her nose. He turned her head gently; her ears were free of blood. She talked to him, still thinking he was Mino, half-intelligible mutterings about it hurting more than she thought it should and would he still love her with this awful scar. "*Psst!* Ifrit—come away."

He did that, and Dania shook her head, slid her eyes sideward to where Flak was working his way forward, hands out to steady himself. "Do you think she'll make it?"

Hunt shrugged. Mino came aft, his face white above his scraggly beard, knelt down beside Liz. Hunt went forward, wishing this sort of thing didn't happen, wishing the two of them could have a little privacy. Dania followed, and Flak stopped cursing his left cheek and how much it hurt and how hard it was "to fly this damn thing even without a bullet up your ass."

"Flak, she must have a doctor."

"The hell you say? What can I do about that?"

Dania gave him a heading and asked him if he could make it there and handle the landing. "How the fuck do I know? I'll sure try, lady."

Hunt said, "Get Mino back here. He's had a minute, that's all the time we can spare."

"Cory! Let them have—"

"Dania, get out of my way." He pushed past her, hesitated on the threshold; Trish and Diehl were both staring at him.

He got Mino up. "You're needed forward, captain. Flak can't cut this aircraft. We'll get her to a doctor if you'll fly us."

The pilot turned to him, eyes red, and took a deep breath and one downward look. "Yes, sir. I—" Mino, eyes squeezed shut, leaned against him. Hunt embraced him. "Damn fool," Mino whispered. "Damn fool girl."

"It's not just her, Mino. It's all of us. Come on, let's get her through what we got her into."

It took them thirteen minutes to reach the home of the doctor. By then Liz was drifting in and out of consciousness; each time she revived, she was weaker; each time she sank back into shocky semiconsciousness, she was more violent. First Trish, then Diehl, had to hold her.

Dania had put Flak on the radio; a prearranged signal was called ahead to the trauma team Dania had standing by. Flak had already bled through the bandages swathing his bottom like diapers under his jockey shorts. Hunt's left foot was sticky from the blood that had run down into his boot. He was exhausted; his vision was grainy; he was dizzy whenever he stood. Trish sat unspeaking, staring at Hunt steadily.

Nobody was talking about the take; he had seen the envelope in Trish's clenched teeth, the bulge in Dania's blouse where something was secreted; the cassettes he had taken from Liz were now in Flak's effects bag. He couldn't ask; he had to wait for Dania to broach the subject. He had only ten days to make good his word to Martinova.

After a time, Dania came aft and saw the staring war in progress, stroked the crown of Trish's head and spoke quietly to her. Diehl was propped against the wall opposite Hunt, watching himself bleed, Liz's semiconscious, blanketed body beside him, her hand in his. When Dania rose from Diehl's side, Hunt asked her to help him: He wanted to go up front, to ride shotgun for Mino in case the other chopper came back. He leaned on her, not really thinking he needed to, only wanting to hold her, but almost passed out as he stood, his vision going with dizzying speed from red to brown to black. When gray lightened to visibility, she was asking him to stoop through the partition. Seated, he requested that she get him one of the Mausers. Then he and Mino were alone.

"How's it coming, Mino?"

"Almost there, Cory. Is she—"

"Intermittent. It's too soon to tell."

"I can tell you one thing: I'm not leaving there without her."

"Dead or alive?"

"That's right, sir." Mino had on a one-ear headset with a com mike attached; he pushed it back and looked at Hunt. "I—we— I just can't leave her like that, Cory."

"You'd better figure out what you're going to do if they tell you she'll live if she stays, but die if we take her. I can't spare you, Mino. And we can't jeopardize everyone by hanging around for a week or so until she's well enough to travel."

"Is that what you think it's going to come down to?"

Dania's voice preempted Hunt's reply. "We can't leave her here, in any case, Mino. *I* could not bear it; she would not wish it. The physician I retain understands our special requirements and the delicacy of our situation. Here, Cory." She handed him a makeup-remover pad; he wiped the camouflage black off his face, took the towel she offered, wiped the oil away. "Despite my long acquaintance with this doctor—we call him 'Snow'—it is necessary for everyone to remain on guard and well armed. Diehl has lost his Beretta; my PPK jammed and in the heat of the moment I discarded it."

Hunt gave up his shotgunner's seat. "Mino, give me your auto." He gave Mino's Combat Commander to Dania; Mino still had his snubby. "If we get desperate, there're three Mini Uzis in our Halliburtons. I'll give Diehl back the Detonics; I don't like the way it feeds, but that's his problem. You keep this. I've got extra leather for it." He went to get it, and busied himself apportioning the remaining 7.62x51 NATO ammo for the Galils, the extra .45 clips, filling empties, making sure that everyone knew where everything was.

When Mino took the TiltRotor out of cruise and set it down, helicopter-style, on the lawn before a large, secluded house whose lights were lit, Hunt felt better. "Good," he said to Dania. As she reached up to kiss him, Liz started ranting and he went to help Diehl while Trish slid the door open and from the house two men came running with a stretcher.

By the time Liz was settled on the stretcher, Trish was outside the TiltRotor, an SAR on her hip; Flak was down by the doctor's "office" door in a clean pair of pants and his down vest with the second Galil. Hunt had the third. He had no intention of leaving the TiltRotor. Dania argued with him, but he held firm, telling her to go on in and send somebody out to him.

There were floodlights in the driveway and he could see everything quite clearly. He saw Trish with her Galil, staring at him, and grinned at her. She frowned.

"Go see how your friend is doing if you want; I've got it, here."

She shook her black-haired head and turned away, walking the TiltRotor's perimeter.

It was more than an hour later that a young guy in a red and white coat came out to have a look at him. He watched Trish frisk and pass him. The man had a beeper and long mousy hair. From behind granny glasses, he was attempting to look as if he were taking it all in stride. His shoulder bore a trauma-team patch and he was jovial. "You must be my patient," he huffed, levering himself up and in. "Boy, this is some machine." He put down his kit, squatted down at Hunt's feet, frowned up at the Galil in Hunt's crooked arm. "Would you sit down and put that thing away, mister—"

"Uh-uh. Do what you can this way. There's no slug in it; just clean it up."

"It really would be easier if you'd—"

"But I won't. Hurry up."

Gentle fingers started cutting his pant leg at the knee. The man whistled through his teeth and tsked. "You really should sit down. This is going to hurt and I've got to give you something for the pain."

"No thanks. I like pain. Just cut, pack, and bandage it."

Commenting that his patient didn't understand, the medic began to explain the procedure. Hunt told him he'd looked at the wound, he knew what was involved. He asked about the "shot girl," and ignored the novocaine needle as it went in. By the time the medic was ready to bandage, he knew Liz's chances, if brought with them, were slim; if she was left behind, they were slightly better. The spleen had been nicked, a kidney scraped. An exploratory had revealed that there was no intestinal involvement, hence peritonitis was not a major concern. Shock and trauma were. Internal bleeding, when the medic had left the examination room, had still been too copious to determine more. Hunt had known the bleeding was bad from the yellow/green/blue look of the flesh around her bandage.

"Would you think her chances better if we had a medic along?"

"Some little bit." The doctor stood up. "By rights you should have a pint or two—a transfusion, mister. Don't push yourself too hard if you won't take my advice. If you feel squeamish or dizzy—"

"How'd you like a free trip to—"

"Oh, no. I'm just hired help. I've got a wife and kid. I'd be missed."

It was a warning. Hunt smiled grimly and told him to get out of there while he still had a choice, wishing he had kept the camouflage blackface on a little longer; this guy could give a good description of him, the plane, of Trish, of everything and everyone involved. He hoped Dania knew what she was doing.

His neck hurt; he couldn't remember wrenching it, then decided it had been Liz's death-tight grip on him when he brought her aboard.

Mino came out of the cockpit; one look at his face told Hunt that he'd overheard everything the medic had said. "You knew, Cory, didn't you—from looking at her?"

"I guessed; I've seen lots of shot people, Mino. . . . You've got some choices. You can go in there and hold her hand—that's what she wants, you can bet. You can stay here with me and tough it out, but you might regret it if she cashes in while we wait. You can pick your doctor and I'll help you abduct him; Dania won't like it, but I can live with that. You can force them to leave her, but if she comes through it because you left her, then where is she? Alone, maybe in a private room at some high-security facility, and we won't know whose or where. . . . It's a no-win."

"What would you do?"

"Bring her; do the best you can for her. I think Dania's right about her, there: She's not the sort who would want to wake up and know she's been left behind. If she weren't a lady, if it were Flak, what would you do? Whatever that is, do it for her—give her the respect she's earned and be with her if she checks out."

"I'm—you think—I could just run in there, quick?"

"Sure, go ahead." He knew it wasn't a great move, but he didn't want Mino to have any more to regret than was absolutely necessary.

Trish came up to the door of the TiltRotor when Mino ran into the house. "What's this now?" Her low voice was hostile, disparaging. "This is no time for the pilot to deplane."

"Go tell him; I'll wait."

"Do you realize that Liz and Mino are the only ones who know how to fly this thing? Dania's had a rudimentary check-out, but nothing—"

"Shut up." Hunt listened hard, looking up into the night, starry and noncommittal, and thought that it would be just his luck if the chopper he could barely hear was what he thought it was. He blessed Flak's effects bag and reached behind him, where one of Triage's pocket-size walkie-talkies lay. When Flak answered its beep, he said laconically, "How's your ass?"

"Fair to middling, I'm told. What's up?"

"Something. You expecting anybody, Darling?"

"No, sir....Hey! Mino...?" Hunt heard nothing more. Three minutes later, Mino came dogtrotting out the door.

By then Hunt was pretty sure the chopper was landing, and Trish was looking up. "Hey, Scratch? Give me a Mauser?"

"Let's see what they want; don't open fire unless they do." He beeped Flak again: "Get a move on. Send Dania out, get a Band-Aid on your butt, and tell them to have that girl out here in five minutes. Step on it."

Mino, craning his neck, headed for the TiltRotor at a dead run. Hunt got out of his way, saw a flash of tearstained face, followed the pilot into the cockpit.

Mino was already trying to get an ID from them without overtly threatening or saying anything on the air he might later regret. Hunt sighed and opened the window, propped his Mauser on the passenger seat where Mino could get to it, and said, on his way out, "No matter what happens, get the balance of these people out safely. If that doesn't include me, or Flak, or Liz, you've got to ignore your feelings. Mission first, understood?"

"Yes, sir. And, Cory—"

"Yeah, Mino?"

"You're right."

He didn't stop to ask about what, just got out and gave Trish the Mauser she'd requested, headed off across the grass, SAR in hand. Flak limped out to meet him, Dania by his side. "Get in the aircraft, Dania. Don't argue. Go."

She went.

The chopper was definitely landing. Out of the house came Diehl, lagging behind the mousy medic and another, the two whitecoats bearing the stretcher between them; a third, bearded man held a bottle of plasma as they ran across the floodlit sward.

"Flak, you got anything to tell me?"

"No, sir. I don't know anything more about this than you do."

Hunt had to take his word for it. They designated bushes as cover areas, and landscaping railroad ties as last resorts. Mino got the rotors going; Hunt looked over his shoulder and saw the medics and Diehl maneuvering the stretcher inside.

Worst case, it was KGB. Whoever it was hadn't answered Mino's queries. He and Flak stood in plain view as the chopper, lightless, put down on the macadam driveway and one man got out of it, then two more. The second two had rifles, the first had a lot of guts, striding across the grass toward two armed men without hesitation. He wore a suit and he seemed to be unarmed.

Hunt clicked the safety off his Galil when the big man in the suit was about ten feet away; he wanted to be sure the other heard it, despite the chopper rotors before and behind. The closer the man came, the more convinced Hunt was that he wasn't an Agency type (he knew his old shop) or an Innotech/Triage honcho. His suit wasn't cut right and he had on rubbers.

When he reached them, he walked between them without a word, not even slowing. Flak let out a deep breath and widened his eyes at Hunt, who inclined his head at the two men with the rifles. They crab-stepped along in the suit's wake, trying to look in all directions at once.

Dania bolted out of the TiltRotor and ran toward them, carrying something in her hands. The big man in the suit looked around once at them. Hunt put his hand out to Flak; they hung back.

He saw Dania slow to a walk, the man change direction slightly to intercept her; they came together; whatever Dania had been holding changed hands. Hunt's heart sank and he threw his rifle up to his shoulder. From the chopper he could hear a shouted Russian exchange. He had a perfect shot at the big man's broad back; in the light, he could even see how the suit humped beneath its collar, fat rolling over it.

"Easy, sir. Come on, Cory, a round out of that from this distance could go right through him and kill her. And what's the use? Look at those guys! We'll be dead in the next sixty seconds. Then where will Martinova be?"

Flak, as well as he, knew what they were looking at: a textbook handover. He lowered the SAR to hip level and waited to see what would happen. The man gave something to Dania, he thought; at least he reached into his jacket, and she didn't fall over dead. The two shook hands, speaking softly to one another in Russian he might have been able to decipher but for the TiltRotor and the chopper. The big man turned, came back toward them; Dania shielded her eyes and looked their way, then motioned to them and headed back to their aircraft.

Flak started to follow; Hunt stayed where he was. "Come *on*, fool. So it's a Russian, so what? Are you going to blow this thing because they didn't treat you nice? Cory? Cory? *Sir?*"

Hunt just stood, the KGB agent a beckoning sight picture, his finger sweating on the four-pound combat trigger of the Galil. He turned on his heel as the agent moved past him, ignoring Hunt as if he didn't exist. With him went all hope for Martinova; with him went any justification Cordell Hunt had been telling himself he had for all he had done in the past eleven days since leaving Zürich.

He thought he ought to put the agent down; he could get him and the two soldiers before they could return fire; he was still that fast and the Galil was as quick as could be. But it would be signing Dania's death certificate.

He clicked the safety on as the suited man and his backups got into the chopper and it spun up into darkness. Then he walked slowly toward Flak, who waited, shifting from foot to foot, halfway to the TiltRotor.

When he reached the asset, Flak said, "Hey, Cory? How about the pineapples? We can catch 'em." Flak grinned, Hunt said, "Shit. Maybe you're right," and they sprinted toward the TiltRotor together, oblivious of their anesthetized wounds. Hunt knew they were going to hurt more later because of it, but the hurt inside him was worse: Dania had played him, run him, and, it looked like, won a round for the KGB on his sweat and blood. All that talk about giving him the take, about helping him with Martinova, about love and long-term arrangements was just agent manipulation by a pro. He knew blowing up the Russian's chopper wasn't going to help Martinova, but it was going to take something away from the Soviets that they had gone to a great deal of trouble to acquire. And it was going to wipe that incipient smirk off the face of the big *mokrie dela* agent who had walked by him as if Cordell Hunt did not exist. He and his *boyevaya gruppa*—combat groups (where there was one, there were more)—were going to find out they still had to worry about him. He owed himself that much.

Hauling himself up into the TiltRotor, he sent Flak forward to update Mino and whistled to Trish to get aboard. She came trotting up, her eyes questioning.

Dania and the three medics were clustered over Liz. There was a little cooler of clear, synthesized blood open by her head, an IV bag taped to the cabin wall.

"Dania." Die' l was forward, Hunt assumed. Just as well, he thought. Dania came to him; he had to either convince her or coerce her. He said, "Which of them are we taking?" gesturing to the three medics with his SAR. "Get the others out of here. Now."

"Cory, it is not what you think. I—"

"You can explain to me after we're airborne. I want one of them." He was whispering, but one of the medics, the one with the granny glasses, was watching him with obvious suspicion and concern. The TiltRotor's engines rose in pitch. "For Mino's sake, I have to do what I can, even if you don't care about Liz."

The TiltRotor shivered as if it were beginning to lift. Dania frowned at him, reaching out to touch his face. He jerked his head back. Beyond her, the three medics were hastily rising.

Trish hitched herself up and aboard. The medical people came abreast of him. He picked the oldest one, the portly man with the beard, and told the others to run along. Danià, eyes averted, hands on her hips, said nothing. Trish, looking between them, grabbed the door and shut it behind them.

Everyone was thinking the quarters were too close and the TiltRotor too vulnerable for matters to be allowed to escalate. Dania, watching the medic, who went immediately back to his patient without a word and fussed about her, told Trish to go sit down.

Then she took him toward the TiltRotor's tail; they had to stoop low. She sat down cross-legged. "Cory, sit with me a moment." Diehl was still forward with Flak and Mino. Hunt hoped Flak was being circumspect. "Thank you," she said. "Now, what do you think you are doing?" Her eyes, fixed on him now, were luminous by some trick of the light. Their hips touched in the small space.

She was ready for him, he thought. He said, wishing he hadn't given her Mino's Commander, "We're going to take out the Soviets' Bell. They've radioed back a successful pickup by now. Don't make me proceed over your objections. I can't let this sort of—"

"Did I not warn you: You *must* give up your prejudices, all your vendettas, your personal and private wars? After so much, you still do not trust me? Cory, what I gave them was something I got from Grechko, this is true. But—"

"You promised me—"

"And I have kept my promise. I had wanted to do more. From Grechko I obtained the transcript of your Lubyanka interviews and the Two Can Play material the client previously passed. I wanted—I *still* want—you to see for yourself what Grechko told me: that you got more from Chebrikov than he from you, and how Innotech played you, knowingly, from the beginning, hoping to place you inside KGB as a respondent where the names you gave them, those of supposed penetrations and doubles in their own *residenturas*, and *apparatchiki* who were known to you as contacts, could be dragged from you. But these were in actuality never Western operatives, only your enemies, to whom your dispatcher sent you, as if Western interests had bought them...Do you see?"

"See what? You gave that guy the take—"

"No, I gave him the originals of the copies I will give you, what Grechko gave me to pay for my services—only the minutes of your Lubyanka stay and the Two Can Play deception. The Soviets cannot be sure what Beth Cannard was transferring. When they see what they have gotten, they will assume it is she who betrays them. You must not interfere in this transfer, Cory. It is the only way I can end my involvement, appear to have honored my commitments, and find for us a chance to live in peace together. I still have what Grechko was giving to the CIA handler. Grechko and his controller are no more; the Soviets have decided an autopsy would be inopportune; they go now to create a cleansing explosion at the site. There is no need for you to intervene."

"Or to interfere, you mean. How do I know? How can I trust you?"

She turned toward him, reached out a hand, stopped, blinking. "Did I ask you this, when John Shy's men attacked me? You may view the tape Trish and Liz made. You may see the packet's contents, though what you can make of it, I cannot say—it is software, nothing more. As for trusting me, if you are still asking, perhaps you cannot." She completed her motion, her fingers tracing his mouth. "Cory, Cory, we have so many troubles yet to weather, so much left to do. Don't make this mistake. I beg you. For all our sakes."

"You haven't been straight with me anywhere along the way. You didn't tell me about this. What else haven't you told me?"

"Many things. I must protect you while you are yet weak. Would I be worth all you are risking if I had no talent of my own, nothing to offer? I am worthy of your respect; I didn't think I had to ask for permission to act in our defense. Soon we will have time to sort out blame and triumph. Can't you trust me, until then? Won't you let me help you, a little longer?"

"Whatever makes you comfortable." He got up on his knees, sure he wanted to get away from her, not sure what he was going to do.

"Promise you will not intercept my contact? I cannot allow you to move precipitately; you will hurt us all. I have bent many rules for you, Cory Hunt—those of tradecraft, those of prudence, those of my own making, which have kept me alive so many years."

"Yeah, okay. For now."

He went to call off the helicopter hit, not certain he was doing the right thing, but certain he had to give her some slack. If in the end he found she was just another treacherous independent, he would do what he had to do.

He hadn't expected to see Diehl and Flak faced off in the cockpit. At least it was merely verbal; even Flak wouldn't play shoot-me/shoot-you in so confined a space with so much at stake. Mino was just finishing his check-in with Langley control; they were flying high, airplanelike in cruise mode, rotors perpendicular to the wings.

"Let it go. You two back off. Mino, let's get refueled at Hagerstown and proceed to Hanscom. We've got medical attention on board." Both Diehl and Flak were watching him. He wished he had heard what had gone on in here. Beyond Mino's thankful "Yes, sir. That's great sir," there was no sound until Diehl with a guttural snarl shouldered past him.

"So?" he asked Flak.

"So, he doesn't like me." Flak rubbed his chin. "I can't imagine why he thinks that mess on the road was our fault. Triage equipment doesn't necessarily mean that it was Innotech who interdicted them—not that I'm saying it wasn't; I just think they're awfully quick to blame us. Cory?"

"Yes?"

"I'd like that one, when the time comes." His eyes slid after Diehl.

"Be my guest."

"What did Morales say about the KGB handover?"

"That in order to satisfy as many interests as possible, seemingly, she had to give them something, putatively from Beth. It wasn't what we're after, she swears. Maybe it'll work—who knows? The Soviets will be annoyed with Beth Cannard, that's for sure, when they find out that all this trouble they went to was to reclaim some information that was generated by their own shop. Between them and whatever Shy's cooked up, I don't think we have to do anything additional about her. You let Jack know, and let him take it from there."

"Are we still going with them?"

"Hell, yes. You want Angel Morales, don't you?"

"Yes, sir, sure do."

"Then go back there and patch it up with Diehl. I'm the bad boy on this flight; two of us and they'll get too nervous. Okay?"

"Okay, sir." Flak grimaced and slid out of the copilot's seat. Hunt slipped into it. "Mino, I'm proud of you."

"You are?"

"Yep. I'd take you anywhere, anytime."

"Really?" He looked at Hunt. "Cory... how's Liz?"

"I don't know."

"Whatever happens, sir, I want you to know *I* don't blame you for any of this. Damned lot of faultfinding going on for no good reason. And, sir... any place you want to take me, or have me take you, I'd be pleased... you know."

"Yeah, Mino, I know."

Two hours later they landed at Hanscom, beside the Innotech hangar, and transferred Liz and the walking wounded into the Falcon without incident. Dania received final instructions from the medical man (Hunt had guessed right: The big, bearded one was "Snow") and Flak gave Snow the keys to the Innotech Mercedes Hunt had rejected in favor of the Wagoneer.

They couldn't be overt, flash their weapons or post guards on the airstrip; Hunt's hackles were risen, expecting Helms et al. or Flak and Mino's much-touted SWAT teams. When no one tried to stop them, Cory began to worry more about that than he would have over token or serious resistance. They swept the Falcon for bugs and explosives and interrogated the night man about tampering, but it all shook out fine. Liz was still Mino's first concern, and Dania's eyes were deeply shadowed. No one talked much.

Mino's friend from the helicopter taxi service agreed to pick up the TiltRotor and deliver it to Dania's proxy at Hagerstown field in Maryland near the Pennsylvania border.

Hunt was shivering in the New England cold, the last one left on the tarmac; Flak had made his phone call to Fowler and come out hunch-shouldered and dispirited, but this was no place to talk about it.

He was just backing up toward the ramp when he saw headlights pierce the 0300 dark. They'd filed and cleared their takeoff; the FAA guy shouldn't need to talk to them face-to-face. He backed up the steps and into the plane as quickly as he could. Before the door was secure, the Falcon was moving off between the red and white lights into blackness.

He had forgotten how opulent, how quiet the powerful Dassault was. The corporate jet seemed almost cavernous after the TiltRotor. Cory looked out the wing window for a long while, but he couldn't see the headlights once the Falcon was speeding down the runway. He turned away and went to see how Liz was doing; Trish and Diehl were stretched out, asleep on two of the leather recliners.

Dania was sitting by Liz on one of the couches in the plane's midsection. She smiled at him; he ruffled her hair. They were both pretending it could still work.

Hunt wanted to squat down by the wounded woman's head; tried it, realized neither his back nor his leg were going to permit it, stood back up, letting his gaze roam over the assortment of bottles and bedpans and tubing and feeder clips and hemostats Snow had left. He checked the tape on the drip bag; it wasn't occluding the flow.

Liz's face was waxen and her hair drenched with sweat. He put out a hand, steadying himself against the bulkhead. He had seen people die of less; under her blankets, Liz twitched, then lay still.

"Cory, you know that this happens. One expects casualties."

"Shot is shot? Yeah, I guess so. I've never been good at watching cliffhangers, and I don't see many ladies this bad off—I get 'em either before or after. The Afghan PDP's used to take women and children out behind the police station and shoot them, but that's clean kill. And it's different when it's not strangers."

"It's Mino's affection for her, surely, that concerns you."

"They're in love. Listen, I'm going to kibbitz up there until we're out of American airspace. We've got lots of electronic counter-measures and nice classified radars, all sorts of things no one's going to want to risk losing—this plane's pretty safe, I'd bet, at least until we get where we're going and they can reclaim it un-damaged. But I'm going to have them brush me up on everything in here. I used to be able to handle myself around an aircraft...."

"They can do without you to teach. You have to rest now, and if you have to think, then perhaps that, too, is good. I can give you Percodan; it will lessen the pain and you'll get sleepy. You are as pale as she, and for less reason."

He declined the drug, waved his hand at her, and went forward, where the galley was, to make coffee. Flak came out to get a beer from the bar. "You want to know what Jack said?" he said quietly. Hunt, back to him, nodded. Flak quoted: " 'Son, you've got twelve hours to get your tails out of the country. You've left us quite a mess to clean up. Stay away from the Cannards and Shy's Triage teams, and I'll be hearing from you soon.'" He shelved his Fowler impression, Midwest-twangy and hard-r'd. "Ain't shit to him what it's cost us."

"It's all right. We just need to be able to say under oath, truth drugs, or lie detector that somebody was in on this every step of the way. He knows that and let us bring him in anyway. He's risking as much as we are—in his terms, possibly more." Hunt turned. "If I take any more falls, I'm going to take every one of those sons of bitches with me. And they know it. Up until now, you're probably the only privy party who didn't. You remember the faceless FI—Foreign Intelligence—honcho who was at the Zürich party?"

"Yes, sir," Flak sighed, crossing his arms and lowering his head.

"Know his name?"

"Yes, sir."

"Get hold of him when we land, and tell him if he still wants to talk about Two Can Play, we might arrange a mutual-assistance pact."

"Phew. CIA'll love that. You'd do that?"

"I'll talk about maybe doing it." If nothing more, it would have the effect of convincing one major service that it might be better if he stayed alive, at least temporarily. The KGB's sanitizing strike on the Saudi's estate was surely going to be blamed on him; Triage had lost an A Team and Innotech had lost face and considerable capital; Fowler had ISA's hand to play.

Flak nodded, jacking the top off his beer bottle, then hesitated. "That smells good, sir. Enough for two?"

"Ten. Here." He gave Flak a plastic cup and took one. "Have you any of that Lamb's Breath left—the Jamaican?"

"Up front. I'll get it and . . . you want some of Beth's blow? Real pure . . ."

"Sure. Wait a minute."

Flak paused.

"First, tell Mino Liz's looking better."

"She is?"

"Not really, but he might as well think so. He's got a long night ahead. I'm glad we've got some sort of wake-ups aboard. And, second: If you think that computer in the com console will run it, I'm going to get the software packet from Dania. If Mino can spare you, I'd like you around while I take a look—"

"Yes, *sir!*"

"Which?"

"Everything." He put down his coffee carefully, said, "Cory—Christ, that's great!" and slipped through into the business end of the plane while Hunt went back to try his luck with Dania.

Diehl was awake. "Is that coffee I smell?"

Hunt said it was and moved to pass by him. Diehl put out a hamlike hand. "Sit a moment, Abu Ifrit, and talk with me." Hunt stopped, but did not sit, looking down at Diehl over his cup. The big man had sustained the worst wounds of anyone save Liz; he had needed a lot of blood. His thigh wound had been deep and the bullet in it had exploded, leaving multiple fragments; the neck wound had required seventeen stitches.

"I've got a lot to do, Diehl. What is it?"

"Your people are not certain Innotech sicced those dogs on us."

"They're young; they don't want to believe that Triage would do that." He wondered where Diehl was going with this.

"But you harbor no such illusions?"

"I told Dania Shy was going to come after her, guns blazing, if they couldn't work out a deal. *And* I told her that if she helped me, she was going to catch a little of my heat. I'm paying my way, too." He indicated his leg. "I need a nice quiet place to lie down and pretend I'm a civilian; I don't need night actions and KGB hostiles, and I most especially don't need to have to justify myself to you. If Dania's worried about me, my motives or my dependability, she'll tell me. Until then, stay off my case. I don't feel real good, and I get short-tempered whenever I lose a lot of blood."

"Cory Hunt, you do not want me for an enemy, and I do not want you for one. The world is full of enemies." He spread his fingers, made a fist. "They come and they go"—he snapped a finger—"like that. Your pups—"

"Diehl, Cory, stop it." Dania stood there, between the plane's sections, her hands on the partition and unshed tears in her eyes. "Isn't it enough, without you two at odds?"

"Liz? Is she—"

"Madonna, what is wrong?"

They had spoken at the same moment. Dania replied to both: "I am tired, and Liz is sleeping." She wiped her eyes and sniffled, opened them. "I cannot bear to see you two squaring off. I won't have it."

Cory, by then, had gone over to her. He felt her forehead; it was clammy and warm. "You ought to sit down awhile yourself." He took her face in his hands and looked at the stitches in her hair, kissed the crown of her head. "I'm sorry. Diehl is, too, I'd bet. It's hard to sit up here, wondering if they'll decide to shoot us down and fuck the plane. Listen, I want to run that software. I need to know if we've got anything there worth talking to people about." This last was a whisper. She nodded. Diehl, when Hunt had approached Dania, had turned away, gotten to his feet, and lumbered toward the galley.

Trish, disturbed, was stirring. She put an arm over her eyes, arched her lithe frame, and sat up in a shower of long black hair. "Are we there, Dania? What's happening?"

"Dinner, pet. We must make their dinner. You know men, and fighters are the worst. They will starve if we do not feed them."

"Affirmative. You got that right." She shimmied out of her blanket and went to "find Flak and get him to loan me a line," dressed only in a peach silk teddy.

"I told them to pack extra clothes, field gear. Did they?" Hunt asked her as Dania, who had gone aft, returned with a folded, taped envelope and handed it to him.

"Do not worry, Cory. They have everything they need."

Trish came back and nonchalantly stepped into her fatigue pants, then pulled Flak's black sweater over her head. "Well?" she said challengingly to Hunt, watching. "Do you like what you see?"

"So-so," he said, and went through the galley to the navigator's station. Flak met him there. "Here we go. What do you think? Can we see what we've got?"

Flak slid the floppy disks out. "Should be able to, sir. The language is Basic, it says here. Somebody went to a little trouble to make sure even the Ivans would be able to make use of them."

When the take started to come up, Flak whistled and shut it down almost immediately. Hunt had seen math, algorithms and numbers, and the heading and cryptonym, that of Innotech's cryptography department.

"Duals?"

"Yes, sir," the asset whispered, "the log of every published dual code for the last year, maybe longer." He leaned toward Hunt. "The top one was the French data code from their new spy satellite. I'd heard it's got a hunter/killer option, but basically it intercepts and monitors, decodes and relays other people's transmissions. This is worth a *fortune*, just the *first* one. You can run the satellite, tap the data, any damn thing you want to do. Should get you Martinova, sir, no sweat."

Chapter
18

John Shy poured himself a Jack Daniel's and Grover a highball
glass of Saratoga water from the stretch limo's wet bar as the
Innotech class-six armored Cadillac sped through the morning
light toward Boston. Since Zürich, he had been careful not to take
the armor classes of his cars lightly. He ordered this one to meet
his chopper at Hanscom when he had finally gotten free of the
ongoing Crisis Committee meeting at Innotech on Madison Avenue to race Hunt to the Falcon. He had lost by a nose—he had
gotten there only in time to see the Falcon taxi into darkness—
but he *had* been in time to intervene for his team's sake and
personally override Sid Cannard's sanitizing directive.

Shy had been a fool to trust Sid when the old man assured him that he would "take it from here. She's my daughter, after all. I'm the one to solve it. I simply needed to be sure." The old bastard hadn't had even the good grace to act surprised. They were two of a kind, father and daughter: Beth was still insisting that she could solve her own problems without any help from him, thank you, when a Triage A Team jumped out of the Maryland bushes and ambushed Dania and, so one survivor thought, Angel Morales. Two pistols had been recovered, one a 9mm Walther, one a Beretta 92—Angel's file noted his fondness for that manufacturer. Both side arms had been wiped of prints.

The wire services were having a field day with this "resurgence of terrorism on U.S. soil." Luckily, so were the would-be terrorist groups; better than a dozen callers had already claimed responsibility on behalf of divers factions. Since the casualties of the evening included Saudis, Soviets, Turks, and South Americans of three nations, as well as one CIA contract agent fielded out of a Dominican mission, many groups vied for the credit, enough that no mention was likely to be made of the tangential issue that fully half of those invited guests unfortunate enough to have been caught in the explosion had been diplomats assigned to the UN, whose presence so far outside of New York was strictly forbidden.

No government agency privy to the truth of last evening's events was anxious to make public what was best left unexplained. Innotech/Triage was content to suffer its losses in silence; not a Saudi nor a Soviet would mention the type of explosion or the method of the ordnance's delivery. Nobody wanted to talk about air strikes in Maryland, or anything else actual or pertinent. The FBI was charged with primary investigative responsibility for domestic affairs of this sort; the new CIA charter allowed it to follow up and "assist" in matters of domestic espionage; 18 U.S.C. 1116, which statute covers murder or manslaughter of foreign officials, official guests, or internationally protected persons, states in subsection (d) that the "Attorney General may request assistance from any Federal, state, or local agency, including the Army, Navy, and Air Force...." What the attorney general had done was to call the Soviet and Saudi ambassadors, CIA's deputy director, and Innotech/Triage's North American regional director and give them an ultimatum: either nobody pressed charges or leaked information, or everybody went on record (and on "Nightline," "Face the Nation," and Reuters) with the whole sordid story of internecine intrigue.

The conditions under which the attorney general himself was willing to refrain from demanding a full explanation, as NSA's head honcho had asked *him,* were "that:(a) no further newsmaking violence occurs in the continental United States which can in any fashion be construed to relate to the destruction of Turki-al-Faisal's Maryland estate and (b) that *apparently* full cooperation be tendered my operatives in making a 'quick and efficient' investigation—i.e., case closed by noon today." The attorney general had a golf game he couldn't postpone.

Shy held the glass steady for Grover, who was better now; the B-Z had been flushed from his system; the red Doberman no longer shivered at a sudden noise or leaped at an unexpected touch. He wondered what the half-life of the drug was; the half-life of this botched operation was going to be a long one, that was certain.

Shy should have expected Cannard to pull something like this, but he hadn't. Hindsightedly, what happened during Two Can Play's run—Hunt being blown despite the amount of information he carried in his head, or because of it; operatives being routinely eliminated as soon as their work was done—indicated that Cannard had long known Innotech wasn't secure, that Sid might even have known from the outset that Beth was the guilty party.

Shy was about to find out. The person he was meeting was Sid. When Sid had refused point-blank to move his trip forward by even twenty-four hours, Shy had realized that he might be dealing with a delaying action. Still, one didn't advance accusations of this magnitude cavalierly. One wanted to confront the putative enemy face-to-face.

Sipping his drink, he slumped back in his seat. His best merino Savile Row suit smelled and looked as if he'd slept in it, which he had. He should never have stopped drinking; one doesn't alter a proven formula before a trial—not for an assault team, a race car, or an intelligence operation. He'd been thinking more lucidly since he'd resumed his practice of moderate intoxication. With his brain lubricated, he had no trouble seeing his next moves clearly: Keep Beth Cannard under twenty-four-hour surveillance;

confront her father with his personal ultimatum; resolve matters satisfactorily before things could proceed to the point where public acknowledgment, denials and admissions, had to be made.

Dropout was running true to form: exorbitantly expensive, unexpectedly effective, unconscionably irrevocable in methodology and repercussions. Still, Cord got things done.

What Dropout's team had with them in the way of hard evidence was of crucial importance; it was all Shy could do to stay off the scrambled communications line that could put him in touch with the airborne Falcon. He'd have to wait. He had to be able to convince Cordell Hunt that he, John Shy, had had nothing to do with Sid's attempt at an executive clearing of Beth's unsightly decks. To boot, he had to be able to offer guaranties, incentives, make conciliatory gestures. To that end he had already been in touch with CIA's deputy from Foreign Intelligence; a sad-eyed general from Afghanistan's Military Intelligence Directorate; and an old friend from Inter-Services Intelligence (ISI), who agreed to act as an intermediary with ISA in the matter of one Anastacia Martinova. He hoped, as did the intermediary, that it wasn't too late. He could have gone to Jack Fowler for clearer, quicker results, but considering the insertion of "Darling" into Shy's shop and Dropout's team, Shy felt Jack to be more a wild card than an ally. He didn't want to engender any more "Cosmic" notations with his name on them; he couldn't risk letting Fowler know how he was getting on.

Shy had put Beth under round-the-clock surveillance. He'd tried assigning men to her overtly, calling the coverage "a precaution," but she would have none of it. So, after the air strike in Maryland, when he knew he couldn't keep her in sight himself, he'd had her picked up by some borrowed talent from SIS, promising the British diplomat who doubled as their Washington station chief information on the disappearance of an outstanding agent of theirs, code-named Ali Baba, and a look at the Two Can Play take relevant to the Hindu Kush in exchange for the use of a six-man team of crack ex–Special Air Services commandos. The ex–SAS 22 "bodyguards" were now on their way with Beth to the Shys' Cape Cod retreat, where he was going to keep her until after his showdown with Sid.

To do so, he had had to secure Michele's permission. And to

get it, he had had to be very forthcoming. At this point in his life, he had wanted to be, anyway. Michele was bound up in this as well as he; he couldn't give her five thousand a month in American dollars if he was only making fifty-five hundred. If he had to leave Innotech and, because of Sid's hostility, couldn't secure another similar job in the private sector, he would have to go back into government intelligence work. Pay ceilings and restrictions, if a man disdained becoming a "five-percenter," would then limit his income to less than he had become accustomed to allotting for his three children's support.

This was no time for them to get a divorce. He had said that.

She had looked at him over her tortoise glasses, then slowly taken them off. "Really? Why is that?"

They had been walking on their little stretch of sand-whipped beach, a spit adjacent to National Seashore conservation on the bay side of the Cape, Grover happily but murderously intent on bringing down at least one fat, young, mottled gull. He didn't answer directly. He said, "I want your opinion on something. A hypothetical case." And he had told her, without naming names, the mess he was in.

She knew exactly what he was saying. Michele's intellect was occasionally a problem between them; she was overpowered as an analyst, tending to make emotional judgments based on valid but idealistic conclusions reasoned from a life-conserving base. They almost never discussed politics or even the more pragmatic facets of intelligence-community matters. She had her work with Rand and similar consultancies, where think-tank abstraction tempered her radical bent; she wrote inflammatory pieces for small-circulation journals when she had to salve her conscience. If not for her tendency to become outraged at what her accurate projections of trends indicated, she would have made a formidable intelligence professional.

Even while he was briefing her—obliquely but thoroughly enough that if anything happened to him, she would know what to do and have the leverage to do it with—he was second-guessing himself: wondering if he had been right to spend the last four days personally baby-sitting Beth Cannard, jetting back and forth across the prime meridian in seemingly random fashion, incommunicado to all but his assistant Hubble, merely to provide a rationale for not pulling his team off the Maryland go, as Sid had instructed him, and to do what Hunt had asked him—keep an eye on Beth.

So when Michele had broken into his monologue to tell him that he had received a call on the "green phone" early Wednesday morning, "someone named Flak—that's your new pilot, isn't it?— who was very disappointed that I didn't know where you could be reached," he was caught off-guard.

"Message?" he had snapped, saw her reproving blink, saw her pat her sand-dusted hair, sigh as if giving in to a persistent, nagging child, then heard her reply, "Yes and no. He said to tell you *'carpe diem; mea non culpa,'* if I heard from you by Friday" as he turned away to call Grover to heel.

When the dog had bounded up, showering them with mud and seawater and sand as he shook himself by Shy's knee, he put an arm around his wife and squeezed her shoulder. "I want you to go back to Zürich—for a few days, anyway. Until this is over."

"Isn't it enough that I've agreed to have her here?"

"No. Surely I don't have to spell it out for you." He put his hand on her cold one; she was wearing an Irish sweater and jeans, hardly enough to keep out March sea wind, gray and sharp. Her expression replied that he did. "Michele, that call was one from my team, telling me things were on line but out of hand. That assessment still holds true. My team hasn't heard from me since I managed to isolate the problem. I've been sourcing in Europe and keeping up with the subject in question, but my team leader is wondering right now whether *I'm* behind the sanctions someone attempted to levy on his people. When a field team walks into a fire fight, they don't tend to shrug it off, especially when the subscription list of privy parties is this exclusive. I—"

"Is it Hunt?"

"Michele, I couldn't tell you if it were, you know that. I—"

"If it is, I won't be any safer one place than another—or any less safe. You should stick to covert action—destabilizing governments from afar, anonymously. That's what you do best. If it is Cord, or someone of that caliber, why are you worried that he'd turn on you?"

"I can't discount the possibility, especially after the call you got. I wasn't there for them when they needed me, Michele. The only thing I could have done, had they reached me, was scrub their go, as I was ordered, but they don't know any of that. And... you know how complicated these things get. Will you go to Zürich? Paris? Any—"

"So you're going to try to pull it out, is that it?"

"I have no choice but surrender, otherwise. I'm down to the last-ditch stuff—tactical nukes, as Dropout would say. Either you'll collect my pension or I'll collect a fat pay raise along with a promotion—at which point if you still insist on divorcing me, at least you'll be able to do so in style. Until then, bear with me—please?"

"Anything to hear the end of Beth Cannard. It's not easy to be one-upped by a clinical psychologist, or whatever those witch doctors call themselves. And publicly, I—"

"Let's not get into it; I have to do my job."

"And she's part of it?"

"Right now she's the most difficult part of it. Will you let me arrange a flight for you? You can board at Otis, you won't even have to go to Boston. Just tell me where—"

"John?"

When he looked squarely at her, she had taken off her glasses again and her eyelids were fluttering rapidly. "I'm sorry," she said. "I assumed it wasn't—I mean, I thought she was your..."

He let her make whatever assumptions she was willing to make, concurred with her that divorce wasn't for "people like us," and agreed that she should call her parents and tell them that "everything's fine, we're all right" from the air base before she debarked. He was even polite when she reiterated her father's standing offer to reinsert him into the Pentagon should he come to his senses and be "willing to work for a living." When they reached the railroad ties that led up to the house among bare beach-plum bushes, she began to worry about his safety. He diverted her with the children's: She should have them all flown over to Zürich as soon as she was settled in; Hubble would handle the arrangements.

He sent his one backup with her; he would be safe enough with Grover and the single driver. He instructed the servants to prepare the house for his "British guests'" arrival before they left and was out of there thirty-five minutes after Michele waved goodbye from the passenger seat of her Audi Quattro.

In retrospect, he had succeeded with Michele better than he

might have hoped. His Cape house was the only safe place he could think of for Beth's debriefing. He told Grover gravely, between phone calls, "Well done. I couldn't have managed it without you, boy," and the Doberman wagged his stump of a tail uncertainly, then stretched out, paw before paw, on the limo's taupe carpet until his jaws rested against Shy's foot.

It was as much truth as lie, as everything from here on had to be. He didn't have much time, and few advantages. But he also had little choice—he couldn't take a cut in pay, a de facto demotion. It wasn't just hubris, it was necessity: He had responsibilities to his children, to his co-workers, to Innotech and the intelligence community as a whole, which he couldn't abrogate— not to mention Dropout et al. He had let operations fizzle in the past, let assets be lost when circumstances dictated, when national security was at stake, or when no other choice was possible. But always there had been reason enough; he had never thrown away a life without a fight. This time the reasons weren't good enough and the lives at risk were more than code names and work designations. If none of the above was true, tradecraft was still built on a crucial assumption of trust: The agent had to be able to trust his agency—his case officer, his controller and/or handler, his couriers in the field. Without such assurance, no fieldwork was possible. The operative word, *trust,* had to have meaning, or his entire career would then be open to reevaluation as a series of petty bureaucratic intrigues with no inherent value—ditto for all the fifty-cent words in whose service he labored: liberty, democracy, freedom, excellence.

Boston inevitably brought back to him all the reasons for the decisions and determinations that had shaped his career. Across the Charles, MIT sat—its squat dome and granite columns evoking all the rhomboids and tetrahedrons of his youth. He remembered Michele and a dozen other Cliffies, long of hair and flashing of eye, occupying the Harvard men's rooms in protest. He recalled their first tryst, here, where he was just being deposited, at the Ritz-Carlton on Arlington facing the Boston Common. Nothing had changed; the creaking, creepy, anachronistic elegance of the hotel was unmitigated; the doormen in their long coats and caps festooned with braid could have been the same who had served him nearly twenty years ago, when he had first conceived his dislike for this place, in which a conscious conspiracy to ward off progress was under way. There had been an addition built since last he had come past the brace of black limousines through the brass revolving door into the musty elegance of High Boston, but he was willing to bet that the dress code—"no jeans, no denims, ties must be worn"—still obtained, unshaken by the passage of time since he had found out, with Michele, that even for them, the young lions, lunch could not be had in comfort, despite the premium price he had paid for their lodging. He had never forgiven the hotel its peccadilloes: Over the question of whether or not to change their clothes, Michele and he had had their first argument.

Looking for Cannard's shaggy leonine head in the café with its pink tablecloths and obligatory single roses, he felt uncomfortable all over again. The maître d' delegated a subordinate to escort him to Sid's hidden table, far from the street-facing windows, invisible from the door. The room was dotted with late breakfasters: a group of six black-jacketed men and women, surely part of the trade mission from mainland China with whom Sid would be meeting this week; three tables of placarded conventioneers from the "Silicon Necklace," the assemblage of high-tech companies lining Route 128 with which Innotech/Triage did business. He wondered if any of them were from Northrop Aerospace in Norwood—some of the missing technology from the New York EO had to do with the air-to-air guidance system, good to thirty G's and capable of midair course correction, Northrop was developing for a NATO missile program.

Crossing the patterned broadloom, he saw Cannard's gnarled hand wave and found himself thinking about the Chinese businessmen he was passing—his former ChiCom enemies were now sought-after allies. Boston's mayor, at the administration's behest, was deeply involved in innocent-seeming cultural-exchange and trade programs. Innotech was setting up a branch here to accommodate the increasing security and production demands of the area. Between 128 and Woods Hole Oceanographic's Soviet interaction and classified think-tank involvement, his old turf was more than ever the hub of innovation, with its concomitant political and security concerns. Innotech could make a seven-figure yearly profit just vetting prospective employees of genetic-engineering firms and research-and-development complexes.

The prospects were very "exciting." To be a part of that excitement to come, he was going to have to handle this meeting exactly right. He checked his Rolex. It was nine-thirty. He was precisely on time. Hunt would not yet have landed on the Côte d'Azur at Cannes.

"Hello, Sid. Thanks for making time for this." His solar plexus twitched, drying his mouth with a rush of adrenaline, so that he knew his hand would be cold when Cannard took it in his big, wrinkled, dry one.

"Don't be ridiculous, John."

The waiter disappeared as Shy, seating himself, ordered tea and juice, poached eggs on toast. Cannard was still telling him it was "good to see you, no matter the circumstances or how terrible you look," when Shy fired his opening salvo: "Sid, if I look like I've been up all night, I shouldn't have to tell you why. How could you do something like this? Have you seen the damage report—"

"I've heard. Containment, naturally, must be our first concern. To that end, I've heard you're doing marvelously." Sid Cannard looked like Shy felt: exhausted, wizened, ill. He took off his glasses and began to clean them on the linen napkin, waiting for Shy to concur. He didn't. Cannard put down his glasses carefully beside his cup and pulled out his pipe. "Do you mind?" Shy didn't. The smell of Cake Box tobacco filled the air. "You asked me how *I* could do something like this? How could you ignore *two*—not one, boy, but *two*—direct orders?"

"I don't count it that way. In the first case, I couldn't reach my people to pull them out—by the time I'd finally gotten through to you, they were on-site and out of contact. I told you *then* I thought that might happen. But you didn't tell me why you wanted them out of play. All that wet work in Maryland is your doing. There's no way to clean this up, Sid. You can't silence everybody who knows. You shouldn't have tried." It was Shy's turn to wait for Cannard's response: there was none. "As far as Hanscom goes, I acted on my own best judgment. Given that you'd failed in reappropriating the desired material on-site, and precipitated an overt incident, a second action in the continental United States for questionable purpose was simply unacceptable—that was not only *my* estimate, but that of the Justice Department." He bared his teeth. "What the hell did you think you had to gain? Or do you *want* to discredit the company so completely that it's useless?"

"I'll ignore that." Cannard didn't look, however, as if he could. His face was so pale, liver spots showed like spattered mud. His small, sharp eyes were watery. "That aircraft is now in the hands of acknowledged international terrorists, you realize—"

"Not so. You can't assume that."

"They *stole* it! Your *team* and the Moraleses. It's got more classified ECM aboard—"

"I gave it to them for the duration. This is a sad excuse for so many casualties, and for making me a possible target of the Moraleses' retaliation. Sid, what's wrong with you? Are you in more trouble than I know? Eliminating Morales and Dropout's team wouldn't have solved anything—"

"Wouldn't it?" Cannard leaned forward. "My daughter's problems are my problems. Unfortunately, she doesn't realize one can't simply renege on a commitment to interests such as she was dealing with. Think a moment, John. She prevents the transfer, reinserts the material where it belongs—then what? How can I protect her from the opposition? No, this was the only way—I had to take responsibility out of her hands, stop the transfer myself. It was the *only* way."

"It didn't work."

"That's so, I'm afraid. At least, so far. I still have a card or two to play—"

"Jesus, Sid, can't you see you're thirty years behind the times in methodology? All you're doing is compounding our errors. *What* cards have you got left?" He had pounded the table. Cannard's eyebrow went up; the old man sat back in his chair. The waiter arrived with Shy's tea and juice. He squeezed lemon over his cup until the man moved away. Then he continued. "No more attempts at executive action. I won't put up with it. This is my team, my operation, my reputation. You stay out of it or I'll *get* out of it—leave you holding a very nasty bag full of compromised daughters with large drug habits and Soviet boyfriends. Do you *know* what the object in dispute is?"

"Do you?"

"Duals; the encoding and decoding library. The whole thing from index to cryptographic matrix generators. Do you know where that would put us? Or do you want us to become Soviet proxies, lock, stock, and satellite down-links?"

"Hush."

"It's too late for that. Sid, I wasn't sure you realized. Now I want you to realize this: Either we do this my way from here on in, or when I get up from this table I'm going straight over to State and play my own aces."

"And what are they?"

"Beth. I had her picked up. Now hold on, don't jump to conclusions. *I'm* willing to be civilized about this. She hasn't been interviewed, she's on a record nowhere as a respondent. I have to get a list of what she's passed, of course—"

"She swore to me, John, that without this final installment, all the previous transfers are useless."

"That may be so. We need to find out, don't we? Then, if you agree, we'll send her to some nice sanatarium to dry out, or whatever they do with drug-abuse cases."

"I assume you've fallbacks and contingencies in place to support this sort of threatening behavior?"

"Believe it. The best. And I haven't even begun to suggest—"

"You aren't thinking about blackmailing *me*, I hope? The packet and the operatives in question are still of interest to friends of mine in the business. I suggest you go back to your desk in Zürich—while you still have one—and forget about Dropout and the Moraleses. The world will, soon enough."

"What have you done?"

"Nothing. Nor will I have to. I simply suggested to certain customers where they might find them...."

"Whoever gets those codes gets Innotech, Triage, and heaven knows what else—"

His eggs came. He assured the waiter he desired nothing additional. Then he said, "Sid, look here...OSS tactics just aren't going to work."

"*You* look here. No one is going to control Innotech but me. I've worked too hard to build it. If I have to go to every customer personally and hand-deliver new encoding matrices, I'll do so. I'll call it new policy on our part."

"And no one will ever believe it, or trust us again."

"Perhaps so, perhaps not." Sid Cannard clamped his pipe between his teeth, sucked on it, found it had gone out, and relit it with trembling hands. "Consider my position, John. Beth's *apparent* misbehavior is central to the continuance of Two Can Play. It may look to you like I betrayed our Mr. Hunt's team, but I can't take the chance that the Moraleses will keep those data for themselves, especially when no one is sure exactly what is in the packet—not you, not anyone. Perhaps Beth doesn't know. She's no mathematician. You've put me in a position verging on untenable. The Soviets are going to want to talk to my daughter. I hope you haven't provided them with the very opportunity they seek."

Something inside him knew that Cannard was covering his ass, that the old man was lying to him. "What are you saying? That Beth's a provocation? That the information and the technology passed is unimportant? She *told* me she got out a VHSIC chip—a Very High Speed Integrated Circuit."

Sid Cannard shrugged. "Bona fides, my dear john. Bona fides."

Shy, hands below the table, wiped sweaty palms. "If that's so, or you think that it's so, it's time for you to retire. Gracefully. Quietly. I'll handle the rest of this. If there's a chance to pull it out, believe me, I'll do it."

"As Innotech's director?"

"*Pro tem*, anyway. The permanent appointment should still be up to the board. Unless you'd welcome a referendum by the community on your handling of this affair. Executive action against our own people is something no one will publicly sanction—even privately you'll get nothing but disavowals. No agency is going to applaud surgical strikes like Maryland—not in America, not for any reason, not when diplomats were involved."

"Who? A KGB station chief? A CIA contract agent, a Salvadoran or Dominican or some such? Saudi muscle and hired ex-commandos with gold-plated guns? Come now, John. Not one word of this is going to leak unless *you* leak it."

"So it *was* purposeful on your part?"

"For the good of the shop—of course it was purposeful. I told you; I warned you to get your team out of my hair. If you've lost them, it's hardly my fault. Now, where is Beth?"

Shy said, "Somewhere safe, I told you that before." He pushed back his sleeve and held out his Rolex for Cannard's inspection.

A little LED glowed red on its face. It was a Triage standard transmitter.

Cannard knew what he was seeing; he seemed to shrink smaller. He'd incriminated himself quite thoroughly in the last few minutes, and he knew it. He blinked, sighed deeply, rubbed his eyes with his fingertips, and put on his glasses. "You know, John," he said, and his voice was tremulous, "I've never been able to help her. When she was twelve, she had a bout of obesity. We tried everything—equestrian diet camps, summers abroad, schools with strict regimens. You see, it was a glandular imbalance.

"We hospitalized her for six weeks when she was thirteen. Her mother and I did everything we could. When she was fourteen, we began to try to understand how our sweet little girl had become so difficult—almost psychotic, one might say. It turned out, we later realized, to be a side effect of the weight-control medication—Preludin for a sluggish thyroid, amphetamines for appetite control. We *made* her into a drug abuser. When she'd run out of her pills, she'd call me in tears, John, *tears*. We'd have to send them to her, wherever she was. She couldn't function normally without them anymore.

"It was different in those days; no one really understood the dangers. Diet pills...the whole thing seemed so innocuous. Her mother wanted her to be fit to debut, you understand....She was so difficult a child. But she never had a chance to be a child—at least not a teen-ager. She was too intelligent to make the usual mistakes. She didn't get into trouble of the mundane sort; she never attempted suicide. Oh, she'd call from Paris, when she was supposed to be studying for finals at Dana Hall, and threaten me with exorbitant credit-card purchases if I interfered....One makes excuses.

"When she entered Columbia, we thought she'd conquered it. But they never do, I suppose. You should have a certain sympathy—I've seen how arduous it's been for you to curtail your drinking."

Shy spread his hands. "This is hardly pertinent. She's not involved in collegiate caprice, she's funneling our best material to Soviet sources."

"I want to know where she is, John." Sid's eyes, behind his glasses, were filled with tears.

"I'll tell you in good time, Sid. Right now, why don't we go up to your room and make a few phone calls. I don't want to try to deal with the consequences if the customers get to that packet before Dropout can secure it."

On the way to the elevators, Shy was wondering whether it would be possible to restrain the customers now that Cannard had loosed them—*if* he had. There was no telling how much, if any, of what Sid had said was true. For Shy's purposes, it hardly mattered. The tape in the car had recorded all the wrist transmitter had broadcast; Sid Cannard was finished as Innotech's director. Shy had had no choice: Someone in a suitably high place always took a fall over an error of this magnitude. It was a "him-or-me" situation. But he wasn't relieved. Not yet. There was too much hanging fire.

When Cannard had Telexed his resignation to the appropriate desks, complete with Shy's temporary appointment as his replacement, they began trying to undo some of the damage Sid had done. Shy had thought, waiting for Cannard to fumble for his key and open his door, that there might be a kicker waiting for him inside—a backup or two, some nasty OSS precaution, antiquated but effective. Percy Hunt used to have knife sheathes tailored into his pants pockets; that whole bunch had given the term *cowboy* its derogatory meaning—anything for law, order, and the American Way. Anything.

But no brusier came lumbering out of Sid's sitting room; no nerve-gas canister, produced from Cannard's voluminous pockets, dropped him to his knees. Shy chided himself for thinking like Hunt. This wasn't that sort of confrontation. This was the hard stuff—a word here, a tiny detail there, and somebody ceased to exist. He had to make sure that Sid's interference hadn't mushroomed into some scenario where the Falcon would be denied landing privileges, or its occupants denied entry, met with anti-terrorist squads, treated as hijackers, and pried out of their plane like sardines from a can. The international consensus, since the late Seventies, had been that terrorists were killed out of hand whenever feasible; this denied them the publicity that kept them viable as an anarchic force. Every agency made use of this free-hand policy when it suited them; Sid and his friends could wield it with impunity.

Luckily, the Falcon was virtually invulnerable in the air, or, Sid admitted, the French could have been prevailed upon to shoot it down for them: no Dropout, no Moraleses, no sensitive intelligence take in the wrong hands, no electronic countermeasures console for rival though friendly government intelligence services to analyze before handing it back. The Falcon had jamming and counterjamming, every passive defense technique of the electronic sort, plus diversionary flare launchers and antiaircraft-quality armorplate on her belly and fuel tanks. One of Shy's first priorities was to make sure that Innotech/Triage, and no one else, got that aircraft back. Another was going to have to be revising the French satellite's cryptographic security: Aérospatiale was going to love that. Mitterand's brother was nobody's fool.

But neither was he. All the way back to the Cape, he took notes. Foremost in his mind was the suspicion that no one was going to win this one unequivocally: Life had a way of piling things on one side of your desk, while you were busy clearing the other. Among the Falcon's many capabilities was that of data duplication. If he were Hunt, he would make safeties of every piece of intelligence in that packet; with that done, his options would be limited only by insufficient boldness and imagination, neither of which Cordell Hunt was lacking. Having come to this realization, he had to admit that Sid's seemingly disproportionate actions had had a strategically sound basis: Given Dropout's capabilities, those of the Falcon, and the Moraleses' international connections, total annihilation was the only sure way to counter the burgeoning momentum of this operation. But he still couldn't justify it.

The most worrisome thing he had learned in the last few hours— the one that had him scratching away on a yellow pad in the March haze that no courtesy lamps could dispell—was that the Falcon hadn't landed on schedule at Cannes, but had diverted to Marseilles, purportedly experiencing fuel-line problems. They had made an emergency landing and disappeared in a waiting Kombi van. From Marseilles, it was unlikely that anyone could extract them; the French port was the premier safe haven and favorite whore of black-market arms dealers, terrorists, pirates, and thieves. From there they could go anywhere: Spain would swallow them up; Sicily would embrace them; Libya was accessible through Algeria or by air. Unless Hunt chose to surface, he had lost him.

Only ISA's possession of the Martinova woman cast a ray of hope through Shy's internal gloom—that and Darling, Fowler's penetration, on-site and ready to go at Jack's signal. He had had to talk not once but twice to Fowler; they had a lot of preparations to make.

At the house he was met with Beth's stony silence and a surfeit of British good cheer from the baby-sitters. He sent two into town in the Mondial to lay in stores—whatever they wanted that Michele didn't have on hand, plus lobsters and clams for a pot dinner. Two others were walking the perimeter and two he sent to reconnoiter the guest quarters above the free-standing garage; mildew was a constant problem at the beach house—they'd need at least to air out the place and wash their sheets.

He knew he was forestalling the inevitable, but he puttered around in the kitchen, feeding Grover, who was spooked by the strange house that smelled of sea and cats (he'd have to be careful to segregate the Himalayans when they came in from foraging; Michele wouldn't be pleased if Grover killed the house cats) while Beth leaned against the white-painted moulding, saying little, looking on.

She was as beautiful as ever, but pale in her Fila ski sweater; it seemed to him she had lost weight—or perhaps it was despair that pulled in her flesh, making it hug her cheekbones and causing her tailored slacks to hang too loosely. She stared out the window, picking at a broken edge of one blood-red nail. When she spoke at last, she had been silent so long that he started and Grover skittered backward along the vintage red linoleum.

"Surely you don't expect to get away with this?" Her voice was modulated, genteel; she might have been discussing the view or his dog—there was just that much dismissal in her tone: She disliked the Cape (too crowded) and all dogs (the pervasive odor). She took an atomizer of Molinard from her purse and squirted some behind her ears.

"I shall be surprised if I don't. Your father seems to think I have sufficient grounds. He's tendered his resignation." If a fight was what she wanted, he was willing to give her one. He barely held back from the accusatory clause: *because of you.*

"After all *my father* has done for you? How *could* you? And in such a tawdry fashion. Class will tell, I suppose...."

"Beth, this isn't etiquette; it isn't a matter of what *I* can get away with, or should do, or even what I want." He had been running the taps; he shut them off. A dish towel in hand, he turned to face her, though her reflection in the window was easier for him to watch. "How could *you* get yourself into such a position? How could you do it to Sid, to me, to everyone who cares about you? And, most important, how do you expect us to get you out of this mess without your unreserved and full cooperation?"

"Is that what your cockney bullyboys represent, guv—my unreserved and full cooperation?" But her upper lip trembled; she licked it, reminding him of Sid, earlier. He *was* taking unfair advantage of this unfortunate family skeleton, perhaps.

"Look, Beth,"—he took a step toward her—"we can work this out. Just help me take care of you. Let me know what exactly you've done—with whom and to whom and for whom—and I can promise you we'll find a way to minimize the damage." He had a bad taste in his mouth, but he moved closer to her. Taking her in his arms seemed like just the wrong thing to do, but he had to get things on some sort of tenable basis. It was going to take far too long to do this if she wouldn't cooperate. He was sorry, holding her, feeling her tremble and hearing her mock him bitterly: "In the interests of security? What shall it be, a frank and full discussion? Or shall we have a fruitful exchange of views? Can we settle for a joint communiqué on the subject of my fall from grace, or will I have to resign my position as First Daughter and Ambassador to your bedroom?"

He tried to push back from her, to see her face, glean something from her eyes that might help him understand her, but she held him close, her breasts impossibly hot against him. Women confused him, he had to admit. If he could just not mind doing things this way, he was going to get farther, quicker, with affection than with imprecation. He'd never interviewed anyone who wanted him to pretend, as she was now demanding, that he still loved the respondent. He wanted her to sit on one side of the desk in his bedroom while he sat on the other—to do things in an orderly, realistic fashion.

"I never thought I'd be here," she whispered, her head buried against his throat, "in *her* precious family 'cottage.' I thought, when you two separated, that we'd make things public—official. I suppose there's no chance of that now."

Then he did extricate himself from her embrace. "I told you long ago I'd never divorce. It has to do with my children, with what I want for them. Not you. Not us. Surely this is beside the point, at this time. Best intelligence says you got into this out of love for some Soviet agent—is that so?"

"Love?" Fiercely blinking, bright-eyed, she backed away from him. A thick chuckle came out of her; she seemed to try to stop it with her spread hand, blue with high-standing veins and trembling. He thought, *She's terrified,* and felt ashamed. "Love?" she repeated. "How about personal worth? Or feeling like something has to be done about the parasitic class of which I'm a prime example—and you. Did it ever occur to you that I'm simply sick and tired of the abuses of unbridled capitalism? That I'm doing my little bit to even the score for a failing, idealistic society in which one out of five persons is employed in agriculture yet four out of five are hungry?

"The big, bad Soviet menace—*you* don't believe that propaganda. The only sophistication those poor people have is in weaponry, and that's because they're frightened to death we're going to destroy them. And we just keep on pushing them toward moral and physical bankruptcy, forcing them to keep up with us at the expense of everything else. Even you know that when a Soviet agent is debriefed, they have to replace all their codes—they don't even have computer-generated duals. Don't you see, *we're* forcing nuclear war, simply because it's profitable to the diplomats and the primary contractors and the politicians to keep tensions at a maximum. Don't you—"

"And *you're* going to change all that?" He shook his head at her, running a hand through his hair. It was worse than he'd thought; she was unhinged, demented. He recalled the drugs and began to treat her more carefully. A nice long rest in a sanatarium was what she needed; as soon as he could get the specifics he needed, he'd see to her. At least half of this mess was his fault. He should have realized from the way she behaved in Zürich during Dropout's debriefing that something was seriously wrong with her, but he hadn't taken the time. And neither had Sid.

He took her upstairs. He could promise some things: He could promise that she wouldn't endure public censure; he could promise her father's reputation would remain unblemished. He couldn't, however, promise to "make everything all right," or that they could continue on as they had been, or that she could walk away from this free and clear if she told him what he needed to know. Later he thought that must have been what had pushed her over the edge. She *was* exceptionally attractive today, so frightened and yet haughty. He had never before seen anything truly touch her, or shake her aplomb. Covertly, as he was unpacking with Grover's "help" he watched her by way of his dresser's mirror as she combed the disarray from her hair.

He laid out clean trousers and shirts; found the ISA scratch gun Dropout had pressed on him, lying between two pairs of socks; opened his drawer to start putting things away—an admission that this was going to take more than the couple of hours he had hoped. She had already unpacked, as he had instructed the baby-sitters she should. Dawdling, he was beginning to draw her out, to broach possible dangers: Soviet revenge—did she think it was possible? Would Angel Morales try to even the score? That was why he had brought the British boys into it—for her own protection.

It was Grover's growl that warned him. He saw the blur of red Doberman flash by out of the corner of his eye. Right then she was saying something about them "going for a little ride," and her voice was inappropriately combative. He couldn't fathom why he hadn't been paying more attention. He saw in the mirror, just before he turned, that Beth had been holding a gun on him when Grover leaped, doing what his training dictated.

Beth's first .25-caliber round didn't faze the Doberman, but Shy couldn't seem to make the dog hear his repeated order: "Cool! *Grover!*"

He thought calmly, analytically, that he shouldn't have sent all the men out of the house at the same time. Then he thought he should have let them treat her like a prisoner, not a diplomat in protective custody, when they brought her up here. Then there was just the screaming woman and the snarling dog locked in a macabre embrace and arterial blood spurting and two more handgun reports, which would surely bring his backups running. Later he thought it must have been the B-Z, some residual flashback potential of the unpredictable drug Grover had been given.

He stood uncertainly, frozen in time and place, as woman and dog thrashed on Michele's pale Aubusson carpet, the silenced

Ruger Hunt had given him wavering in his hand.

Finally, after what seemed like minutes, he shot his dog through the braincase and pulled its convulsing body from Beth's, Grover's shattered skull oozing cranial tissue and his jaws still locked on Beth's arm.

There was a tremendous amount of blood—on Beth's face, all over him, on the furniture and the wallpaper where arterial pressure had caused the bright red spurts to arc far and wide. He was crying: It wasn't Grover's fault—Grover had been trying to protect him, responding to his training, doing everything right. Beth was hysterical, moaning, splattered with foam he couldn't be sure wasn't hers. He wanted to retch, but he called the Rescue Squad first.

All this because of some floppy disks, because Beth was crazier than he had given her credit for, or just more desperate—because he was in over his head. In the bathroom he stooped, and when he had finished vomiting, he realized he still had the little Ruger in one hand, and that it was empty. He could have sworn he had only fired once...but then, that was common enough—in the moment of adrenaline-prompted action, instinct took over. He, too, had done what, years ago, he had been trained to do.

He wondered how long it was going to take his Britishers to get up here from the garage; almost certainly they'd heard the shots—unless they were in the laundry.

He couldn't wait. He had to see to Beth himself. Poor Grover. He saw again, as he washed his shock-white face before the mirror, his dog's loyal leap. There had been no way to explain to Grover the difference between a woman's grandstanding and real danger. Beth would never have shot him, never have done anything more than threaten and rant and try to bully him into driving her wherever her addled brain told her she might be safe—she just wanted to run.

He was still wiping his reddened eyes and wondering how the hell she could have gotten herself into such a pitiable mess and how, without her cooperation, he and Sid were ever going to get her out of it when the bathroom door, ajar, swung wide and he saw her in the mirror, gory and wild-eyed, her right arm dangling loosely, lean against the doorframe, prop her left hand there, and fire at him from point-blank range. He even saw the orange flash from the Browning's muzzle as he was opening his mouth to object. And then the bullet slammed into his ribs as he was turning and all the pile-driving trauma of its impact knocked the breath out of him.

As he fell toward the mirror, cracked by the bullet that had passed through him, he saw the exit wound blossoming red and wide on his chest and thought that if he hadn't reached an accommodation with Michele concerning Beth and the beach house, none of this would be happening. Then he thought the hole in him was much too big to be survivable.

Then it started to sting everywhere inside him and he was glad not to feel anything at all, to fall into a brown/orange painless well like the tonsillectomy spiral he had slipped down so many years ago when he—what? He couldn't remember, except that there were men at the edges, as there had been then, peeking over into the pit/tunnel/nonplace through which he was falling, telling him it was "going to be all right, old man, don't you know?" and not to worry, to just lie still.

He thought that was nice; he didn't want to worry. He hoped he was lying still, he couldn't tell. He was willing to "forget it," as a voice from far above suggested; he was ready to forget ... except ... he really wished he could have finished what he had started— whatever it was—something about Dropout and Sid Cannard and somebody—Jack ... somebody ...

Chapter
19

A burly, gray-bristled man in a pea coat and Greek fisherman's cap sat alone at one of six tables before a Valley of Auffes café, his crutches propped beside him, an unlit cigar in one hand, picking at the red-checkered oilcloth on the rickety sidewalk table. At the table next to him, three young toughs sat drinking red wine, bright scarves at their necks, a huge Japanese ghetto blaster on their table filling the air with American rock 'n' roll. Beyond them, two men in sunglasses, plaid jackets, and thin ties sat quietly, eating plates of cold fish.

From the café's dingy interior, an aproned man smelling of

bouillabaisse and aioli brought the solitary seafarer with the weathered face and overlong crew cut two cups of oil-slicked French roast and a basket of crusty bread, offered a match, received his gratuity, and disappeared behind the fly-specked brown windows of his establishment.

Jack Fowler wished momentarily, as a briny gust came in off the sea, that the meet could have taken place before Marseille's Monument aux Morts d'Orient, as he had first proposed, or anywhere along the relatively clean five kilometers of the Corniche Prest. J. F. Kennedy—anywhere but here, beyond the bridge in this sinister little fishing village. He hadn't been out in the field under cover in years. It was probably the best medicine for what ailed him. Since being wounded, he'd been coddled to distraction. Save for the urgency of this encounter, he might have let the endless stream of specialists and aides convince him that at his age, in his condition, he had to take things easy. The last forty-eight hours had convinced him that "easy" was poison. He felt better than he had since some damn kids had reminded him the hard way that it was dangerous to fall into routine, fatal to feel comfortable.

He watched the trio come ambling up the quayside street full of lorries and fish scales and crates and dock workers, not certain until one waved that the three clean-shaven young men in sweaters and tennis shoes with knapsacks over their shoulders were headed his way. Then he lit his cigar and the "fishing boat" that had brought him here hooted twice: the captain on the motor sailer, responding to Fowler's signal. If he stubbed out his cigar in the ashtray, help would pour from the ship's hold; if he ground it underfoot, the young toughs with the motorbikes would tail and engage the three approaching; if, as was his custom, he let his cigar go cold and put the remainder in his silver case, they could walk away with no interference from Jack's soldiers. He really hoped that was going to be what happened.

When the three reached the half-dozen sidewalk tables, Darling and Mino Volante took an empty one. Cordell Hunt alone came up, shook his hand, slipped into the wire chair opposite him, and stirred the second coffee Fowler had ordered with the lemon peel from the cup's thick, cracked saucer before lighting a cigarette. "How're tricks?"

No "sir," no "Jack," just a steady stare and nervy quietude. "Pretty good, son, considering I'm just getting used to being a gimp." He indicated his crutches. "What have you got that's so sensitive we couldn't handle it by phone?"

"Problems. Doubts—at least Flak has. A missing case officer. Something to trade for Martinova. A proposition. You said you wished I'd come to you. Here I am." He sat back. Shaved, he resembled Percy more—Percy when Fowler had first met him, on the Berlin tunnel project, guy-wire tight and full of imperatives. "You *can* negotiate with me about her...?" Hunt prodded.

"Whoa, there, Cory. Let's clear the air first. One thing at a time. Start with the problems."

"I've got the Soviets' transcripts of my debriefing. They're in Russian. My Cyrillic isn't great, but it looks pretty exhaustive to me. I want you to pass copies to the various services—Innotech/Triage customers, whoever else thinks they've got bones to pick with me. I want them to leave me alone, and when they've got this, they will. You were supposed to bring that Foreign Intelligence guy. Did you?"

"How did you manage to get your hands on that?" Fowler sat forward, elbows on the table, forgetful of posturing or strategy.

"You're not answering my questions. But I'll tell you. Dania Morales. She got the original copy from Grechko—you know who he was—and made photocopies. That's what I've got."

"Nice of her."

"She likes me. She wanted me to know that it wasn't as bad as I thought. It isn't. It's worse for Chebrikov, but there's nothing I can do about—Don't look at me like that."

"Don't you know that Nikolai Chebrikov blew his head off with an AK? Kabul, I think it was, when he was reposted...." Fowler saw Hunt blanch, drag on his cigarette, looking at its coal. Then Hunt pushed back his chair and got up. "Cory, boy, I can't go hobbling after you—" The asset had reached his companions' table. He leaned on it, stiff-armed. Fowler couldn't tell whether he was talking to them or not. If he was, his words were drowned out by the tape deck, meant to protect Fowler from any surreptitious recording of what transpired.

Jack's cigar had gone out. Carefully, he relit it, holding it high, thinking fast. If Hunt walked, he was going to let him. Surprised at himself, he wondered how guilty he actually felt about Percy's death. He couldn't allow Cory to manipulate him. But what he was seeing now he'd seen before in other agents: The relationship between interrogator and respondent, developed over as long a time as young Chebrikov had worked with Cordell Hunt, was a close and complex one. Hunt's hunched shoulders and the frown on Darling's face as the slick young asset reached out to pluck at Cory's sleeve told Fowler that Hunt was deeply shaken, probably assuming responsibility for Chebrikov's death. As Fowler had assumed it for Percy's death, when he had had to refuse, as per American policy in those days, to negotiate with Percy's terrorist kidnappers, and refuse furthermore to send an antiterrorist squad led by his son to try to recover him. Instead, he had sent young Cory to Shackley in Laos, as far as he could from Aden, where Percy Hunt was being held, minus increasingly more appendages, which had come to his office piece by piece.... Belatedly, Fowler had sent another team leader, who was unsuccessful.

All these years he had watched over Cory, as Percy had once made him promise to do, as best he could without being overt or letting the promise cloud his operational judgment. Sending Hunt to Innotech/Triage to infiltrate Two Can Play had been a decision taken by the Joint Chiefs, an assignment offered Cory through a delicate and nearly invisible chain of intermediaries, one of whom finally made the "suggestion" to the asset. But ultimately, the whole muck-up was Fowler's. He wasn't shirking responsibility, but it saddened him to have lost Cordell Hunt, as far as Western intelligence services were concerned, because of it. That much was clear: Cory, as his father never could have done, had decided to strike out on his own.

He sat calmly, quietly, until Hunt turned around, then came slowly back. "Shit, Jack. How do you know he did that?"

Fowler winced theatrically. "You're not going to like my answer. Promise to sit still and hear me out."

Hunt met his eyes, nodded.

"Martinova, Anastacia. Then we checked it back through channels. I've sourced it exhaustively. You're right about those interviews having a negative effect, not only on the reputation of the deceased, Nikolai Chebrikov, but also on his patron, KGB Chairman Chebrikov. But I shouldn't be surprised that you've brought home the bacon—that's what we sent you in there for. If what you've got here supports best intelligence—that you debriefed young Chebrikov more thoroughly than he you—the old man'll resign KGB, and even his secretariat appointment may not be enough to insulate him from the resultant loss of face when we surface those transcripts, thanks to you."

"Don't thank me. I wouldn't have done it if anybody asked me. I just had a run of luck." Hunt's voice was guarded. His dark hair, grown longer since Fowler had last seen him, danced on his forehead in the wet sea wind. He rubbed his face. "But if you're so grateful for this, give me Martinova and I'll call us even."

"You don't want her."

"The hell I don't, Jack."

"You think you do. But, Cory, that girl's a Soviet infiltrator, a pure penetration who has spent as much time at Odessa as at the Sorbonne. NTS doesn't know her; the Afghans don't list her anywhere—not in their *Biographic Register,* as they would if she were the diplomat's granddaughter she told you she was, not even as an 'enemy of the people,' as they would if she were the revolutionary she claimed to be. And she's admitted all this to—"

"Jack, I don't give a shit about her politics. I don't even care if she lied to me. She wouldn't be where she is except for me, and if you won't release her as a favor, or trade her to me for some take I can guarantee you'll salivate over, then I'm going to come get her."

"Cory, we're going to trade her back to the Soviets. We can get Two Can Play people back for her, people who are hurting the way you were hurting. Do you want us to let them sit there, stewing in their own psychochemical disruptions, so that you can ease your conscience?"

"I—Jack, I've got to do this. Turn her over to me in Morocco. Let me talk to her; tell the Soviets that's where you'll release her. I won't screw up your trade. I'll go as baby-sitter—take Flak and Mino and we'll do the whole handover, get the assets they're trading, whatever you want. I promised her."

"Good God, boy, you don't give up, do you? Will you wait a minute while I think of some objection to that? No, I didn't think so. Why aren't you telling me I can't let the Soviets have her?"

"What good would it do? If what you say is true, they'll take good care of her—better than the Americans took of me."

Fowler puffed deeply on his cigar, grimaced, pulled a piece of tobacco from his lip. "You must have known about this. Before I told you, I mean. Did you know all along? According to her, you never even suspected. She gives you a clean bill of health."

"Shit, I thought you'd know better than this." Hunt lifted his cup to his lips, sipped, and took a pack of Camels from his khakis' hip pocket. Fumbling one from the pack, he added, when Jack did not respond, "You've got some hot talent—that one, anyway." He inclined his head, gesturing over his shoulder to where Darling sat with Volante. "If you let me do what I've suggested, I'll do something for you in return."

"What's that?"

"Stay where I am, work out of Morales' shop, send you all sorts of goodies."

"You can do that?"

"Easily."

Fowler licked his lips. "It's tempting."

"I mean it to be. I'll keep those two and we'll do you proud."

"What about Innotech/Triage?" Cautiously, Jack drew him out.

"They sent an assassination team after us; we don't owe them anything. I've got enough grievances to justify putting that shop out of commission permanently, and the ammunition to do it with."

"I don't doubt that you have. We don't want that, Cory. A while ago you mentioned your case officer. Perhaps I'd better explain to you what happened." He detailed what he knew of Sid Cannard's fiasco and subsequent resignation, Shy's strategy and Beth's resultant "shock-induced psychosis," which led to her attempt on Shy's life. When he had finished, he said, "Innotech/Triage is too valuable to lose, even if Shy doesn't recover sufficiently to become its permanent international director. Now that we understand each other, what's this about Flak's 'doubts'?"

"He needs to know that Innotech's turning on him doesn't mean anything as far as you're concerned. I could tell him what you've told me, but under the circumstances, it'd be better if he heard it from you. Regarding Morales, he'll want clarification of his orders. Something's bothering him—more than just Shy dropping the ball warrants. He's good enough that I don't know exactly what. You want to talk to him? You've been Shy's collaborator in this whole business...."

"Assuredly. If I'm going to have you and yours on my payroll—"

"Easy there, Jack. I said I'd send you information from time to time. That's the furthest I'm willing to commit. We're independents trading for advantage—that's all anybody, especially Darling, can know. Any disbursements have to look like we're extorting them from you. The money I want to collect is from Innotech/ Triage: We're down a fifty-thousand-plus-before-armor Mercedes; everybody's taken hits—Flak's is in his butt. We figure that the Falcon ought to be about right as compensation."

Fowler whistled.

"Can do?"

"Cory, I don't know."

"Find out." Hunt reached around; his hand disappeared into his knapsack. Fowler stiffened, then relaxed as the hand re-emerged clutching a nine-by-twelve manila envelope. "Here's a taste of the good stuff. Where's my Agency contact? I'm going to enjoy giving him his personally."

"Behind you. Blue plaid. Don't give them more than the Soviet transcript—please."

Hunt grinned at him. "Now, would I do that?"

Before he had framed a reply, Cordell Hunt was on his way to the table behind Fowler's, where his contact waited.

Jack noticed that his cigar had gone out. He reached into his breast pocket, fetched out his silver case, and placed the half-smoked cigar within. Then he put the case carefully away. Percy would have been so proud of that boy....

As Mino came back into the cabin of the Gates Learjet Longhorn 29, Flak fell silent. Mino, grinning, announced, "Just cleared Frog airspace, sir—no thanks to me," and stretched out in one of the small turbojet's eight swivel seats, opposite Hunt, who was looking out the rear window over the plane's swept wing.

"I told you this thing wouldn't fall out of the sky unless we let *you* fly it," teased Flak, across the aisle, his feet up on the facing seat to keep pressure off his wounded buttock. Mino had balked within sight of the Gates Lear this morning at Sardinia's Olbia Airport, insisting on vetting its pilots himself, explaining to Hunt that *he* wasn't entrusting "all of our asses to some guys I never met who might have passed their check ride below fifteen thousand feet and don't know squat about turbojets up where they play their tricks. Takes an ex–fighter pilot to fly a Lear good, at least the older ones. I heard the Longhorns are easier, but in the old days you had to be damn quick at figuring out what one was trying to tell you." Mino had stalked up the ramp, hands on hips, only to wave them aboard ten minutes later, saying that the pilot was an ex–Israeli Air Force squadron leader and the copilot had "cut his teeth in Mirages. I'm game if you guys are."

Hunt had been relieved; they had been on a roll, starting when Dania's people had met them at Aéroport Marseille-Marignane in the Kombi van five days ago. Things had been running like clockwork. Her villa on Sardinia's Costa Smeralda was a perfect place for rest and recuperation. Her medical and security personnel and provisions were first-rate. Even Liz's touch-and-go fight for life had turned out to his advantage: Everyone was so concerned with her that it pulled the team back together. Flak and Diehl were patting each other on the back once Liz had been off-loaded and secured in the Kombi, their earlier squabble forgotten as Diehl's part of the operation went smoothly into gear. It was almost too good to be true.

So when Mino had stood this morning, arms akimbo and freshly shaved chin set, in the Longhorn's fuselage, Hunt had been thinking, *This is it, this is where it's going to fuck up.* Diehl had wanted one of them to stay behind at the villa as an article of faith; Mino had been hard-pressed to leave Liz, conscious now and gaining strength; Hunt and Dania had prevailed: He needed his team intact. For four days Mino had stayed by the wounded girl's bedside; he'd even tied a red string on her bedstead to "ward off the evil eye." Evidently the string had done its work: Even this second sortie into Marseille had gone off without a hitch—and it had been doubly dangerous because Fowler was the best of the old OSS boys, capable of anything.

But every detail of the meet was in order: The ID's Dania had provided his team passed muster; contacts were waiting with a Porsche 928 and Citroën SM follow car; no one asked questions or failed to perform professionally. Hunt had chided himself for being too jumpy—this was Marseille, after all. The last leg, on foot, had been covered by local types; if anything had happened to him, Dania would have known promptly what, how, and probably where he would have been taken. Still, walking around town with knapsacks full of handguns, stun grenades, flash hoods, and walkie-talkies wasn't his idea of deep cover. Despite the pitfalls, nothing untoward had occurred.

Yet he was as spooked as Mino, who admitted to being a terrible passenger as he darted forward to the cockpit every few minutes, snapping at Flak, when he complained Mino was making him dizzy, that "*some*body better keep tabs on what's going on up there. Somethin' happens, there's not shit me *or* you's gonna be able to do about it, except shoot those hot rodders before we hit the ground."

Hunt said, "I'm as glad as you are, Mino, to be out of *French* airspace," as much to cover the sticky silence as to explain his obvious case of nerves. Flak, sensing it, had periodically offered him a joint, a line, coffee, or magazines as if he were some paramilitary flight attendant. Only minutes ago, when Mino had last headed forward, had Hunt broached the subject on his mind, asking Flak, for starters, if Fowler had satisfied his doubts. Flak had replied, "I guess so, sir. If you're happy, I can live with it."

"But...?" Hunt had prodded.

"*But*—I don't know what he said to you. Don't you think it was a little too easy? He didn't ask about the packet—at least he didn't ask *me*. And he's giving me carte blanche to 'aid and abet' you in whatever. That read right to you, Cory?"

Hunt had been about to take it from there when Mino returned. Now Flak pulled his sweater over his head, revealing the blue/gold/green Hawaiian shirt beneath. "Hey, Mino, Cory wants them to overfly the house on the way to Olbia. Can you get them to do that? If I ask them, they're going to start that 'pilot's prerogative' bullshit...."

Mino replied that he could get them to "strafe the Vatican for a couple of lines. Dania told 'em, 'Do whatever Cory says,' anyway. Come on up, I'll intro you. We've been finding out we've got lots of things in common: They've been rooked by that no-win Asteroids machine in the Guam airport—"

"Okay if I do, sir?" Flak was threading his waistband holster onto his belt.

"Go ahead, Flak. I'll be here when you get back."

Hunt thought that Flak, too, was a poor passenger. He didn't blame him: Nobody likes to have things taken out of his control. For his own part, he was trying to figure out why he felt so woozy; he was usually a good flier. He hadn't felt so fragile since leaving Moscow. It must be that he was moving around too much. They had moved him a lot in Russia—in cars, planes, vans, trains—always blindfolded, often at night. Or they hadn't moved him at all, but taken him on dislocating excursions and then back into the Lubyanka—same address, different cells. But wherever he was, Chebrikov was. Chebrikov had always been there, the one stable feature of his world for interminable months. Hearing of his death from Fowler had been like losing a younger brother: an adversary, a rival, often hated and silently cursed. He felt sad about it. When you blow your own head off, you've not only given up, you've given strength to your enemies—a propaganda victory. You're proof that they can take it all away: will to live, self-respect, hope and courage. You give the other side the ultimate victory: They can use your suicide to scare others into submission. Bastard. He'd left Hunt a legacy: one more casualty on his account.

He shelved it; he'd shed tears for Chebrikov in too many dreams; he could carry all the guilt the world had to offer—it was part of his job. "W—What, Mino?"

The pilot had come back: "I said, 'Is there some reason you're worried?' I mean, how come we're overflying the house? Is there something I ought to know, sir? That Fowler said, or anything?"

"No, Mino, there's no reason I'm worried. I'm just being my paranoid, overcautious self."

"So it's not gut instinct?" The pilot put one leg up on the facing seat, steadying himself.

"Might be. Sit down, will you? I want to ask you something."

Mino did, one leg folded under him, his face screwed up. "I'm sitting."

"Does it bother you that you're always the last one to know what's going on?"

"You mean like with Fowler?" He fumbled in his pants pocket, pulled out a stick of gum, unwrapped it. "That's not my area. I've got it worked out with Flak pretty good now. Guys argue." He popped the gum in his mouth. "Ninety percent of that intrigue stuff is just wheelspinning, anyway. The other ten percent, what's really going to come off—I'm getting where I can suss it out pretty good."

"Would you like to keep doing it—after Morocco, if that goes down and we come through the Martinova handover all right?"

"With you, yeah—you know I would. That's what Fowler's up to?"

Hunt was aware that Mino was more reserved than might have been expected. "Out of the Morales organization, it would be. Independents. That's what *I'm* up to."

Then Mino's eyes sparkled. "Stay with Dania—Liz and all? And you and Flak? Is this for real, Cory? I was sort of thinking about marrying her or something."

"Your decision, Mino. But married, you two are anybody's leverage on one another. I can't tell you what to do, but unless you're ready to fly cargo and make babies—"

"*Babies?* Aw, Christ!" Flak, coming aft, interrupted.

"Flak, Mino and I were just talking about staying on with Nirvana—"

But Flak was continuing, avoiding Hunt's eyes: "Mino, *uomo,* ain't you got *enough* troubles? You think that bitch is going to put away her 'Teflon-coated Enforcer' and put on an apron for *any*-body, you're dreamin'!"

"You shut up. I was talking to Cory, not you—"

"Proud poppas can't go out on these kinds of missions, fool. Cory, tell him...."

"All right, all right, you two. Flak, please let me explain it to him. Get me some coffee. And lay off that blow, both of you. Neither one of you can afford to get so far off center."

Flak, throwing Mino a disgusted glare, disappeared forward toward the galley. Hunt said to Mino, "We need you, Mino. Nobody wants to break up a good thing like this. For once, Flak's finding out he's depending on you for more than flying."

"Yeah, I know that. But if I'm going to be a full-fledged agent, it's my decision, not his. I'm doing it for me, not him. What I'm trying to say is, it's nice to be consulted. I'll lay off cocaine—it's more his thing than mine. But my personal life's my own—okay, sir? Can you just count on me to be there when you need me?"

"That's good enough for me, Mino."

Flak, coming back from the galley, a plastic coffee cup held elaborately high, was mimicking a commercial pilot's spiel: "...to your left, forty-one thousand feet below, you'll see the southern-most tip of Corsica—that's Bonifacio there, sir, and the Arcipelago della Maddalena coming up over there." Sniffing, he wiped away the white powder dusting his nostrils and held out Hunt's coffee. "Hey, sir?"

Hunt took the cup. Flak sank sideways into the seat across the aisle.

"Flak?"

"I'm sorry I jumped in. Mino, it's just that I want you aboard for the long haul. I don't dislike Liz, it's just sort of—she's got designs on you, it seems to me. Women have a way of breaking guys up. But you're smarter than that. And I've got foot-in-mouth syndrome today. Too much blow, like Cory says. I promise I'll be good—"

"'S okay, man," Mino said, chewing his gum. "Either of you find out when, how, and if Innotech's going to pay us?"

"I'm going to make sure I collect from them, but from now on, Mino, *I* pay you."

"That's nice to hear. I've got about fifty French francs—that's ten bucks—and my emergency American C-note. Don't like to break it—bad luck."

"When we get home," Hunt promised, and saw Flak's eyebrows raise at his choice of words. "Since we're all officially committed to this now, Flak, why don't you explain to me your objections to Dania's idea that we withhold the duals permanently—tell Shy or whoever replaces him that their own A Team fried 'em along with Dania's SEC."

"Well, sir—Dania's a nice lady. I'll even admit she's smart. But computers aren't her specialty. Since they had that dish and sufficient storage, you know I worked up a way to store all the encoded traffic we were capable of monitoring with that equipment. If we want to keep doing it, it'll be expensive, just in the number of disks, and then we'd want a bigger, more powerful satellite dish than that thing she's got on the bluff. We can make certain that *we've* got any new *en*coding programs for the French satellite: They have to send the new codes in the old codes. But the *de*coding portions—if they're hand-delivered or even sent by mail, we'll be out of luck.

"So, since I'm now actively engaged in subversion against a number of governments, including my own, the least I can do is make a perfect job of it. If my reputation's going to the dogs over this, even just as cover, then I've got to keep my moves up to spec—got to awe the fuck out of 'em. So I'm gonna give it all the candlepower I can." He tapped his temple. "That says we give Innotech back the originals and just keep our copies. Don't give out any other copies, either—no agency, not even CIA, could resist trying to use them as grounds for a takeover. For us to make anything out of this, Innotech has to be comfortable. Then we can sell bits and pieces of what we get—judiciously, of course—and get rich while Innotech pats us on the back for a job well done."

"I'll buy that," Hunt nodded. "And I'll argue it with Dania. We'll probably do it your way, but let *me* convince her. She's worried that they'll figure we did just what you're suggesting unless we swear up and down that the whole packet was destroyed." Hunt got up, thinking he'd visit the head, careful not to bump his calf, still bruised for inches around the hard scab, which felt, as he put weight on it, as if a bullet were embedded in his flesh. The jet angled downward; he steadied himself on the seatback and looked at Mino.

"Just the beginning of our descent, sir. Hurry back. They're going to light the seat-belt sign in—"—he looked at his watch—"—seven minutes or thereabouts."

Hunt did. When they approached Costa Smeralda, Mino went forward to make sure the pilots put them over the right house, promising Hunt that they wouldn't buzz the premises; "We don't want or need to scare them, Mino. It's just recon."

When they flew over the seaside villa, dipping to a thousand feet, the sun had set. Hunt peered through field glasses in the gloom. The cement and granite house, perched behind its swimming pool on the bluff, was quiet; there was no sign of life. He handed the glasses to Flak; just then, lights went on inside the house.

"What do you think, Cory?" Flak said, putting the glasses down. "They didn't put down the umbrella on the table by the pool...."

"Yeah, I know. And the cars aren't in the garage. The pool lights aren't on, either."

"You thinking what I'm thinking?" Flak asked. "We always took in the umbrella. They always do."

"They didn't today."

Mino, unfastening his safety belt, stood in the aisle. "Something's wrong, isn't it? I'm going to have them swing over again. Fuck SOP."

"No," Hunt said. "That's no good. We don't want to flush them yet. I was hoping nobody would be this stupid. Let's figure out what we have to work with."

"Work with?" Flak echoed. "Just us? We don't know what, if anything—"

"Ever read *The Prince*, Flak? 'Only those means of security are good, are certain, are lasting, that depend on yourself and your own vigor.' Just us, and maybe our pilot friends, if Mino can convince them."

"I might have known sooner or later you'd quote me Machiavelli. Cory, we've got copies of the duals right here—"

At the same time, Mino, flopping down into the seat he had just vacated, was saying, "Sure enough, they'll give it a go, sir. They're *Dania's* guys. The Israeli was tellin' me about his Saiyeret days—how they could never have pulled off Entebbe without Kenya lettin' them refuel at Nairobi." Then: "Machiavelli, don't he make perfume?"

"*Mino!*"

"Flak, man—Liz is in there. Trish. Dania. *Women*. We can't just leave 'em."

"Why the fuck not? We don't even know if any of our people are alive in there."

Hunt knew what was bothering Flak. "We're going in there. You're up to it; Mino's up to it. We'll do fine. We can't let anybody get those codes, you said so yourself." Flak looked away, out the window. Hunt had to let him come the rest of the way on his own. He was grateful when Mino spoke up.

"Don't worry about me, Flak. I can shoot better than ninety percent of *anybody's* army."

"Okay, you two, listen. *Somebody's* in there. Maybe it's some enemy of Dania's who just happened to pick the wrong moment, somebody who doesn't know us from Adam, but I don't think so. Mino, go ask your friends if they'll fly up there with us in Dania's Dauphin Two. We'll just need them to sweep for heat signatures—cars or guys in the woods—and maybe a diversionary action."

Dania's chopper, parked at Olbia, was an Aérospatiale twin-engine executive transport with single-pilot IFR capability; it was fast and maneuverable. He wished it had a couple of machine guns, inboard or door-mounted, but it didn't really matter. The Costa Smeralda villa was a fortress, built to the Aga Khan's standards and in the local tradition of solid granite-and-cement construction. To that, Dania had added bulletproof sliders and windows of the same military specs as F-16 windshields, able to withstand up to 50mm fire, and an electro/seismic intrusion-detection perimeter that wound through the brushwood among wild roses and asphodel, eucalyptus and cork, and along the sheer drop from the bluff to the sea. He had had the full tour; he didn't see how anyone could have rushed the house or surprised its inhabitants. They were too cautious, too well prepared. It had to have been a ruse of some sort, the substitution of hostiles for the butcher or the baker or any of the stream of medical types who had been constantly coming and going.

"Find out what they can lay their hands on in the way of smoke—how many flares—and what they're willing to do."

"Yes, *sir!*" Mino bolted upright just as the "fasten seat belts/no smoking" diagrammatic indicators lit.

"Flak, what have you got in your bag that'll help?"

"An oscilloscope—we can scan for transmissions by walkie-talkie or radio. Whatever kind of sweeps you want. I've been trying to scope whether we ought to just call them on the phone before we go in shooting. I mean, what if they just didn't bring in the umbrella and forgot to garage the cars?"

Hunt, digging in his pocket, came up with a set of house keys Dania had given him. He dangled them before Flak's eyes. "We're going to sneak up on them if we can. If whoever's in charge there is smart, our only chance is to walk up to the door, open it, yell to our people to hit the deck, and shoot everybody still standing about three seconds after that."

"You're going to walk in the *front door?*"

"I said *sneak* up. You'll be trying the back-door key. That is, assuming we're all ambulatory after we've cleared the perimeter—Hi, Mino. Are they game?"

"Yes, sir, they are. They say we have good surveillance capability in the Dauphin, just need Flak's frequency choices."

"Flak, want to go forward?"

"In a minute, Cory. How do we know we're shooting the right guys?"

"Anybody in there coercing our people or holding our wounded hostage are the 'right guys.' Every government in the free world shoots hostage-takers out of hand. You want to speculate about who's in there? I can't think of any 'wrong guys.' Shy's in the hospital, so this isn't his go. Maybe Hubble's feeling his oats, with Shy down and Sid having retired so abruptly. Or maybe it's Sid's swan song, maybe he's tired of sitting by his crazy daughter's bedside, but I—"

"*What?*" Flak interrupted, while Mino, strapping in as the plane banked for its final approach, said, "Shy's sick?"

"I thought Fowler talked to you." Hunt replied to Flak first.

"Not about that."

"The way I heard it, Shy brought Beth in for interrogation, she took a shot at him, Grover jumped her and got his ticket punched. Looks like no casualties, but they're both out of action."

"No casualties?" Mino looked pale. "*Grover's* dead. That's a damn shame." He stared out the window at Olbia below, parallel red and blue-white lines in the dark.

"That hound *bit* me, remember? They're going to be okay?"

"Do I look like God to you? I'm more concerned about us being okay. Anyway, that leaves Sid by proxy; maybe Fowler, but this isn't his style—if he wanted us, he had us in Marseille; the Soviets or their proxies; or friends of Flak's."

"*Sir?*" Flak objected.

"*Flak's?*" Mino echoed.

"DIA, CIA, ISA, whoever."

"That's not fair!" Flak flushed, then looked out along the wing as the flaps came up.

"Maybe not, but if you can't go in there and take down anything on two legs without qualms, I'll have you trade slots with Mino's Israeli friend. Any Israeli with gray hair is a stone pro; the others don't live that long."

"The fuck you will. This is *my* go, *my* op, *my* team...." Flak shook out a Marlboro and lit it, disregarding the "no smoking" indicator. "What happens after we yell to Nirvana to hit the deck?"

"I wish I'd had a chance to put you guys through a fun house in Zürich. When we get in there, remember what I taught you: fire and roll. Keep moving and *keep low* or we'll be picking each other off with our own cross fire. Take your head shots first; then

wo-shot bursts to the chest if you have to...." He relaxed, talking
hem through it. They'd be fine; he'd make sure of it. By the time
Flak had found a pencil and paper, he was certain they weren't
going to need diagrams, but he sketched the villa's floor plan
quickly and gave them three contingency plans before the Longhorn taxied to a stop.

By the time they had transferred to the Dauphin, he was pretty
pumped up. Dania's pilots' handled the single airport official on
duty; all he had to do was smile and be nonchalant and present
his papers to be stamped while the Israeli warmed up the chopper.
The way he was feeling, it wasn't easy. Mino soothed, in *sotto voce*
English, that Dania's pilots daytripped in and out of here all the
time. But what Hunt was worried about was a welcoming committee, and he couldn't look like he was expecting one.

He was angry and he was shaky, but his leg didn't feel sore and
his back didn't ache and he knew he was going to be able to pull
himself together. He had thought for a few minutes he might be
too tired to handle this, but the thought of Dania being held in
her own home on his account had done its work. He thought of
what she must be thinking—and what Diehl, if he was alive and
kicking, must be saying about the advisability of keeping Hunt
round when everywhere he went his ghosts came following after,
and the more he thought about it, the angrier he got. He remembered what she had said about waiting to see whether she was safe
in New York when their joint venture was completed. The ques-
ion was, he told himself, whether she could be safe *anywhere* as
long as she was associating with him.

He was no longer filled with moral reservations about her Soviet
connections or whether he could truly play the independent game.
she had done more for him than anyone outside his family had
ever done. The transcripts of his debriefing had not only salved
his conscience but given him a new lease on life, hope that he
could get out from under the various agencies wanting to sit on
him permanently, a way to think about the future and not cringe
or have to make it a joke.

The Dauphin 2 had lots of window area; it wasn't an assault
vehicle—it wasn't armored, it wasn't armed. Its fifteen-seat capacity had been cut in half by the addition of electronics gear just
ft of the cockpit. The biggest problem they found they had was

getting enough com headsets together that everyone could hear
and talk back to everyone else. He put them through one jamming
drill with their Combat Commanders and wished he had brought
the Mini Uzis, then thought that Dania et al. might have made
use of them, and, second, somebody like Mino was likely to empty
his whole full-auto clip of thirty-five rounds in seconds, doing
little damage to more than the villa's decor. It was better this way
Cool heads and placed shots were going to make or break this
mission.

He was just realizing how dry his mouth was and hoping that
Dania's visitors weren't Soviet friendlies when Flak reached out
and touched his arm. "Yeah?" He spoke into his headset's mike

Flak pointed to the screen in front of them: "I said, 'That's n
sheep, Cor.'" Flak tapped another, bigger greenish-white spot
"Here's a car."

Stretching his imagination, Hunt could just relate the display
to Dania's five-acre grounds below. "And there's the house?"

"Yes, sir."

He nodded. "There's a second 'sheep'?"

Mino chuckled. "Don't teach him no more, Flak, or we'll both
be out of jobs." Then, calling the pilot by name, he told them to
keep his altitude steady: "We don't want to flush 'em—at least
not yet." Mino turned in his swivel seat and Hunt noticed he had
taken off his sweater. Under it he was wearing a Triage T-shirt
The logo on his back, a radar display in scope green, sweeping
along the Berlin wall so that the West was defined but the East
in shadow, looked like a cluttered bull's-eye as he leaned forward
the front, Hunt knew, bore only the legend, in futuristic computer
script, *Helping Those Most Likely to Survive.*

He sank back in his own chair, watching obliquely to see if more
humans became visible on the villa's grounds, banishing the nag
ging doubt that he might be interrupting some meeting Dania
had wanted to have when he wasn't around. Ephemerally, he saw
her face overlaid on the radar screen, the impish smile, her mis
chievous habit of brushing her nose with a finger when she was
ready to reveal some outrageous piece of executed tradecraft. He
had come to terms with her habit of holding back information
until she felt the time was right for him to know. Her address in
Cannes had turned out to be only a dead drop. He couldn't blame

her; he did the same thing himself. But the guys in the bushes
told him his instinct was right. Having seen the hidden blips and
the secreted car's position, he felt vindicated. He would have gone
in on full auto, had he the capability, and not given it a second
thought.

They took fixes, dividing up the targets. Mino would disable
the car on the west flank and try to get up on the roof, from
where he could drop a stun grenade down the living-room chimney; Flak would be dropped on the north—seaward—side. With
the wind blowing northwesterly, the chopper, running without
lights, might be able to get in and out without being heard. So
far as Hunt could see, the wind was their only advantage—that
and what surprise they could muster.

For his part, he had to come up the driveway and through the
open gates to get to the sentry hiding among the little stand of
fig trees and parasol pines shielding the house from the road.
With luck, he wouldn't run into any of the local privileged in their
Maseratis, or their servants, who still led the occasional stunted
donkey and loved to gossip in rapid-fire Italian about their sons
and daughters, making "fortunes" in the luxury hotel complexes
here or in the industrialized South.

Flak remarked that he wished he had thought to bring the night-
sight goggles, but "I didn't think we'd be needing them, not in
Marseille, anyway."

Hunt didn't answer. He had checked the suppressor on his
Commander and made sure it was spotless and ready to go. He
snapped it into his shoulder holster—no hip scabbard made could
accommodate its low-signature device. He hadn't shot it since he'd
taken it away from Bowser in the Baur Au Lac; in the Zürich safe
house, he'd been working the bugs out of his accurized Detonics
and used that until he'd had to discard it.

They were dropping him first. He had half a mile to walk. The
pilots had their orders; everything was synchronized, from walkie-
talkie frequencies through diversionary action if called for. In
good order he was deposited in a clearing near the road. He
winked at Mino, waved to Flak, and spoke test phrases into the
walkie-talkie strung on his shoulder harness. Then he was alone,
walking up the hillside toward the road, flash hood and gas mask
on his belt, handgun cocked and locked.

He found himself thinking about Dania, recalling her airily waving away his gratitude over the transcripts—"It is nothing. I have friends everywhere"—and her implication that he, too, would have such friends soon enough. She had risked some of those friendships for him, handing the Soviets their own Two Can Play material and the Chebrikov transcript originals instead of the Innotech codes. But when he mentioned it, she explained that the cassettes of Grechko "clutching his chest and gurgling, falling over dead of a 'heart attack' in Trish's embrace, will make the First Directorate very happy. Think of its value as a training film, what a fine object lesson they will make of it. This poor, misled Slav will be immortal as a prime example of what happens to a good party member when he dares allow himself the temptation of a Western degenerate. And, too, such grisly Soviet snuff film are sought after for their entertainment value alone by higher ups. Don't worry, Cory—to have such friends, one must understand what makes them happy."

If the Soviets were to get their hands on those floppy disks, they would be even happier. In the single case of the French battle station/spy satellite, the possibilities were sobering. The French felt they had to have something since the Soviets had tested hunter killers in orbit. The extant A-sat treaty covered only "weapons of mass destruction in space." Lasers had limited value as offensive weapons. Mirrors or highly polished surfaces could deflect them; only ten percent of short-wave and less of long-wavelength energy actually reached the target. The best way to destroy something with a laser, as far as Hunt knew, was still to drop one on the target—the energy requirements for use made them incredibly heavy.

Nevertheless, lasers were being developed as a legal alternative. Every free-world country felt it necessary to come up with some defense against the Soviet's exploding hunter/killers. The West was much more dependent on satellites than was the Soviet Union—for communications, weather, and military applications. Anyone holding the encoding matrix could simply reprogram the satellite in question to accept only his own instructions. Properly done, it was tantamount to acquiring total control of the satellite. If Dania *was* hosting ComBloc representatives who were there to take that intelligence, either by force or by invitation, he would move heaven and earth to stop the transfer.

Reaching the road, he headed toward the villa, wondering if he could ever stop feeling that the Soviets were his mortal enemies. Even in the worst of his Lubyanka time, when he had wanted to say yes to Chebrikov, defect, and save himself unending agony, under truth drugs his partisan faith was unshaken: West was right and East was wrong and there was nothing he or they could do to change the way he felt. He hoped to hell she hadn't decided to give it to them. The thought of what he would do then scared him more than any other.

A car came up behind him; he heard it before he saw its lights; he stiffened and reached for his Commander, his fingers in a shooting grip before the car drove on by. When its taillights had disappeared around the curve ahead, he found that his heart was pounding and his breathing short. Wonderful. It had been all he could do not to dive for cover in the brush. If it had slowed, he would have, and shot first. He knew all the variations—a window rolled down, a muzzle in a gunport, the car itself used as weapon to sideswipe or flatten you on the pavement. He trudged onward steadily, thinking pleasanter thoughts. The Falcon, if he succeeded in acquiring it, would not only please Dania but allow him to buy into her operation at a respectable level: The Falcon 50 listed for nine million-plus in American dollars and was built just before Dassault had been nationalized.

He switched on his com set and checked the watch the pilot had loaned him: They had another seven minutes of radio silence, after which they were going to do a lot of talking on Flak's favorite shielded side band. He worked on lowering his pulse rate and felt it come down. This was going to be easier than Maryland—almost anything would be. He was controlling it; it conformed to his maxim that when there was going to be trouble anyway, you might as well choose when and how it starts. This go would be head and shoulders over cleaning up Diehl's mess. It was going to be *his* mess.

He checked the flash hood's radio connection; the hood-and-gas-mask combination served a twofold purpose: He would be safe from the concussive effects of Mino's grenades and anonymous. Somebody breaking down your door in hood and mask also had the advantage of looking very scary—the combo had good shock value, as well as providing stabilizers for the small headset/com mike beneath. He patched the cord into his walkie-

talkie, tested it once, got a laconic acknowledgment from the Israeli pilot that he was being heard, and was told that "Two"—
Flak—was "in place."

Once Mino was on the ground, Hunt knew he was going to
have to keep talking to them; Flak had gone to too much trouble
to convince him that it would be safe to do so: "SAS Twenty-two
guys use this system. I heard that it was you in the London Iranian
Embassy thing—the one maverick with the forty-five among all
those Hi-Powers?" Hunt had asked who had told him that, and
Flak had answered "Trish." He had neither confirmed nor denied
it, only agreed that he would give the system a try.

He came up to the final curve and rounded it. The house looked
unremarkable from this distance, just lights haloing the trees, a
paler dark in the sky. The gates were open. He had to flatten
himself against the granite posts to get through while remaining
in the surveillance's blind spot. By the front door of the house,
there was another, similar error in camera placement: The unit
had been set into a space provided for it above the lintel, but the
stone niche itself was not properly squared off, so that to the left
of the front door an area three feet deep and five feet long wasn't
monitorable. All he had to do was get that far.

He sidled around the post, feeling the granite, scratchy, through
his shirt. He looked around to get a good fix and set off toward
his target. He didn't want to put on all that headgear until the
last possible moment; once his ears were in the phones and the
flash hood on his head, he wouldn't be able to hear the night
sounds around him. All his silent-kill training depended on becoming a part of nature; he didn't want to separate himself from
it until he absolutely had to—if not for Flak and Mino, he would
have waited until he had made it to the doorway. He checked his
watch again: He had three minutes left.

There was a lot of landscaping to deal with—Japanese-style
rock gardens of raked gravel and mosses and all sorts of damn
bushes of one kind or another. It was real pretty, but tonight he
wished it weren't there. He worked on feeling as if it were all
effortless; he picked out the darker mass of the fig and pine grove
from the less-solid black of night; stars were beginning to twin-
kle—he was lucky the moon was in its dark phase.

His sneakers were doing him good service and he heard the
sentry before he saw him: a sneeze in the night. He turned off

his walkie-talkie, hoping his team would forgive him, and zeroed in on the sound. The man was sitting on a rock eating something— a gust of wind brought him the smell of garlic and herbs. He could hear paper crackle, and the sentry's breathing, and then the staticky snap of his target's walkie-talkie. He crouched where he was and let the man check in: "All clear, Fred." Then: "Not a damn squirrel, nothin' but bugs. Yeah, a car about five minutes ago— didn't even slow down. Can't somebody come out and relieve me? I'm gettin' bit to death."

The querulous young voice, speaking American English, gave Hunt pause. The sentry, signing off now, was just a kid. Even in Afghanistan, it happened often that the enemy turned out to be alcoholic, semiliterate eighteen-year-old conscripts. There you roasted them in their tanks because there were so many and you were fighting those tanks from camel- or horseback, or on foot, jamming ancient Enfield rifle butts down their turrets or smearing their periscopes with your own feces because there just isn't any mud in Kandahar during winter, when the Soviets traditionally mount their fiercest offensives.

But this kid was a threat only if Hunt didn't manage to put him down before he could run toward the perimeter fence and trip the seismics, or grab his walkie-talkie and call for help. He was less than ten feet from him now. His "weapon" made—stiffened fingers out straight—he sprang forward and struck the kid's right mastoid process, above and behind the ear, while pulling him down and backward with a left-handed choke hold, using the momentum of his swoop to drag the unconscious body back toward the stand of pine and fig. When he stopped, he patted him down for weapons and ID; pocketed a snubby, wallet, and passport; and got out a roll of two-inch surgical adhesive he had found in the Longhorn's first-aid kit. Using the knife he had secured under his tennis sock with the elastic Leech, he cut strips, gagging and binding the prisoner. He pulled the kid's pants down to his knees for good measure, backtracked and found the boy's com unit, clipped it to his belt.

Then he switched his walkie-talkie on, checked his watch, and called in: "I'm headed toward the house. One down, no sweat."

"Where *were* you?" Flak's voice demanded, angry and relieved. "You okay?"

"Fine, Two. Three?"

"Yes, sir." Mino's voice came to him indistinctly.

"Talk into your unit," Flak snapped.

"Can't. Almost got this distributor cap out."

As Hunt moved back the way he had come, careful to stick to the gravel and mosses, mindful of the seismic sensors along the walk and the perimeter fence, disguised as clods of earth and buried in the ground, he heard a sharp intake of breath, a grunt, then Flak's voice, "You want to die, or you want to be reasonable?" coming faintly over the com line. He slipped the headset, tight as a clamp, the hood and then the mask over his head, patching the cord into his shoulder-strung com unit. When his jack made contact, he heard "...motherfucker, sleep tight."

He asked Flak if he was all right, received a curt "Affirmative" and Mino's estimate of "time-to-roof."

"Two," he asked Flak, "do you know anybody named Fred?" The kid he had taken down was a native American-speaker; the documentation in his pocket, the heft of the snubby, and the size of the wallet felt American. He didn't have a flashlight, but he had a suspicion.

"No... shit!"

"Flak! You all right? Flak!" Mino demanded, forgetting to use Flak's number.

"Yeah, yeah, just stubbed my damn toe. Hope I didn't trip any alarms. Worse than the goddamed fake-bamboo seismics we used to drop along the Ho Chi Minh trail."

"Hey, sir? We're one minute to smoke," Mino's voice whispered, "and diversionary chopper action and I'm in sight of the house, here... I think maybe I know who Fred is."

"Wait where you are until the fireworks start. We want the best odds we can get for this. If they all watch the chopper play mayday, you can hop up there unnoticed.... You going to tell me, or am I supposed to guess?"

"No, sir. Helms, Frederick. Here's the chopper, sir, right on time. Commencing climbing."

Flak chimed in that he was in position and that the key fit the back-door lock just fine.

"Don't try it until Three gives the word." Mino's flash-bang grenades were specially made to temporarily stun and blind without lasting damage; the concussion grenades' casings flung no shrapnel, disintegrating harmlessly. About the size and shape of a can of shaving cream, they had been developed to facilitate actions where minimum fire was indicated to protect hostages from injury. Mino had three. If the damper was closed, he'd need all of them. When he dropped the first one into the chimney, Hunt and Flak had to be ready. By then, the chopper's theatrical antics hopefully would have drawn everyone to the living room, where they could watch the Israeli pretend to ditch his Dauphin in the sea through the sliders on each side of the fireplace. It wasn't foolproof—the hostiles could miss the show entirely, or be so enthralled they had their noses to the bulletproof glass, in which case only the "bang" and not the "flash" would have full effect— but Hunt hadn't had much time or choice of strategies. You worked with what you had on hand.

He was walking as nonchalantly as he could across what he remembered as the "safe" part of Dania's lawn when Mino's whisper, excited and clipped, came through his phones: "Oh, ain't that *beautiful*! There they go, guys. Just like Fourth of July. Man, you'd think they're really crashing."

"You cool, Three? *Ready?*" Flak demanded.

"Yeah, yeah, don't get snippy."

"Then *say* so. You think this is some fucking drill?"

"Hey, sir? Anytime you tell me." Mino spoke to Hunt, ignoring Flak's rebuke.

He had his own key in hand by then, facing the choice of hopping over the bushes to avoid the seismic motion detectors that might be there or taking the chance that the wide-angle door cameras would pick him up. This was no time for second thoughts. He jumped, his foot slipped, and he slid on a rocky patch; he cursed and hugged the wall. "Whenever you want, Three. It's all yours."

Somebody smart might be waiting behind the front door with Hunt's own Uzi. At least they couldn't shoot through it; it was centered with armor steel. He snapped loose his Commander, hoping Flak's man had had a chance to check in before being put out of action, and then there was no more time to think. Key in left hand, pistol in right, he hit the doorstep on both feet as Mino called out: "Go!"

He never remembered putting the key in the lock, only his relief that no one had thrown the dead bolts.

He got in there just as the first flash-bang rocked the room and turned everything white, even through his treated lenses, and tried to pick out possible targets: Anyone faced away from the blast he might have to shoot.

There were four in the living room: Diehl, trussed like a turkey in the corner; Trish, stripped to the waist on the couch; two big guys in sport coats by the windows, guns in hand but blinking and groping. He saw all three Uzis and a pile of side arms on the coffee table even as he was somersaulting to his feet and realizing Dania wasn't in the room and Flak came bursting in from the kitchen, doing as he'd been taught—keeping low, rolling across the floor in a good imitation of a commando, his auto already cycling. One of the standing men went down, clutching his ear.

Hunt yelled into his mike, "You don't have to shoot them if they can't see you, asshole!"

"But you said—How can I tell who can see me?"

Hunt was already headed toward Dania's bedroom, an awful sense of foreboding coming over him. "Mino, get your ass in here. Cover Flak—he's got prisoners to render harmless. On the double."

He was running down the hall by then. When he burst through the door into Dania's bedroom, the slider to the pool was open and the curtains blowing inward. "Shit."

"Sir?" Mino's voice came to him.

"See anybody out there?"

"Ah...no. Yeah, yeah. Big guy, with one of the ladies—Dania maybe. Want me to take a shot? Throw another stun grenade? He's headed toward the dish, sir. Sir?"

He was through the sliders, headed out into the night. "Two, get those damn pool lights on, I can't see shit!" The dark was impenetrable to his light-contracted pupils. He ran on anyway, counting on his instincts to avoid the pool and leap the planters on the low cement wall.

He tore off the mask with his left hand, discarding it, not liking the labored sound of his own breathing in the confinement of the flash hood. As the lights came on, he heard a report ahead of him, saw a flowerpot to his left explode, ripped off the flash hood, the headphones.

He could see them, Dania in front of the big man, his arm across her throat as he dragged her backward. The floodlit poolside was behind him, but the dish caught the light and he could see clearly enough, as he ran toward them, that the man was making for the bluff. What the hell good was that? Unless there was a boat...Maybe there was a boat down below. Maybe the Scarab was back from the shop; maybe they'd brought their own damn boat. The Maddalenas were only a good speedboat's ride away; Corsica was an hour at best with any kind of horsepower.

Or maybe it was do or die.

He slowed to a walk. He didn't want to force the issue.

The big man slowed, too, silhouetted in front of the satellite dish. Dania wasn't struggling. She seemed calm enough. If she would just stay still, he could pull this one out yet.

He called out: "Helms, is that you?"

"Dropout? What the hell is this, Halloween? Be a good boy and throw that piece down. I've got what I want. Go crawl in one of your holes somewhere. I'll be in touch."

Hunt kept walking, Commander at his hip, until he saw Dania's face: Helms was holding a little auto to her temple.

"Which is that? The take or my friend?"

He had to know if Helms had the disks.

Dania's eyes met his. "Cory," she called. "Don't do this. I understand. You must, too—" Then he remembered Flak's copies and he stopped stock-still, wanting to get Helms to take a shot at him. The distance was about fifteen yards—not point-blank, but perfect pistol range.

Helms started to edge sideways, pulling Dania with him. The muffled choking sound she made decided him. Moving with them, he brought his Commander up, his other hand along with it, as if in surrender. When his hands reached eye level, he told himself he'd done this countless times, in practice and in real life.

Then, as quickly and smoothly as possible, he brought his gun into position, leveled his sights, and took a headshot, going for the point between Helms's brows; and as his muzzle came back down, he took another, at the gun hand holding the little auto to Dania's temple.

Helms was already reeling back from the first round, so close to Dania's head it parted her hair. She threw herself left and down, lunging forward as the second shot spat from his silenced Commander.

Hunt was running, not sure what all that blood on her face meant, watching Helms's body as it careened into the dish and fell there, spread-eagled.

By the time he reached her, she had gained her knees. He pulled her to her feet, brushing her hair back, wiping the blood away. When she grabbed him and clung to him, he knew she was all right, that no wound was hidden by her hair. She couldn't talk; choke holds can do that. He couldn't think of much to say himself. He just stood holding her, feeling her heart beat and hearing her breathe.

After a time, he said, "We're too old for this shit. I don't know about you, but I'm tired of it. Let's go inside."

Hoarsely, she replied, "Not yet." She pulled away from him. He let her. He didn't understand why she had stiffened in his arms. She went to the dish and took a packet from Helms's corpse. "Here. This is what you want." She held it out to him.

"I—You're wrong. It was you—*is* you I want."

By then Flak was calling him, wanting to know what they were going to do about the casualties and prisoners, and he heard Diehl's "Madonna, are you well?" punctuated by heavy, running footsteps.

He went to her, brushing the packet so that it fell from her hand. "I don't care what you think, or what Diehl told you, or what Helms told you. I didn't know about this." He spread his hands. Behind her, over the bluff's edge, he could see her black Scarab bobbing at the end of the dock.

She looked at him steadily. Her shirt was torn and her mouth was bruised and swollen. Then she sighed tremulously. "Fool that I am, I believe you. Come—we must call my friends, the carabinieri. And convince Diehl you are not his . . . enemy—not the traitor he wishes you were, so that we needn't admit we have grown too comfortable, too sure of ourselves—that we, too, can make mistakes." She was looking beyond him as she spoke. He could feel Diehl's bulk behind him, hear the huge man's harsh breathing.

He put an arm around Dania's waist and turned slowly to face Diehl, his Commander's silencer pointed groundward, the pistol loose in his hand.

"Cory Hunt, you and I must reach an understanding."

"Whatever engages your safety."

"Next time, you must let *me* rescue *you*." And he began, uproariously, to laugh.

Hunt, looking behind Diehl to Flak, leaning against the house with an Uzi on his hip, trained on Diehl's back, blew out a deep breath. Snapping his Commander into its holster, he reached out to shake Diehl's hand. "Next time, Diehl, I'll hold you to it.

"Flak, what's the body count in there?" he called.

The asset pushed himself off the wall and joined them. "Just the one wounded. He'll live. The target I put to sleep in the bushes ought to be waking up about now, but he'll keep." He squinted at Helms's corpse, askew in the radar dish. "Don't have to check *him* out. Did I hear something about friendly cops? The suit with the shot ear told me Helms is still officially on vacation and this was all for brownie points. I think you might want to talk to him, sir. The name Cannard came up in his conversation."

"A little later, Flak. He'll keep, too."

Dania frowned, rubbing her swollen lip. "And where is Mino? I must thank him, too, for not destroying my house." She smiled at Flak. "Don't worry, my friend. These are terrorists. They'll be a conundrum, as terrorists often are, to the local authorities, who will receive them without their papers. They shall sit long in jail before their identities can be established. Then..."—she shrugged—"it's a matter for their embassy, which must make profuse apologies. From your expression, you don't believe me. Diehl, explain to our friend Flak how many other friends we have, and how strongly *all* our friends feel that terrorism cannot be tolerated on this island."

Diehl, still chuckling, put a beefy arm on Flak's shoulders.

Dania called after: "Flak? You haven't told us—where is Mino?"

"With Liz. Where else?" Flak called back.

"Where else indeed," Dania said softly, sliding out of Hunt's embrace to take him by the hand. "And us? Can he say that about us?"

"I hope so. I have a lot to tell you, and I'm dead tired."

"Hush. Don't say such a thing. Come, let me see to you."

He was glad to do so. In the morning he was going to tell her about Martinova; tonight, he wanted nothing to worry her.

Chapter
20

KING Hassan II's representative in Rabat had been so effusively apologetic over the "mix-up" that allowed Cordell Hunt to bring flowers to his own grave in Marrakech that he invited Hunt and his party to stay at Bahia Palace, where only relatives of the king and VIP's ever stayed. The war with Algeria was hotting up again, the Polisario guerrillas roused by new Soviet arms shipments into fervid activity. Hunt declined to stroll the "Brilliant Palace" gardens, Moorish and smelling of jasmine, green all year long with water from an artificial lake. He was content to have his Moroccan passport back; he didn't want to get so involved here that it would be impolitic to leave.

The little cemetery was Catholic, walled with ocher stone, his headstone modest, the letters of his name incised in red granite. He and his companion from British Special Intelligence met "Jerry" there. It had been easier to find Ali Baba's former case officer than the elusive agent from Long Island: Hunt still had friends in SIS, but to contact the pseudonymous American he'd had to look under "Foreign Officers in Reserve" in State's *Biographic Register* and then phone all those listed in Marrakech until he heard the voice he remembered, sardonic and rife with glottal stops. He was mildly surprised that the American showed at all; Hunt was getting no cooperation from the Marrakech station. Whether this was to protect the agent's identity or just make Hunt's life difficult, he couldn't say. But he knew *they* knew that the confrontation would be sticky at best, so he really didn't blame the local station chief for stonewalling him.

Hunt threw the jasmine he had been carrying for appearance's sake onto the grave before him while the English gentleman beside him tapped his walking stick against his chukka boot and Jerry, on the far side of Hunt's headstone, hooked his thumbs in his web belt and widened his bandy-legged stance, inscrutable behind mirror shades.

Cory introduced them and then couldn't think of anything to say. The letters of his name wriggled in the heat like some well-trained snakes. He heard the SIS man clear his throat, then grope for words: "I say, old man, this is disconcerting, despite everything.... Blast, Hunt, I've trotted along without asking a single question, as you asked of me, but really... what *is* the purpose of all this?"

"You want to tell him?" Hunt spoke to Jerry, not looking up.

"Tell him what? Man, you'd better have—"

"Tell him about shotguns and covers and takedowns and planting my ID on Ali's—"

"What's this?" the Briton demanded, then let out a long, windy sigh: "Bloody hell. We *have* got something to be on about, then, don't we. The man you call 'Ali' has been—"

"Look, Hunt, what are you getting out of this?" Jerry demanded. "What's the point, cocksucker?"

"The point is this guy was a friend of mine and a good Muslim, despite his Oxford accent, and it's a shame to bury him against the tenets of his faith. Get him the hell out of here into a good unmarked grave the way he deserves—" He broke off. It wasn't as satisfying as he'd thought it was going to be, though the SIS man had summoned all his righteous indignation and Jerry was beginning to squirm. Hunt left them together, phrases like "international incident" and "unfortunate necessity" and "widow's compensation" following him on the hot, fetid breeze. He couldn't stay there, looking at that gravestone, no matter how bad he felt about Ali. The place gave him the creeps.

So did everything about his return to Marrakech. Rendezvous of the Dead seemed to apply not only to the Djemaa El Fna, the great square where "Ali Baba" had worked at his cover trade of black-market currency dealer, but to the whole town.

The day before vernal equinox, it was hot as hell, and that made things worse. Mino had been disappointed that Hunt had turned down the invitation to enjoy Bahia's turn-of-the-century splendor. But for Hunt, being able to choose the Ourika, twenty-eight miles southeast of Marrakech in the Atlas foothills, was excess enough. From his bedroom, with its view of the snowcapped mountain range and the Ourika Valley road below the ledge on which the hotel complex was built, he had made his phone calls and completed his arrangements. It remained only to take delivery of Martinova and execute the handover.

He felt like a degenerate Westerner, lounging around the terrace or watching Trish swim in the pool or dance with Mino (Flak didn't dance) in the antiquated disco on Saturday night. This wasn't Morocco—it was International Tourism, a world apart. He asked himself what he had wanted, and the answer was that he had wanted exactly this. He had to keep at bay the feeling that the last six weeks had been a dream; that he still lived down in the casbah with Martinova with no hope of ever putting his life back together; that someone was going to come along and tap him on the shoulder and turn him back into a fugitive: no validated papers, no credit cards or money, no Flak, Trish, or Mino, no Falcon waiting at the airport. He would be trapped here forever, trying to explain to a senile old king with culture shock that even American weapons and Soviet money weren't going to make the Polisarios go away.

To shake the feeling of unreality, he took his team into town and into the square, guiding them through the *suqs*, finding the finest Chichaoua rugs for Trish, the best silver daggers for Mino, the softest camel's-hair blankets for Flak, making sure they bartered hard enough, even taking them to another tourist trap, La Zagora on Route de Casablanca, for a true Moroccan dinner in the Palm Grove. It was a hacienda-type complex that hosted folklore shows—from Berbers on horseback to belly dancers. They ate under a great tent while the horsemen in their flowing robes brandished sabers and did their stunts and the desert drums played.

Trish, beside him, her hip-length black hair unbound over a colorful robe from the *suq*, could have been a local girl. Her face was tanned and bare, though, so that she got many burning looks from the Berbers, who well knew that any Moroccan girl over twelve who walked around barefaced was a whore. This one, by the costliness of her clothing, the perfection of her teeth, and the three rich Westerners fawning over her, must be an excellent one.

He ordered what he knew would please them: lemon chicken, pigeon pie, *tagine* (lamb with olives and artichokes in savory sauce) almond milk, and pastries, assuring them they must eat with their fingers, properly, right hand only, and drink endless cups of mint tea at every stage of the meal. When the others were ready to join him in his favorite vice, strong Moroccan coffee, the Soviet envoy appeared, squat and sanguine, a Mongol sweating in his tropical worsted. Beyond him, in the tent's center, the belly dancers were done and the musicians packing up. Magicians and jugglers had the stage, while palm readers and flame eaters and money trainers circulated among the diners.

He didn't invite the Mongol to sit; he didn't rise. The man stared openly at Trish, and Hunt let him. That was what they were doing here, after all. He touched her arm and whispered in her ear and she stopped eating and folded her hands in her lap, her eyes downcast. They fixed a time and determined coordinates. Both were content with the general site—the Atlas foothills—that Fowler and his opposite number in KGB had determined; but for security, the specifics had been left up to the operatives.

Finished, Hunt summoned a waiter and asked for the check, ignoring the perspiring Mongol. When he looked around, the agent was gone, seemingly. Still, he got his people out of there, and during the twenty-three-mile drive in their rented Land Rover through the foothills to the Ourika Valley, he spent his time staring into the rearview mirror, expecting anything, his knuckles white on the wheel and his imagination setting ambushes.

When they passed the desk, he checked his messages. The little white slip of paper in his box gave a room number only. He breathed a sigh of relief and turned to see Trish watching him, her dark eyes amused. "Another unwinnable war?" She stepped closer. "How did I do back there?"

"Maybe he bought it. Your guess is as good as mine. Don't get your hopes up. There's nothing definite, as yet. Go on, make Flak know I'm not trying to hit on you."

No one but he and Trish knew what Hunt had up his sleeve. She was along as the obligatory matron, a female officer who could see to Martinova's health, strip her if search was necessary. Flak was glad to have her; Mino had asked no questions. The first test was putting her in front of the Soviet agent. As far as he could tell, she had passed it with flying colors; tanned, in her embroidered robe with her hair down, she looked the part. It had first occurred to him when he had tried, one last time, to get a picture of Nasta in Paris. Failing, still hoping there was some way around it, he had gotten Trish to go with him to the passport photographer. Any black-haired girl, rail-thin and sultry, would have done for his purposes by then. He had her part her hair in the middle and proceeded from there to use the thirty thousand U.S. he had been carrying around in his belt to buy Martinova a Dominican passport. (The official who usually demanded an additional twenty-thousand-dollar fee waived it as recompense for a favor Hunt had once done him.) He was going to give Martinova a choice.

Nasta. He wished he knew what shape she was in, what was true and what was disinformation, what he was going to find when he knocked on door 109.

Like the Falcon's disposition, nothing was settled yet. He had possession of the plane, as he would soon have possession of Anastacia Martinova, alleged Soviet spy. He could develop scenarios and plan for contingencies. More than that he couldn't do.

In Paris he had drawn money from four banks—his money, that his attorney had deposited for him over the years, paid to him through his old friend's French office so that no taxes could be levied by either the French or American governments as long as his American tax-exemption form's validity went unchallenged and he claimed he was going to spend that money in France. With it, he had paid Flak and Mino each a hundred thousand French francs—not what Innotech had agreed to pay them, but what he felt they had earned. He wrote it up as hazard pay and bonuses and submitted a bill to Shy's office. He hadn't heard from Hubble about it yet, or about his own money. But they had plenty to work with, since Jack Fowler was picking up the tab for this handover—from fuel to hotel and per diem—as an ISA gambit.

He had also seen the NTS spokesperson in Marseille. How it was all going to fit together was anybody's guess.

When he was sure that Mino, Flak, and Trish had had plenty of time to settle in, and that no one who looked remotely Russian came following them into the lobby, he put down the *Paris Match* he'd been thumbing and went up to his room. He showered, checked his Commander, shrugged on a nylon windbreaker. Opening his door to step out into the hall, he noticed that his palms were sweating. At Flak's, he knocked.

When the door opened, blue *kéf* smoke billowed into the corridor. Holding his thumb over his pipe's bowl, Flak blinked at him, red-eyed.

Hunt asked him to do a bug sweep in his room and held out his key. Something must have shown in his face.

"This is it, I guess, sir." Flak took the key and zipped up his jeans, squinting at him.

"Yep. I've got to check it out alone. If I'm not out of 109 in twenty minutes, get Mino and break the door down. Understand?"

"Sure do, sir. I'll wait in your room until then." He checked his watch. "Hey...Cory?"

"Yeah, Flak—" He had been walking away. He turned, came back.

"It'll be okay. We're right with you, I mean—no, that's not what I mean." Flak leaned against the doorjamb. "You cool, sir? You don't look real happy. Are you okay?"

"I don't know, Flak. I really don't. Let's hope so."

"Is there something I should know about? Something you haven't told me? If some shit's going to hit the fan, or anything...Trish's got some sort of bug up her ass. Do you have any idea what—"

"Beats me. Just make sure the room's clean."

He turned and walked away, hearing Flak cursing "black ops" and calling him an "uncommunicative son of a bitch" as he headed the other way toward Hunt's room.

Before room 109, he told himself that even if she *was* a Soviet penetration, she might not relish the thought of protracted debriefing at the hands of her masters. He wondered if anyone had offered her the option of defection. Probably not. She wasn't the sort they'd ask, not station personnel.... He still didn't know how he was going to handle this, but he could think of nothing else to delay it.

He knocked. The door opened. A suit with a crew cut stood at technical ease, barring entry and occluding his view. He introduced himself as "Dropout" as he had been ordered, the taste of it sour in his mouth.

The man's square-jawed, thirtyish face was already breaking into a grin. "Hey, Scratch, don't you remember me?"

He didn't. He faked it. Some ex-Delta guy, maybe. They shook hands and he was ushered in and still he didn't see her. It was a suite and there were two others, standard baby-sitter issue.

"Let me have her. Then get out of here. Watch out for the Soviets with Totes rubbers and jet lag."

"Easy, man. What's the rush?" the crew cut, code-named "Zero," wanted to know.

"Just trying to keep everything on schedule. Anything I should know about her? Drugs, health problems, care-and-feeding stuff?"

"Naw, she's a perfect lady. Never says a word."

One of the other two said something in Spanish about her being "too quiet. A fuse."

Zero said, "That's right, she checks everything out. You wouldn't want to push her hard—she might go bang in your hand. You're sure you don't need any help? We're off now until midweek, if you want backup..."

"No, no. Just give her to me. How about baggage?"

"She didn't come in with any, she's going out about the same." Zero pointed to one ripstop flight bag in the corner. "That's it." Then he told the Spanish-speaker to get her.

Hunt stood up and braced himself, legs a little apart, her flight bag over his shoulder.

She came through the door unaided, walking slowly, her long hair ratted and dull, her eyes downcast. She couldn't have weighed more than ninety-five pounds and she didn't look up until the man guiding her by her elbow stopped, three feet from him.

She blinked, her pupils dilated. "Kori? Kori?" She took a step forward. He thought she was going to faint, fall against him. He shook his head minutely and she stood, uncertainly, weaving on her feet.

He said, "Okay, thanks guys." Then he reached out to her, taking her by the elbow as the other man had, and somehow got her out into the hall before he was tempted to shoot everybody in that room.

Once their door had closed and he was out of peephole range, he put an arm around her waist and let her lean on him, a finger to her lips when she said, "Malik, I thought—you could not—"

It was an interminable distance down that hallway; he could feel her bony flank, the jut of her hip against his thigh. He looked back twice but saw no one watching them from an open doorway. He whispered in her ear: "It's just a little farther."

Flak, holding up a finger, showed him the Soviet-type transmitter taped to the doorframe. Hunt made a motion with his head and Flak pulled it away from the wood, holding it distastefully, as if it were actually an insect. "You can't see 'em when the door's closed. Lots of these in East Berlin hotels—" Then he stopped. "You two need anything?"

She had sagged against him, her head on his shoulder. He snapped at Flak: "Privacy."

"Okay, okay. I've got a pot of cold coffee in my room, and dope and drinks. You want any, just ask. Her stuff's all here, the stuff Dania got for her." He pointed to the Hermés valise Dania had bought and filled in Paris while Hunt was off with Trish getting the passport photos. Hunt had forgotten all about it; he'd never looked inside it, only told her, when she asked, that Nasta was about the greyhound's size.

He said, "Flak!"

"I'm going, I'm going. You call me if you need me. Miss Martinova, we're really sorry—"

"*Out!*"

Flak headed for the door on the double. Hunt never heard it

close. He was holding her against him, her bag dropping from his shoulder unnoticed, feeling her all over, looking for harm, kissing her, smelling her fear and her exhaustion and feeling everything he thought she was feeling, his own heart skipping beats, his eyes filling with tears he couldn't blink away.

"*Bismillah*, malik," she said, her face against his chest, her trembling frightening to him so that he, too, began to shake. "I fooled them. The Schurawi want me, they did not make the lie to it. Oh, Kori, so glad you are come, seeing again that you are—"

"God, Nasta, what are we going to do? *Why* did you lie to—"

She seemed to shrink, to fold, to lose all strength, and he held her upright while she murmured brokenly in Pushtu that her *khel* (clan) was not betrayed, that the Durrani tribes must be protected, that he must kill her and then, by *pushtunwali*, avenge her death upon the schurawi (Russians) because "Malik I have no more strength for lying, no more fight is in me. Only sleep I need. Safe sleep, no harm—one night, do we have? One night for spending? Then—"

"Shut up. By God, shut up. Nasta..." He felt her sagging, picked her up, and carried her to the couch. He crouched beside her and opened the throat of her denim shirt. Her eyes were streaming tears and her lips were cracked and he very slowly slipped his shoulder holster off and put it behind him on the coffee table. He didn't want to be tempted. He needed to do something, not look at her face, her eyes, trusting that he would help her cheat the Russians.

"So good that you came. Tomorrow, New Year's Day. I feared to hope for it." She reached out and touched his face. She was so tiny in jeans and a workshirt; he kept getting angrier and angrier. He couldn't. He mustn't. He said, "Look, I've kept one promise and I'll make you more. You don't have to go there. You don't have to die. I have it all worked out. Don't be afraid. I'll take care of you, Nasta. I love you—*Shit.*"

He bolted up, got the case Dania had packed, brought it to her, holding it out, feeling helpless. "Look in here. We've got all sorts of stuff for you. You take a shower and I'll explain to you. Are you hungry? Did you eat? Do you—"

"No, no, Kori. Just sleep, and peace tomorrow. Peace, no more questions. Many... Kori, do not cry. And before I said, there is no loving one who is what I...have become. I do not love myself. You must not, either. *Plan*, or *anasha*, or *chefir*—do you have these?" The first was Russian for an opium-based drug; the second Soviet hashish; the last a boiled-tea-leaf stimulant.

"No. Yeah. Wait a minute." He got up and called Flak's room. "Bring me some *kéf* and anything like pain-killers or blow that you've got." He hung up.

She had risen to a sitting position. One hand to her face, fingers drifting over her lips, she was looking through the valise's contents, touching a Sanchez voile robe, holding the sheer, gold-striped fabric up to the light. He had admired Dania's; he hadn't realized she had gotten him one to give Nasta. As he watched, she doubled over, hugging the case of silk underpants and shirts and good trousers and he didn't know what else, weeping freely now.

He got up, went into the bathroom, ran hand towels under cold water, and brought two back—one for himself.

Scrubbing his face with it, he wondered how he could have said *twice* that he loved her—it was a different love from what she thought he meant. He tried to justify it, explain it, cursed and broke off. He didn't like her telling him how foolish he was, how hopeless it was, how it was all going to end.

Flak came knocking on the door. He was relieved to answer it. "How's it going? Ah, sir, maybe I better come in—"

"Get out of here." He took the paper bag Flak had in hand and slammed the door in his face.

Then he sorted out the analgesics and the little bill with the cocaine in it and showed her what to do with it, how to sniff it. "You'll feel stronger in a minute. When you want to be reasonable, we'll talk this out." She blew her nose on the tissue he handed her. He paced back and forth and at last went to his jacket and got out two envelopes. "Look here, Nasta—" he started in English, then switched to Arabic. "Tickets to Peshawar by way of Athens. Passport. Money." He put down the first envelope, picked up the second. "A letter from NTS, outlining their arrangements. You must choose."

He put them in her lap and went to the window. He didn't hear her put the valise down, or get off the couch, or even hear her click his safety off; it was made for that—a combat safety, inau-

368   *Casey Prescott*

dible more than six feet away, and he was at the window, trying to compose himself, when he heard her say, "Kori, you will not let me explain. It is *pushtunwali*. One must be strong. I am not strong—" Then the silencer spat and he lunged for her, but it was too late. His hot handload at point-blank range had gone straight into her brain and there wasn't a flicker of life left in the wide-open eyes below her shattered forehead.

He sat there a long time, until nearly dawn, while her blood dried on him and he sorted it all out. *Pushtunwali.*

Then he put away broken dreams of air-dropping with her into the Kush or hiding her with Dania and all the intricate preparations he had made with NTS for her, let her slip from his arms, and called Flak.

"You ought to come over here. There's been a change of plan. Bring Mino and Trish, too. On the double."

He was going to salvage what he could. It was a lot simpler now.

There had been some difficult moments when Flak, Mino, and Trish came running through the door he had left ajar and saw him cleaning his field-stripped Commander of Nasta's blood, her corpse carefully arranged behind him. Flak had waved the others back and come forward alone, murmuring placatingly, "It's me, Cory, Flak, remember? It'll be okay. We'll take care of you, sir. You want to just tell me what happened?"

Mino, ignoring Flak's orders, went over to Martinova and stood staring open-mouthed down at the corpse. "Jesus, God. Leave him alone, Flak. I'd have done the same thing. Ain't you never heard of 'mercy killing'?"

Trish, her lizard boots muffled on the kilim rug, followed, backed away, sat on the coffee table where Hunt was just fitting the Commander's slide lock back into place. "She doesn't look much like me at all, Scratch."

"People look different when they're dead." He answered Trish first. He was tired, he had a lot to do and so little time. "Trish, explain to Flak what we're going to do while I get myself together—" He had made to rise. Flak had reached out and grabbed his wrist.

"Cory, I want to know what happened here. Fowler's going to

have a shit fit. How could you sell out those two assets we were
going to get for her—and *her*, after all we went through?"

He had tried to explain what he only partly understood: Perhaps she hadn't believed that he would or could help her; perhaps
she had been afraid that he could. Certainly she was tired of
fighting, sick to death of questions, longing for freedom, ready
for peace. That was what she had wanted: peace. She had it now.

While he changed into clothes free of blood, he heard Trish
outlining the scenario he had worked up with NTS to spring Nasta
from her Soviet keepers: Trish would pass for Nasta, who, in the
best of circumstances, couldn't have been expected to take part
in this. "I was going to go meekly, wait until we were out of sight
of the hotel and you guys had the Two Can Play trades and were
headed in the other direction. Then, when the NTS cars showed
up, I was—I guess I still am, I don't see what else Scratch can
do—going to hit the Soviets with my trusty prussic-acid spray gun
and, bingo, I'm free and clear. I've got my antidote pills and slap-
injectors of amyl nitrate, if it takes longer than the half-hour the
pills are good for to complete the handover and get out of sight.
NTS was going to pick me up and get me back to the Falcon."

While he had changed in the bathroom, first running his head
under the cold tap, he could hear Flak arguing, accusing, and
Trish's husky laugh: "Sweet Jesus, I do believe you're worried
about me. Don't be. I'm not sweating this, Flak, I'm looking forward to it."

Twenty minutes later, in the Land Rover headed toward the
site, Flak had maintained a nervy silence, punctuated only once
by "I don't believe you were going to do this to me without more
than a last-minute warning." Hunt, in answer, had asked him for
the high-intensity flasher, which would nullify any sniper's night
sights and cut down the effectiveness of any other sort of scope
in the tricky predawn light. He reached out the Land Rover's
window to slap the magnetized unit on the car's roof.

Mino, when they were leaving the hotel, had offered Hunt his
"condolences" gravely and honestly, and Hunt had clapped him
on the back. Flak, now, as they waited in the car, pulled off the
road on a little ledge above the valley floor, checked his Mini Uzi's
clip. "So she was NTS all along? Why wouldn't they try to help
her?"

"They helped her. They didn't make her any more attractive to either side. She was holding on to her single triumph: She'd managed to keep her column's existence, the indentities of her cell's members, secret. I don't think she'd even had made it this far without that to hold on to. NTS isn't rich or powerful or well equipped. Since the Fifties they've been anybody's pawns. They know enough to know that the best thing they could do was wait and hope. They had a little money to work with, on this one, that somebody gave them—enough to help a militant splinter group set up their part of this when the opportunity arose."

"How did you get in touch with them? Even *we* didn't have the specific drop point until last night at the restaurant."

"The waiter. I wrote it on the back of the check."

"Oh. Hey, Cory? Were you going to go with her?"

"I was going to meet her in Peshawar and make sure she got back in—by air drop or what have you—when she was strong enough. I thought maybe we'd take her home with us— Ah, forget it. It doesn't matter. It's done. We'll just get our guys out of this last little—"

Mino, outside with field glasses, gave Hunt the signal.

Hunt started the Land Rover's motor and the flasher began to pulse. "Ready up, Flak."

"Sir, I'd like to work something out with you—about Jack Fowler and my orders...in case this screws up somehow. Jack's not the sort to listen to excuses."

"Go ahead, then."

Hunt, watching the road, saw a single pair of lights approaching from the northwest. He lit a cigarette, drew deeply, watching the coal.

"Well, sir. You know Jack wants you on his team real bad. That's my primary objective, to reel you in. They don't want you working for anybody else. I could say you said yes, Cory, and they'd never know the difference. Nobody'd see you, run you, or collect from you but me. You'd have an open pipeline for equipment and special favors, virtual immunity. We'd both be on the books, collecting vouchers from Uncle Sam.... Especially if something does go wrong here...I mean, Christ, they could reactivate my original orders any time: to bring you on home, even if I have to blow every friend and every safe haven you've got. Fowler suspended the kill order on the Moraleses indefinitely—you probably know that—but he could change his mind anytime...."

"Thanks, Flak, for telling me. But this isn't going to screw up."

"Is that a yes or a no?"

"Tell them whatever you want, whatever makes it easy for you. Just make sure it doesn't mean that one of these days we're going to find ourselves on opposite sides of the fence. I'm not anxious to lose any more friends—not you, not Dania, not anybody. The way I heard it, you're assigned to me for the duration. If that starts seeming like too long a hitch, we'll get you out of it, off the hook. Until then, just take it one step at a time. Okay?" He ground out the cigarette butt in the Land Rover's ashtray.

"Okay, Cory. What do you want us to do?"

"What Trish told you. Be cool. Let me hand her over, help Mino get our two into this car, and don't say anything about NTS—not in your report, either."

"Martinova's body?"

He had brought it with them, wrapped in Flak's new camel's-hair blanket. It was in the follow car, behind a rockfall that reminded him of some Afghan *sangar*. He looked at his hands. "I'll be taking it in the other car when you've gotten the trades out of sight. We had much more complicated arrangements when we thought she'd need...different...care. But if it's agreeable to NTS, I'm going to put her in the car with the Soviets before we set fire to it. She won't mind, and it's neater. It's not like she was born in the Tribal Trust lands or anything. It's just a body—Nasta's gone." He cleared his throat. "Then I'll drive into town and meet you at the Mamounia bar, for old times' sake. I'll have Trish with me. Okay? You know as much as I do now."

"Okay, sir."

"Good." He got out and walked back to the second car, an ancient Volvo wagon. He'd thought of it as just a follow car, not a hearse. He leaned against it, unspeaking, as the Soviet car approached and the sky started to show tinges of blue above the Atlas's jagged peaks. Trish, inside, knocked on the window. He moved away from the door and she opened it. "Did you talk to Flak?"

"Yep. Are you ready?"

"Sure thing, Scratch."

"Do you want a backup gun? I'll give you mine...?"

"No, thanks. I don't want to chance it if they pat me down." She had the gas gun fixed to her thigh with his Leech; it was undetectable under the flowing Marrakech robe.

"Even if they do, don't worry. That's what I'm here for; that's what the follow car is for. Even if NTS gets cold feet, we've got it covered. If I can't get to you, Moroccan authorities are going to find your Dominican passport isn't in order. I've worked real hard on this. With Martinova out of the picture, I've got more fallbacks than we need."

He looked at her, lit by the courtesy lamps of the open car. She was the best operational mind of his party. He had seen her work in Maryland and he had no doubts about her. Few had her shooting eye or her instinct for action. He thought about chucking her under the chin, and shook her hand instead. "All right, lady, this is your acting debut."

Still holding his hand, she let him help her out of the car, feigning disorientation, weakness, her head hung low. As he closed the car door; she stumbled and leaned against the fender, then giggled, then straightened up. "How's that?"

"Pretty good. Don't overdo it—just enough that they won't expect you to chatter in Russian or curse in Pushtu." In the last five minutes, he drilled her in the few Pushtu phrases he had taught her. She had good Arabic, and he reminded her that Nasta customarily spoke it.

Then the Soviet car was there, and in the intermittent illumination of the flasher, he saw four men pile out of a Microbus. "This is it. Let's go."

He took her by the elbow and led her to the drop point, letting her lean against him after an artful stumble, as Martinova would have done. He knew he was shut down, and he was grateful. Otherwise the temptation to shoot the Soviets right there might have been too great to overcome. But he mustn't. They needed to let the NTS splinter group claim the hit if nobody bought the "accident." The bullet in Nasta's brain was a problem, perhaps, but fire cleanses errors; there might not be enough of her left for the deformed bullet to come to anyone's notice. Marrakech autopsies weren't painstakingly thorough, especially in cases where cause of death was not in doubt. If the Soviets demanded an investigation and the bullet was found, no one could trace it to a particular country or manufacturer: Hunt had gotten lead wherever he could find it, and commercial hydroshock slugs, with a hollow point centered by a sharp, narrow prong, were made for a dozen markets, including illicit ones. He had had nothing better to do in Marrakech than load his own....

For a moment, in the flasher's light, Trish seemed to *be* Nasta, black hair blown by a dawn breeze, slim and fragile, yet defiant. It was her spirit he had loved, the wild creature in her. Maybe they could never have overcome their cultural differences; he had come to think so. But the world was a lesser place without her. He had wanted only to turn her loose in her mountains, to see her free. He had never thought to hold on to her. It was that kind of love he had meant. He was glad enough she was going to end on a fiery pyre; he knew she wouldn't have wanted to be buried in the Tribal Trust lands or in any man's cemetery. He wiped his hand across his eyes and stopped, kissing Trish one time for Nasta, as he would have if it were she—as the Soviets must see him do, or suspect something was wrong.

He didn't say anything when he handed her to the tall Soviet with the fat rolling over his collar. It seemed to him to be the same one he had seen at the trauma center, taking a package from Dania, but he wasn't sure that anything, right then, was what it seemed.

They put her in the car and he heard "Kori!" and a blessing in Arabic. It was all he could do to walk slowly away. He passed the two assets Flak and Mino were helping into the Land Rover without a word. He didn't want to know them, to meet them or assess them or have to care about them. He was just about played out. He wanted to go home.

Instead, he started up the Volvo follow car and drove a mile in the wrong direction before he turned it around and headed toward Marrakech on the valley road. Flak and Mino were to check out, feed the trades, make sure they didn't need medical attention, and delay long enough that whatever was going to happen on the road would have happened before they drove by.

He got five miles, driving slowly, coaxing the old Volvo through its gears, before he saw or heard anything. He talked to Martinova's body a little, trying to let his physiological grief cycle. You

had to do that. Grief was a physical reaction. You had to let it
out, let it go by, let it burn through you like fever. He wished she
hadn't done it, he told her, but he was able to forgive her. He
said he thought he understood, and hoped he did.

Firelight and a volley of shots brought him back on line, and
he gunned the car to its limit. Around a curve he saw the Soviets'
Microbus, askew on a little ledge, a couple of strewn bodies, two
NTS jeeps.

Screeching the Volvo to a stop, he jumped out, running, calling
out in Arabic for Trish. He saw her behind a rock, and she waved.
Then three NTS radicals, full-bearded and dark in sunrise, helped
him with Martinova's body. Trish had explained everything. That
was good; he didn't want to argue. They got Nasta close to the
Microbus and the heat was daunting. They couldn't touch the
doors, but the slider was open. One commended her to Allah,
and all together they swung the blanketed corpse three times for
momentum and cast it aside. Then they all ran back to the rocks
and one of the NTS boys handed him a radio detonator: "For
you to do."

He did it, and they covered their heads from the shower of
sparks and metal and death. Then he grabbed Trish and said,
"You okay?"

"Sure, Scratch. I was out the back before the guys in front knew
what happened. You?"

"Yeah." He was looking behind her, at the burning Microbus.
Pushtunwali. "Yeah," he said again. "Let's go. It's better than twenty
miles to town and I sure could use a cup of coffee."

"Me, too." She tugged at the jellaba. "And I want my jeans back.
You've still got 'em, I hope?"

"In the car." They trotted toward it together. He knew he was
going to make it: He could drive away and not look back.

Chapter
21

"ARE you sure this is going to be okay, Cory?" Flak unwound his long legs from the Porsche 928's passenger seat and got out to help Mino, coming down a bluestone drive with a big box in his arms and a bigger grin on his face. Zürich was stubbornly resisting spring, the hedges lining the driveway grudgingly budding, the sky a noncommittal gray above their heads.

He didn't answer, just watched Mino and the road behind as Flak opened the rear hatch and they positioned the box, about two feet square, in the cargo area behind the back seats. None of them had shaved since Marrakech; they were scruffy and unkempt and bundled against the Swiss chill. Hunt hadn't been able to avoid talking to the newly traded assets on the trip from Marrakech to Brussels: Somebody had to baby-sit them; Flak and Mino had had their hands full flying the Falcon. Trish had kept telling him she could handle them alone, but, after Martinova, he wasn't taking any chances. He couldn't tell them anything about what awaited them, he couldn't promise them anything, he couldn't help them readjust. He could make sure they didn't hurt themselves and that they realized neither he nor Trish was going to give them tune-ups or interrogate them. He was glad they had never heard of him nor he of them. Two Can Play had involved many actors.

He kept remembering his own flight north from Marrakech when Shy wouldn't let him sleep and Bowser was biding his time so obviously. He made sure these two slept, giving them the last of Flak's Lamb's Breath and an untouched bottle of Courvoisier from the jet's well-stocked bar. Whenever they woke, he and Trish tried to get them to eat. They were burnt, exhausted, frightened, and weak. A real nice business, theirs. He thought it would be better for them with Jack than it had been for him with Innotech, but he wasn't certain. It wasn't lost on him that they weren't looking on this trip as liberation. Even transiently, he didn't like being taken for anybody's jailer.

He was relieved to turn them over to ISA in Brussels, comforted that Fowler himself met the plane, jacked up on his crutches, inarguably in control. They didn't talk then. Jack knew where to find him. Fowler was a professional's professional. He didn't make a single move that could in any manner compromise Hunt's team's legend, just "picked up his packages" and went on his way, the little NATO flags on his limo's fenders whipping in the morning breeze.

They had made the short hop to Zürich as soon as they were refueled. Dania's people had met them with her Porsche and a sealed noted for him, which said only that if there was a change of plans, he should drive to Marseille and expect to be met there. She did have a lot of friends.

Trish had stayed with the Falcon; no one knew whether they were going to fly it out of here, but if they did, it would be nice to know it hadn't been tampered with while they were in town.

"You didn't answer me, Cory," Flak reminded him as Mino

scrambled into the back seat muttering, "Damn, that was expensive. I didn't know they cost so much."

"I'll split it with you, Mino," Hunt offered as Flak jackknifed in and slammed the door saying, "Yeah, that's a good idea. Me, too. From all of us."

"Thirds? That's great, guys." Mino stretched out along the back seat, his knees up, a hand on the box.

Hunt keyed the ignition and the powerful eight roared to life. "You *still* haven't answered me, sir," Flak said again as Hunt pulled out of the driveway and headed for Shy's along the lakeside drive.

"Because I don't know what to tell you. I'll do the best I can. As far as Mino's present, I think it's a great idea. Michele might not—"

"He's cryin', sir. Can I take him out?" Mino interrupted, brows knitted.

"Sure thing. Let's see him."

"If he pisses, make certain it's in your lap and not on this leather fucking upholstery," Flak warned as Mino opened the box and, crooning, brought the red Doberman puppy, legs flailing, uncropped ears flapping, out for their inspection. "Damn, look at those feet! He's gonna be a monster." Mino thrust the puppy between the front seats. It sniffed Flak, curled its lip, and growled at him.

"Fuck the feet. Look at those teeth." Flak shrank back against the car's door. "Christ, get it away from me! What is it, Grover's full brother?"

Hunt, watching the road and behind them for uninvited follow cars, grinned despite himself. Flak just didn't like dogs, and they knew it.

"Naw, it's better bred than Grover. Grover was a States Doberman. This here's the real thing, championship—"

"Just how much is my third going to *be?*" Flak asked suspiciously. By the time Flak had gotten over his shock at the number of Swiss francs involved, they were slowing to turn off toward Shy's.

At the gate, Flak rolled down his window and handed an armed guard a little leather ID folio Hunt had never seen before, while Mino, having put the puppy back in its box, whispered in Hunt's ear: "They never had any security like this before. He really must be in bad shape."

"Maybe just nervous."

"We should have called first."

"I don't think so," Hunt replied, trying to hear what Flak was saying to the guard, who saluted him smartly and went to phone the house from the little gate station, which hadn't been there, Mino assured him, a month ago.

"Let's see that." Hunt held out his hand for the folio when Flak took it back from the guard.

"Just my SOG, sir. Nothing you don't already know about."

Hunt took the ID wallet and looked at Flak's Studies and Observation Group card: Military Assistance Command Studies and Observation Group Counterterrorist Activities, which authorized the person identified on the obverse, as one acting under the orders of NATO's supreme commander, to "wear civilian clothing, carry unusual personal weapons, transport and possess prohibited items, pass into restricted areas and requisition equipment of all types including weapons," and instructed whomsoever not to "detain or question bearer." Hunt flipped it closed and handed it back. "When I had one of those, it was under the authority of the Joint Chiefs."

"Times change; this one does me better service in Western Europe."

"I bet." He drove on in.

Michele met them on the doorstep. "Cord, I'm so pleased to see you." Behind her, he saw a teen-ager, a tall boy with residual acne, peer at him from the shadows, then disappear. "You've never met my son...." She turned around, saw no one, turned back, smiling, her tortoise glasses in her hand. "He was here a minute ago. You know kids.... Flak, isn't it? I know Mino. Come in, come in. You're here to see John, of course...."

She chattered determinedly, leading them into the living room until the puppy in the box whined. "Oh, God." She stopped in her tracks on the living room's threshold.

Hunt thought that secretly she was relieved to have something specific to talk about. He didn't understand why she was uncomfortable with him; it had all been so long ago.

"It's a dog, in there? Isn't it? Mino, tell me it's housebroken. Well, let's have a look at it. Maybe it'll perk John up. God knows something's needed."

He let her spend a moment more pretending to be whatever she thought was appropriate, offering to take their coats and asking if they were hungry or thirsty, then interrupted. "Michele, I haven't got much time. Can I go up and talk to him?"

"Well, yes. Of course." She was chewing the stem of her glasses. "But we've moved him into the library; he's happier pretending he's working...Cord, can we talk privately a moment?"

He went with her down the hall. "What's up?"

"He's insistent on business as usual. Don't tire him....Are *you* all right?"

"Never better."

"There's no problem between you two?"

"None that I know of, Michele."

"I've been asked to join Innotech's staff, you know."

"No, I didn't know."

She smiled again, a strained, faked grin. "You're happy for me?"

"I guess. Michele, I've got to—"

"I know, I know. I just want you to know that if there's ever anything I can do...John can be terribly difficult when he wants to be...."

He didn't know what she wanted. He nodded gravely. "Thanks, I'll keep it in mind."

"Good." She put her glasses back on. "We'll want to be seeing you more often. Perhaps you'll come for dinner tomorrow? Bring your two—"

"I'm leaving the country right after I talk to him. Which has to be now. I hate to rush you, but I'm on a tight schedule."

"Fine." She turned brusque. "Do give him a good reason to let you have that aircraft. Jack's been burning his ear off about it. Don't make me regret all the nice things I've said about you. He's about to be confirmed as Innotech's international director. He wants it so much. We wouldn't want to spoil it for him."

"Okay, Michele."

"Your word?" Her intelligent eyes held his steadily.

"Now, would I do a thing like that to him?"

"After all he's done for you? I don't know. That's why I'm mentioning it. Come on, I'll take you to him."

She went in first, alone, closing the door softly behind her. Mino, beside him in the hall, had the box in his arms. Flak was intent on staying behind; Hunt had left him watching the driveway through the living-room window.

Almost as Mino said, "What's *with* him? We should *all* give it to

him. Unless he doesn't want to pay his share..." Hunt decided
to go back for him.

"I don't think that's it, Mino. Go on in if you want. We'll be
right along."

Flak was at the window where Hunt had left him, one hand
parting the sheer curtains, a cigarette in the other. "What's the
trouble, Flak?"

"Sir?" he turned, stubbed out his cigarette carefully in an im-
maculate ashtray by the couch.

"Come on, let's see Shy."

"Uh-uh. No, sir."

"Why?"

"Why?" Flak rubbed his stubbed jaw. "I don't want to screw
you up. I don't know what you're going to tell him, what you're
going to hold back. I might say the wrong thing. Our system's
up and running, so we're covered, whatever you do about the
disks—" He shrugged. "Christ, Cory. I'm confused. No—I'm
scared to death. I've lied to everybody—him, Fowler, you name
'em, I've fucked 'em. If I say the wrong thing up there—about
Martinova—"

"Don't say *anything* about that. Just be your charming self—
noncommittal, earnest, honest. You know the rules. Now come
on, I won't let you make any mistakes."

Flak sighed deeply. "What about *me*—you going to blow the
Darling thing to him?"

"'We won't mention it unless he does. If he does—that's life. If
Innotech can't vet an agent properly, it's their problem. *Cavea
emptor.* Okay?"

"Yeah, I suppose. But—"

"Come *on*, Flak. We're keeping everybody waiting."

"Just one thing. I've got to ask you—what would you have done
if I'd had to go all the way with the executive-action order on the
Moraleses?"

"Hypotheticals don't count. If you want to know for future
reference, my advice is never cut off your own avenue of retreat.
Morales is our best shot right now. Like you say, you've fucked
every one of those nice guys who cut your orders without caring
whether those orders are feasible or even survivable."

Flak took a step toward him: "This isn't how I wanted it. I mean is this what I do for a living? Where's the sense of honor in it? I mean—what's the point?"

"Oh, boy. You're alive, aren't you? You're asking questions, aren't you? You've got to be alive to do that. Maybe that's the point: exercising your option to doubt, to think for yourself, to act on your own." He shrugged and Flak came up to him, squinting.

"You meant that about being your own country? About—"

Hunt touched Flak's shoulder. "Come on, Flak, you know the answers. Everybody takes care of his personal space, controls his immediate environment, keeps things straight up, and nobody's got a problem. You and I won't have any, that's for sure."

"Okay, Cory. Thanks," Flak whispered, and they hurried down the hall to join Mino. Hunt thought he saw the tall kid he had glimpsed earlier duck back into the kitchen, but he wasn't certain. It didn't matter, anyway. He'd said nothing he regretted.

Since his brush with death, John Shy had been doing a lot of thinking. He didn't feel the same. Little things mattered; abstract goals had lost their substance, as if in a dream a cement wall in front of his speeding car had turned to mist at the last possible moment, and he had driven through, conscious of the privilege of life as he had never been before, aware that he was cheating death by a hair's breadth.

When he had wakened in the hospital, he had realized it was true, that the dreams were his mind's attempt to make sense of his body's trauma. He had never been so glad to wake.

His pragmatism rejected such concepts as transcendental or even spiritual experience. He hadn't died, even ephemerally—his heart hadn't stopped beating, no clever doctor had brought him back from the dead. He needed his quotidian practicality, his business-as-usual approach to everyday problems, the attention to detail and the commonplace that made him so good at what he did. He was striving to regain that focus, working as hard as he could, stretched out on the library couch, though it took him a long time to get comfortable; his incision hurt and his ribs ached and he still tired too easily. But each day he was better.

He could drink in moderation now, his doctors said. The

security-cleared male nurse was willing to leave him alone to work
six hours a day. Bringing Michele aboard had been a necessary
adjunct to his working convalescence. Hubble was needed at the
office; Shy had to have somebody. The press of events wasn't
heeding his doctor's advice that everything must be taken slowly,
that he shouldn't get upset, that the world would wait. It wouldn't.
He couldn't. They were making do as best they could. He rather
liked being able to discuss business with her. She was knowledge-
able and incisive, a valuable addition to Innotech's staff, now that
he could offer her the sort of salary she was worth. He thought
he might have solved their personal problems by extending their
mutuality of interest, too. He didn't have time to gloat about how
neat a solution it was: Confirmation hearings were only a week
away—a formality, since he was already familiarizing himself with
Sid Cannard's files and acting with his authority, but one he must
be prepared to pretend to take seriously.

The library was large and cypress-paneled with a southern ex-
posure that gilded the built-in book walls. He was anxious to be
able to sit at his desk again, but they had moved the computer
terminal over to the huge Oriental coffee table, and he had the
keyboard on his lap, his feet up on the table, and the monitor
scrolling beyond his crossed ankles when Mino Volante, Flak Godwin, and Cordell Hunt came in, looking like they'd been up for
a week, three of a kind in their flight jackets and fatigue jeans.

Michele told them they mustn't stay long, and left.

He said, flippantly, "Well, well. Our most expensive assets. It's
a good thing Innotech's been commensurately increased, or I'd
never dare initial these vouchers of yours, gentlemen. Pull up
some chairs, if you will. I'd get up—it's not every day I have a
chance to congratulate my people on having done the impossible—but my doctor's nerves are shot as it is. You'll forgive me
of course."

Hunt waved a hand; they all pulled up the Federal side chairs.
Flak found two ashtrays and put them on the coffee table; Hunt
came around and looked at the monitor. Shy tapped a key and it
went blank.

Mino had a strange look on his face. In truth, all of them looked
odd: Hunt seemed to be committing Shy and all about him to
memory; Flak looked at his hands, at his cigarette, at the etched

brass coffee table; Mino seemed about to burst out laughing. He said, "Hey there, sir. We've got somethin' for you." He tapped the box balanced on his lap.

"Not a bomb or someone's head, I hope."

"No, sir. You open it." He leaned forward, putting the cardboard box next to Shy on the couch. Dropout was still nosing around.

"Sit down, Cord, please." Shy knew he wasn't up to any mental sparring match; he hoped Hunt wasn't going to pull any rabbits out of his metaphorical hat.

Then the box quaked and he heard a noise in it. Carefully he reached around and grunted as the movement made his stitches pull. Then he had the top open and two liquid eyes appraised him, tan paws reached for him, and a flop-eared Doberman puppy, crying ecstatically, tried to lick his hand and jumped up so that the box tipped and the pup scrambled into his lap. "My, my, my ...look at you!" In spite of himself, he was touched. Then the puppy tried to climb his chest to lick his face, and he winced, grabbing it with both hands. He meant to say he couldn't accept it, but he was holding it against his neck, appraising its perfect head though the pup's paw on his wound had made his eyes smart with pain.

Mino was saying something about leaving it up to him "about the ears—you know, if you want to crop them, they said they'd do it for you." He glanced up and Mino was holding out the puppy's papers. He took a look and whistled softly, letting the squirming pup down to explore the room.

"I truly don't know what to say, gentlemen. You shouldn't have done it, of course, but I accept with pleasure and gratitude."

"That's okay, sir. Just so you like him. We're all real sorry about Grover. This little guy's as close to warrantied as Dobermans get. He's got a German name, there, but I sort of thought maybe you'd call him Grover Two, or something—"

"All right, Mino," Hunt quieted him as Flak said, "It's *his* damn dog; he'll name him."

"It's perfectly all right. That's a fine name, Mino. Now, let's get down to business. I assume you're here to report...?"

Hunt reached into his jacket and pulled out an envelope. He dropped it on the table. "We're here to collect. We're done. We've neutralized Morales—you'll have no more trouble there. We've identified your leaks. You've seen my vouchers. Can we settle up?"

"Certainly. I'm all ready for you. Jack Fowler was very sure you'd be coming to see me today or tomorrow. There are three brown pay envelopes there—cash; I assumed you'd prefer it. I've included the hazard pay and bonuses you so cavalierly handed out, Cord. But next time, consult me first."

Hunt read the names typed on the envelopes and handed his assets theirs. "I tried to get hold of you. So did Flak. All we could reach was your assassination team—"

"Antiterrorist team," Shy corrected. "I didn't have anything to do with that."

"We know that, sir," Flak said, then flushed and sat back.

Hunt was watching Shy with those flat agate eyes. Shy said, "How did Jack's handover go?" carefully, studying Hunt's face.

"Perfectly, so far as our part of it went."

Out of the corner of his eye, Shy saw Flak pull out a pack of Marlboros, mouth one from it, light it with great concentration. He wanted to talk to Hunt alone. He said, "Jack left something with me for all of you. You'll find another envelope, a white one, there somewhere. This apparent mess is actually a very efficient system...."

"What's in it?" Mino asked as Hunt opened it.

Shy saw Flak shoot the pilot a reproving look. But Hunt answered: "'Get out of jail free' cards—SOG's. Here you go, Captain Volante—NATO loves you." He held out a small laminated card. "And you, Flak—you got a promotion, too. You're a light colonel, according to this—very light."

"What's yours, sir?"

"*Mino!*" Flak whispered.

"It's okay, Flak. My old Agency grade, Mino." He flipped his card casually into the pilot's lap. "Hold on to it for me, will you? And go out and warm up the car? I need a minute or two alone with the director here. You don't mind, Flak?"

"No, sir," to Hunt. "Thanks, sir," to Shy, "for everything. We'll be in touch, I guess." Mino echoed him, stepped forward and shook Shy's hand, and they were gone.

"What was that about—'We'll be in touch'? Cord, he's very probably Fowler's 'Darling.'"

"I know that. He knows you suspect him. I'm not worried about him at all."

"I see. Jack says you want to stay where you are and keep them on the payroll. I have no objections, but some reservations—"

"I don't care what you've got or haven't got."

"Cord, if it's Martinova... She was on a hunger strike most of the time. Everybody makes a mistake in judgment once in a while. She'll be better off with the Soviets; she's a formidable personality, fanatically loyal, capable of nearly incredible feats of resistance—"

"I don't want to talk about her. Let's talk about the Falcon, and what Jack's told you."

"I rather assumed that you were using him to transmit to me Morales' fee—that the Falcon is their price for a cease-fire. It had better be pretty long-term if you expect to walk out of here with a title transfer. I have a board of directors, you know."

"I want the title in my name. I'll keep Morales honest, they'll have the use of it. You'll have your own personal troubleshooters, me and my team, available to you without any vetting procedure or Innotech oversight. Total deniability. Capable of almost anything as long as we're under the Morales umbrella."

"For how long?"

"No telling. A few months, a few years. If it doesn't work out, we'll both know it. You don't have to keep any of us on your payroll—in fact, I don't want you to do so. This is severance pay, as far as I'm concerned. You know how to get in touch with me—" Hunt stood up.

Shy got slowly and carefully to his feet. "Wait a minute."

Hunt nodded. "Okay. I'm listening."

"Perhaps you'd like to see Godwin's file. It's there under that R&D report."

Hunt bent down and leafed quickly through it. "So?"

"I just thought you should know what I know."

"I knew this in New York." He dropped it, reached inside his jacket. Shy tensed in spite of himself. He could feel Hunt's tension like a physical, low-voltage current. "I wasn't going to do this unless you showed some signs of playing me straight." He shrugged. "I guess you've qualified. You know that Helms—DIA—came after us and that we took care of it, I assume. Do you know why?"

"The agents who came back didn't have the specifics," Shy admitted, beginning to feel uncomfortable. The puppy, crying, came over and tried to climb his leg. He started to bend down, slowly, as it squatted.

Hunt darted forward, grabbed it, and put it in the paper-filled box: "Just in time. Michele would never forgive him."

"Thanks.... You were saying?"

"Yeah. About the intelligence—the take all this fuss was about." He extracted a folded manila envelope from his jacket pocket. "You folks were so interested in what I told the Soviets, I thought I'd give you a transcript. I blew some people, there's no denying that, but maybe not as many as I'm being blamed for." He handed it to Shy.

"That's not the total story—all that you recovered?"

"That's right. I've got a whole lot of encoding programs, some decoding ones, too. My system's up, running, and suitably redundant. Don't try to take it out, and there's no problem. Dania thought you'd rest easier if you thought it had been destroyed, but I don't think so."

"That's in here? The originals?"

"You got it. Even worst case, if we—or you—were to leak some of the take from future coded transmissions, the onus could be shown to fall on Arianespace, not you."

Arianespace was NASA's competitor, the European consortium that handled satellite launches, an "evenhanded" business firm that had been taking a lot of NASA's customers. They had just launched satellites for Italy and Japan in a new and important frequency range, 30/20 gigahertz, with which the U.S. had little familiarity and, until now, no way of overseeing without overt espionage. "You're saying we could give some of the thirty/twenty data to NASA and blame it on Arianespace?"

"Flak wants to give it to CIA, yeah. We'll do it through Fowler. I just thought you should know that anything like this can be played as the competition's liability—we're not going to hurt Innotech with it, or let Jack get any kind of stranglehold on you."

"Cord, I don't know what to say."

"How's Beth?"

"Doing pretty well. I think when she's well enough, she'll be getting a new face in South America, so watch your women. You'll let Sid alone? He only offered to pay Helms's expenses."

"He's got lots of misery ahead. I wouldn't want to deprive him of it—as long as he doesn't mess with me again."

"I'm sure he won't. I'd know about anything like that before the fact. We'll be talking intermittently, I presume."

"If you like. I've got to go. I just wanted you to know we brought it in with a perfect score—your op, I mean."

"*Almost* perfect."

"How's that?"

"Angel Morales—you never did—"

"*Flak* never did. Angel's out of the picture permanently. Dania and I aren't telling anybody that. If you mention it, we'll just have to stage some overt operation only he could have masterminded, to prove you wrong."

"Cord, I never meant—"

"The fuck you didn't. But it's okay—now."

"That's it?" He looked at Hunt's face, saw no emotion, no hostility visible under the forty-eight-hour shadow of beard.

"It's a wrap," Hunt confirmed. "Stay out of trouble—and out of ladies' sight pictures." He held out his hand. Shy shook it, wondering whether he had won, lost, or managed to draw.

That evening, when the puppy tried to climb the bedpost and he carefully reached down to bring him up, he was still wondering whether Hunt had forgiven him for engendering the series of actions that led to Martinova being traded to the Soviets. If he hadn't, he was still a problem. But if he hadn't, he wouldn't have given Shy the duals back. And with those duals, he was going into that confirmation hearing with guns blazing.

Hunt, he decided, had been worth all the trouble and money he'd cost. The puppy—Grover II—licking his face, was doing wonders for his spirits. He had known that in a way he was going to have to start all over again, turn Innotech inside out and wash it thoroughly, but he hadn't seemed able to summon up the energy to get started. Now, he couldn't wait for tomorrow, when he could begin dropping his bombshells. Any agency that thought it could revert Innotech to a proprietary company was in for one hell of a surprise.

CORDELL Hunt was still out on the bluff, though the sun had set an hour before, when he heard Dania's car drive in. The pool lights were on, and the floodlights illuminated the dock below where the Scarab speedboat bobbed at its slip.

Costa Smeralda was truly beautiful; the mixed scents of brush-wood and sea were just what he needed.

In Marseille, after they had seen to the Falcon and he had recouped what money he had advanced Flak and Mino, he had told them to either arrange for long-term locker space at the airport or rent a deposit box at a bank where Hunt customarily kept a bailout package—two pistols, four clips, five thousand U.S., and a set of papers—under lock and key. In a situation as desperate as his had become once Innotech scooped him off the street in Marrakech, the lockbox had limited value because banks took pictures, but the SOG cards Flak had gotten from Fowler by telling him Hunt had "said yes" were probably liabilities in as many situations as they were advantageous. In black, your cover was all-important. Should the wrong people see those cards, they'd be death warrants. If Flak or Mino found they needed them, they could give the authorities concerned the keys to their boxes; in dire straits, the one-phone-call sort, they'd have to ring Jack Fowler anyway. Grudgingly, Flak had agreed. Mino, who wanted to flash his to Liz, was disappointed, but did what Hunt suggested— rented a box at Cory's bank.

Trish had come with them, party to all. Hunt wasn't worried about her. She had asked him, when they deplaned at Marseille, if her work had been "up to snuff. Cory, anytime you want to use me again, I'd be pleased to sign on." He had said he'd keep her in mind. She had looked at him askance, holding her hair at the back of her neck; Marseille was in the grip of a mistral, and the wind was fierce and wet. "We did great back there, Scratch. All of us. What's wrong? Is it the lady—I only look a *little* like her. You don't have to keep avoiding me...."

"Sorry. Shot women always bother me. Some genetic thing, maybe. A shot girl makes me feel like I fucked up. But if I need you, I won't hesitate to ask. I liked what I saw back there. Nobody could have done better." He knew she wanted something more, so he promised that from then on he'd "think of you as one of the guys."

Satisfied, she had moved off, approaching Flak, who was definitely not thinking of her as one of the guys since she'd made such a fine showing in the Marrakech op—or maybe since he'd seen her and Hunt with their heads together. He didn't know which, and he didn't care. If Flak had a steady bed partner who didn't need to be vetted, it was going to make all their lives easier— *if* things worked out the way he hoped.

He turned around. Dania should have come out to find him by now. Through the sliders he could see Flak and Trish, taking turns at a video game in the living room. Earlier he'd heard some laughter and singing—off-key but enthusiastic. Dania had a baby grand and Flak had brought his guitar from the Falcon. Liz was ambulatory, after a fashion, stretched out in jogging shorts on the couch. He didn't see Dania. She'd been in Porto Cervo when he and his team had put her chopper down on its pad beside the garage. Diehl was with her, which had suited Hunt. They'd tied down the Dauphin and raided the refrigerator; then he'd changed into jeans and his old Airborne sweatshirt and come out here to think things through.

He'd always loved the sea. It made sense of everything he believed in—the nonverbal imperatives that guided his life. It gave him proportion and sometimes, he thought, lent him strength when he was tired. His back was complaining off and on again, but it was nothing worrisome. He wasn't a kid anymore. He had to be willing to pay as he went. With his shot calf and his deep-seated frags, he was still in better shape than most guys his age. He discounted his dreams and knew he was right to do so; they weren't as bad as they'd been. He'd almost forgotten *how* bad they'd been until Flak had assumed he didn't know what he was doing when they'd walked into his room in the Ourika and seen him with Martinova's corpse. That had hurt.

There was a buoy out there; he heard the bell and heard the foghorns soughing. *It's okay,* he thought. *Even if we have to look for a new base tomorrow.* He knew where to look, how to put safe havens together. He'd give Monaco a shot—no income tax and good facilities; he knew three arms dealers there, one who did lots of business with the Pentagon. He could hook in there in a matter of hours.

He crouched down, slowly, carefully. It hurt a bit, but he could handle it. He picked up some pebbles and threw them, counting the seconds until they plunked in the sea. He had to clear his decks, go straight up with her, or he'd be forever wondering when Flak was going to drop a hint in conversation, inadvertently, innocently—or Mino, who couldn't be counted on to think before he spoke. Any little reference to Bogotá or even Brazil might do it. Dania's tradecraft was unexcelled. It was always a tiny piece of information, out of place, that killed people, unmasked agents, blew whole networks in the field. This thing wasn't going to keep forever.

He wanted to get it over with. It was one thing that was in his power to settle. So many things weren't. Martinova hadn't been. Flak had asked him what was going to happen if Zero and the rest of Fowler's delivery boys saw the burnt-out car. "That's NTS's problem, not ours." *Pushtunwali*, he had thought again then. He hadn't really explained it to Flak properly. The Pushtun Way: One's allegiance went first to clan, then to tribe, then to nation; wherever those of Pushtun blood happened to be, the whole infrastructure was behind them, ready to support, rescue, or avenge.

Though he was expatriated, he still felt that way about America, about the ideal America he carried in his head, about the Constitution and what he felt all Americans abroad must embody: the right to *pursue* happiness with no free ride, no guaranties. The right to bear arms. The unspoken but ultimate obligation to extend the American concept of a fighting chance to anyone willing to dedicate his life to it. He knew those ideals were out of favor, forgotten, swathed in comfort, complacency, and greed at home, but he *was* his country. He was his America, to all intents and purposes. He and all his fellow, fragile humans, so far as he could determine, lived in a world that was ninety percent subjective. For his part, he felt responsible that his ninety percent meet his standards. The ten percent was beyond his control.

He was glad Two Can Play was over, the nets rolled up, the after-action reports being written, the books being closed. Given what he knew of it, even Martinova's death had a positive interpretation. If she had lived and he had managed to put her back in place and convince American interests that she was a loyal NTS operative, well connected with the Afghan Jirga, it might have started things rolling again. He had been very careful, after that initial debriefing in the Zürich chalet with Shy, not even to allude again to knowing that CBW's (chemical/biological weapons) were the weapons the defense community and the intelligence community most wanted to see deployed against the Soviet occupation force in Afghanistan. That was what Sid Cannard and his "customers" were afraid Hunt had figured out, why they were so anxious to debrief him until he admitted knowing, or until they were satisfied that he didn't know, or, best of all, became a vegetable in the process, so that no one would ever have to worry about what he might know from the Soviets or what he'd found out on his own.

America's Virginia stockpiles of outlawed chemical shells were shrinking even before the production of binaries was approved by Congress. The new binary shells didn't fit the old weapons-delivery systems. He'd heard from Chebrikov what the Soviets had seen, and what they suspected but couldn't prove: that the old systems were being "disposed of" as they were certified "faulty; leaking; debilitated"—transhipped into the Kush. Agencies were so curious about the effectiveness of the old single-compartment shells, it seemed a shame to just bury them. Nothing could be proved of test insertions, but with the binary shells in production and so many old stockpiles due for destruction as the binaries came on line, the Soviets were justifiably worried.

With the arms conduit Hunt had been trying to "initiate" for the most paranoiac administration his country had ever seen would have come the ability and the opportunity to make use of the old stock. He was glad it hadn't happened. He didn't want to be a party to it. He'd have had to go back to the Joint Chiefs with some sort of report if it had looked as if that particular facet of Two Can Play had any chances of success. With the end of Martinova, it was over, as far as he was concerned. The Soviets would still feel the pressure—even the remotest possibility ensured that. But the reality was now very unlikely. There was just enough about it in the Chebrikov transcripts to stop any further feasibility studies dead and give those who'd signed off on the inception orders cold sweats for the next five or ten years.

That was the nice thing about intelligence work: Every now and again, you came across something that let you grab the big boys by the balls. This time he'd done it without a word, by implication and innuendo—the best possible way. There was no way they could sterilize all the records, all the actors, all the sources. It was an abort, a no-show. He had hoped it would go this way.

It might not have if DoD hadn't wanted so badly to know what did and didn't work against sophisticated Soviet CBW delivery, defense, and decontamination systems that they were sloppy, overt, careless. It might not have if the intelligence agencies involved hadn't been crippled by their hereditary fear of walk-ins: Any types who came to you asking for help were trying to set you up for a penetration, for blackmail, for a consummate fall; the only people you could trust in a foreign country were those who hated your guts, whom you had to woo extensively, buy if you could, manipulate through black networks if you couldn't. The more strongly a revolutionary group resisted Western blandishments, the more certain the Agency and all other related agencies became that these were the right—in fact, the only—factions to support. It never worked; it was always the same; they never learned.

He heard a slider open; sounds were louder, momentarily, from inside the house, then muted again. He heard Dania call him. *Damn* Martinova for sending him into this tailspin when he should have been concentrating on what he was going to say to Dania, how he was going to handle her.

He got up slowly, stiffly, calling out, "I'm over here." She was dressed in something white and flowing that whipped around her knees; she had a rope of Roman gold at her throat and a tray in her hands; her gait was sensuous, almost mincing, due to the height of her heels.

"Cory! What are you doing out here! Come take this, *per favore*." Then, when he did: "*Grazie*. Now, what's this I hear, that you haven't eaten enough to keep a bird alive, that you've been out here by yourself since before sundown?"

On the tray was a metal pot of espresso, cold veal salad, a small plate of pastries. "I'd thought we would have our first picnic tomorrow—drive to one of the *nuraghi*—you have not seen our prehistory. They are fortified stone dwellings, circular, some from the nineteenth century B.C. You're always spoiling my surprises...."

She was chattering: *Nervous*, he thought. He said, "I'm not much of a tourist. Should you be out here like that? It's getting cold. I want to talk to you. If you think you ought to change, I'll wait."

"No, no. Let's sit by the pool."

"All right." He put the tray down on the poolside table's glass top. The umbrella was in. She sat demurely, crossing her legs. "There. That's better. Shall I pour?"

He nodded and lit a Camel. "Where's Diehl? In the house?"

"I had a meeting, you know. Diehl went along with the clients, back to Beirut. We think we may do something there with the Falangists. You are friendly toward them, yes?"

"Yep." At least it wasn't the Soviets or the PLO. "What are 'we' doing? I just got off one go. I need a few days—"

She brushed her nose with the knuckle of her forefinger, her eyes glinting mischievously. "Nothing physical. Just ordnance and intelligence coordination. One does need rest from fieldwork. I, too. I have not yet recovered from being rescued by a man in a frightful mask who has many unpleasant acquaintances who shouldn't have been able to visit here."

"We've been through all that." She had had doubts, she'd later admitted, primarily that his team had been too well prepared for their rescue mission for it to be the impromptu action he claimed. He'd said then, "That's me, regular Boy Scout," and redirected the conversation to the flaws in her own security procedures that had made it possible for Helms to beat the information he needed out of one of the local paramedical types she had vetted so off-handedly.

"Yes, you are right." She handed him his coffee. "There, this will change your mood. Did you miss me? Or hadn't you time?"

"I missed you." He sipped, sat back, watching her hair blow and the spill of light along her angular cheekbone. "The handover got a little complicated, but it worked out well enough in—"

"Trish called me from Zürich, Cory. To confirm arrangements. I'm sorry about your friend. Grechko could find no KGB file for her—he said she was not their agent."

"Yeah, I know."

"It wasn't your fault."

"I know that, too. I've got title to the Falcon."

She raised an eyebrow. "So?"

"So, if we're going into business together, maybe you'll help me with the maintenance costs. I've never owned anything like that before. It's wreaking havoc with my bank balance, and I've only had it a few hours."

"*Sì*—yes, of course. You know that's no problem." She sipped from her cup. "Cory, what is it? What do you need? Assurances? Money? A proclamation of my undying love?" She made it a joke, teasing him, though he wasn't sure she was joking.

He didn't answer, just turned his cup in its saucer. Mino had said, when they arrived here, that it was the only place he'd been in months where he wasn't afraid he'd break something, and felt that "if I did bust somethin', it's okay."

"I have spoken inappropriately, so soon after your loss? If so, I am truly sorry."

"No, no. It's just that I don't want to tell you this, but I have

to, if we're seriously considering going into another project together."

"Then tell me." She picked up a fork, slid veal salad onto a
plate, handed it to him. "Don't keep me in suspense."

"Shit. Okay. The Bogotá thing. I was still working for the Agency
then. I was their penetration. When it got overt... I was at the
airstrip. I fired on the Cessna. It was part of my job...." He pushed
his chair back, ready for anything. She had an evening bag, a little
chain-mail pouch slung over her shoulder. She could pull out her
new PPK and take a shot at him. Maybe he deserved it. He wasn't
going to shoot her, no matter what she did.

"Cory!" She, too, sat back. She took a deep breath, then fumbled
in her bag. She took a handkerchief from it, head down, and
wiped her eyes. "He, too, shot at you? You exchanged fire? And
there were others there?"

"Yeah."

"And the plane, I know, took off. *I* was there when it landed—
when it crashed."

"Oh."

She leaned forward, her slim arm outstretched. "Are you still
working for them? For any of them? Are you about to arrest me
or do away with me?" Her eyes were steady, very earnest; her
brows were knitted.

"No." He thought of trying to break the tension, of telling her
he'd have to fuck her to death. He wanted this so much; he hadn't
realized how much. If he could have called back his confession,
he would have. But it was too late.

"So, you only *think* that you may have had a hand in his...
death. You can't know for certain. So why do you tell me this?"

"I don't want you to hear it from someone else." He couldn't
read her face with her hair blowing around it; her voice was
careful, calm, and just a little tremulous.

She got up and came over to him. He craned his neck. She
touched his hair. "Cory, what is it you want me to say?"

"Nothing, I guess." He got up, too. "Do you want me to go?"

She raised her hand and tapped his nose, shaking her head.
'You are not going anywhere. You shall stay and do penance,
earn my forgiveness. We have lost lovers, both of us. I, for one,
would not go through that pain again."

He reached out to her then, uncertain, unbelieving, looking for hate in her face. He had seen doubt there previously, and he didn't find even that. She stepped in against him, shivering. "You are right. It's cold. Hold me.".

He did, and all the things he'd thought to say were extraneous: She kissed him and he knew that, finally, no tradecraft was required.

"*Bene?*" she whispered eventually.

"*Bene.* It's good to be home."

Historically, Western nations tended to assign such tasks as covert action to their diplomatic corps; and, from the fiction of Shakespeare to the reality of Talleyrand, an ambassador was expected to know the arts of Machiavelli as well as the rules of the racquet club. But in our more civilized era, diplomats bargain over the riches of the seabed, while subterranean chores are more often left to intelligence services on the premise that the latter have relevant "assets" in the forms of existing networks of secret agents armed with the equipment and training for underground politics.

Frank R. Barnett, Intelligence
Requirements for the 1980s: Covert Action

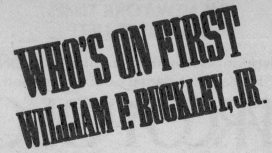